Freshman Pledge:
The Magic of Love

Freshman Pledge: The Magic of Love

Larry Coles

P.D. Publishing, Inc.
Clayton, North Carolina

ISBN-13: 978-1-933720-21-0
ISBN-10: 1-933720-21-2

9 8 7 6 5 4 3 2 1

Cover design by Darrin Kimball/Barb Coles
Edited by Day Petersen/Penelope Warren

Published by:

P.D. Publishing, Inc.
P.O. Box 70
Clayton, NC 27528

http://www.pdpublishing.com

Acknowledgements:

First and foremost to my partner, Darrin, whose own artistic creativity rubbed off on me in ways that I never imagined. His love, support and encouragement provided me with the stamina to continue typing after a hard day's work. To my Uncles Dave and George, whom I have admired since I was a teenager struggling with being gay. I thank them for all the support that they provided and for being positive role models in my life. I have aspired to have the type of loving relationship that they have had for over thirty years. To Ma-K for allowing me to share her son's life, and for being such an open, accepting and cool mother-in-law. To my sisters, Barbie and Linda, who were the first to read this story and tell me what needed to be done (*less narrative and more action*) to make it publishable. To my sisters, Lori and Sheri, for being themselves and learning that they are strong and independent women. To the Maholics (Connie, Sheila, Stacie, Deborah), the ladies I have been meeting with after work on Friday nights for over sixteen years. I thank them for all of their support and encouragement during the "dark" years. To my dear friend, Faith, who supported my efforts and helped me with editing the story before I submitted it. She has been there for me as much as I have been there for her. To Andra who read one of the very first versions and provided feedback and encouragement. She can escape to France, but she will never be forgotten. To my many friends and co-workers (they ALL know who they are) who have provided support and inspiration. To the many authors that I have read over the years, who have inspired my love of the written word and provided me with rich worlds in which to dream and fantasize. Last, but certainly not least, to my Mother, who brought me into this world, and who taught me to be myself and do things that I enjoy no matter what others might say or think! Her strength and support after our father walked out provided inspiration for my own life.

Special thanks to PD Publishing for having faith in me and trusting that I would follow through with their suggestions. To Day, my first editor, for all of her suggestions and comments; for finding the words that I couldn't; and for making editing fun. She smoothed out the rough edges, brought out the best and worst of the characters, and eliminated much of the smiling, laughing and cheering! <g>

Finally, I would like to thank Darrin (again) for creating the paddles that grace the cover of my book. Thanks also to Barbie and Linda (again) for designing the look of the cover. I love all three of you!

Dedication

To Darrin: for coming into my life and providing the positive energy that had been missing; for allowing my creativity to come forth; and for your love and support, especially during the process of writing and editing this story. It's because of your love and creativity that I was able to write this love story. We'll always have Etta! *At last...*

And to all the lovers in the world who understand the magic of love!

Author's Note:

There are unexplained mysteries in our world that will forever remain unexplained. To the believers of those mysteries, there is no evidence that they can use to prove such mysteries, nor is there evidence that can be used to disprove them. We have to rely on our own personal faith to believe.

The power and energy of nature is an unexplained mystery, although it can be witnessed in such events as hurricanes, volcanoes, earthquakes, etc. Centuries ago, people believed that the natural energy contained within plants or crystals or the wind, which surrounds the Earth, could be used for healing or for evil.

Modern-day self-help gurus and twelve-step programs tell us that we can change our own lives by using the energy that exists within us. If you have ever lived with an alcoholic or drug addict (or both wrapped up in one), you know that they exude a negative energy – it is noticeable to all of those around them. These people will not admit that they have a negative energy about them, because they do not believe that it is negative. But it is especially palpable to those who use their own positive energy in an effort to change their lives for the better. Using your own personal positive energy can change your life for the better – once you have removed the negative energy from your life.

God, magic, the belief that Earth's natural energies can be used for healing, the belief in the use of crystals for healing, the belief that we can communicate with the spirits of the dead, the belief in an afterlife, the belief in reincarnation, the belief that we can feel connections between and with others – cannot be proven or disproven. They are individual beliefs and truths unto the individual.

While this story is a work of fiction, made up in my mind, a lot of my own beliefs and truths are contained within. The most important of those beliefs and truths is that Love is the single most powerful energy on Earth – and that it can connect two people and change their lives. It is magic!

MEMORIUM

In memory of my grandmother, whose spirit and love I still feel to this day. The memories of coffee brewing (in that avocado green percolator) first thing in the morning, and the delicate scent of lilacs blowing through my bedroom window on warm spring nights, will never be forgotten.

1: SCHOOL DAZE

Tommy Ford smiled happily as he looked around the noisy dorm lobby. Heinz Hall, a four-story red brick building, was the oldest and only all-male dormitory on the Timian State College campus, and it had no air conditioning. Even with all the windows and doors open, the lobby of the Fdorm was hot and stuffy, crowded with students and parents fanning themselves with papers or magazines. A dozen students waited in line to check in and receive their room keys. Older students greeted one another with easy familiarity, while excited yet nervous freshmen like Tommy quietly surveyed their new surroundings.

As he patiently waited for his room key, Tommy looked around at the people in the lobby, overhearing portions of the assorted conversations going on around him. Suddenly, he felt the atmosphere in the lobby change. Everyone appeared to stand still, and the noise faded to silence. He watched as a handsome, well-built young man walked through the lobby with another student. The guy was tall and muscular, with black hair, mustache and goatee, a slightly crooked nose, sparkling blue eyes, and a smile that seemed to brighten the room. Wearing a pair of black jeans and a white t-shirt, he strode through the lobby with an air of confidence and assurance. He glanced toward Tommy and smiled. Struck by the attractiveness of the man, Tommy turned his head to watch the two men as they left the lobby.

"Yo, Ford, Thomas. Here are your keys," a young man called out, looking up from the dorm room assignment list.

Tommy blinked and shook his head as the noise from the people milling about the lobby returned in a rush. Episodes like that had happened to him before. His grandmother, a Wiccan practitioner, had explained that some people's life energy could be strong enough to overwhelm a person who was a sensitive. During the years that he had lived with her, she had trained him to control his own energy and how to recognize it in others. Nevertheless, it was rare enough that he was still surprised when an episode occurred. Hearing his name called again, he stared down at the person who was speaking.

"Welcome to Heinz Hall. You're on the third floor in room 301. This is your dorm key, your room key, and your mailbox key," he rattled off, pointing at each key. "Try not to lose them." He chuckled as he handed the keys to Tommy.

Tommy read the name badge. "Thank you, Jay. I'll make sure to keep them with me." He held the keys tightly. *At least Jay has a nice smile to make up for that bad hair.* Tommy smiled at the guy with the shaggy-dog look.

"I'm the resident assistant for the third floor. I'm in room 310, which is in the middle of the hallway," Jay said. "If you notice any problems on the floor, or if you have any problems with other students, please let me know. It's my job to keep things orderly. Serious issues will be handled by our resident director."

"Okay. Thanks."

"One more thing," Jay said, stopping the young man. "Your roommate is a freshman named Scott Smith. He hasn't arrived yet, so you get dibs on which side of the room you want."

"Cool." Tommy picked up his suitcase and turned.

"Don't forget to go to the student center and get your class assignments," Jay called after him.

"All right. Thanks," Tommy replied, then left the lobby to find his dorm room.

Tommy walked up two flights of stairs and to the end of the third floor hallway. Standing in front of the door to his room, he looked down the noisy hall where other students were moving into their rooms, happy that he would be in the end room on this side. There was one room next to his, number 303, and then a stairwell leading down and out of the dorm, separating the two end rooms from the rest. He hoped that it would be quieter than the center of the hallway, surrounded by other rooms. He opened the door, looked around the twenty by twenty room and started to laugh.

The walls and ceiling were beige, and the floor was covered with light green tiles. The steam heating unit and north facing windows, covered by dark beige curtains, were located on the wall opposite the door. The wall to the right of the door contained two floor-to-ceiling cabinets for hanging clothes and storage, and there were two four-drawer dressers located between those units. Two desks with shelving units above were situated in the middle of the floor, helping to divide the room in half. There were two desk chairs, one for each of the desks, and one large ugly green chair for guests. One twin bed was located next to the windows, and the other was against the corner of the walls to the left of the door.

The room was stifling, even without direct sunlight coming through the windows, on this late August Sunday morning. Tommy was grateful that he had first choice, as it appeared that the side of the room next to the windows would be the more comfortable. After putting his suitcase on the bed, Tommy opened the three windows to allow air into the room. He sat down on the bed and smiled wryly. It wasn't as comfortable as the queen-sized hotel bed he had slept on the previous night.

An hour later, after two trips to his car, Tommy had finished putting all of his clothes and personal belongings into his half of the room and making his bed. He placed his grandmother's old wooden trunk next to the head of the bed to use as a nightstand. It was a small trunk made of oak that had darkened over the years, with black owl-head metal handles on each of its sides. He had inherited the trunk and its special contents after his grandmother's death. On top of the trunk he placed a small white vase containing a single red silk rose. Then he stood back, wiped the sweat from his face, and looked around the room.

"Well, that's a little more livable."

A tenor voice spoke up from the hallway behind him, where he had left the door open to allow the air to circulate through the room. "It would be better if the walls weren't so damn ugly." The young man dropped his duffel bag on the floor and stood by Tommy's door.

Tommy laughed as he turned to see who had spoken. "Hi. I'm Tommy Ford." He walked over to shake hands.

"I'm Welby, Kyle. Freshman. Room 302. Don't lose the keys," he stated robotically as he held the keys up in front of him and then laughed. "It's nice to meet you, Tommy." He shook Tommy's hand. "I'm getting tired of hearing my last name first."

"I hear you, Kyle. And I still have to go pick up my class cards."

"If you wait up, I'll walk over with you. I have to do that too." Kyle picked up his bag, unlocked the door to his room, and took his bag inside.

Following Kyle into room 302, Tommy noted that it was a mirror image of his own. "Your room is much brighter than mine."

"It's also much hotter because of that damn southern exposure," Kyle replied, as he began putting his things away on the side of the room away from the windows.

Tommy walked over and looked out the windows, where the sun was shining in. "But you have a beautiful view of the dining hall," he teased.

"I hope we don't get the beautiful smell from the dining hall as well," Kyle responded wryly. "Are you ready to go, Ford Tommy?"

Tommy laughed. "Yes, I am, Welby Kyle."

"I love this campus, all these trees and grass courtyards. There are a lot of places to sit and watch the world go by." Tommy took a deep breath of the pine-scented air.

"It certainly helps to have all this shade on such a hot day," Kyle replied.

"I wouldn't have thought it got this hot in the mountains," Tommy said as they walked through the campus on their way to the student center.

"Heat rises, although we do have all these beautiful shade trees that help keep the heat contained."

Tommy glanced around the area. "I never thought about it like that. I'm from South Jersey, where it's always hot and humid during the summer, even in the shade."

Walking by the college radio station, they noticed a group of students and parents trooping after a woman from Administration. Tommy recognized her from his orientation visit during his high school's spring break in April. Kyle stopped, and he and Tommy stood back to listen.

"Timian State College began its history in 1867 as a seminary and normal school, educating and training men to become teachers. In the mid-1920s, it began training both men and women and became a teachers' college. As this area grew, and more students began coming here, Timian became fully accredited in the state university system," the woman lectured.

As they left the group behind and continued their stroll to the student center, Kyle smiled at Tommy and mimicked the stock presentation. "Over here on your left is the library. It was built in 1920."

"No, dude, that's the science building. It was built in 1974." Tommy laughed and slapped Kyle on the back.

"Are you sure it's not the English building, built in 1953?" Kyle asked facetiously.

"Obviously, we shouldn't have been daydreaming as she was telling us about all of the buildings."

"They must have missed orientation this summer." Kyle smiled sympathetically toward the group.

"Signing into the dorms, getting the class schedules, *and* having to listen to her on the same day — that's brutal," Tommy said as they reached their destination.

Tommy and Kyle looked around at the hundreds of students standing in lines snaking throughout the inside of the student center. Most of the students were talking and laughing, raising the decibel level way beyond loud. The majority of the lines were for those who had not pre-registered during summer orientation and now had to select from whatever classes were still available. A smaller section of the center had lines for the students who had pre-registered. Tommy and Kyle walked over to that area and stood in their respective alphabetical lines.

"Last name?" the young man asked without looking up from his seat behind the table.

"Ford, Thomas," Tommy replied, looking down onto a head of wavy brown hair. He smiled as he watched the guy's long fingers flip through the stack of envelopes.

"Here we go — Ford, Thomas." The young man looked up and smiled. "Check out the class cards inside and make sure they are the classes that you selected."

Tommy stood there for a second, staring into a pair of sparkling emerald eyes. "Uh, okay," he stammered as he accepted the envelope.

"I'm Jack," said the young man with the striking eyes. "I notice from the envelope that we'll be in the same psych class."

Tommy was having difficulty keeping his mind off Jack's eyes as he thumbed through the six cards that listed the class, its day and time, and the professor. "Uh, that's cool," he managed to mumble. "Sorry. These all look right to me."

"It's okay, Thomas."

"Tommy," he said quickly. As he looked away from Jack's face, he saw the red and black Kappa Lambda Pi crest on the black t-shirt.

"Relax, Tommy. It's the first day; freshmen are always a little nervous. I'll look for you in class this week."

"Okay, Jack. Thank you." He turned away, shaking his head and feeling stupid about getting caught staring. Although Jack didn't appear to be offended by his attention, he couldn't believe he had acted like such a fool.

Kyle rejoined Tommy outside the student center. "Did you get all your classes?"

"Yeah, it's a tough schedule," Tommy said, still distracted by his actions inside.

"Try being pre-med." Kyle slapped Tommy on the back. "Let's go get lunch. I'm hungry enough to try the cafeteria," he said with a laugh.

After lunch, Tommy and Kyle walked over to the campus bookstore to purchase their textbooks. Tommy also bought a pair of shorts, a muscle t-shirt, a short sleeved t-shirt, a pair of sweats and a sweatshirt in the school colors of navy blue and gold. As they returned to their rooms, Tommy saw his door slightly ajar. Bidding good-bye to Kyle, he walked into his own room.

"Hi, I'm Tommy Ford." He tried not to look startled by the pale young man's spiked hair — dyed black with blue tips — or the pointy stud sticking out beneath the young man's lower lip. He put out a hand to greet his roommate.

"Hey, dude. Scott Smith." The young man smiled brightly at Tommy and shook the offered hand. "I'm finally getting some freedom from my parents. It's so cool."

Tommy returned the smile. "It is cool." Tommy noticed that he and Scott were both six feet tall, but Scott was much thinner and paler. "What's your major?"

"Business administration. What about you?"

"I'm hoping to get degrees in psychology and sociology."

"Whoa, dude. A Brainiac!" Scott teased as he continued putting his belongings in their place. "How'd you get stuck in the jock dorm?"

"I'm going to try out for the tennis team in the spring," Tommy answered.

"Good luck. I'm hoping to make the varsity baseball team as a shortstop. They'll probably put me on the junior varsity, though. Some people have a bit of a problem with my Goth look." He briefly stood in the middle of the room with his arms spread out and waited for a reaction.

Tommy chuckled. "It is different, but we'd have a pretty boring world if everyone looked and acted the same."

"That's cool, dude, an open-minded Brainiac. I like you. I hope you don't mind my techno music."

"As long as you don't mind my country music," Tommy returned with a laugh.

Over at Kappa Lambda Pi House

"*Hola, hermano*," a deep Mexican voice called out from the third floor hallway of the Kappa Lambda Pi fraternity house. "The goatee and mustache look good."

Mark Young looked up from his computer and smiled at his friend and fraternity brother, Oscar Jimenez. "*Hola*, Oscar. Welcome back." He walked over and shook hands.

"How cool is this? We're finally seniors, with our own rooms on the upper floor of the fraternity house." Oscar's teeth gleamed a bright white as he smiled at Mark.

"It's pretty cool, man," Mark said, following Oscar into the room next door.

"I'm gonna be right here, buddy. Better keep the sex noises down." Oscar grinned.

"That won't be a problem," Mark said frowning. "Sally and I had a disagreement during her family picnic on the Fourth of July. It was a disaster." He shook his head as he sat down at Oscar's desk. "I just can't figure that chick out."

"What's that now, three or four break-ups since you two met last fall?"

"I lost count, dude. I don't think she knows what the hell she wants from me, and I certainly don't know what she wants. She said that she'd have to think about our relationship and would talk to me when we got back to school." He sighed as he thought about Sally Brown. She was a senior, a beautiful young woman with blonde hair and blue eyes. He had been intrigued with the Delta sorority sister since they'd met at a Greek mixer the previous year. They seemed to have a lot in common during their first semester together. They liked dancing and going to the movies, and enjoyed having sex. Sally seemed interested in him, but would not make a commitment to their relationship for reasons she wouldn't explain. There was a small part of him that was glad that she wouldn't commit to him, but he would have liked to understand her motivations.

"I'm sorry to hear that, *hermano*." Oscar patted Mark on the back. "On a lighter subject, how's your knee? I certainly hope you're ready for the season."

"The knee is fine. I've been rehabbing it since last season." Mark gave his knee a whack for emphasis. "It's been holding up through these first two weeks of practice, and the team is looking pretty good."

"Let's hope you guys can win the first game and draw in some pledges for us," Oscar teased.

"So, you appear ready to lead us, Pledge Master. How many pledges are you looking for this semester?"

"We'll discuss that tonight, when the house council is all together. Now get out of my room so that I can finish unpacking."

"All right, brothers, the sooner we get this meeting started, the sooner we'll finish," Oscar shouted over the noise in the third floor meeting room. He waited as the other eleven members of the Kappa house council found seats and quieted down.

As Kappa Lambda Pi's pledge master, Oscar was in charge of making sure that the national rules for pledging new members into the fraternity were followed.

The twelve members of the Kappa house council had been chosen at the end of the previous semester. They would vote on which new students would be allowed to pledge the fraternity, and then vote again on which of those pledges would be accepted at the end of their probationary period. The four senior members of the ruling council were automatically members of the house council: Dave, the president of Kappa; Joe, the vice president; Brent, the secretary; and Rick, the treasurer. If enough pledges were accepted during Rush Week, each of the senior and junior members of the house council would select one of the pledges to be his little brother for the duration of the pledge period.

"Welcome back, brothers." Oscar looked around the room. "Rush Week begins in two weeks, and our first rush party is scheduled for the 15th. We need to start looking for and considering new students as pledges for our fraternity. We'd like to have between fifteen and twenty in the pledge class."

"We need to get some lively candidates," Mark commented from the back of the room. "Last semester's group was pretty bland." Mark saw Paul, the second semester freshman, turn around and glare at him before smiling.

"I concur." Dave laughed and others joined him. "We need to find some interesting guys to add some flavor and life to this house; otherwise people will think we've become a group of bookworms."

"Should I scout the drama department?" Jack asked, a big smile on his face.

"No," several members called out in unison.

"We don't want that much flavor," Dave said.

"That's discrimination, big guy," Jack replied, still smiling.

Dave brushed that aside with a laugh. "Sorry. We need guys who want to be brothers, not guys who want to sleep with brothers."

Jack and Oscar smiled at one another and shook their heads while the others laughed.

"We'll do our best to find good candidates," Jorge said.

"Great. I'm in need of a housekeeper," Mark said.

Oscar laughed along with the rest. "I pity the pledge you get for a little brother, Mark. You were a sloppy roommate; our room was always cluttered with your stuff. I'm glad you have your own room this year."

"So am I, Oscar. Your snoring was loud enough to wake the dead," Mark responded, causing another bout of laughter.

"Okay, brothers," Oscar called out over the laughter. "I'll run down the schedule for you. Sunday the 13th, Rush Week begins. Tuesday the 15th, our first rush party. Saturday the 19th, our second rush party following the football game." He looked to the back of the room at Dave, Mark, and Donald. "Hopefully, it will be our second win and hook us a few recruits."

"Go to hell, Oscar," Dave replied, as the room broke out in laughter again.

"Sorry, brothers." Oscar smiled and then quieted the room. "Let me go over the rest of the schedule, and then we're done. Sunday the 20th, the house council meets to review the students and select those we'll invite to pledge. Monday the 21st, we begin inviting those selected. Friday the 25th is the first meeting with our new pledges. And, finally, Saturday the 26th is our first mixer." He looked around the room at the others making notes. "Are there any questions, comments, or concerns?"

"No," the Kappas yelled.

"All right, then, go out there and find some good recruits. Make sure all the other brothers know that they can assist us in the search." He looked around the room and then slammed down his gavel. "Adjourned."

Getting Started

"Holy shit, dude!" It was Monday morning and Scott was preparing to go to the shower room. "Is that your fucking schedule?"

Tommy looked over at the schedule he had taped onto his dresser. "Yeah. It's a little heavy, but I think I can handle it." He had been awake since before six o'clock, gone out for a run, and had already taken his shower. Now he was getting dressed to go to breakfast.

Scott stood naked by the dresser and read down Tommy's schedule.

Monday, Wednesday, Friday:
      6:00 Run
      8:30 — 9:30 Euro History
      10:00 — 11:00 English 101
      12:00 — 1:00 Algebra 101
      4:00 — 5:00 Personal Time.
Tuesday, Thursday:
      6:00 Run
      8:30 — 10:00 Sociology 101
      11:00 — 12:30 Psych 101
      2:00 — 3:30 Earth Science
      4:00 — 5:00 Personal Time.

"You are crazy, dude. You didn't leave enough time for partying. That's why I took the minimum number of credits this semester, and none of my classes start before ten o'clock. I'm going to ease myself into the party scene and *then* deal with the academics."

Tommy laughed. "Whatever works for you, Scott. I'm hoping to get out of here in four years." He turned away from Scott's scrawny, naked body. He thought his roommate looked anorexic, but realized his skeletal frame might be attributed to too much partying.

"I'm thinking more like five years, dude. Gotta party on!" Scott put on his bathrobe and opened the door to go to the shower room. "See ya in English, Brainiac."

"Hey, teacher's pet, wait up." Tommy heard a loud voice yell as he was leaving his Tuesday psychology class. He turned and looked at the tall, muscular guy walking toward him. Tommy had noticed the guy's dark brown hair and brown eyes during class; he had always been a sucker for dark good looks.

"I'm Brian Walker," the young man said.

"Tommy Ford." Tommy noted the long fingers as he grasped Brian's hand and looked up at him. "Nice to meet you. Did you want me for something?"

Brian smiled, a mischievous gleam in his eye. "How did you know all those answers already? It's just the first day of class; I haven't even cracked the book."

Tommy thought he noticed a strange look in Brian's eyes, but decided to ignore it. "I took some pre-college courses in high school, and I cracked the book for a sneak peek at what I was getting myself into."

"How about joining me for lunch?" Brian asked.

"That would be great," Tommy responded.

"Why do you sit in the front row?" Brian asked, putting on his sunglasses as they made their way to the dining hall. "You know that's where profs always pick people to answer questions."

Tommy laughed. "Why do you sit in the back of the room? If the professor gets tired of hearing me answer his questions, he's going to start picking on you."

Brian slapped Tommy on the back and laughed. "Then, let's hope he doesn't get tired of listening to your voice," he said softly, glancing over at Tommy with a smile.

Tommy looked at Brian suspiciously, wondering whether the guy was coming on to him. As much as he hoped to have a relationship at some point, Tommy was more interested in getting his academics in order before dealing with emotional involvements. Deciding that it wasn't bad to have somebody flirt with him, he smiled over at the taller man. "Stop teasing the freshman."

Brian led the way through the cafeteria line and then to a table in the back of the dining area. The cafeteria was divided into two separate halves, with the kitchen work area in the center of the building. Two large salad bars separated the dining areas, making it easier for students to enter or exit from either side of the cafeteria.

"So, let me tell you a little bit about myself." Brian glanced over at Tommy. "I'm a sophomore, majoring in general education. I'm a guard on the varsity basketball team and hope to coach basketball someday. I'll probably start in my hometown high school and then work myself into the college ranks."

Tommy sat quietly eating lunch as Brian rambled on about basketball. He smiled from time to time, hoping that Brian thought it was because he was listening. There were two other reasons for his smile. One, he found Brian's long fingers arousing. He also thought Brian was a self-absorbed jerk, albeit a good-looking jerk. *Too bad the first reason isn't enough for me to stop thinking of Brian as a jerk.*

"And I'm a brother with the Gamma Theta fraternity. If you're interested in joining a fraternity, ours would be a good one to pledge. You could be my little brother." He winked.

"I'm still getting myself acclimated to the campus and my classes. I really haven't given thought to joining a fraternity."

"You know, being a part of the fraternity system is a great way to network for your future. The brothers of Gamma Theta would help you, and so would I."

Tommy pondered the pointed comment and the look that Brian was giving him. He was about to respond when they were joined by another student.

The new guy looked over at Tommy and winked as he sat down next to Brian. "Bri. New meat?"

"Tommy, this is one of my fraternity brothers, Andy. Andy, this is Tommy. He's in my psych class."

Andy reached over to shake Tommy's hand. "Nice to meet you, Tommy."

"You too, Andy."

"Trying to recruit already, Bri?" Andy asked as he nodded his head at Tommy.

"It's never too early to start looking for new guys," Brian responded, with a wink at Andy.

Despite the fact that they were both trying to be discreet, the tone of their voices and the way they were glancing over at him led Tommy to understand exactly what wasn't being said. When Tommy was twelve and realized that he had a preference for boys over girls, he talked with his gay uncle about his feelings and to get advice. His uncle talked to him about being gay and how guys acted around one another.

"Gentlemen," Tommy stood up, "if you'll excuse me, I have a class to attend." He looked at Andy. "It was nice meeting you, Andy." To Brian, he said, "I'll see you in class on Thursday." With that, he took his tray and walked away from the table.

Brian and Andy watched as Tommy walked away from them.

"Nice ass," Brian said as he watched Tommy.

"Sweet," Andy replied. "You going to try for that one?"

"Pretty boy, smart in class, but clueless to the ways of the master." Brian sat back smugly and pulled his sunglasses down over his eyes. "I should have him nailed before rush week."

"Hi, Tommy, Jack Rosenberg." They were walking out of their Thursday psychology class. "We met when you were getting your class cards on Sunday."

"I remember. I was a nervous wreck." Tommy smiled and politely shook hands.

"Would you like some company for lunch?"

"That would be great." He felt a sense of déjà vu as they quietly walked toward the dining hall.

As Jack led the way through the cafeteria line and to a table in the back of the dining area, Tommy hoped that this lunch wouldn't be a repeat of Tuesday's with Brian.

"So, why don't you tell me about yourself: where you're from; what your major is; how you're enjoying the college experience so far. That kind of stuff." Jack looked over at Tommy expectantly.

Inwardly appreciating that Jack was not self-absorbed, Tommy nodded. "I'm from South Jersey; I'm majoring in psychology and sociology; I have an interesting roommate; and, so far, I'm really enjoying my experience at college."

"What's so interesting about your roommate?"

Tommy chuckled. "He's Goth. His spiked hair is black with blue tips, he has a stud through his lower lip, and he listens to the strangest techno music I've ever heard."

Jack laughed. "Yep, that's definitely interesting."

"What about you?" Tommy asked. "Tell me about yourself."

"Let's see. What's interesting about me? I'm a junior, pre-law. I'm a pitcher on the varsity team with eight wins last season. I have too many friends and not enough time to devote to them. And that's about it. No strange piercings or anything like that." He looked over and smiled. "So, what vampire clan do you belong to?"

Tommy was taken by surprise. "What?"

"The tattoo on your left calf. I noticed it when you left the student center on Sunday. It's *White Wolf's* vampire ankh for the role playing game."

"You recognize it! Most people don't know what it is!" Tommy exclaimed. "I'm Ventrue," he said with a smile.

"Same here," Jack replied. "Did you watch *The Kindred* on TV?"

"Yeah. I was disappointed when they cancelled it."

"Hi, Jack," a voice called from another table. Jack waved an acknowledgement.

Tommy shot a quick glance, then watched the handsome, black-haired guy sit down two tables away from them. It was the man he'd seen when he was checking into his dorm, when he'd had the sense of time standing still. "Who is that?"

Jack followed Tommy's stare. "That's Mark Young, senior quarterback on the football team. When he hurt his knee last year, we lost the final game of the season. Then we lost the western division game, which kept us from going to the state championship."

"Is that his girlfriend with him?"

Jack considered. "They've been dating, but she's not sure what she wants."

Tommy looked at Mark's profile. *I know what I'd want with a guy like Mark.*

"Hey, Jacko." A deep voice startled Tommy out of his thoughts. "How's it going?"

"Good, Ken." Jack made the introductions.

"Nice to meet you, Tommy." Ken reached across the table to shake hands.

Tommy looked directly into Ken's eyes. "That's a good grip you've got there."

"It better be." Ken pulled his hand back with a chuckle. "I'm a tight end on the football team. I better be able to grip the football and keep hold of it." He began eating. "So, what were you guys talking about before I interrupted you?"

"Just getting to know each other." Jack looked over at Ken and smiled.

"I don't have to worry about competition, do I?" Ken whispered in Jack's ear.

Jack chuckled. "No. We'll talk later."

Tommy discreetly watched the interaction between the two similarly built men. They made a good looking couple, Ken's blond hair and blue eyes contrasting with Jack's brown hair and green eyes. He smiled to himself as he realized that there was a connection between the two; he could see it in the way they looked at each other.

Ken glanced over at the other table. "Is Mark back with Sally again?"

"Yeah," Jack grunted in response to Ken.

"I wonder if that bitch will ever decide what she wants," Ken said roughly, and then looked over at Tommy. "Sorry, man, I didn't mean to be rude. I'd have dumped her after the first time."

"What do you mean, first time?" Tommy inquired.

Jack shook his head. "She keeps him on a string like a yo-yo. When she needs him, she keeps him close. When she's through with him, she pushes him away until she needs him again."

Ken looked over at the other table. "I just can't believe that he lets her play him like that."

Tommy followed Ken's gaze. Mark was a very handsome man, especially with the mustache, goatee, and stubble of growth on his face.

"Well, that's enough about Mark," Jack stated. "There's got to be something else we can talk about."

"Are you recruiting pledges yet?" Ken asked.

"We're looking around," Jack replied evasively.

"Tommy, be careful around this guy. He can be very convincing when he wants something." Ken smiled at Jack to remove any sting from his teasing.

"I haven't talked with Tommy about pledging."

"Good. Maybe I can convince him to join Gamma," Ken declared.

Jack shot a wry smile at Ken and then looked over at Tommy. "Now you're in trouble. He's the president of Gamma. Talk about convincing others, he's a pro."

"I didn't convince you, did I?" Ken teased.

Jack's face turned pink and he lowered his head. "Not about joining Gamma," he said, glancing shyly at Ken, who laughed and slapped Jack on the back.

"I have to get to my next class." Tommy stood with a smile. "You guys are good together."

Jack frowned. "I hope you'll keep that to yourself, right?"

"Of course, I will. It was nice meeting you, Ken."

"Think about pledging Gamma," Ken called after Tommy.

Tommy raised a hand and waved good-bye to both of them. *I could be friends with those guys*, he thought as he walked away.

"I'm sorry about what happened this summer," Sally said sweetly. "My parents lectured me for half an hour after you left the barbecue. They told me that I was being a spoiled brat and that I shouldn't have treated you the way I did." She glanced shyly at him. "Will you forgive me?"

Mark looked into Sally's blue eyes and smiled broadly. "How can I say no to those beautiful eyes and pouty lips?" No matter how many times she broke up with him, he always took her back.

Sally giggled as she gently slapped him on the arm. "Stop. You sure know how to make a girl blush." She looked up at him through her lowered lashes.

"What's the problem with us, Sally?"

"I don't know, Mark."

"What do you want after we graduate?"

Sally looked away from him, took a deep breath and let it out. "I want to get married and have a family, but I also want to have a career. I don't want to end up being just a housewife."

"I have a feeling that housewives of the world would rebel against you for that comment," he said with a smile.

"What I mean is that I don't want to be stuck at home with children while my husband has a career. I want it all, Mark. I just don't know what I want first."

Mark reached over and held her hand. "My mother has it all, Sally. She married after college and began a family. She sold cosmetics and worked her way through grad school, earning her doctorate in psychology. She was a wife, a mother, a businesswoman, and a student. And I believe that she did a damn good job."

"I can't do what your mother did, Mark," she stated firmly.

"How do you know that?" He thought she might be lacking in confidence.

"That's too much for me to do by myself."

"My father gave her all the support she needed to get through it."

"I'm sure he did, sweetie. But, I want to do one thing first and then let the others follow into place. I can't decide which is more important to me." She smiled sadly at him. "That's why I'm scared about making a commitment to you. You seem to know exactly what you want."

Mark chuckled softly at the comment. "Yeah, well that's all a façade, Sally. I want to have a career, and a family, but most importantly, I want to share my life with somebody. I fell in love with you last year. You're beautiful, smart, and sexy," he said, watching her smile. "I thought we'd make a good couple, and not just because our fathers know each other. I enjoy being with you. But ever since New Year's, I don't understand all the break-ups we go through."

"I'm really sorry about that, Mark," she said, looking away as he scowled. "I enjoy being with you, but I'm not ready to make a commitment. And I won't be ready until I decide what I want."

"I can respect that. Besides, my dad told me that I need to be patient when dealing with women."

Sally giggled. "Why don't we take it slowly this semester? You've got football and your fraternity, and I've got my sorority events. We'll get together when time allows."

"Okay, I can agree to that." He looked at her solemnly. "But I don't know how many more times I can deal with our break-ups."

Sally leaned over and kissed him on the cheek. "You need to shave."

Mark shook his head in disbelief. He would probably never understand the control she had over him. "Yes, boss, but the goatee and mustache stay on." In the back of his mind, Mark wondered if getting back together with Sally really was the best thing for him.

It was fairly quiet around campus during the Labor Day weekend, since many students had gone away for the three day holiday. Tommy spent part of the weekend running through different areas of the small town of Timian and getting a head start on his classwork. He spent some time in the library doing research for a paper and some time sitting outside reading or watching students around campus. The weather had been hot and humid, and there was little relief in the warm breeze that blew through the window.

"Come in," Tommy yelled from his desk in response to the knock on his door.

"What are you doing in here on such a gorgeous day, Ford Tommy?" Kyle asked as he entered the room.

Tommy smiled. "I'm working on a paper that's due on Friday, Welby Kyle."

Kyle made a face. "I know it's Labor Day, but you're not supposed to be laboring."

"I can't help myself. I didn't have anything better to do."

"Well, come on. Let's go down to the river." Kyle looked over at the other side of the room. "Where's your roommate? I never see him around."

Tommy laughed. "He's partying with his off campus friends this weekend."

"See? Even your roommate knows the meaning of Labor Day."

"You don't understand, Kyle. He parties every night. That's why he only has four classes this semester, and none of them start before ten o'clock."

"Oh, I see, *every* day is Labor Day." Kyle pulled back on Tommy's chair. "Come on. Let's get out of here and have some fun."

"All right. Lead on."

"I really have to thank you, Tommy," Jack said as they sat down to eat lunch following their psychology class. "I was pretty sure I had the right answer, but I started questioning myself when Professor Kimball said I was wrong. Then you saved me."

"Come off it, Jack," Tommy said modestly. "I simply explained how your answer could also be correct."

"Yeah, right. That's why he looked shocked when you challenged him. Did you get in trouble after class?"

"No. He just wanted to talk," Tommy replied briefly. He noticed Jack wave at somebody.

"Mark," Jack yelled, "come join us." Jack smiled at the faint blush that rose to Tommy's cheeks. Tommy lowered his head and continued eating his lunch.

"Hey, Jack." Mark sat down across the table from Tommy.

"Mark, I'd like you to meet Tommy." Jack waited for Tommy to lift his head. "Tommy, this is Mark Young, the school's star quarterback."

"Stop it, Jack." Mark held out his hand. "Hi."

"Nice to meet you, Mark." As Tommy reached over to shake Mark's hand, he looked up into a smiling face and bright blue eyes. All the noise in the cafeteria seemed to disappear for a brief moment.

"It's good to meet you, Tommy," Mark said as he shook Tommy's hand and felt a charge of energy rush through him. Mark glanced quizzically down at their clasped hands, then up at Tommy. He smiled faintly as he settled back in his chair.

Tommy wasn't sure how that had happened. He hadn't been practicing any magic since before his grandmother's death. He smiled back at Mark across the table.

"Tommy is in my psych class," Jack said. "He's a brilliant student and saved my ass today."

Tommy blushed and lowered his head. "It wasn't that big a deal, Jack."

"Somebody is always saving your ass, Jack," Mark commented with a laugh. "Good for you, kid. There's nothing wrong with being ahead of the rest of the class."

"Thanks." Tommy looked at his watch. "I need to leave for my next class. See you later, Jack." He stood up and grabbed his books and tray, then looked over at Mark. "It was really nice meeting you, Mark."

"You too, Tommy."

Mark watched as Tommy left the table, then looked back at Jack. "A curious young man. Humble. Unlike you."

"Go to hell." Jack laughed. "He really is a smart kid."

"Are you going to recruit him for Kappa?"

Jack shrugged. "I haven't asked him about it. He didn't seem too interested when Ken mentioned pledging Gamma."

Mark smiled at Jack. He suspected that Jack and Ken were more than just *buddies*, but that wasn't something that concerned Mark because Jack was his friend. "He might make a good pledge," Mark persisted as he continued eating his lunch.

"At least think about it," Brian pleaded.

"I don't know, Brian," Tommy demurred. "I have a full class load. I'm not sure I could devote the necessary time to pledging."

Brian leaned closer. "But I'd be your big brother; you wouldn't have to worry about anything."

I'd only have to worry about you. "All right, I'll think about it, but I'm not promising anything."

"That's fine. I'm just glad that you've agreed to think about it. In the meantime, would you like to go with me to the first football game on Saturday?"

"I'm sorry, Brian. My roommate asked me to join him and his friends for the game."

"Come on, Tommy. I promise you'll have a lot more fun at the game with me than with your roommate."

Tommy looked pointedly at Brian. "If I didn't know better, I'd think you were coming on to me. But we all know that jocks don't play with boys." He gathered his books and stood up. "I'll see you later." Tommy smiled to himself as he walked away.

"Damn kid is going to be harder to crack than I thought," Brian mumbled as he watched Tommy walk away. "I'll get him, though. One way or another, I'll get him."

Are You Ready For Some Football?

Excitement was rife on the campus as the first game of the season arrived on a warm Saturday afternoon in mid-September. After two full weeks of classes, the everyday routine was finally broken. Timian State College was a small Division II school with roughly five thousand students. The old-style football stadium had originally been built in the early 1960s on an open field at the other end of town from campus. The home team seating was on one side of the field, and the visiting team seating was on the opposite side. The students and fans of Timian filled the fifteen levels of metal benches built onto a concrete base that stretched from one 20-yard line to the other. The students and fans for the visiting team had to be content with seven levels of metal benches that went from one 30-yard line to the other.

As they walked through town toward the football stadium, Scott and several of his friends passed a joint back and forth. When it came around to Tommy, he passed it along to the others. Some of Scott's friends also had flasks filled with vodka hidden under their shirts. Tommy was more interested in enjoying the game than in getting high or drunk.

He was excited. While he enjoyed the sport of football, his true fascination was with the muscular players. His best friend had been a linebacker on their high school team. They had grown up together and had started fooling around when they were young boys. His best friend's becoming a football player had been the catalyst for his obsession with the sport and the men who played it. Tommy knew that he wouldn't overtly make an advance on a straight college player; that could result in retaliation. That knowledge didn't dampen his enjoyment of the game or appreciation of the players.

Tommy, Scott, and his friends sat in the center of the first row of the stands, where they had a terrific view of the players on the sideline. From that vantage point, Tommy was able to watch Mark throughout the entire game. After a series of plays that set up the team's first touchdown, Mark took off his helmet and grabbed a cup of water behind the team bench. With the aid of binoculars, Tommy could see the sweat running down Mark's face and muscular neck. He watched as Mark's long, thick fingers combed through the sweat-dampened wavy black hair matted to his head. As he talked with another player, the smile on Mark's face softened the hard look that the black mustache and goatee gave him. Tommy saw the bright blue eyes glimmer as Mark talked to and congratulated other players on the sideline.

While Tommy watched Mark, he was being watched by others in different sections of the stands.

"Tommy Ford. That's the guy I think would make a good brother," Jack said to Oscar as he pointed toward Tommy.

"He's with the potheads," Oscar said, recognizing a couple of the older guys in the group sitting around Tommy. "We don't tolerate drug addicts in the fraternity."

"Trust me, Oscar, he's not a pothead. The kid with the freaky look is his roommate, Scott. I'm sure he's with them just as we're with other Kappas, to have somebody to go to the game with," Jack countered. "Tommy is a bright student and has a demeanor that causes people to like him. If he were a pothead, he wouldn't have that kind of attitude, and he wouldn't be so well-prepared for class."

Oscar looked at Tommy, then back at Jack. "Are you sure?"

"Trust me. He's in my psych class. Whenever Professor Kimball asks a question, he's the first person with his hand up. The professor has even started to ignore him and pick on those of us trying to avoid being called on. Tommy saved my ass once by correcting the professor when I gave an ambiguous response that could have been either right or wrong." Jack grinned. "The other students in class really like him. Most of us feel a little jealous that he knows all the answers, but he doesn't come across as a know-it-all, and he doesn't flaunt his intelligence. Seriously, Oscar, he's a good kid; he'll make an even better brother."

As he studied the freshman, something about the young man caught Oscar's attention. Tommy looked toward the group of Kappas, and Oscar felt a rush of energy go through him as their eyes connected for a brief moment. He nodded thoughtfully.

"Invite him to the party on Tuesday, and we'll see how the others feel about him," Oscar said to Jack.

In a different section of the stadium, several members of Gamma Theta rooted for their brothers on the team. Brian had been watching Tommy. "There he is, front row center, sitting with some of our pot buddies." Brian pointed toward Tommy for the benefit of his senior brother, Andy. "I really think he'd make a good brother."

"Have you made a move on him yet?" Andy asked, looking toward the potential pledge.

"We've had lunch together a couple of times," Brian stated. "I'm still trying to get to know him better."

"I bet you are, dog." Andy chuckled. "Invite him to the rush party on Wednesday night. Since sweet-talking hasn't worked, maybe if you got him drunk and high first, you'd get him into your bed."

Brian smiled as he watched Tommy cheering for the team. "The thought had crossed my mind."

Timian's football team won the first game of the season in a 35-32 upset of Antelope State, their biggest conference rival. Fans were ecstatic as they left the stadium.

"What a fucking great game!" Scott exclaimed. The group walked along a back street so that they could smoke a joint on the way back to the dorms.

"Mark was on fucking fire, man," Bill shouted, passing the joint to Tommy.

Tommy passed it on to one of the other guys without taking a hit. "I was impressed with the running touchdown that he made."

"Yeah, man, that was so cool. Who was that tight end that caught those two touchdowns?" Scott asked.

"Ken," Tommy immediately supplied. "That second catch that he made in the end zone was amazing."

"It was awesome." The joint came around again, and again Tommy sent it on its way without a toke.

As the rest of the guys smoked and talked about the game, Tommy's mind lingered on the one moment of the game that had meant the most to him. While the offense was getting ready to go back on the field for the winning drive, Mark had been standing near the water table behind the team bench. He had been scanning the stands when their eyes met for a moment. The crowd noise seemed to vanish as Tommy looked into Mark's eyes. That instant had been long enough for Tommy. He would be fantasizing about Mark for a long time.

"Why don't you come over with us and party?" Scott asked his roommate.

"Thanks, but I'm going back to the room and finish my class work."

Scott laughed as he slapped Tommy on the back. "All work and no play makes Tommy a dull boy."

"That's okay, Scott. Somebody has to be dull. It's not going to be you, so it might as well be me."

"All right, see ya later." Scott gave him a wave as he and the others turned down another street.

Tommy walked through town alone, whistling the school fight song, and thinking about Mark.

Tommy's morning routine began with a run at six o'clock. He loved being outside as the sun was beginning to rise. The air was fresh, and there were few people to get in his way. During the first few days at Timian, Tommy had run through campus, learning where all the buildings were and finding shortcuts to his classes. After he was familiar with the campus routes, he started running through the residential areas and then widened his scope and began running along Main Street, through town, and out to the stadium. He loved his morning jogs through the small town.

Donning his navy blue and gold running shorts and muscle t-shirt, shoving his feet into his sneakers, and placing his CD headphones over his ears, Tommy was ready to set his mind free. The only distractions were the occasional coal trucks rumbling through town, blowing dust around the street and sidewalk.

Leaving his dorm behind, Tommy ran north through campus to Main Street and then turned west. He ran through the center of town, five blocks of businesses on both sides of the street and a movie theater at each end, then past City Hall and the little central park. The rest of the town was residential. He ran along the tree-lined Main Street for a mile until he reached the turnoff for the cemetery, his preferred route. If he had continued forward, he would have passed the football stadium and then would have had to go downhill toward the river.

The cemetery, surrounded by a stone wall around its perimeter, was located three blocks off Main Street. There was a slight incline up to the black iron main gate. Inside, Tommy could sense the peace and quiet, as if all noise was kept outside the gate. He loved the scent from the pine trees that were scattered amongst the gravestones and the sound of the birds singing in the early morning light. Running up the inclined dirt road and around a bend, he passed the graves of soldiers who had died during the American Revolution and the Civil War. The worn gravestones were overgrown with moss and barely legible. He rounded another bend and ran along the road in the back end of the cemetery, looking out over the open fields of grass toward the wooded areas half a mile away. A dozen pine trees lined the central spine of the small hillside where he ran. Tommy's favorite meditation spot was at the top of the hill, between the pine trees, looking out over the open western fields.

As he ran out the front gate, Tommy turned right and began running uphill, passing the masonry buildings where the grave-digging equipment was stored.

Beyond the peak he ran downhill and around the bend that led into the trailer park at the end of town. Over the music of his CD player, he could hear dogs barking, and he smiled at the familiar early morning distraction.

Tommy ran through the trailer park and back into the nicer residential areas of town. On Saturday and Sunday mornings, he often turned right and continued out toward the mall and freeway, adding two miles to his route. On weekdays, he kept to the residential areas. He ran down the quiet, tree-lined neighborhoods leading back toward the campus. He was looking forward to the sight of all the green leaves changing to bright reds and golds once autumn arrived.

Tommy had a lot on his mind this beautiful Sunday morning. He had loved the first couple of weeks of classes and the new friends he had made. His roommate, Scott, was strange, but the two of them had been getting along well, especially since Scott was always out partying. Kyle was a really great guy, and the two of them had quickly become friends. He also liked Jack a lot and believed that they had a secret in common, especially after meeting Jack's friend Ken. Tommy wasn't sure how he felt about Brian. He sometimes felt uncomfortable around him, as if he were being sized up. Other times, Tommy enjoyed his company and didn't mind the attention Brian paid him.

As he reached the end of the trailer park, Tommy decided that he needed to run the extra distance out to the mall. There were still a few things on his mind that he needed to mull over. Both Jack and Brian had invited Tommy to their first fraternity rush parties, one on Tuesday and one on Wednesday. Tommy wasn't sure he wanted to pledge any fraternity, but it wouldn't hurt him to go to the parties and see what they all were about. If he did decide to join one of them, he knew which one he would pick and the primary reason for pledging it. Mark Young.

Tommy had not been able to get Mark off his mind since the first time he'd seen him walking through the lobby of his dorm. He fondly remembered the day that Mark had joined Jack and him for lunch, when Tommy had felt the charge of energy that surged between the two of them. He had also enjoyed watching Mark on the football field. From the little he knew, there were a lot of good things about Mark, so Tommy couldn't figure out why he put up with his girlfriend's behavior. He deserved someone better, even if that was another woman. Tommy smiled to himself. *I'd be happy just to be friends with Mark.*

2: FRATERNITY RUSH WEEK

"Hey, Ford Tommy," Kyle called through the open room door.

"What, Welby Kyle?"

"Wow!" Kyle stopped and stared at the print hanging on the wall above Tommy's bed. The art deco painting was of a man in a black overcoat and white scarf, holding a top hat. "Great painting. De Lempicka, right?"

Tommy closed his textbook. "Yeah. I bought it the other day to brighten up these walls. How'd you know?"

"My parents have several of her pieces, but not this one. It definitely looks a lot better than Goth posters." Kyle glanced over to Scott's side of the room. "Are you ready to go to the Kappa rush party?"

"I am." Tommy let Kyle precede him out of the room, then locked the door.

"Who invited you to the party?" Kyle asked as they started walking the three blocks to the Kappa house.

"Jack. He's in my psych class. I'm not sure about pledging because of my class load, but he said just come to the party and decide later."

"I was invited by Dave, the Kappa president. He assists the professor and helps the students in my chem lab."

"A guy from Gamma also invited me to pledge his fraternity, but he was putting way too much pressure on me to join. Jack didn't seem to care one way or the other."

"Same here. There was no pressure from Dave to join, just the invitation." Kyle added, "I thought that was great."

"Have you been to the Kappa house before?" Tommy asked. "I don't usually run this way."

"Me neither. I guess we'll both be seeing the house for the first time."

At the end of the third block, Tommy and Kyle stood in front of Kappa Lambda Pi. The three-story wood and brick house was located in a quiet residential neighborhood, in the center of a grassy lot surrounded by oaks and pine. A roofed porch with a wooden railing went around the entire house. Lights blazed from all the windows, music blared from inside, and a lot of people were milling about outside.

Kyle whistled. "Wow, that's a big house."

"It's a bit intimidating." Tommy had second thoughts about going inside.

"If anyone can handle intimidation, it's you."

"Thanks," Tommy said as he steadied his nerves, calmed his mind, and walked up to the front door with Kyle close behind.

As they entered the house, they were met with warm handshakes by several brothers. Jack walked over to the two potential pledges and greeted them. "Welcome, gentlemen. I'm glad that you both decided to make it."

After Tommy introduced the two men, Jack asked Kyle, "You were invited by Dave, right?"

"That's right. Is he around here somewhere?"

"I saw him in the kitchen." Jack nodded in that general direction. "Come on, we'll find him."

Kyle stayed with Dave in the kitchen, while Jack led Tommy downstairs into the basement. He got them each a beer, introduced Tommy to some of the younger members of the fraternity, then led Tommy back upstairs and showed him around the first floor. As they re-entered the living room, Jack called a greeting to a group of senior members in the far corner and led Tommy over toward them.

"Hello, brothers. Let me introduce you to Tommy Ford," Jack said. "Tommy, this is Oscar, our pledge master; Rick, our treasurer; Brent, our secretary; and Joe, our vice president. And you've already met Mark."

Joe was the last of the brothers to shake Tommy's hand. "It's really nice to meet you, Tommy. We heard that you saved Jack's butt in psych class. It's not easy to keep him from looking like a fool," Joe said, causing the others to laugh.

"Thanks, Joe," Jack said with a wry chuckle.

Tommy could sense Mark's anxiety, but didn't have time to think about it as the other guys were beginning to ask him questions.

Rick was first. "What's your major?"

"Psychology and sociology. I'm hoping to specialize in therapy geared toward young adults. The teenage years are the hardest years to survive."

"Amen," several of the guys muttered.

"So, what's your class schedule like this semester?" Joe asked.

"I'm taking eighteen credits. I have fairly good study habits, and don't think it should be a problem."

"You'd have to have good study habits to handle eighteen credits."

"When you have free time," the other guys chuckled, "what are your interests?" asked Brent.

"I like to run first thing in the morning and enjoy an hour of meditation in the afternoon."

"What type of community service do you participate in?" Oscar queried.

Tommy held the pace of the rapid-fire questions. "I worked as an assistant at a senior housing center, keeping elderly people company and reading to them. I did that for the past two years while my great aunt was a resident, and also during my grandmother's last months. It started with just being there for them, and then I began helping others, since I found I had the time. I've also helped to raise money for research foundations, in the hopes of finding cures for diseases." Tommy decided not to indicate that the research foundation that he helped raise money for was an AIDS foundation. He wasn't sure how the Kappas would handle that information.

"What types of books and movies do you like?" Rick asked.

"I'm a horror and science-fiction fanatic, with both movies and books."

"I bet you're an Anne Rice fan," Joe added, "since she has that vampire series."

"You'd lose that bet." Tommy smiled brightly. "I prefer Chelsea Quinn Yarbro's historical novels about a 3,000-year-old vampire named St. Germain. They are more intriguing to me because of the historical research and settings of each story. Those books are the main reason I'm taking European History this semester."

"You're taking Euro History?" Oscar commented. "That's usually a class you take later, like junior or senior year."

"Well, that was the only history class that interested me and was available when I pre-registered at orientation."

Mark interjected for the first time. "What's your favorite sport?"

"Participation sports would be tennis, swimming, and running. Viewing sports would be football," Tommy responded.

"What did you think about the game on Saturday?" Mark inquired.

Tommy thought for only a second before looking directly into Mark's bright blue eyes. "I thought you started off the game a little flat." Tommy noted the looks of surprise from Mark and the others. "Then again, your line wasn't holding the pocket long enough for you to get set, which is probably what caused that interception. The line play got stronger by the end of the first quarter, and then you lit up the field. That 40-yard pass to Ken was a beautiful spiral right into his hands, and the timing couldn't have been better. But my favorite play was when you ran for that eight-yard touchdown. It reminded me of Steve Young." He tilted his head. "You wouldn't happen to be related to him so that I could get *his* autograph?"

The group of guys started laughing, while Mark favored Tommy with a smile. "That's an impressive assessment. And, no, I'm not related to Steve Young."

"I love football. I watch as often as my time permits." Tommy nodded at Mark. "By the way, I thought you were awesome."

"Thanks."

"Since you're from Jersey, are you an Eagles, Giants, or Jets fan?" Jack asked.

"None of the above." Tommy turned toward Jack. "I'm a Forty-Niners fan. Joe Montana was one of the greatest QBs during the 1980s."

"Dude, Marino and Elway had better arms and far more yardage. Their stats were much more impressive," Joe argued.

"If I owned a football team, I'd much rather have a QB that can win when it counts." Tommy focused on Joe. "Montana's stats may not be as impressive as Marino's or Elway's, and yet he won four Super Bowls. And I do believe that he beat Marino and Elway both in two of those four Super Bowls." Oscar, Jack, and Mark started chuckling. "If we use your comparison, Terry Bradshaw wasn't the better QB compared to Marino and Elway, but I recall that he also won four Super Bowls. Bradshaw and Montana both had great running backs behind them and great receivers in front of them. They also played on teams that had amazing defenses. I'll take wins over flash any day!"

Hoots and howls of laughter sprang from the group. "He got you on that, Joe," Jack said, patting Tommy on the back. He remained close to Tommy for the remainder of the evening, making sure he was introduced to all the members of the house council.

Mark stood by his bedroom window, watching as Tommy and Kyle left the house around eleven o'clock. He had felt a rush of excitement, followed by a wash of fear, race through his body as he shook hands with the young man. He remembered the rush of energy he had felt the first time they shook hands in the cafeteria, and also remembered looking up into the stands during the football game and seeing Tommy amongst the crowd.

During the conversation at the party, Mark had enjoyed listening to Tommy and had even noticed a sadness in Tommy's voice when he had mentioned his grandmother. He had started to wonder why he had found himself so interested in this young man's life, and had become uncomfortable standing next to him. Something about the positive, confident young man made Mark nervous. Recalling the smile he received from Tommy, as he left the room, he wondered what would happen if Tommy was invited to pledge Kappa. A slight smile crossed his face as he turned away from the window. *This could turn out to be a very interesting semester*, was his last thought about the young man before getting into bed.

Gamma Theta Aftermath

"Mind if I join you?" Ken asked.

Tommy was sitting at his favorite table in the back corner of the dining hall, eating breakfast and preparing for his Thursday morning class. "Of course not," he replied.

Ken sat down in the chair next to Tommy. "I know that Jack hopes you'll pledge Kappa, and he said that you went to their rush party on Tuesday, so I'm glad you took the time to come to the Gamma party last night. But I couldn't help noticing you didn't stay long. I'm sorry if you felt uncomfortable at the party."

While Tommy tried not to judge the behavior of others, the openly sexual goings on in the Gamma house weren't to his liking. "No offense, Ken, but the Gammas were a little too intense, and Brian was a little too pushy."

"Gamma is a little more open-minded than most fraternities; nobody has to feel as if they have to hide who they are."

"From the antics going on throughout the house, it appears you guys are a *lot* more open-minded."

Tommy had left the Wednesday night rush party after only half an hour. Gamma's party had been louder than Kappa's, there had been more than just beer being served, and the smell of pot had been prominent throughout the house. Students were paired together in every combination imaginable, necking in any dark corner they could find. Brian had been high and drunk, and making blatant advances on Tommy.

"Our parties do tend to get a little out of hand, but we make no pretenses about our feelings and desires." Ken waited for a reaction.

"I'm not sure that I'm ready for that much openness in my life. I'm a little more old-fashioned about my behavior." Tommy preferred the privacy of one-on-one relationships. He understood that being able to be out, and not having to continue to hide his sexuality, would probably make him feel better about himself. However, he didn't want everyone to know he was gay, nor was he interested in seeing how many other guys he could catch.

"I understand," Ken said. "You should know that some of our brothers are faithful to one another. I wouldn't consider cheating on my partner, even with all that sexual activity around me."

"That's nice to know."

"You are aware that Brian is interested in you."

Tommy was surprised by Ken's directness. "I got that impression from our lunches, the way he kept rubbing my neck last night, and the invitation to spend the night," he stated, not indicating a reciprocal interest in Brian.

Ken smiled. "I think I understand. You're not as interested in Brian as he is in you."

"Brian can be a nice guy, but he can also be a jerk. I'm not interested in a one night stand or being a notch on his bedpost."

"Most guys don't catch on to Brian's act until the morning after."

Tommy chuckled. "I'm not like most guys. I learned a few of life's harder lessons when I was a little boy. Plus, I have an uncle who explained the birds and the bees to me when I realized that I was different."

Ken studied the young man. "Open, honest, and sincere. How did you get to be so mature at your age?"

"I'm not that much younger than you are," Tommy replied. "I listened to my wise old grandmother and my uncles."

"Smart, too." Ken complimented, as he returned to the original subject. "Are you going to join Kappa?"

"I believe you have to be invited to join before you can make that decision."

"Yeah, but I know that Jack is your sponsor into Kappa. If the rest of Kappa likes you as much as Jack and I do, you're a cinch to get in."

"Thanks," Tommy said shyly.

"I'm going to be honest with you."

"I thought you were before, Ken."

"I was," Ken replied, taking a deep breath and slowly letting it out. "I joined Gamma with two good friends, and we're all part of our fraternity council now. When we joined, it was a great fraternity. Gamma and Kappa were the top two fraternities on campus, with the highest GPAs and best athletes. However, over the last couple of years, more guys who enjoy partying and being open have joined Gamma. I don't think that's necessarily a bad thing, but if I had to choose to join Gamma or another fraternity today, I'd join another fraternity."

Tommy was surprised by Ken's comments. "I can't believe you're saying that about your own fraternity."

"Neither can I, but it's true. I haven't been happy with this group of guys." He looked directly at Tommy. "I'm a senior, and it's the last year I have to put up with a bunch of jerks like Brian. You're a good kid, Tommy, and you might be able to help change Gamma back into a better fraternity, but I don't want to see you get caught up in this mess. Jack's in a good fraternity, and if I were you, I'd pick Kappa over Gamma."

"Thanks for your honesty, Ken."

"It's a part of who I am, Tommy." Ken smiled at last. "Besides, Jack would be pissed at me if I tried to talk you into joining Gamma, especially knowing how bad it's gotten."

"I'm really sorry about last night, Tommy," Brian said as they were walking out of their Thursday psychology class. "I had a few too many drinks and got carried away. I hope you'll forgive me."

Tommy shook his head. "I was irritated by the way you came on to me."

"Tommy, you're a sweet guy. I couldn't help myself." Brian's eyes begged for understanding.

Outside, Tommy situated himself so that the sun was shining on his back and into Brian's eyes. Brian had to squint because he was not wearing his sunglasses, and because he was obviously still suffering a hangover from the rush party. Tommy enjoyed the discomfort on Brian's face.

"Brian, you're a nice enough guy and I don't want to hurt you, but I'm just not interested. Someday I hope to meet a man that I'll fall in love with, and we'll spend our lives together."

"That's a fantasy, Tommy. Happily ever after doesn't happen between two guys."

"Sorry, Brian, but I'm not a one-night stand and I'm not a weekend fling. I'm the type of guy who wants a relationship. I'll wait until I find the guy that makes me feel all gushy inside."

"Gushy? You are a crazy kid." He gave Tommy a quick hug. "Good luck finding that prince," he said, laughing as he walked away.

"What was that all about?" Jack asked as he caught up to Tommy.

"Just a little apology from Brian for his bad behavior at the Gamma party last night."

"You went to the Gamma party?" Jack asked.

Tommy was wise enough to know Ken would have told Jack what had happened at the party. He was also smart enough to let Jack pretend to be surprised. "Sure. I need to check out all my fraternity options, don't I?"

"I guess you do." Jack smiled with understanding. "So, what did you think about Gamma?"

"Not exactly my cup of tea." Tommy shrugged.

"Good." Jack put an arm around Tommy's shoulder and led him toward the cafeteria for lunch.

Dinner tray in hand, Oscar looked around the dining area for a table. He spotted Tommy sitting by himself in a corner and walked over to his table. "Would you mind if I joined you?"

"Of course not, Oscar," Tommy said, looking up from his textbook. "To what do I owe the honor?"

"I saw you sitting by yourself with a textbook open in front of you, and I thought you could use some dinner company."

"That's really nice of you," Tommy said skeptically. He sensed there was more than one reason for Oscar joining him. "I'd enjoy the company."

"I was quite impressed with your responses to the questions you were asked the other night," Oscar said as he sat down in the chair next to Tommy.

"I was just answering simple questions."

"No, you weren't. You were being baited," Oscar said with a smile.

"What do you mean?"

"Personal invitations were only given to twenty of the people who attended the party Tuesday night. The brother who recommended the student for the invitation provided us with background information." Oscar looked at him for a response. When there was none, he continued. "Jack told us about your major and the number of credits you were taking, and that you were prone to keeping to yourself. So you were considered the bookworm of the group. Some of the guys thought they could catch you giving bullshit responses or trying to kiss up to the brotherhood."

"I'll have to be a little more careful around Jack," Tommy said with a wry grin. "But I don't understand how I became the bookworm."

"We're looking for interesting students to become brothers, outgoing people who work well with others, who don't mind grunt work tasks, and who are interested in serving the community. Several brothers didn't think you were the type to fit into our fraternity."

"Were you one of them?"

"No. My instincts tell me that you would be a make a good brother."

"What was so impressive about my answers, then?"

"The honesty with which you answered them, without stopping to think about your answers first." He started laughing. "But when you told Mark that he started off flat in the football game, you won them over. None of the brothers would have dared to tell him that he was anything less than spectacular."

Tommy wondered if he had misjudged Mark. "Is Mark that egotistical?"

"On the contrary, he's the exact opposite. He doesn't take compliments well, but he also doesn't take direct criticism well. You just laid it all out there."

Tommy was concerned that he had made a mistake at the party. "Was he mad at me? He left rather quickly after I made those comments."

"Oh, no," Oscar reassured him. "I believe he was quite surprised that you had made an accurate assessment, and I also think he appreciated the candor. Not that he would have told me, one way or the other."

For several minutes, both men ate their dinner without speaking.

"Is there another reason you joined me for dinner?" Tommy asked quietly, looking over at Oscar.

Oscar was only slightly surprised at being called on his ulterior motive for joining Tommy. He could now confirm for himself that there was more to Tommy than most people realized or understood. He made a mental note to contact his grandmother and speak with her about the potential pledge.

"Well, a friend of mine was at Gamma's rush party last night and mentioned that he saw you there."

"I was there. I thought students were allowed to attend more than one rush party."

"You don't like beating around the bush, do you?" Oscar laughed. "I was curious as to your thoughts about Gamma. I didn't get the sense from you on Tuesday night that Gamma would be the right fit for you."

"What do you mean?"

"There's something about you. I haven't figured it out yet, but you don't appear to be the type of guy—"

"Maybe your spy didn't tell you I left that party half an hour after arriving. I'm an old-fashioned boy, and the Gammas are a little too open and outgoing for me."

"I'm sorry if I offended you. That wasn't my intention," Oscar said sincerely. "I was just curious about whether or not you would accept an invitation to pledge Gamma."

Tommy pondered his next comments for a moment. He didn't want to hurt his chances of being invited to pledge Kappa, but he was not happy about having his activities reported on by others.

"It is my understanding, from reading materials provided by the college administration, that during rush week students are allowed to go around to the various fraternities or sororities to see whether they would want to join any. It is also my understanding that outside influence was not supposed to be placed on students to sway them away from a fraternity before a fraternity sent out their invitation to pledge."

"Well, well, well, Mister Ford, you've done your homework regarding fraternity pledging. I'm impressed!" Oscar complimented.

"I'm not going to answer your question." Tommy looked directly into Oscar's eyes. "Even if that means I lose the chance to join the only fraternity that I would consider pledging."

Oscar burst out laughing. "*Amigo*, we are going to get together again. I haven't been this entertained during a meal in a long time. Thank you for your candor." He winked at Tommy and stood up from the table. "And for correcting me with regards to my attempt at influencing your choice of fraternity." He was still laughing as he walked away.

Timian's football team won its second game of the season at home, 17-13. It was a hard fought game, with both defenses playing well. Mark threw one passing touchdown to Ken, one interception, and was sacked four times. Dave had a spectacular game at his linebacker position, with three sacks and two interceptions.

"Are you going over to Kappa house for the party?" Kyle asked as they were leaving the game.

"I was thinking about it," Tommy replied.

"It's our second chance to make an impression on them."

"I know it is," Tommy said dejectedly.

"Are you worried about not making it into Kappa?" Kyle asked, as he started walking backwards, looking at Tommy. "Dude, you're always smiling, you get along well with everyone around you, and they all seem to like you. You're the most enchanting guy that I have ever met, and I don't say that about guys." He smiled.

Tommy smiled back. "All right, I'm sorry. It just makes me nervous, being checked out by all these guys and trying to make a good impression on them."

"Just be yourself, Tommy. You're a great guy to be around. And it usually takes me a while to warm up to new people."

"Okay, you've made your point. But I'm still nervous about all of this."

Kyle put his arm around Tommy's shoulder. "It's okay to be nervous. I'll be there with you. Don't worry about it."

On their way over to Kappa house, Kyle and Tommy talked about the game and laughed and joked about some of the people in their classes. They were greeted by several brothers as they entered the front room, then went into the kitchen to get something to drink. Kyle got a beer, and Tommy got a 7-Up.

Tommy found Jack in the living room and joined the group talking with him. He was introduced to a few new brothers and answered some of the same questions that he had been asked at the previous party. He found it easier this time, and soon discovered that he was really enjoying himself. The Kappa brothers were making him feel comfortable and welcome.

An hour later, the brothers who were on the football team entered the house to rousing cheers from all those in attendance. They greeted people on their way through the living room and upstairs to their rooms to put away their personal football gear. When they came back down, Mark made his way through the group to Tommy. "I was pretty flat again this week," he said with a smile.

"Well, their defense was tough on you guys," Tommy said.

"Don't sugar-coat it, kid," Mark stated firmly but with a smile.

"You ended up winning the game, so I won't nit-pick this week."

"Thanks." Mark turned as Sally walked up to him. "Hey, babe." He hugged and kissed her.

Tommy quietly left the group and went into the kitchen to talk with some of the other Kappas. He wasn't upset that Sally had arrived, but he didn't want to watch her and Mark together. He was envious of the closeness between them. Tommy knew that he had to keep such feelings hidden deep inside so that they wouldn't interfere in his becoming a member of the fraternity.

"We're going out to dinner. We'll see you guys later," Mark said to Dave and Oscar as he and Sally were preparing to leave.

"Have a good time," Dave said to the couple.

Tommy watched Mark leave the house from where he stood in the back corner with Jack and some other Kappas. Tommy smiled and waved at him. Mark returned the smile, but as he escorted Sally out of the house, it vanished from his face.

Invitation To Pledge

It was a warm Sunday morning, and there was a lot of activity on the first floor of Kappa house. Twenty-five members of the fraternity were preparing to discuss the students who might receive invitations to pledge Kappa.

"Brothers," Oscar rapped his gavel against the table, "let's come to order so that we can get started." He waited until those gathered had quieted. "Thank you, brothers. As you can see, we have placed thirty student photos around the room. The pictures were taken during the parties on Tuesday and after yesterday's game. These are the students who have shown the most interest in becoming Kappa brothers. All of them have been sponsored by at least one current brother. We'll spend the next hour discussing the pros and cons of each candidate before taking our first poll. A minimum of half the brothers present today must approve the student before he can be considered for an invitation to pledge."

Dave and Joe passed out sheets of paper that listed the name of each student. There was enough space on the paper by each student's name for the brothers to take notes.

"Once we finish discussing the students, you should vote only for those that you believe would make good brothers. The names of those who get enough votes will then be placed before the house council, which will make the final decision as to who will be invited to pledge. Are there any questions?" Oscar looked around at the brothers, then pounded his gavel on the table. "Then let the games begin."

During the next hour, small groups gathered in front of each photograph and discussed that particular student. There was a lot of discussion about some of the candidates and quite a bit of laughter about a few others. Few of the brothers in attendance could find fault with either Tommy or Kyle, as both of those young men had made good impressions.

When the hour had passed, Oscar banged his gavel on the table and instructed the brothers to cast their votes. The ballots were then gathered and given to the Kappa ruling council to count. Dave, Joe, Brent, and Rick took the votes into the smaller office, while other brothers meandered around the house.

"You're looking a little green around the gills," Jack teased Mark as they walked into the kitchen.

"I had a bit too much to drink last night." Mark grabbed a bottle of water from the refrigerator.

Knowing that Mark had been with Sally the night before, Jack nudged Mark with his elbow. "You devil."

Mark shook his head. "Unfortunately, it wasn't all that good." He took a huge gulp of the water and swallowed. "We had a good dinner together, then we bought a bottle of wine and went back to her room at Delta house. The wine went straight to my head. Not only did I get a bad headache, but there was no performance."

Jack tried not to laugh, but he couldn't help it. "I'm sorry. I know it's not funny." He put his arm around Mark's shoulder. "It happens to the best of us."

"And I still have the headache," Mark grumbled.

The house council met in the private living room on the third floor to vote on the twenty students selected for consideration by the brotherhood. Along with the four members of the Kappa ruling council, the other members were: seniors Oscar,

Mark, and Walter; juniors Jack and Jorge; sophomores Donald and Steve; and the lone second semester freshman, Paul. They stood in a circle, holding hands, with their heads bowed as Dave said the fraternity prayer for guidance. The television channel was turned to a football game, but the sound was muted. A mini-refrigerator in one corner of the room was stocked with plenty of beer and soda, and bowls of chips and pretzels had been placed around the room. The council members took seats and began reviewing the candidates.

Once the list of twenty names had been winnowed down to fourteen, the house council took a half-hour break before reviewing the finalist and holding the final vote.

"All right, brothers, before we take the final vote, are there any concerns or comments that you want to make about any of the students?" Oscar asked.

"Just one," Brent called out.

"Which student do you have a concern about, Brent?" Oscar asked.

"Tommy."

Jack glared over at Brent. "What's wrong with him?"

"How can anybody be that fucking positive and happy?" Brent's objection made the brothers laugh.

Mark gave a sigh of relief. He'd briefly been concerned that the brothers would not want to invite Tommy to pledge. "There's nothing wrong with a positive attitude, Brent. You could use one."

The brothers continued laughing, and Brent joined in.

"Any *real* concerns?" Oscar asked. "All right, by a show of hands we'll vote on each of the remaining fourteen. Remember that it takes at least ten votes for the candidate to receive an invitation."

As each student's picture was shown, the house council members raised their hands to offer that student an invitation. Tommy, Kyle, and one other pledge, Carlos, received unanimous votes for acceptance. Six other pledges received eleven votes; while one, Herbert, received the minimum ten votes. Four remaining students did not receive enough votes to be accepted into the fraternity pledge group.

After the last round of voting, Oscar said, "All right, brothers, now it's time for the members to pick the students they would like to have as their little brothers. It will be your responsibility to invite your prospective little brother to pledge Kappa, and then to help guarantee that he makes it through the process. Normally the ruling council would get the first selections; however, they informed me earlier that they were going to give the first choice to our star quarterback." He looked over at Mark. "Mark, you've been an exemplary member of the brotherhood since you first pledged, and you've never had a little brother. And because you're the best quarterback this school has ever seen, you have the honor of making the first choice."

Mark looked at all of the student pictures on the table, but kept looking back at one in particular. He pulled the picture off the table and held it up. "I'll take Tommy," he said quietly, wondering if he was making the right choice.

"Damn," Jack said under his breath.

As president of Kappa, Dave received the next choice and picked Kyle. The other four senior members made their choices, followed by the two junior members. Pursuant to fraternity rule, the two sophomore and single freshman members of the house council were not allowed to have little brothers. As pledge master, Oscar did not have a pick because he was responsible for overseeing the entire pledge process.

The last two candidates would be offered to two of the senior members of the fraternity.

"Okay, gentlemen, tomorrow you should go meet your potential little brothers, give them the applications, and make the invitations to pledge Kappa Lambda Pi," Oscar said. "After we have their applications and fraternity dues, they will be admitted to the pledge class. Please ask them to provide us with their applications before the meeting on Friday night."

At seven-thirty Monday morning, Mark knocked on Tommy's door. Mark smiled as he waited for an answer. Despite his feeling of unease around Tommy, he would now have an opportunity to learn more about the intriguing young man. He wondered how Tommy would handle the ordeals he would have to endure during the pledge period.

A sleepy, naked Scott answered the door. "Hey, dude, if you're looking for Tommy, he already left. You might be able to catch him in the cafeteria, getting ready for his eight-thirty class."

"Okay, thanks." Mark departed quickly, hiding his grimace, appalled by the sight he had just seen.

In the cafeteria, Mark left the serving line with his breakfast tray and looked around. It was still early enough that the large dining hall was not full. He spotted Tommy sitting at a table near the back wall in the center of the room, his head lowered over a book. "Mind if I join you?" Not waiting for a reply, Mark sat down.

"Not at all," Tommy said, a blush spreading over his cheeks.

Mark was glad to see that he had caught Tommy off-guard. "I'm here to invite you to join Kappa Lambda Pi."

"Wow!" Tommy's eyes sparkled as they met Mark's. "I was hoping that I would be asked. Thank you."

"There are a few things you need to know before accepting our invitation." Mark took a sip of his orange juice.

Tommy shut his book and looked over at Mark. "Okay, you have my full attention."

Mark handed him a sheet of paper, which Tommy glanced at before slipping it inside his notebook. "We need you to fill out the application before Friday night. Fraternity dues are also required, but we will accept payments throughout the pledge period. There will be a meeting at eight o'clock on Friday night, and all the new pledges are expected to be there on time," he said firmly.

"That won't be a problem, sir." Tommy had overheard the younger brothers calling the older brothers "sir" at the Kappa parties and used it.

Mark was impressed by the immediate and proper response. "Are you sure you can handle the demands of pledging a fraternity in addition to your class load?"

"Yes, sir."

"We expect a lot from our pledges, especially where grades are concerned."

Tommy looked directly at Mark. "Again, that won't be a problem, sir."

"We expect our pledges to participate in all house events and any meetings that they are told to attend." He watched Tommy for any signs of apprehension or doubt.

"Yes, sir."

"Good." He ate a forkful of eggs before continuing. "I'll be your big brother."

Tommy held his emotions at bay while absorbing this news. "Yes, sir. I won't let you down."

"That's good to hear. I'm not going to make it easy for you, but I'm not going to be a slave driver, either."

"I don't expect it to be easy, sir."

"I'm going to need a copy of your schedule so that we don't interfere with your classes," Mark said before concentrating on the remainder of his breakfast.

Just as Tommy was mopping up the last of his eggs, Brian walked up to the table and sat down next to him, directly across from Mark. "Good morning, gentlemen," he said brightly, and then focused on Tommy. "I'd like to invite you to join Gamma Theta."

"Wow! Two invitations in one morning."

Brian frowned at Mark. "You invited Tommy to join Kappa?"

"You know what they say about the early bird, Brian," Mark said with a smug smile.

Brian turned to Tommy. "Take your time and think about your decision. The right fraternity would set you up, be a support system for the rest of your life. We're a great fraternity, and we would love to have you as a brother." He glowered at Mark. "We have more to offer than sports."

"Both of our fraternities are three-quarters jocks, Brian." Mark chuckled. "And I'm not going to debate the opportunities that each could offer a guy like Tommy. I believe Tommy's smart enough to make the decision on his own."

Brian and Mark were quietly finishing breakfast when Mark felt Tommy's eyes on him. He looked over at Tommy and smiled.

"I need to go to my class," Tommy said. "Thank you both for the invitations. I'll consider them seriously." He stood and picked up his tray.

"Have a good day, Tommy," Mark responded.

"Thanks, Mark. You have a good day, too."

After Tommy had left, Mark smiled at Brian. "I believe it will be a good day."

Brian smiled smugly. "There's one thing that I can offer Tommy that you can't."

Mark looked amused, knowing Brian's reputation. "Maybe so, but is it something that Tommy wants? We'll have to wait and see what he decides," he said confidently.

Brian's eyes narrowed and he glared at Mark as he picked up his tray and walked away from the table.

Dave smiled when Mark walked through the kitchen door of the fraternity house late Monday afternoon, and held a piece of paper above his head. "Your pledge returned his application," Dave said, chuckling.

Mark wondered if he had misread the young man, if Tommy had decided to pledge Gamma. "Did he change his mind?"

"Nope. It's completed, and he paid his dues in cash."

"Really?"

"He brought it over earlier this afternoon. He's the first one to return his application."

"But I just gave it to him at breakfast." Mark was perplexed. "How much thought could he have put into the answers on the questionnaire?"

"Quite a bit, by the looks of it," Dave said. "Here's the other sheet of paper that gets attached to it, along with a copy of his schedule." He handed the sheets to

Mark. "I need those back when you're finished reading them."

Mark glanced over the neatly written responses. "Jesus!"

"It's an interesting application. He's a little weak in sports, but does like to play tennis and run. However, he's not here on an athletic scholarship. He's here on a full academic scholarship. He was in the top five of his class all four years in high school and was his class valedictorian. He's also had quite a bit of community involvement," Dave said with approval. "Looks like you might have a really good pledge on your hands."

"We'll see how he handles himself during the pledge period." Mark placed the application inside his notebook. "Gamma made an offer to him this morning, as well. I think Brian is going to be disappointed that he didn't get his boy."

Brian sat down to join Tommy for lunch after their Tuesday psychology class. "So, have you given any thought to pledging Gamma?"

"Yes, I've thought about it. I'm going to pledge Kappa."

"No, dude," Brian whined. "You're making a big mistake joining Kappa. They're just a bunch of dumb jocks."

Tommy stared at him incredulously. "Gamma is also full of jocks, Brian. The only difference is that Kappa has the best GPA of all the frats."

"They aren't as...accepting as Gammas." Brian smiled suggestively.

"I'm joining a fraternity, Brian, not an orgy. If what I cared about was getting laid, I'd join Gamma," Tommy said angrily.

Brian glared at him, then smiled. "Whoever they give you as a big brother won't treat you nearly as well as I would, sweet boy."

Before Tommy could respond, Mark and Sally walked by their table. Tommy noticed that neither of them looked happy. Brian watched as the couple sat down at a table near the back of the cafeteria. He looked over at Tommy, and saw that he was also looking at Mark. "As hot as Mark Young is," Brian said softly, "and even though he invited you to join Kappa, you'll never get the time of day from him. He's a pussy-whipped straight boy, who would only fuck your pretty little ass if he was drunk."

Tommy's heart raced, and he could feel the blood rushing to his face. He stood up and grabbed his tray, but before picking it up he leaned over to Brian. "You're a jackass, an arrogant, self-centered jackass." He took his tray and walked away from the table, still seething from Brian's comments.

3: PLEDGING A FRATERNITY, WEEK 1

"You're early," Jack said, opening the front door for Tommy and Kyle. "That's a good sign." He smiled at the two young men as he led them into the living room. "Have a seat up front while we wait for the others to arrive. May I get you something to drink?"

"A 7-Up would be nice," Tommy responded as he walked toward one of the ten chairs that had been arranged at the front of the living room.

"Same for me," Kyle replied.

Jack left them sitting in the living room and went to get their drinks. Several members of the fraternity walked through, but nobody spoke to the two pledges.

"Did you notice that there are seven clocks in this room?" Kyle whispered.

"Yes, and they all show different times." He looked over at Kyle. "What do you think that's all about?"

"I don't know." Kyle looked at his watch. "What time do you have?"

Tommy looked down at his watch. "Seven forty-eight. I set my watch according to the time from the college radio station."

"Same here." Kyle looked around the room at the various clocks. "That clock on the mantelpiece has the same time we have."

As the other pledges arrived, they were seated up front with Tommy and Kyle. The brothers who were coming to the meeting ignored the pledges and talked amongst themselves. Tommy and Kyle noticed that the brothers were all checking the clock on the mantel. When it reached eight o'clock, the same time as on Tommy and Kyle's watches, the pledge master stood up and began the meeting.

"I notice that we have two pledges that are late to the meeting." He looked sternly at the pledges who were present. "One of the first rules you will learn is that we do not tolerate tardiness. You are expected to be on time to every meeting and every event."

"Yes, sir," Tommy responded.

Everyone quietly waited until the last two pledges arrived. The two late arrivals made their way to the last remaining seats at the front of the room.

Oscar glared at the two young men. "Tardiness costs you one point for every minute that you are late. You each have five points against you. Now, let's begin this meeting." Oscar turned to address everyone in the room. "First, several members of this fraternity are members of the football team and are traveling to Erie for tomorrow's game." He looked at the pledges. "For the three of you who have football players for your big brother, I'll be their proxy when they are at away games." He waited for any response; when there was none, he continued. "Along with being on time to all meetings" — he looked pointedly at the two pledges that had been late — "all pledges are expected to assist in cleaning up the fraternity house and yard. You are also expected to clean your big brother's room and do his laundry each weekend. Any questions?"

"No, sir," Tommy and Kyle said quietly. None of the other pledges responded.

"All pledges are expected to obey any order or task given to them by other members of the fraternity." Oscar waited for somebody to complain. "Failure to obey any order or to complete any task given to you by your big brother will result in your losing five points. Failure to obey any order or to complete any task given to you by a member of the house council will result in your losing four points. Finally, failure to obey any order or to complete any task given to you by any other member of the fraternity will result in your losing three points. If you amass fifty or more negative points, you will be dropped from this pledge class. Is that understood?"

"Yes, sir," Tommy and Kyle responded. Again, they were the only ones to answer.

Oscar smiled at them before continuing. "All pledges are expected to design a paddle." He pointed to several fraternity paddles, made by previous pledges, hanging on the walls of the living room. "You will have four weeks in which to complete your paddle. They will be examined by the house council for approval and acceptance before your initiation into the fraternity." Again, he looked around at all the pledges. "Four weeks from Saturday night will be your formal initiation. If your paddle is not accepted, then you will have one opportunity to fix it so that it will be approved. Any questions?"

One of the pledges raised his hand. "Yes, Victor."

"What do we have to put on this paddle?" the pledge asked naively.

"I suggest you take a look around at the walls in the house and figure it out for yourself." Oscar again pointed toward some of the paddles hanging on the living room walls that had been left by previous brothers. "Does that answer your question?"

"Yes," Victor answered.

"Yes, what?" the pledge master asked.

The pledge looked at him, perplexed, then responded, "Yes, sir."

"Good. This task is to be completed by you alone; you can't ask for any help." Oscar glanced at each of the pledges. "Finally, pledges will be required to work with the Delta sorority sisters in creating our joint Homecoming float. Failure to assist with the building of the float will cost you ten points. You will also be required to ride on the float with the Delta sisters during the Homecoming parade, or you will lose ten points."

"Yes, sir," the pledges responded in unison.

"Great! We'll be standing along the parade route cheering for you." Oscar laughed. "Now, on to other business."

During the next hour, Oscar discussed fraternity business, new rules for fraternities passed down by the Intrafraternal Council and by Kappa's national committee. At times, the pledges looked confused by the information that was being provided, but several of them were taking notes.

"Before we adjourn," Oscar said, "there is a mixer tomorrow night at eight o'clock." He looked over at the pledges. "We expect you to be here at seven forty-five sharp. That's it, brothers. We are adjourned." Oscar brought the gavel down on the podium.

"That was fun," Tommy said as he and Kyle were walking back to their dorm a couple of hours later.

"Now I'm the one who's nervous."

"We can help each other get through this." Tommy put his arm around Kyle's shoulder. "You helped support me during the second party."

"We could make it even more interesting by challenging each other as well as supporting each other."

"Oh, a competition, huh?"

"Why not?"

"You're on, Welby Kyle."

Hoping that he would not disturb his roommate, Tommy entered his room quietly. He wasn't particularly surprised to see that Scott was not there. He turned on his desk light and began to undress for bed. As he looked out the window and finished a bottle of water, he thought about the events of the evening. His last thoughts before falling asleep were of Mark.

Tommy was excited when he woke up Saturday morning. He was ready to show the Kappa brothers that he was serious about pledging. He went out for his regular six o'clock run, staying on the short route rather than going out toward the mall. After returning, he went down the hall and took his shower. From previous experience, Tommy knew that Scott would not return to the room until the weekend was over. That would allow him to do the things that he needed to do before starting his day.

Tommy put on a pair of shorts and sat down in the lotus position in front of his grandmother's trunk, placing the white vase with the red silk rose on the floor next to it. He closed his eyes and placed both hands over his grandmother's clear quartz crystal, which hung around his neck and lay against his heart. He concentrated as he chanted: *Out with all things negative; I banish negativity. In with positive; I accept calming, cleansing and healing energy. Only pure stays in; purity is my magic.*

He then reached out for the trunk and gently lifted the lid. The energy that his grandmother had put into the trunk came forth and lifted his spirits. The smell of lilac pleasantly assailed his senses, and he smiled at the reminder of his grandmother. He slowly opened his eyes, then looked inside for the items that he needed.

Tommy pulled out the piece of royal blue velvet from the top of the trunk and laid it on the floor in front of him. Inside the trunk were twelve velvet pouches, six black and six red, containing crystals sorted by shape, size and color, along with several empty black velvet pouches. Each pouch had a protective symbol sewn onto it with gold thread. The crystals inside were each used for a particular purpose, such as the amethyst crystals that his grandmother had specifically empowered for healing. Tommy selected the two that he was looking for, pulled them out of the trunk and placed them on top of the blue material.

He moved several things out of his way — the other pouches, as well as a crystal ball, a dragon dagger, a deck of Tarot cards wrapped in red silk, sticks of sage and incense, small vials of oil of pennyroyal — and he reached for his grandmother's journal of spells. Underneath the journal were four other books on crystals, spells, magic, and alchemy. Also on the bottom of the trunk was a 16th century manuscript that Tommy's grandmother had treasured. The manuscript had been purchased by her own grandmother from an elder druid priestess in London before she moved to America.

Tommy put everything back in place, except for one vial of pennyroyal. He opened the journal and found the incantation for empowering crystals, then pulled a four-inch clear quartz crystal from the first pouch. This crystal had never been used, and it needed some assistance to bring it to life so that it would accept energy from the person for whom it was intended. He dripped three drops of pennyroyal onto the crystal, and then began the chant to empower the crystal. He smiled as he began to rub the pennyroyal along the length of the crystal. He opened the second pouch and pulled out a four-inch yellow topaz, which he had worn until he inherited his grandmother's crystal. He performed a variation of the empowering incantation on the topaz crystal, as it had been previously empowered. When he was finished, he looked inside the trunk and pulled out an empty black velvet pouch. He put the two newly cleansed crystals inside the bag and placed it in his lap, then returned the crystal pouches and pennyroyal to the trunk and covered them with the royal blue velvet. He closed his eyes and said the closing chant, then carefully closed the lid, sealing the trunk shut.

When he was finished, Tommy stood up and placed the journal and pouch on his desk. He put the vase and rose back on top of the trunk. He was ready to begin his day.

"Ford Tommy, where're you going?" Kyle called out as he returned to his room from taking a shower.

"Good morning, Welby Kyle." Tommy locked his door and turned around. "I'm going to breakfast, and then I'm going over to the house to clean Mark's room."

"Great idea. I'll join you in the cafeteria as soon as I get dressed." Tommy nodded, and Kyle quietly entered his dark dorm room.

After breakfast, Tommy and Kyle passed through the unlocked back door into the kitchen of the Kappa house. It was quiet inside, since most of the members who lived in the house were still sleeping. Tommy and Kyle went up to the third floor and located Mark's and Dave's rooms at the top of the stairs, across the hall from each other. Kyle entered Dave's room, but Tommy stood in front of Mark's door, staring at the wooden name marker, feeling a bit of trepidation as he reached for the doorknob.

He slowly opened the door and glanced around. The bed was unmade, and clothes were scattered on the bed and floor. There were stacks of papers and books on the desk next to the computer and on every other available top space, and there were empty take-out boxes and dirty dishes scattered throughout the room. The bookcase was filled with books, CDs, and picture frames. Tommy smiled as he shut the door behind him.

Before starting the physical cleaning of the room, Tommy performed a spiritual blessing, cleansing, and protection of the room. He hoped that the spiritual cleansing would provide Mark with physical and mental peace and strength. He lit a candle and walked around the room, chanting as he paused at each corner: *By my will I call forth the light to banish all darkness.* Using his own crystal, he lightly scratched a pentagram on the North facing wall, and chanted: *From the north I call for blessings of nature's positive energy to be upon this place.* Then to the East, South, and West facing walls, changing the blessing according to the direction he faced. When he finished, he stood quietly in the center of the room, feeling the energy of the room and projecting a symbolic white light outward, mentally filling all the nooks and crannies of the room with the spiritual blessing. When he felt the spiritual energy had filled the room, he chanted: *This room is protected. Tranquility and serenity replace chaos and confusion. Healing replaces hurt. Light replaces darkness. So let the goddess allow.*

After finishing the spiritual blessing of the room, he began organizing and cleaning up Mark's mess. He threw all the dirty clothes into a pile near the door and stripped Mark's bed, adding the bedclothes to the pile. He gathered all the used plates, glasses, and silverware and placed them in a stack on a small table by the desk. All the trash went into the trash can, and he organized all the loose papers into a neat stack on the desk by the computer. He gathered loose CDs and books and put them on Mark's bed, then dusted all the furniture and reorganized all of Mark's books and CDs.

He was surprised to see so many country CDs in Mark's collection, and would have to change his opinion about jocks, or at least his opinion about Mark. Tommy smiled as he recognized country and other albums that he had in his own collection; music by Reba McEntire, Dixie Chicks, George Jones, Alan Jackson, the Eurythmics, and Chris Isaak. More surprising than Mark's similar taste in music was their similar taste in reading material. Mark had the Pendragon novels, a series about Merlin and King Arthur written by Stephen Lawhead, a series that Tommy also owned and cherished. Tommy wasn't just surprised, he was shocked to see a dozen *White Wolf* vampire novels amongst Mark's collection. He realized that he and his big brother had a lot more in common than he had first thought.

Tommy put all but one piece of the dirty laundry into a laundry bag and placed the bag outside the door. He took the dirty dishes and the trash down to the kitchen, then returned to Mark's room to finish dusting and tidying up. After he had made the bed, he pulled the black velvet pouch out of the pocket of his jeans. He took the two cleansed crystals out of the pouch and wrapped them inside the jockstrap he had left out of the laundry, then placed the crystals between the mattress and box spring at the head of the bed. If the crystals couldn't absorb any of Mark's personal energies by using the jockstrap as a conduit, then Tommy's plans for his paddle would be a lost cause.

He looked around the room, happy with the job he had done. There was only one last thing to do. He stood quietly in the center of the room and concentrated on Mark.

> *For you, through the will of the Goddess, a helmet of light.*
> *For you, through the energy of the Goddess, strength that is growing,*
> *Strength to strength; ease and easeful sleep; gladness spreading,*
> *Thankfulness spreading through all of your Body, all of your Mind, all of your Self,*
> *By the power of the Goddess; through the power of the Goddess.*

Tommy left the room and met Kyle in the hallway, and the two young men picked up the bags of laundry before heading downstairs.

Sitting at the kitchen table with a cup of coffee in front of him, Oscar looked up as he heard somebody coming down the stairs. He was surprised to see Tommy and Kyle come into the kitchen.

"Good morning, sir," Tommy said cheerfully, as he put his laundry bag by the back door.

"You're both here awfully early," Oscar grumbled, his head still pounding as a result of the previous night's binge.

Tommy went over to the sink and began washing Mark's and Dave's dirty dishes. "Sorry, sir. I've always been an early riser."

"Same here, sir," Kyle added, putting his laundry bag next to Tommy's. He joined his fellow pledge at the sink and began drying the dishes.

"It sounds like you're both damned morning people."

Tommy and Kyle laughed as they finished up the dishes. Although there was a small laundry room in the basement of Kappa house, Tommy and Kyle had decided to wash their own clothes at the same time they did their big brothers'. "We're going back to our dorm and do laundry, sir." Tommy went to the back door and picked up his bag.

"We'll be back later to help with the rest of the housecleaning, sir," Kyle added, following Tommy out of the house.

Oscar stared at the two young men until they had disappeared. He shook his head and took a sip of his coffee.

The members of the football team returned to Kappa house around six-thirty Saturday evening. Mark and Dave trudged up to the third floor of the house, exhausted after a hard fought game that had ended in a loss.

Mark opened his door and dropped his bag on the floor. "Holy shit!" he exclaimed, glancing around the room. He hardly recognized it as his own.

Dave moved into the doorway beside Mark and looked inside. "Dude, looks like somebody's pledge is serious about joining the fraternity." Dave clapped Mark on the back and went over to his own room. "Damn. It looks like my pledge is serious, too," Dave said, entering his room.

Mark took his bag into the room and set it on the bed, then looked around the room. Everything had been cleaned and organized. As he was unpacking his bag and putting away the extra set of clean clothes that he always packed for traveling, he noticed that his dresser drawers had been organized as well.

Passing by to his own room, Oscar stopped in Mark's, looked around and whistled. "If you had any leftover pizza under your bed, it won't be there," Oscar teased. "The kid cleaned it all out." He slapped Mark on the back.

"When did this happen?"

"Tommy and Kyle were here *early* this morning. I was barely awake, and my head was pounding, but they were bright and chipper." He gave Mark a look of disgust. "And they were smiling! I think I hate both of them."

"Well, Tommy did a great job in here. Now get out so I can take a nap before tonight's mixer." He pushed Oscar out into the hallway and shut the door. Still smiling, he lay down on the bed and fell asleep.

Kappa Mixer

Mark woke up from a sound and dreamless nap, feeling more refreshed than he ever had from just a short sleep. He pulled on jeans, one of his football jerseys, and a pair of sneakers. He took a look in the mirror, ruffled up his hair, and then left his room to join the party.

The Kappa mixer was with another fraternity and two sororities, neither of which was Delta, since Kappa and Delta were involved in other events during the school year. Mark slowly wound his way through the groupings of people, listening to bits and pieces of conversations as he passed through the living room. Several sorority sisters stopped him to ask about going out sometime. The women weren't shy, and he smiled and chatted with them briefly as they gave him their phone numbers. Depending on whether he was on-again or off-again with Sally, they might come in handy.

Downstairs to get a beer, Mark was surprised to see that there were about twenty people talking in small groups around the basement. The room was usually dark and dreary, but burnt-out light bulbs had been replaced, and a radio was playing near the bottom of the stairs. Tommy was standing in the back corner pumping beer from a keg.

Mark joined the queue by the keg, behind a sophomore. Tommy finished pumping a cup of beer and handed it to Mark. Apparently Tommy had already learned that in the fraternity pecking order, big brothers and senior members always took priority over other fraternity members.

Mark stood off to the side while Tommy pumped another beer and gave it to the sophomore. When Tommy looked over, Mark was smiling broadly. "What's up with that smile?"

"You did a great job on my room today."

"Thank you, sir."

"No, thank you." Mark saw Alex, another pledge, coming down the stairs. "You, pledge," he called across the basement. The pledge immediately came over. "Take over the tap; Tommy's on a break."

Mark led Tommy upstairs, through the kitchen, and out the door into the backyard. He leaned against an old oak tree, staring at Tommy. "What is it about you, Tommy?" Mark took a drink of his beer as he waited for an answer.

"I don't understand, sir."

"You've officially been a pledge for two days, and you're already doing everything properly, including your responses to the brothers. You have the most optimistic attitude that I have ever seen in anyone, even Jack. And you are way too mature for a freshman. Heck, some of the seniors in this fraternity aren't as mature as you."

Tommy chuckled softly and looked Mark directly in the eye. "That's how I was brought up; it's who I am," he said seriously. "Being a member of this fraternity is something that I want, and I don't intend to go about it half-assed."

"That's good. Because doing things half-assed around here won't get you into the fraternity. You've already made quite an impression on several members, including me. I think I'm going to have to find ways to make it a little more challenging for you." He winked.

"I believe I'm up for any challenge, sir."

"You'd better be." Mark had a disquieting feeling that Tommy was going to create havoc in his life, and he wasn't sure why. He wasn't sure if he was ready to deal with the disruption, either. "I think your break is over; get back to that tap."

"Yes, sir," Tommy responded with a smile. He turned smartly and marched back toward the kitchen.

Mark watched Tommy walk away. Other than quick glances in the locker room, he hardly ever paid attention to other guys' physiques, but now he found himself taking notice of Tommy's backside. As a young teen, he had fooled around with boys, but once girls came into his life, he had stopped. *Maybe that's what's making me feel uncomfortable around Tommy. I don't think I'm gay, but being gay might not be so bad with a guy like that. Or maybe I'm just fucking horny.* He smiled to himself and turned away.

Jack joined him a few minutes later. "Everything okay?"

"Everything is fine."

"Tommy didn't do anything wrong, did he?"

"No, he didn't do anything wrong." Mark looked back at the house, letting out a sigh. "As a matter of fact, he's doing everything perfectly. You recommended a really good kid. I think he's going to make a great brother."

"Cool."

The two men stayed outside talking for a while before going back inside.

There they separated and mingled with the other people at the party, including several of the sorority sisters.

"Ugh, this place is foul," Kyle groaned as he and Tommy looked around the Kappa house basement on Sunday morning.

The smell of stale beer assaulted their noses even before they reached the bottom of the basement steps. Bowls of chips and pretzels, empty cups, partially filled cups, and spilled beer littered the basement floor and any available holding space.

Tommy laughed. "Now aren't you glad that we got all that fresh air during our run this morning?"

"Why are we the first ones at the house?" Kyle grimaced as they began picking up the trash.

"We're morning people, and we don't drink as much as the rest of the guys."

"Maybe we should start drinking more." Kyle laughed but stopped abruptly at the look on Tommy's face.

"That's not an option for me, buddy. I'd rather do all the cleaning than become a drunk like my parents."

"Sorry, Tommy," Kyle said quickly. "Let's get the rest of this crap cleaned up."

They finished bagging all the trash and put the bags near the bottom of the steps. Kyle started sweeping up the floor, while Tommy looked for a bucket so that he could mop.

"All right, the floor is all yours, buddy," Kyle said as he brought the broom back into the furnace room, where Tommy was filling a bucket with warm, soapy water. "I'll take the trash upstairs and start cleaning up the living room."

"Okay. I'll be up to help you as soon as I finish this."

Finished with the mopping, Tommy turned and saw Oscar sitting on the steps, watching him.

"You make me sick, kid." Oscar laughed. "Already up this damned early in the morning, and you've actually mopped the fucking basement floor."

"I'm sorry, sir." Tommy smiled up at Oscar. "I thought it was one of our responsibilities to clean the house."

Oscar shook his head. "You and Kyle are going to make the rest of the pledges look bad."

Tommy grabbed the mop and bucket and followed Oscar up the stairs. He emptied the bucket out in the back yard, then took it back down into the basement. While Oscar sat at the table with his coffee, Tommy started cleaning up the kitchen.

"Yeah, I'm pretty sure that I hate both of you." Oscar laughed as he stood up. He wrapped his big arm around Tommy's neck and rubbed his knuckles over Tommy's head. He smiled as Tommy stood up, laughing and rubbing the top of his head. "After you've finished the dishes, I want both of you to get out of here. Go back to your rooms and do whatever you need to do."

"But we should be helping the other pledges clean the house."

"Do you see any other pledges here?" Oscar asked.

"No, sir."

"Then you can't help anybody clean the house. Besides, you and Kyle have already done the basement, part of the living room, and the kitchen all by yourselves," Oscar said seriously. "The other eight guys can take care of the rest of the first floor without you. I'll have Mark and Dave call you if they need anything.

There's going to be a meeting on Monday night at eight o'clock."

"Thank you, sir." Tommy shook Oscar's hand.

Oscar just shook his head as he went into the living room. "I'll tell Kyle to finish up and leave."

"I slept like a log." Mark said to Dave as they walked into the first floor den. "I don't remember ever sleeping that soundly."

"Good morning, Oscar," Dave said. "We appear to be missing a pair of pledges."

Oscar was sitting at the desk, working at the computer. He swung around in his chair and faced his brothers. "While the two of you were upstairs, comfortably sleeping in your beds, and those lame-ass pledges out there were sleeping in theirs, Kyle and Tommy were in the basement, living room, and kitchen cleaning up." He smiled. "Tommy boy even took it upon himself to mop the basement floor."

"What? He mopped the floor?" Mark shook his head. "When was the last time somebody mopped the basement floor?"

Dave laughed out loud. "That would have been last semester during pledge."

"I told Tommy and Kyle that they could go back to their rooms; that you guys would call if you needed them for anything."

"But won't the other pledges get upset if they think Tommy and Kyle are receiving special treatment?" Mark asked.

"I thought about that, but I don't really give a damn what they think. Tommy and Kyle were here working while those guys were still sleeping," Oscar said. "Those two are showing a lot of initiative. They remind me of us, when we were pledges."

Dave chuckled along with Oscar. "I remember Mark made the rest of us look pretty lame."

Oscar looked over at Mark. "See, Dave and I don't hate you for making us look like those lame asses in the living room."

When Tommy returned to his room he sat down at his desk and began to flip absently through one of the books on symbology that he had borrowed from the library. He was looking for the right symbols to put on his paddle; something that most people wouldn't recognize, but that Mark might. Having seen Mark's book collection, Tommy thought that using druidic symbols and runes would be a nice touch. They might help him connect with Mark. As he began creating the paddle's design, he checked his calendar to see when the next full moon would occur and saw with dismay that it wouldn't be until the middle of October. There was going to be a new moon, however, during the fourth week of rush in early October, on a Tuesday night. Tommy's grandmother had often reminded him that while the full moon got all the glory, a new moon could be an even better time for starting something new. He would have to work fast to complete his paddle by then but was confident that he could do it.

While he worked on his paddle preparations, Tommy was hoping that Mark would call, though he wasn't surprised that he hadn't. As much as he wanted to let Mark know how he felt, he knew that would be the worst thing he could do. Instead, he would do everything he could to make Mark proud to have chosen him as his little brother.

That evening when Tommy left the cafeteria food line, he saw Mark and Sally having dinner together. Looking at the two of them sitting next to each other and talking intimately, Tommy felt a little stab of pain in his heart. He wanted to be the one sitting next to Mark. He moved to the other side of the cafeteria and found a table by himself. Looking over at Mark and Sally, he saw that there was a darkness shrouding Mark. Mark appeared angry, his features menacing, which both scared and excited him. Tommy grinned as he imagined how Mark would look wearing leather.

Pledge Responsibilities

"*Silencio!*" Oscar yelled out as he started the Monday night meeting at exactly eight o'clock. He had discovered that using simple Spanish words rather than the English equivalents drew more attention. "We had a very successful mixer Saturday night. Thanks to everyone who was here and helped make it a success." The brothers in the back of the room clapped and cheered. As Oscar was about to continue, the last pledge came running into the room. "Thank you for deciding to join us, Herbie," Oscar said sarcastically, using a nickname that he had learned the tardy pledge didn't like. "That's three more points against you."

Oscar looked at each of the other pledges. "Pledges, you need to start helping each other, which means that you need to help Herbie here get to these meetings on time. One thing about joining a fraternity is that it's a brotherhood. That means helping one another and not letting anyone down. Do you boys understand that?"

"Yes, sir," Tommy and Kyle responded. The other pledges sat quietly with their heads down.

Oscar looked around at the other pledges. "I don't think I heard the rest of you," he shouted.

"Yes, sir," all the pledges said in unison.

"That's better." He looked to the back of the room at the brothers who were snickering at the pledges. "The first order of business is to inform you that one of the tasks you need to consider completing before your initiation is getting a tattoo." He anticipated the shocked looks on the faces of some of the pledges. "You should consider getting the fraternity crest tattooed on your body. For those of you who decide to get a tattoo, Doctor Reynolds, our faculty advisor, or Al Martin, a Kappa alum, will accompany you to the tattoo parlor and wait while you get it." He smiled at each of the pledges. "Anyone who has a problem with the idea of getting a tattoo doesn't have to complete this task. It will only cost him ten points."

Some of the pledges grumbled, but Herbert spoke up, loud enough for Oscar to hear. "That's so unfair."

Oscar glared at him. "Well, Herbie baby, life ain't fucking fair, but it goes on. Considering the ten points against you yesterday for not showing up to do your fair share of helping your fellow pledges clean the house, I can understand why you would think this is unfair."

"I was too sick," Herb responded defensively.

"You didn't look too sick on Saturday night while you were putting away all those beers," Oscar commented. "Tommy and Kyle didn't look too sick yesterday as they cleaned the basement floor by themselves. And your fellow pledges didn't look too sick while they were cleaning up the first floor yesterday without your assistance." Oscar was coming down hard on Herb. "It's only been three days, and you already have eighteen points against you. You may not make it through the pledge period, and I'm sure you won't think that's fair, either." He glared harshly at

Herb. "Now, do you have any further comments that you would like to make about fairness?"

"No, sir," Herb responded quietly, staring at the floor.

"Good." He turned away from Herb and looked at the other members in the room. "Let's get on with business."

Once the meeting was adjourned, the TV was turned on and most of the guys stayed to watch *Monday Night Football*. Tommy was sitting with Kyle and a few other brothers when he saw Mark walk through the living room and head upstairs without saying anything to anybody.

Despite a miserable Monday night, Mark woke refreshed on Tuesday. Built into his schedule was going to the gym to work out on the exercise equipment before running through the southeastern neighborhoods of the city of Timian. He'd had the same routine for the past three years and, until recently, hadn't considered revising it.

When Tommy provided Mark with a copy of his class schedule, he'd been curious whether his little brother routinely ran at six o'clock in the morning or whether that was just there in the event that Tommy wanted to run. He had learned through Kyle that Tommy did, in fact, go running every morning. As Mark was getting ready for his morning run, he looked at himself in the mirror and then wondered why he was doing so.

Over the previous couple of weeks, Mark had found himself distracted by the personal issues between him and Sally that had once again become problems in his life. Football workouts and practice were everyday time consumers for him. Kappa rush and pledges had taken more of his time this semester because of his having a little brother for the first time. Moreover, Mark's confusion regarding his little brother had become the biggest distraction of all.

Mark felt good as he ran the three blocks to campus and then through campus to Heinz Hall. He became nervous about his decision when he saw Tommy running out of the dorm at exactly six o'clock. He lagged behind long enough to allow Tommy to get a good lead before he began following. He figured Tommy wouldn't hear anyone running behind him because of the headphones that he was wearing, and that thought made him wonder what Tommy was listening to. Mark smiled as he noticed and recognized the ankh tattoo on Tommy's left calf.

Tommy set a casual pace as they went through town and out toward the stadium. Mark was surprised when Tommy turned off the road and ran up the incline toward the cemetery. Tommy's pace continued steadily as he went into the cemetery and around the back hillside. Mark found it quite easy to keep up with him, and even had to slow down a couple of times for fear of overtaking Tommy.

As they left the cemetery and started downhill toward the trailer park, Mark was surprised to realize that he was focusing on Tommy's body, watching Tommy's long, lean, muscular arms and legs as they pumped with each stride. He saw sweat tossed from Tommy's hair as it bounced with each step, watched the back of Tommy's shirt getting wetter as the material soaked up the sweat from Tommy's neck and back. What shocked him was that he was getting excited as he watched the flexing gluteus muscles stretch and pull Tommy's shorts tight against his buttocks.

Even when he was a teenager, he had never found himself sexually attracted to another guy. Fooling around with his best friend had been a phase that he had gone through and grown out of. However, Mark now found himself being drawn to

Tommy's body. Rather than continuing to follow through the trailer park, Mark abruptly turned around and headed back toward the cemetery, then along Main Street back to Kappa house, where he bolted up to his room.

Just five days into the program, the Kappa pledges were discovering more of the tasks they would have to endure during the four-week pledge period. Tommy and four other pledges had gathered for dinner on Wednesday evening.

"I can't believe we agreed to do this," Jason grumbled.

"I don't think it's going to get any easier on us." Kyle looked around at his fellow pledges.

Tyler shook his head. "I was sent shopping for a bag of chips and a soda this morning."

"That's nothing, Ty. I had to buy a box of condoms. Not the little three pack, the big box with a dozen inside." Carlos laughed at his own embarrassment and the others joined him.

"I haven't minded the little chump chores, but the time demands are rough," Tommy said. "Trying to go to the store, take the stuff to the house, and return to campus for class in only half an hour is really tough."

"I hear you, Tommy," Jason sympathized. "I've had to decide whether being on time for class or completing a task was more important. However, I managed to complete the task and get to class," he smiled at them, "with a minute to spare."

"At least there's a time period during which they can't bother us," Kyle added. "If they were allowed to call us after ten at night and before eight in the morning, I might have to reconsider pledging."

"I'm not sure they're being fair with those time constraints," Tyler observed.

"Nobody ever told us it was going to be fair," Tommy said. "I'm sure they all went through the same thing when they pledged. Now it's their turn to do it to us." He smiled at his pledge buddies. "Next semester it will be our turn." Murmurs of anticipation came from the others.

"Do you know what I dislike the most?" Tyler asked. "The calls where you're told that there's going to be a special meeting, and you need to be at the house in fifteen minutes. And when you get there, a bunch of brothers are sitting on the porch laughing." All the other pledges mumbled agreement.

"It can be pretty humiliating," Jason chimed in. "Rick invited me to join him for dinner last night, and I thought that would be cool." He looked around at the others. "I had to follow him through the line and gather the food that he selected onto the tray. Then I had to follow him through the dining area as he looked for a table. There were plenty of tables, but he walked me back and forth through the cafeteria. After he decided on a table, I was allowed to go get my dinner."

"I had the cafeteria walk this morning at breakfast," Carlos said, a smile on his face.

Tyler laughed. "I did the lunch walk yesterday."

"Oh, goody. I'm having breakfast with Dave tomorrow," Kyle stated wryly, as all the pledges burst out laughing.

Tommy felt a little left out, since he had seen little of Mark. He had received the shopping tasks and the special meeting calls, but they were done by other Kappas. Even though he felt ignored by Mark, he was intent on making it into the fraternity and getting Mark to notice him.

"How's it going, pledge?" Jack smiled as he sat down next to Tommy for dinner on Thursday. He followed Tommy's gaze across the cafeteria where Mark was having dinner with a new girl. Jack wondered whether he should say anything about Tommy having a crush on Mark. He decided not to, yet.

Tommy turned his glance away from Mark and looked at Jack. "It's going okay, sir," he said quietly.

"You've almost made it through your first pledge week. How has it been so far?" Jack asked as he started eating his dinner.

"It's been a little crazy. I was really thrilled to have to buy a *Hustler* magazine for Larry the other day. I was lucky to get a compassionate cashier who allowed me to buy it."

"Ah, one of the thrills of pledging. I remember those days," Jack said with a chuckle.

Tommy sighed. "May I ask a question?"

"Sure."

"I don't want to get Mark into any trouble, but I've barely seen him this week. All of my task requests have been from other brothers," Tommy said. "Also, several of the pledges are having meals with their big brothers. They're talking about being paraded around the cafeteria while their big brother looks for the right table. Mark hasn't done that." He looked directly into Jack's eyes. "Have I done something wrong?"

Jack glanced at Mark and then focused on Tommy. "No, you're not doing anything wrong. Mark's going through a tough time right now." Jack debated whether he should discuss Mark's personal life, then decided that the pledge needed to know. "Sally broke up with him again."

"Why would anyone break up with Mark?" Tommy looked over at the quarterback and his new girl. "He seems like a really great guy."

"Mark is a good guy, Tommy," Jack started. "He's a dedicated student, with one of the best GPAs in our fraternity. He's the best quarterback that's ever played at Timian, and should set several team records before the season is over. And he's a good friend to a lot of the brothers." Jack hesitated before moving on to the hard part. "When he met Sally last year, he fell head over heels in love with her and became slavishly devoted to her. During last year's winter recess, they had their first break-up, but they got back together in the spring. There was another break-up, but they were back together for spring break. Another break-up after spring break, and then back together before the end of the semester. He ends up depressed after each break-up, then he starts indiscriminately dating non-stop. But even then, he's so loyal to Sally that he doesn't allow himself to fall in love with any of those other girls."

Tommy glanced over at Mark and then looked back at Jack. "Why would she keep doing that to him?"

"I don't know. She's a self-centered bitch?" Jack blew out a deep breath. "I had a hard enough time trying to figure out gay guys; there's no way in this world that I could ever attempt to figure out women."

"But he's so..."

"Hot?" Jack supplied. "Yes, he is. And if I were Sally, there's no way I would ever allow any other woman to even touch him."

"Then why?"

"There's some speculation that it has to do with Mark's..." he leaned closer to Tommy, "endowment."

Tommy raised his eyebrows and stared at Jack.

"You have to promise to keep this a secret."

"I promise."

"Mark is a big guy," Jack whispered, winking at Tommy. "When Sally's horny, Mark is the only guy that can satisfy her. Then, for whatever reason, she lets him go. But whenever she wants him back, he's there for her. I know he was in love with her last semester, but I think he's starting to get tired of her game playing."

"So, Sally is a size queen only when she's horny?"

"You got it." Jack laughed ruefully. "Don't forget that you promised to keep that a secret."

"I won't say a thing," Tommy affirmed. "I was just worried that I was doing something wrong, and that's why Mark has been ignoring me."

"You just keep doing what you've been doing. A lot of brothers at the house have noticed your good work. We're very impressed, even if Mark is oblivious." Jack playfully punched Tommy in the arm. "One more thing, Tommy," Jack said seriously. "Don't let that crush you have on him get out of control."

Tommy blushed crimson. "How'd you know?"

"I could see it in the way you look at him." Jack took in the shocked embarrassment on Tommy's face. "Don't worry, you've been very discreet. I could tell because I'm a gay guy and notice such things. Mark's a straight jock and..."

"They don't switch teams," Tommy finished, a sadness in his voice. "My uncle warned me about jocks when I first came out and fell in love with one of my high school buddies."

A smile spread across Jack's face. "If you want to keep your fantasies about Mark, you can. I'd certainly fantasize about him, if I were single and needed to."

"Thanks." Tommy looked at Jack. "You're not going to tell anybody, are you?"

"I put my trust in you, Tommy; you did the same thing with me. What we just discussed here at the table will stay between the two of us." Jack raised his hand, three fingers pointing up. "Scout's honor."

"I'll rein in my crush on Mark, and I'll keep my mouth shut about what we talked about." Tommy raised three fingers in the air. "Scout's honor."

"We might lose a pledge," Jack said as he walked into Oscar's room on Thursday night.

Surprised at the lack of preamble, Oscar looked up from the book he was reading. "What do you mean?"

Jack shut the door and sat on the chair by the desk. "Mark's been ignoring Tommy. He hasn't been doing anything to support the kid's efforts at making it into the fraternity. He doesn't have meals with him, he hasn't sent him on any tasks, and he's rarely around for any amount of time at house meetings or parties. I know he has football and that he's had issues with Sally, but he's completely overlooking his little brother."

"What makes you think we'll lose Tommy?" Oscar asked as he absorbed the information.

"We had dinner together. He feels as if he's doing something wrong."

"Shit," Oscar growled. "He's one of the best pledges we have this semester. I like that kid's attitude, and he's a lot of fun to be around."

"What should we do about this situation?" Jack asked. "I recommended

Tommy to be a pledge, and I don't want to lose him."

"I don't want to lose him, either. He brings a positive energy into this place. Not to mention that the basement floor has rarely been so clean." He paused for a moment. "I'll talk to Dave about it, and we'll come up with something. Just be prepared to support us in whatever we decide."

"I'm with you. Thanks, Oscar."

4: PLEDGING A FRATERNITY, WEEK 2

"Please come to order, brothers and pledges." Oscar waited while the room quieted for the regular Friday night meeting. "Congratulations, pledges. You have survived your first week, and you even managed to get Herbie here on time." He smiled at the pledges as the brothers burst into laughter.

"We will be attending a fraternity mixer on Saturday night. Pledges are expected to be at the house by eight o'clock sharp. Got that, Herbie?" Oscar looked directly at the offender.

"Yes, sir," Herbert said loudly.

"There will be a barbecue at the house on Sunday afternoon. Pledges, please be here by noon to help set up," Oscar continued. "Also, you'll be dining as a group with the brothers on Tuesday evening. You should be at the cafeteria by five-thirty. Any questions?"

"No, sir," the group responded.

After the meeting was adjourned, the pledges and brothers mingled around the house as they continued to get better acquainted.

Early Saturday morning, Tommy and Kyle went on their morning run, then over to Kappa house. Because Dave and Mark were at an away game, they had decided to do the room cleaning and laundry early. Now they were walking back to their dorm. "I don't know if Herb is going to make it."

"He's the only one that's keeping us all from looking good," Tommy agreed.

"All the other pledges are getting pissed at him," Kyle said sourly.

"So am I. It seems like he's pledging just so he can drink at the parties."

"I agree." Kyle looked over at Tommy. "It was good of Adam to make sure he was on time last night, but Adam doesn't want to be stuck being his babysitter."

"Do you think there is anything that we can do to help Herb?" Tommy asked.

"I don't know, buddy. We may just have to let him fail."

Inside his room, Tommy sat in front of his grandmother's trunk and meditated. He opened the lid and pulled out the envelope that he had placed inside. He pulled a second envelope from the pocket of his jeans and added the new hairs to those in the first envelope, smiling as he closed the lid of the trunk. The plans for his paddle were moving along nicely.

"Brothers and pledges," Oscar called to those mingling around outside Kappa house Saturday night, "we'll be going over to Theta Chi for the mixer. Pledges, please pair up." Oscar smiled as he watched the pledges comply. "Now, hold hands as you skip over to Theta Chi." The pledges groaned, but followed orders.

An hour later, Jack stood talking with a couple of friends in one corner of the Theta living room. He had been watching Tommy throughout the evening and had noticed an air of quiet solitude surrounding the young man. Jack thought that maybe he should try talking with Tommy, then thought better of it. *This might be Tommy's way of coping with Mark not being around.* As he watched Tommy laughing with a group of people, he had to admit that the neglected pledge still exuded a positive attitude.

Sam, Jack's closeted friend and poli-sci classmate blatantly leered at Tommy as the young man walked by on his way to the kitchen. He followed Tommy's every move, letting his gaze wander up and down Tommy's body. "Damn, that boy has one helluva cute ass," he snickered softly. "Wouldn't mind getting a piece of that."

A couple of the other guys in the group laughed with him, until Jack grabbed the front of Sam's shirt and pushed him back against the wall. "First of all, he's one of Kappa's pledges," Jack hissed in the guy's face. "Second, he's Mark's little brother. Third, don't ever let me hear you make comments like that about him again." Jack glared directly into nervous eyes. "He's not a piece of meat, and he's not available to you or anyone else. Understand?"

"S-s-s-sorry," Sam stammered. "It won't happen again."

Jack released him abruptly and stalked outside for some fresh air. He couldn't believe how defensive he had gotten regarding Tommy. He really did like Tommy, and he didn't want to see anything happen to him.

It was about eleven o'clock when he saw Tommy leaving the mixer. "Hey," Jack called out, hustling to catch up. "Where're you going?"

Tommy stopped and turned around. "Back to my dorm so that I can get some sleep."

"Are you okay? You seem a little down."

Tommy nodded. "I'm fine, just a little tired."

Jack looked at him intently. "You've seemed distant the past couple of days," he commented, hoping to get something more.

"Just studying."

Jack wanted to do something to help Tommy, but he wouldn't intervene unless he was asked. He put his arm around Tommy's shoulder and looked into his eyes. "If you need to talk with anyone, I'm a good listener. And I promise that I can keep a secret."

"Thanks. I'll remember that," Tommy replied as he turned away and left Jack standing alone.

As Tommy and Kyle arrived at Kappa house on Sunday, they saw some of the members outside, preparing for the barbecue. Oscar started the meeting at exactly noon, with all the pledges present. "Pledges, you will be assisting with our barbecue today. Find your big brother and get your instructions from him. That's it, boys." He quickly adjourned the meeting.

Tommy hadn't seen Mark outside when he arrived, so he assumed that he was inside the house. He walked down the hall toward the stairway, thinking he would first check in the den. He saw Jack, Dave, and Oscar in the room, talking quietly, their backs to the doorway. Hoping to get a chance to ask them where Mark was, Tommy waited by the doorway and unintentionally listened in on the conversation.

"You gotta feel for the poor bastard," Jack said softly.

"He seems to be getting more depressed," Oscar agreed.

Dave sighed. "Someday he'll find somebody that won't walk away from him."

"Well I hope it's real soon, because he's becoming a total pain in the ass," Jack said.

"We're going to have to do something if he doesn't snap out of it soon," Oscar stated.

Tommy quietly moved away from the doorway and went upstairs. He knocked on Mark's door and waited with his hands clasped behind his back and his head down, as pledges had been instructed to do.

Mark had been lying on his bed, thinking about all the time he was spending dating a variety of women. The knock on the door interrupted his pity party. He considered not answering, hoping that whoever it was would just go away. Then he realized that it might be Tommy looking for him because he had Tommy's instructions for the day. His spirits rose when he opened the door and saw Tommy standing as ordered. "Come in, pledge." Mark stood back from the door.

"Thank you, sir." Tommy walked to the center of the room and stood there, awaiting further instructions.

Mark shut the door. He grinned as he looked at the top of Tommy's bent head. *What if...* Mark quickly dismissed the thought. "Relax and have a seat, pledge."

As he complied, Tommy smiled up at Mark. The smile sent chills down Mark's spine. Despite the overwhelming positive energy he felt coming from Tommy, Mark's mood was still sour.

"I've been told that you have my instructions for today, sir," Tommy said softly.

"While the brothers are watching the football games on TV, you'll be serving food and drinks during the first game. After that, you'll be free to stay and watch the second game or leave," Mark said with little interest. "Pledges will be having dinner with their big brothers on Tuesday. You should be at the front doors of the cafeteria at five-thirty. You can go now," Mark directed, more sharply than he had intended.

"Yes, sir," Tommy said. He stood up and moved toward the door. "Are you okay, sir?"

"Yes, I'm fine," Mark said softly. "Just go, please." Watching Tommy walk dejectedly out of his room, Mark felt a pang of guilt at having been so short with his little brother. He knew he shouldn't take his frustrations out on the pledge, but he was there, and Mark couldn't help himself. He grabbed his phone and called one of the girls that had given him her phone number.

Tommy went downstairs, disheartened by Mark's abrupt treatment. He tried to focus on the fact that he was simply a pledge, and the brothers could treat him any way they wanted, without question. By the time he went outside to join some of the others, his spirits had rebounded, and he joined in the joviality of the afternoon.

Tommy stayed at the house that afternoon, helping to serve food and drinks to the brothers during both Sunday afternoon football games. Taking a break and sitting outside under one of the oak trees, Tommy was thinking about Mark when he heard somebody approaching from behind.

"Marie Laveau," a booming voice said from above.

Tommy looked up at the large African-American man, holding a plate of food and smiling down at him. "Samantha Stevens," he responded.

The man let out a howl of laughter and sat down next to Tommy, leaning against the tree and balancing his plate on his lap. "Oscar warned me about your sense of humor," he said. "I'm Al Martin. Kappa alum, class of '81." He held out his hand, trying to get a read on the young man.

"Tommy Ford. Freshman pledge." Tommy shook the big man's hand and felt a soft charge of energy. "Are you related to Doctor Irene Martin?"

"Yes, she's my wife. We met fifteen years ago while we were here at college and married before starting our graduate work elsewhere. I received my nursing degree, and she received her doctorate in history. We returned to Timian because of all the great memories it held for us. Now I work at the hospital, and she teaches here at the college."

"I'm taking her European History class. She doesn't teach from the point of view of the upper class, but from that of the working class and slaves. I think she's an amazing professor."

"I kinda think she's amazing, too," Al stated with a smile. "My work schedule is four twelve hour days, actually nights, followed by three days off. I love all the time that I get to spend with her."

"Why aren't you with her now?"

Al chuckled. "Well, I like coming to Kappa house, keeping in touch with the older brothers and meeting the newer brothers and pledges. Being an alum has its advantages, especially when Irene loads up the CD carousel with Etta James."

"What's that mean?"

"It means that my darling wife is preparing tests for her classes, and I should either go into my den to watch football on television or get out of the house." Al smiled at Tommy. "It's a beautiful day to get out of the house and attend a barbecue."

Tommy laughed along with Al, then sat quietly eating.

Al looked over at the younger man. "*Unto thee have I given knowledge.*"

"*Unto thee have I given Light,*" Tommy returned.

"*Hear ye now and receive my wisdom,*" Al continued.

Then in unison they both said, "*brought from spatial planes above and beyond.*"

"Very impressive for someone of your age to be familiar with Toth's *Key of Mystery.*"

"My grandmother was Wiccan," Tommy revealed, sensing a camaraderie with the stranger.

"Ah, that's what I sensed," Al replied. "Did your grandmother teach you to close your mind to others?"

"Yes. But she also taught me to keep my mind open to knowledge."

Al smiled again, showing off his bright white teeth. "I can also sense the energy coming from the crystal under your shirt."

"It belonged to my grandmother until her death in June. She taught me about cleansing and empowering crystals. She told me I was too young to put my knowledge to use, that I would have to wait until I was older before she taught me how to use it properly. All I can do is play with my crystals and read Tarot cards." He refrained from mentioning what he was planning on doing with his paddle.

Al sat quietly eating and mulling over Tommy's comments. "But there's more to you than just Wiccan knowledge."

"I spend an hour meditating at the end of the day, which helps my mind recover and settle down. It also helps to clear my mind before going to bed at night. Then, when I wake up after a peaceful night's sleep, I run for about half an hour." Tommy felt comfortable around the big man. "And I spend a lot of my free time reading about the ancient mysteries, as well as reading novels that incorporate ancient mysteries into their storylines." He leaned closer to Al and whispered into his ear.

Al chuckled. "Merlin's *Charm of Making*. You know that's not a real spell. They made it up for the movie *Excalibur*."

Tommy winked at Al. "I know that, and you know that, but it's fairly intimidating to the uninitiated when spoken in a serious tone."

"Is that how you scared bullies in high school?"

"I used the chants in elementary school. In high school, I scared them with judo and karate."

"Hm. A skilled as well as learned young man."

"I was a skinny little boy and had to handle myself the best way I could, whether it was with my brains or what little brawn I could muster."

Al nodded and continued eating. After a short pause, he looked over at Tommy. "You don't plan on using any of that *knowledge* on anyone, do you?"

Tommy shot a look of curiosity at Al. "I'm a student, not a practitioner, and would never use it on others. Bad juju as the vodun would say, yes?"

Al's laughter rang out over the yard, causing some of the other brothers to look toward them. "You read too much. Knowledge can be a dangerous thing." He stopped laughing, but smiled at Tommy. "My family is from New Orleans. My grandmother told me that her great-grandmother was friends with Marie Leveau."

"There are no big name witches in my family."

"That's not important. What is important is what you learn and how you use your knowledge. You seem to be doing well."

"Thank you," Tommy said. "This conversation is strictly between us, right?"

"From your lips to my ears and no further, pledge."

The Intervention

Oscar, with Dave and Jack for backup, confronted Mark when he returned to the house that evening. Despite the look on his face and the foul mood he was in, they pulled him into the living room on the third floor. Jack closed and locked the door behind them.

"What the hell is going on?" Mark complained. "I really don't feel like any bullshit right now."

"That's just too damn bad, buddy," Dave growled back, standing directly in front of Mark. "This is an intervention, and you're going to listen to us whether you like it or not." He glared at Mark.

Oscar put his hand on Dave's shoulder and pushed him away from Mark. Dave looked at him, then moved to take a seat.

"Sit down, Mark," Oscar commanded. Mark did, all the while glaring at Oscar. "You can do whatever you like regarding your personal life, but you've been neglecting your responsibilities as a big brother, and it needs to stop."

Mark stared angrily at each of them. Then the look in his eyes softened from hatred to resignation. "I'm sorry," he whispered.

"I'm sorry?" Dave mocked. "That's all you have to say?" He frowned at Mark from across the coffee table. "You have one of the three best pledges this semester, a kid who has been busting his ass to make it into our fraternity because he believes in this brotherhood. A kid who has the best damned attitude and personality that I've seen in a long time. And a kid who is more than willing to do anything that is asked of him. But all you can say is 'I'm sorry'," Dave spat.

Mark dropped his head and stared silently at the floor. Jack knelt down next to Mark's chair and put his hand on Mark's back. "This may sound corny, but let me explain this in terms that I know you'll understand. You and I love to read vampire novels." He **waited for Mark's** nod, as Oscar and Dave watched quietly.

"As a big brother, **you are like** the vampire sire that has taken a newborn childe under his wings. Now **it is up** to you, as the sire, to nourish and train this new childe in the ways of **the coven.**" Jack's voice was soft but authoritative. "As you nourish and train this **childe, he** will learn the ways of the coven and will become a better individual within **the coven.**" Dave and Oscar watched Mark's face for a reaction and saw that Jack's **words** were sinking into his thick head. "If you don't nourish and train this **childe, he** will fail to integrate into the coven. He will become an outcast and perish." Jack looked directly into Mark's eyes. "Is that what you want to happen to Tommy?"

"No." Mark's voice was barely audible.

Jack stood up and looked pointedly at Oscar and Dave, then moved away so they could have their say.

"Mark," Oscar began. Mark looked over at him. "The three of us know better than any of the other guys in this house that you're hurting. You've confided in us, and we do understand what's bothering you. But right now, you need to put that hurt and pain behind you and think about your responsibilities as a member of this fraternity."

Dave smiled encouragingly. "We really need you to be a part of this pledge period and help get your pledge initiated. Put the ladies on hold for now and concentrate on helping Tommy. I bet if you spent as much time with him as you have with these chicks, you'd feel a helluva lot better than you do right now." Oscar and Jack chuckled in agreement.

Mark looked around at his three best friends. "You guys are right, of course. I've been a complete asshole lately. I was short and dismissive of Tommy earlier today, even though seeing him standing outside my door lifted my spirits." He shook his head. "He really didn't deserve that. I hope he'll forgive me."

"I don't think you'll have to worry about that," Jack said. "He told me that he was worried about you. He knows there's something bothering you, so he overlooked your boorish behavior."

Oscar looked down at Mark. "And you'd better do something before he begins to think that he's done something wrong," Oscar warned. "We won't get another pledge to mop the basement floor this semester." All four men laughed.

"All right, all right. I've been put in my place. I'll make sure it gets fixed," Mark promised.

It was a warm, sunny Monday morning, and Mark watched Tommy run past the corner from his vantage point half a block away. Tommy was wearing headphones and running at a relaxed speed. Mark began to follow, noting the even strides of Tommy's long legs. He caught up to Tommy and kept pace next to him. "Mind if I join you?" he asked as he smiled over at Tommy.

"Not at all." Without breaking stride, he turned off his CD player and took off his headphones.

"What were you listening to?"

"Dolly Parton," Tommy stated, not ashamed to mention his favorite singer.

"I love Dolly. Which album?"

"*Here You Come Again*." Tommy looked puzzled. "I didn't see her in your collection."

"I was embarrassed to have her around, for fear of being teased by the guys,"

Mark confessed.

They turned left off Main Street and went three blocks before turning right to go up the incline and through the gate into the cemetery. Mark decided that the peace and solitude inside the cemetery would provide a good setting for him to talk to Tommy. "I've been informed, by several of my brothers, that I have been negligent in my duties as a big brother." Mark glanced over at Tommy. "They're worried that you might be considering dropping out of the pledge program."

Tommy quickly looked over at Mark, then turned to watch where he was running. "I'm not going to drop out of the pledge group. I'm not a quitter," he said. "I was afraid that I might have said or done something to offend you because all of the other pledges have been spending a lot of time with their big brothers."

"First of all, I want to apologize for neglecting you." Mark smiled. "You haven't done anything wrong. As a matter of fact, you've been the perfect little brother." He saw the blush that rose in Tommy's cheeks. "I've been distracted by other things, so don't blame yourself for my behavior."

Tommy glanced over at Mark. "I don't blame myself for anything."

"You're a bit of a smart ass." He laughed as they continued running through the cemetery. "Like when you told me that I started off flat in the first game of the season."

"Well, you did start off flat. Flat on your feet *and* flat on your ass after that sack."

Mark gave Tommy a playful shove. "Knock it off. I'm trying to apologize."

"Your apology is accepted," Tommy said. "I understand about life's distractions; I've had a few myself."

"Thanks. How about if I take you out to dinner sometime to make up for neglecting you?"

"You don't have to do that, Mark," Tommy demurred.

"I know I don't have to do it, but I'd like to do it. Please?"

"All right. That would be great." They turned out of the cemetery and headed up the hill that would eventually lead them into the trailer park.

"You set a really nice pace," Mark complimented. "I usually run along the southeast end of town. How long have you been running this route?"

"Since about three days after starting classes and learning my way around campus. I got bored and decided to check out the rest of the town."

"Which way do you go now?" Mark asked as they reached the highway at the end of the trailer park.

"On weekends, when I don't have to worry about classes, I usually turn south along the highway and run out to the mall before returning to campus." Tommy led the way across the street and back up the hill toward town. He looked over at Mark and gave him an impish grin. "But if you had continued following me last week, you'd know which way I go after leaving the trailer park."

Mark was surprised that he had been spotted. "You saw me!"

Tommy chuckled. "A couple of times, as I rounded the bends inside the cemetery, the one that circles around the hillside."

"I never saw you look back."

"I'm acutely attuned to all of my senses, and I have very good peripheral vision." Tommy smiled at him before returning his attention to the road ahead. "I knew somebody was following me, and that he always turned back after reaching the trailer park. So why did you always turn back?"

Mark kept himself from looking over at Tommy. "I decided that down the hill and then right back up the hill would be a good cardio test before returning to the gym for my workout."

"I never thought about doing that. It would be a good cardio workout. Did you know that Jack and Ken were following you the other day?"

"Funny thing about that." Mark started laughing. "I wasn't aware that they were following me, but they obviously were not aware that I turn around at the trailer park, so we almost ran into each other at the top of the hill. Jack did some pretty quick stumbling and mumbling to come up with a reason why he was there. How did you know they were following me?"

"I saw them standing in the shadows of the mechanic's building when I ran out of the cemetery. They weren't very successful at finding a hiding spot where they wouldn't be seen."

They ran for another block before Mark broke the silence. "So, what clan do you belong to?" Mark asked casually.

"Ventrue," he responded. "And you?"

"Ventrue. That makes us compatible." He nudged Tommy's shoulder with his hand. "When did you get your tattoo?"

"Last summer, when I was visiting my uncles in San Francisco. They're friends with a tattoo artist. I showed him a picture from one of the books, told him what colors I wanted, and he did the work."

"Well, it's awesome." He looked over at Tommy. "I'm sure the new one on your arm is just as nice."

Tommy glanced at his left bicep and realized that the gauze covering the Kappa crest was visible beyond his shirtsleeve. "Thank you."

"How did you get it without having an adult with you?"

"Kyle has an uncle in Erie who does tattoos. We risked a road trip late one afternoon, gambling that nobody would call us to run errands."

"You two certainly are resourceful." Mark thought about the closeness between Tommy and Kyle. "Well, this is where I turn and go back to the house."

"I'll see you later." Tommy waved and continued running down the street.

Mark stopped and watched as Tommy ran down the road.

The Singing Pledges

"Fucking Herb. That worthless shit is late again," Herb's big brother Simon complained. "We should just kick his ass out now." The other brothers nodded in agreement but said nothing.

The other nine pledges were standing at attention off to the side of the front door of the cafeteria on Tuesday evening. Students going into the cafeteria pointed and chuckled at the pledges standing with their hands behind their backs and their faces looking down at the ground.

When Herb arrived five minutes later, the brothers led their pledges into the cafeteria. Each pledge grabbed a tray and shadowed his big brother as he chose his dinner. Then he walked behind his big brother to a table and waited for him to sit down before placing the food from the trays on the table. They were dismissed to go back and get their own dinner.

As the pledges sat at a table behind the big brothers, Tommy picked a seat that allowed him to look at Mark.

"I think we need some better music than what's playing overhead," Dave commented to the brothers, nodding at the speakers that were spouting Muzak into the cafeteria. "Let's have each pledge sing a song for the folks." The other brothers agreed.

Oscar went to talk with the cafeteria manager to ask them to shut off the Muzak and allow the pledges to sing. As he returned to his seat at the table, Dave stood up to address the cafeteria. "Ladies and gentlemen, may I have your attention, please," Dave looked around at the full cafeteria. "This evening, to enhance your dining pleasure, the pledges of Kappa Lambda Pi will sing. Enjoy!"

Simon picked Herb to be the first to sing because he had been the last one to arrive. Herb looked terrified as he stood up at the pledge table and faced the cafeteria. He did not have a good singing voice, and apparently the only song that he could think of was "Row, Row, Row Your Boat". He sang the song too softly to please the brothers and was forced to sing it again.

The Kappas laughed hysterically, as did most of the other people in the crowded cafeteria. The other pledges sat quietly at their table, horrified at the prospect of singing to the cafeteria crowd.

Tommy and Kyle waited and watched as each of the other seven pledges took his turn. Some of the pledges had bad singing voices, and some seemed scared about singing in public so they messed up their songs. The brothers and other diners were laughing heartily at the entertainment.

Kyle was the ninth pledge to sing. He stood up at his table, turned to look at the crowd, and began to sing in a lovely tenor "Nessun Dorma", from Puccini's opera *Turandot*. The entire cafeteria stopped to listen to the joyous voice. The brothers looked at each other in surprise; the pledges were also surprised. Tommy had heard Kyle sing, so he wasn't surprised; he was too busy being scared because he would be next.

The cafeteria applauded as Kyle let the last note end. He turned to the cafeteria and took a bow, and then turned to the brothers' table and bowed again. He sat down without saying a word and began eating his meal.

"You fucker," Tommy leaned over and whispered. "How the hell am I going to follow that?" Kyle grinned at him and shrugged.

Tommy knew that he didn't have the vocal range or talent that Kyle had, but he could sing well. He had decided that he was going to perform his favorite song, a fun song that would tease his big brother. Tommy smiled over at Mark as he stood up. He cleared his throat, looked around the dining hall and began singing "Slow Boat to China". When he came to the line "melt your heart of stone" in the second stanza, Tommy tossed one of his biscuits over at Mark. Although the brothers and students in the cafeteria were laughing, it wasn't because Tommy was singing badly, but because he was making the song funnier with pantomime. After his song, Tommy took a short bow and sat down to finish his dinner. He looked across the two tables and smiled impishly at Mark.

Mark shook his head. "You'll pay for that, little brother," he warned.

Dave was laughing as he stood up to address the cafeteria. "And that concludes this evening's pledge sing with the pledges of Kappa Lambda Pi. Thank you."

Girls Talking

"Can you believe that stupid bitch Sally dumped Mark again?" Connie asked the other girls eating dinner with her.

The four seniors, best friends since they were freshmen, were watching Mark sitting with his fraternity brothers during dinner on Wednesday evening.

"How do you know that?" Sheila asked.

Connie smiled knowingly at her three friends. "Victoria Moss is in my English class, and I overheard her telling another girl."

"Maybe he's the stupid one, taking her back all the time," Deborah commented, glancing over at the table of Kappa brothers. "Look how crazy they are over there."

"Mark has a 3.4 grade point average," Connie stated smugly. "I had a friend in Admin check it out for me earlier this semester. I heard that they broke up during the summer, so I was going to see if Mister Yummy was interested in a girl who was more stable."

"I'm sure he'd do you in a stable," Deborah snapped back.

"Bitch," Connie replied with a smile.

Stacie finally joined in the conversation. "I dated him a couple of times last semester. He's a lot more romantic than he looks when he's hanging around with his frat goons, but once he got undressed and into bed, wow." She looked at her friends. "Size has its advantages."

"Really!" the other three girls exclaimed in unison, then broke out giggling.

"He is a very well endowed man," Stacie confirmed with a nod.

Connie smiled toward the Kappa table. "I'd like to take that for a ride."

"Then you better get on it before Miss Brown decides she wants him back," Stacie warned. "She rarely lets go of him for longer than a month."

"Why does she do that?" Sheila asked.

"Why does he let her is the question," Deborah amended.

"Who knows?" Stacie responded. "I heard they were crazy in love when they first met. He wanted to be exclusive and she didn't, or some crap like that."

"Hm." Connie smiled at her friends. "The guy wanting a commitment before the girl...that's unusual, and something that I would have agreed to on the spot." She looked around the table. "He's just too yummy to allow to roam the streets alone."

"And those blue eyes..." Sheila squealed and was joined by the other three.

For over twenty years, Delta Delta Delta sorority and Kappa Lambda Pi fraternity had jointly created a Homecoming float. Inside an old warehouse near the mall and interstate, the two groups constructed their float on the back of a flatbed truck. Victoria Huffington, president of Delta, and other Delta members were responsible for the design, and were making sure that their pledges and the Kappa pledges didn't make any mistakes in its construction. Tommy, working underneath the platform, ignored the women's talk. He pricked up his ears, though, when he heard Mark's name.

"Sally, you're playing a risky game with Mark," Victoria told her Delta sister as she stuffed tissue paper into a tree made of chicken wire.

"Maybe, Vicky, but he's always there when I want him." Sally giggled from the other side of the faux tree.

Victoria had been dating Kappa's president for three years, so she had the inside scoop. "Dave says he's starting to get frustrated with you."

"It's part of my charm." Sally turned from her task and looked over at two Kappa pledges. "Make sure that platform is sturdy," she directed. "We're going to be putting four chairs on it for the ruling sisters of Delta." She turned her attention back to Victoria.

"You could lose him for good one of these days," Victoria warned. "Where would you find another guy with his...attribute?" she asked with a laugh.

"Well, that would be a loss. It's very fulfilling when you have that deep itch that no other man can get to."

"You are such a bad girl," Victoria scolded. "Aren't you concerned that he'll find somebody else, somebody that might actually be in love with him?"

"First of all, there aren't that many girls who would handle what he has to offer." Sally giggled and blushed. "Second, I never allow him enough time apart from me to get to know somebody that well. I'll get him back in another month."

"Don't you ever get tired of groveling to get him back?"

"I don't have to grovel, Vicky. I just have to bat my pretty blue eyes and pout my lips. He's putty in my hands." Sally laughed as she demonstrated.

Angered by what he was hearing, Tommy despised Sally even more. He thought it was bad enough that guys treated women that way, and some gay guys did the same thing to one another, but he couldn't understand how a woman could treat someone like Mark the way Sally was treating him.

Tommy Tutors Brian

"I'm tired of reading about Freud," Brian complained, looking up from his textbook. He smiled across the library table at Tommy. "I'd rather talk about you and how pledging Kappa is going."

Tommy sighed. He hadn't wanted to be Brian's tutor, but he'd had no real choice in the matter. Their psychology professor, a big basketball supporter who wanted to keep Brian eligible, had asked him to help Brian, who was having a difficult time with the class. There were some benefits to taking on the task: he got extra credit, and the other professors in his major field were taking notice of the freshman.

"Pledging is going fine, Brian, but I doubt that's a question that's going to be on the test. If you want to pass, you'd better keep reading." He shook his head and went back to his own reading. He had enjoyed Brian's attention at the beginning of the semester, but after Brian's pressure to spend the night during the Gamma rush party, Tommy had had to make an effort to even remain friendly. Since pledging Kappa and being around Mark, he found Brian's flirtations downright annoying.

Brian smiled. "Are the Kappa brothers satisfying your needs?" he asked directly.

"Brian," Tommy looked up from his book and glared at the man across the table, "stop being crude. The Kappas aren't like you. They have respect for one another."

Brian batted his eyes. "I promise that I'd respect you in the morning, if you'd just spend the night with me."

Tommy gave him a hard stare and shook his head. "If you don't stop, I'm going to leave. I'm here to help you pass the psych test," he said forcefully, keeping his voice low so that he wouldn't be overheard.

"But satisfying your needs is more important to me. You're a sweet boy, and should have somebody to keep you warm at night."

"I don't need anybody to keep me warm, Brian. Why are you so interested in me? I'm just a freshman, and I'm pledging Kappa instead of Gamma."

"I see a sweet boy, lonely and confused by all these college men. I want to clear up your confusion and keep you from being lonely."

Tommy closed his eyes and shook his head. "I'm not confused or lonely, Brian."

"Ah, but you are, sweet boy. You picked Kappa over Gamma, and you turned me down." He smiled lewdly, leaning across the table to whisper, "I could scratch any itch you have."

"I take a shower every morning so that I don't itch. And I picked Kappa because they concentrate on their studies, not one another's bodies."

Brian sat back in his chair and laughed quietly. "Are you sure you didn't pick Kappa because of that macho stud quarterback, Mark Young?"

"Mark has nothing to do with it," Tommy said, more vehemently than he had intended.

Brian laughed louder. "There's only two ways you'll ever get him into your bed, Tommy: if you have big tits and a pussy, or if you get him drunk."

"I'm not trying to get Mark into my bed." Tommy voiced the same lie that he kept telling himself. He knew the reason he'd pledged Kappa in the beginning was Mark. Now, though, he was enjoying the friendships that he was making, especially with Kyle, Jack, and Oscar.

"Then why don't you let me into your bed? I'm ready, willing, and able to satisfy all of your needs."

Tommy slammed his textbook shut. "I've heard stories about some of your conquests, Brian." He glared across the library table. "I'm not going to end up as a notch on your bedpost or the joke in the stories you tell around your fraternity house."

"I could still spread stories about how hot your sweet little ass is, and how you begged me to keep fucking you."

Anger blazed in Tommy's eyes. "That would be a lie," Tommy snarled, "and I'll never speak to you again if I hear that you're spreading stories about me." He stood up from the table and gathered his belongings. "Good luck on the test," he said as he left Brian sitting alone at the table.

5: PLEDGING A FRATERNITY, WEEK 3

"Congratulations, pledges, you have survived the first two weeks of the pledge process. You're halfway home," Oscar began the Friday night meeting. "We have an exciting week planned for you boys, beginning with tomorrow's Homecoming parade. Make sure you're at Delta house by ten o'clock tomorrow morning, so that you can ride on the float with the Delta sisters. Afterward, you'll be attending the game with your Kappa brothers. There will be no clean-up tomorrow; that will be on Sunday."

Oscar then went on to fraternity business before concluding with, "And finally, before we adjourn for the evening, we have a little surprise for you." Oscar smiled malevolently at the pledges. "Jack, would you please give the pledges their surprise?"

Jack went into the kitchen and returned with ten large burlap bags. He passed one to each of the pledges and then went back to his seat. The recipients looked curiously at the bags, wondering what they were for.

Oscar provided the answer. "You are to design your own undergarments from the burlap bag. That means a pair or two of underwear and a t-shirt. Beginning on Monday, the burlap undergarments are to be worn every day until your initiation in two weeks. And don't think that we won't have surprise inspections to make sure you are wearing them."

Tommy groaned inwardly, as he knew better than to be heard. All the pledges were starting to get worn down under the demands from their classes and classwork, and the additional tasks, assignments and pretend meetings from the fraternity, but none of them were ready to give up.

"All right. This meeting is adjourned." Oscar slammed the gavel onto the table.

The brothers and pledges mingled throughout the house, joking and laughing about the burlap assignment.

"Running errands in burlap underwear is not going to be fun," Kyle observed grimly.

Benjamin nodded in agreement, then turned to another pending assignment. "How are you guys doing on your paddles?"

"I'm doing all right with mine," Kyle said. "It's almost finished. I just need to think of something to add that will make it special. What about yours, Tommy? I suppose you're finished already," he teased.

"I have the design ready; I just have to execute it."

"What about the tattoos? Are you guys going to get one?" Benjamin asked with a shiver. "I hear it hurts."

Kyle looked at Tommy, who nodded. "We already got ours."

"How did you do that?"

"Kyle's uncle does tattoos and lives near Erie. He was willing to do it for me and Kyle."

Kyle put an arm around Benjamin's shoulder. "It doesn't hurt, Benj. It feels like a mosquito bite or bee sting."

"That's right, it's not bad at all," Tommy agreed.

Jack joined the three pledges. "Do you guys mind if I borrow Tommy for a moment?" He put an arm around Tommy's shoulder and walked him away.

"What's up?" Tommy asked when they had moved away from the group.

"A friend of mine mentioned that there was a bit of a fuss while you were tutoring Brian in the library. Is he bothering you?" Jack asked.

Tommy frowned. "Brian has been hitting on me, but I've been ignoring his advances. I'm not interested in him. Still, it's kind of flattering to have somebody pay attention to me."

Jack frowned. "If he gets too pushy, let me know, and I'll have Ken talk with him."

All of the pledges arrived at Delta house on Saturday morning, as instructed. After riding the float through town to the football stadium, they joined the Kappa brothers to watch the Homecoming game. Afterwards, the brothers and pledges went back to their house to prepare for the victory party.

"That was a great game today," Tommy said, handing Mark a beer. He had once again been assigned keg duty.

"Thanks. I'm trying not to be flat," he replied, accepting the glass.

Since the intervention by his brethren, Mark had paid more attention to his fraternity responsibilities, especially those concerning his little brother. He had discovered that he felt better hanging around with Tommy than chasing after fickle girls. He wasn't sure if that meant anything, but he did enjoy Tommy's company during morning jogs. They had talked casually during the week, and Mark had joined Tommy for some meals in the cafeteria. Tommy was coming along well in regards to the pledge period.

Tommy and Kyle were still the first ones to arrive at the house on Sunday morning. They sat quietly in the living room, waiting for the other pledges. It had become necessary for the house council to set a time for the "morning after" clean-ups because Tommy and Kyle had been the only two who arrived early, while the others straggled in whenever they felt like it. Tommy and Kyle were also the only two pledges who never arrived with a hangover. Adam appeared a couple of minutes before nine o'clock, with Herb in tow. Herb had been drinking a lot at the party and had a bad hangover. Adam was furious. "I just want you guys to know that I've had it with Herb. I'm not going to be the one to keep looking after him."

Herb had a hard time staying awake while Oscar gave them their assignments. Just as Oscar finished, Herb threw up on the floor.

"All right then," Oscar said, looking at Herb, "Herbie here will now be cleaning up the rug and floor." He shook his head as he looked at the other pledges. "Get to it, boys."

The pledges scrambled around, clearing up the dishes and cups from the party. Oscar put a bucket in front of Herb. "You can start by cleaning up your own mess." As he walked away, Herb threw up in the bucket. The other pledges finished their cleaning tasks in the basement and first floor, and awaited further orders. Herb was still lying on the living room floor, next to the bucket. "Leave him there," Oscar instructed, "and get on upstairs and clean those rooms."

The pledges went upstairs, and each stood in front of his big brother's door. Each knocked, then remained standing at attention while waiting for a response. The pledges had been instructed that if there was no answer, they were to enter and proceed with the cleaning.

Mark opened his door and smiled at the top of Tommy's head. "Come on in, pledge." He moved aside so Tommy could enter.

From his position, Tommy could only see Mark's lower body. He felt a thrill of excitement at the line of black hair that led downward from Mark's navel and disappeared beneath the towel that was wrapped around Mark's waist. Tommy walked to the middle of the room and waited.

"Relax, pledge," Mark said as he closed the door.

Tommy had never seen Mark undressed, and his breath caught as he looked up at the tanned torso. Lightly covered with black hair, the finely chiseled muscle rivaled that of Michaelangelo's David. As Mark picked up a book from his bed, Tommy noted the red and black fraternity crest on the left bicep. Tommy's gaze moved from bicep to the muscular, hairy forearms, then back to the torso. *I wish I could see what's under that towel.*

Mark smiled at the reaction he thought he'd seen in Tommy's eyes. The "*what if*" questions continued to plague his thoughts. "Don't mess with anything on the desk, please. I'm in the middle of a paper." Mark put the book on his desk and picked up his shower bag.

"Yes, sir." Tommy watched the muscles ripple across Mark's smooth back as he left the room. A small patch of black hair covered Mark's lower back, just above the towel. He took a deep breath and shook his head to banish the thoughts that were scrambling around inside his mind and the bulge that was growing in his jeans. As fantasies danced in his head, he began cleaning up the room.

When Mark came back, Tommy picked up the dirty dishes and quickly left. As much as he desired to see Mark naked, he wasn't sure he'd be able to control himself in such circumstances. By the time Tommy returned, Mark was dressed. They chatted amicably as Tommy went about making the bed. Tommy reached under the mattress to make sure that everything was still secure.

"You'll be free to go after you finish, unless there's anything else to do around the house. I'll be down in the den in a meeting." As he left, he favored Tommy with a smile and a wink.

"Thank you, sir." Tommy knew that he'd never be able to get the image of Mark's partially nude body out of his mind. He smiled as he wondered what it would feel like to run his hand over Mark's hairy chest. He shook his head again and finished his cleaning. When he was done, he slung Mark's laundry bag over his shoulder and left the room.

"Okay, brothers, it's time for the mid-rush assessment of our pledges." Oscar looked around at the ten big brothers and the three members of the house council that did not have little brothers. "We'll leave our discussion about Herbie until last."

The house council began assessing the pledges in alphabetical order by first name. Each big brother assessed his little brother, and then the others each added his thoughts. It appeared that the pledges were surviving the pledge period well.

"All right, Mark," Oscar said, looking over at the quarterback, "give us your assessment of Tommy."

"I think Tommy is a great little brother and maid. He's been doing everything that's asked of him, has a great attitude, and is always on time. No problems with the kid." The only problem that Mark had with Tommy was personal.

One of the senior brothers raised his hand. "Yes, Simon?" Oscar asked.

"I'm concerned that Tommy might be queer," Simon sneered. He was aware that Herbie, his own little brother, was going to be dropped from the pledge group.

Mark, Jack, and Dave looked toward Oscar, while mumbling started amongst the other brothers.

"What makes you think that, Simon?" Oscar called out over the noise. "Has he said something to offend you or made a move on you? Have you seen him doing something with another guy?"

"No. It's just a feeling that I have."

Mark stood up and glared at Simon, who was sitting on the other side of the room. "You're going to have to give us something more to go on," he growled. "I have a feeling that you're an idiot, but I don't hold that against you."

Nervous laughter broke out. Simon had an air of arrogance and was not well liked amongst the other brothers. However, because his father, uncle, and grandfather had been members of Kappa Lambda Pi, he had been accepted into the Kappa brotherhood.

"Fuck you, Mark." Simon looked over at Oscar. "Tommy just seems too perfect, too happy."

"Maybe we need to tell Tommy that he should try being depressed and suicidal," Jack responded tersely.

Oscar chuckled as he looked over at Simon. "So, you think we should cut him because he's happy, does everything right, and because you have a feeling."

"Not just that," Simon replied, taking a deep breath. "I've seen him hanging around with that Gamma fag, Brian. They've had lunch together, and I've seen them together in the library."

"I've seen him at football games with his roommate, so he must be a pothead also," Jack said sarcastically.

Oscar felt the sting of Jack's retort, as he had expressed similar feelings at the first football game when he saw Tommy sitting with some of the college tokers. "Calm down, Jack."

"No, Oscar." Jack glared at Simon. "We all hang around with other people, Simon, but we don't make accusations against one another just because of who we have as friends. Brian happens to be in the same psych class as Tommy and me. Brian is having problems keeping up with the class, and the prof asked Tommy to tutor him. Tommy's not happy about it because Brian is such a jerk. It's even possible that Brian is playing dumb just so he can have Tommy as a tutor."

"I bet there are a few of us who have had that slimeball come on to us." Dave laughed nervously, trying to break the tension.

Jack shrugged off Dave's intervention, remaining angry at Simon. "Another thing, Simon, if I'm going to have a fling with a guy, the last place that I'm going to be seen is in the fucking library."

"All right, brothers," Oscar addressed the group. "Simon, I don't know what your problem is with Tommy, but he's been a great pledge. Nobody else has made this kind of accusation against him, and I've seen him interacting with many of our brothers. He gets along with all of them: Whites, Blacks, and Hispanics. If we had any Asian brothers, I'm sure he'd get along with them, as well."

"Sorry," Simon said sullenly, looking at Oscar and then over at Mark. "I guess I'm a little jealous about having to talk about the best pledge when I have the worst one."

"So, what's up with you making that accusation against Tommy?" Mark asked.

"Are you worried that he'll make a pass at you, or that he won't?"

"Fuck you, Mark." Simon turned away to look out the window while the other brothers snickered.

Finally, the house council began discussing Herb, the only pledge who was failing to meet the fraternity standards for acceptance. He was still lying on the floor in the main living room, in his own vomit. By unanimous vote, Herb was dropped from the pledge group.

After Oscar adjourned the meeting, two of the younger council members picked Herb up off the floor and helped him back to his dorm. He was notified verbally, and with a written note, that he was no longer a Kappa pledge. One of the other pledges, who was still cleaning his big brother's room, was detailed to clean up the rug and floor in the living room. The rest of the pledges were notified by phone that Herb was out, and that there would be a meeting on Monday night.

Dinner With Tommy

On Tuesday evening, Mark hesitated in front of the door to Tommy's room. He was excited about going out to dinner with Tommy. At the same time, he was nervous because of the feelings that had been nagging at him during the previous couple of weeks. He was also curious and concerned because of the accusation that Simon had made. He kept telling himself that this was not a date. It was an opportunity for him to get to know his little brother better. Mark took a deep breath and knocked on the door.

"Come in," Tommy called. He wasn't expecting anyone and had to lean around the side of his desk to see who was there. He smiled brightly when he saw Mark. "This is a nice surprise."

"I would have been able to pick out your side of the room without you being here." Mark looked around, noticing the print hanging above Tommy's bed. "That's a great painting. Who did it?"

"Tamara de Lempicka, an art deco painter. She did her best work during the 1920s." Tommy looked up at the picture. "It's an unfinished portrait of her first husband," he turned and looked at Mark, "but to me, it's my vampire ideal."

"What?"

"He's what I consider to be the ideal vampire. He looks as if he's been around for a long time. And, I wouldn't say no to him if he asked me to spend eternity as a vampire." Tommy laughed. "So, what brings you here? You're certainly not here to discuss artwork."

"I told you that I wanted to take you out to dinner. I was hoping that you might be free tonight."

"As luck would have it, I have no appointments on my social calendar for this evening."

"Great." Mark moved toward the door. "How do you feel about Italian?"

Italian is great, especially if the guy is tall, with dark hair and dark eyes. "Sounds good to me," he responded with a chuckle.

"What's so funny?"

Tommy shrugged. "Nothing. I had a funny thought, but it passed."

As they walked down Main Street toward an Italian restaurant called The Gold Spike, they made small talk and discussed Herb's removal from the pledge group. Mark wanted to wait until they were having dinner before broaching a more serious discussion.

The maitre d' knew Mark well from all the dinner dates he brought to the restaurant. He put them at Mark's favorite table in the back corner so that they could have privacy. The waiter promptly brought them each a glass of water and left them to look over the menu. Mark and Tommy discussed the dinner options, and Mark pointed out some of his favorites. When the waiter returned, Mark placed their orders.

"We'll start with the antipasto, and we'll both have the minestrone soup. I'd like the chicken piccata, and Tommy will have the veal marsala." Mark looked at Tommy. "Would you like some wine with dinner?"

"No, thanks."

"We'll both have iced tea," Mark said, handing the waiter both menus. He looked over at Tommy's broad smile. "Did I do something wrong?"

"I'm not used to having somebody order for me."

"Sorry about that. It's an old habit."

"That's okay. It was actually kind of nice."

Mark took a sip of his water and waited while the waiter placed their iced teas and the antipasto plate on the table. "Why don't you tell me more about yourself; I'd like to know my little brother better. I already know that you're from New Jersey, your tastes in books, movies and music, and I know about your fanaticism for football. But I don't know a lot about your family or who you are beneath that optimistic exterior."

Tommy took a sip of his iced tea and sighed deeply. "Well, my parents are alcoholics. My oldest sister is twenty years older than I am, with twin daughters that are three years older than me. My youngest sister is fifteen years older than I am." Mark's eyebrows lifted in surprise. "Needless to say, I was a surprise for my forty-something parents." He smiled ruefully. "When I was six years old, my father came home drunk one night after having been fired from his job. He was regularly fired from one job or another. He and my mother got into one of their infamous arguments, which usually led to physical violence. I had learned at an early age to steer clear whenever they were arguing. This time, however, I was eating quietly at the dinner table, trying to make myself invisible. As my father walked by the table, he punched me in the mouth and sent me flying into a wall, knocking me unconscious. Apparently in the belief that I was to blame for all of their problems."

Mark stared in shock at Tommy's brutal honesty. He couldn't believe that anybody would do something like that to any kid, let alone his own child. There was deep sadness in Tommy's eyes and Mark wondered how he'd had the fortitude to survive growing up with alcoholic parents. He suddenly understood why Tommy rarely had alcohol at fraternity gatherings.

"After my parents stopped arguing, I was finally taken to the emergency room, where I was treated for a fractured jaw." He looked over at Mark. "My grandmother threatened to file child abuse charges against both my parents unless they agreed to make her my guardian. They took very little time to discuss it before they decided to give me up." He paused for another sip of his tea.

When he was talking about his early years, Tommy's expression showed sadness and hurt. Once he mentioned his grandmother, a decided change came over his face, and a brightness appeared in his eyes. Mark was keen to hear more about Tommy's youth.

"My real life began when I moved in with my grandmother." Tommy smiled happily. "I had my own room, but didn't feel safe sleeping alone for almost a year, so I slept in her big comfy bed; it smelled of lilac. She would lie with me until I fell asleep, and then return when it was time for her to go to bed. Sometimes she would sing me to sleep. My favorite song was 'Slow Boat to China'. It was very comforting for a little kid to know that somebody wanted to be with him." He looked over at Mark, who smiled in recognition. "As I got older, we used to play the states game. We would lie in bed and name all of the states in alphabetical order, or from east coast to west coast, or we would try to name all of the state capitals. It was a great learning experience."

"Your grandmother sounds like a wonderful person," Mark commented as the waiter put their entrees on the table.

"She was great. She taught me a lot of things about myself." Tommy jabbed his fork into the veal and took a bite. "Mmm, that's good." He wiped his mouth with a napkin. "She taught me a lot about dealing with adversity, and how to always have a positive attitude as I go through life. She said that being positive makes positive things happen, and that people would like me better if I was upbeat."

Mark smiled at Tommy. "It sounds to me like she was a wise woman."

"She was wiser in more ways than people knew or understood. She encouraged me to be myself, to do whatever I needed so that I could discover who I was and what I wanted out of life. She took me on summer trips to places like Philadelphia, Boston, and Washington, D.C., so that I could learn more about American history. We also went to a cabin in the Poconos for Christmas." He smiled brightly. "But my favorite trip was when she took me to Salem, Massachusetts. We walked around old Salem and learned about the witch hunts and trials. We went to an old cemetery where they had buried those wrongly accused of being witches. It was awesome."

Mark noticed yet another change in Tommy's face. Over the first few weeks of the semester, he had rarely noticed any changes in Tommy's happy expression, until tonight. Mark saw the sadness return to Tommy's eyes, but not the hurt that had been there when he'd mentioned his parents.

"At the beginning of my senior year, my grandmother had a stroke. I found her on the floor when I got home from school. While she was in the hospital, we discussed the possibility of her going to a senior facility, and she decided to move into the one where her sister already lived," Tommy took a deep breath and let it out slowly. "Anyway, I was the valedictorian of my senior class, and my grandmother assured me that I would have the funds to go to college. She was well enough to attend my graduation in early June, but died of a massive heart attack later that same month."

"I'm so sorry, Tommy."

Tommy gave him a half-hearted smile. "It's all right. She made sure that I would have no financial worries." That thought made him chuckle. "My parents received the shock of their lives when the will was read. They learned that my grandmother had a lot more money than anyone knew about. My parents and my sisters received a pittance from the estate. My uncle, who lives out in San Francisco, received a third of the estate and some stocks and bonds, and became my guardian. He kept laughing during the reading of the will." Tommy smiled at Mark. "I guess I don't have to tell you who got the bulk of my grandmother's estate."

"No, but why don't you tell me anyway?" Mark was mesmerized by Tommy's voice.

"Okay." Tommy shrugged. "I got everything, including her house and the cabin in the Poconos. I had assumed that she'd rented it for us to use, but found out that she owned it and rented it out to others as a timeshare." He finished the last of his meal and set down his fork. "Now I'm here getting my education and pledging Kappa. And that's my life in a nutshell."

"Wow, that makes my life look bland!" Mark exclaimed. "You've been through a lot for a young guy."

"My grandmother used to say that there is nothing we can do about our past or where we came from, but there is a hell of a lot that we can do to make our futures brighter. I'm in the process of doing everything that I can to make my future brighter. I know she's watching over me, and I don't want to disappoint her."

"Well, so far, it appears to me that there's no chance of you disappointing her." He picked up a dessert menu. "Do you want dessert?"

"No, thanks." Tommy rubbed his stomach. "I'm full."

"Are you sure? They make a killer tiramisu!" Mark tempted.

"Are you having one?"

"Naturally."

"All right then, I'll have one too, but just to keep you company."

Mark smiled. He really liked Tommy, despite the reservations he had about the inner feelings that were coming to the fore. He was still scared about what might happen if he acted on those feelings, but more and more he was beginning to wonder what he might lose if he didn't make a move.

"Now it's your turn," Tommy said after their dessert arrived.

"It's really boring compared to your life." Mark marshaled his thoughts. "I grew up in an upper middle-class neighborhood outside of Hartford, Connecticut. My parents met in college and have been married for twenty-five years. I have one sister, three years older than me. After he graduated from college, my father worked for Schwab, then he became this financial wizard for an international corporation. My mother was a salesperson and the state-wide rep for a cosmetics company while she worked to get her doctorate degree." He smiled. "She is very proud of that pink Cadillac, although my sister and I were embarrassed when she drove us to school in it." He laughed. "I've played football ever since I was a little boy, always dreaming of winning the Super Bowl. The reality is that I'm not a great quarterback and probably won't get drafted, which is why my education is so important to me. Computer programming and business administration will help me build a future."

"I think you're a darned good quarterback."

"Even when I'm flat?"

"Yes. Even then." Tommy replied. "If you were hoping to get a shot at the NFL, why did you come to Timian instead of a college with a more preeminent football program?"

"My parents wanted me to go to Harvard so that I could get the best education money could buy and still be able to play football. I was tired of living in our Boston/New York suburb. I wanted to go somewhere small, out-of-the-way, where few people would know my family. I wanted to become my own person without having to live up to the expectations of others." He smiled as he looked over at Tommy. "Besides, you can't beat this setting. The mountains and the trees surrounding this college and little town sold me on Timian. I love nature and the outdoors."

"That's what sold me on Timian, too."

Mark picked up the tab for the meal. "Are you ready to leave?"

Tommy nodded. "I guess so."

6: PLEDGING A FRATERNITY, WEEK 4

"Congratulations, pledges, you have completed three weeks of the pledge period and only need to survive one more week before the initiation." Oscar smiled over at the pledges as he began the Friday night meeting. "How are you doing in those burlap undies?" The brotherhood roared with laughter. He noted that the pledges looked a little uncomfortable after he mentioned the burlap underwear. He remembered from his pledge days that if you didn't think about the burlap, it didn't itch quite as much.

"Just one more week and you'll be able to stop wearing them, if you want to," Oscar said, once the laughter stopped. "But, pledges, before you get too comfortable with that thought, there's a fraternity pledge competition tomorrow. Six fraternities have signed up their pledges to participate in this event. Students will be attending the competition and donating money for the local chapter of Muscular Dystrophy. The last time Kappa won the competition was when the current senior members were freshmen. Dave, Mark, Joe, Brent, Rick, Walter, Simon, Larry and I were the last group of pledges to win the trophy. We'd love to see that trophy taken away from Gamma." Oscar's expression turned serious. "We simply ask that you do your best, and if you should win the trophy, there will be no clean-up duty this weekend."

"Thank you, sir," the pledges cheered.

"Meet here at the house at nine o'clock tomorrow morning. The brothers will escort you through town to the football field." Oscar grinned. "We will allow you to wear a jockstrap underneath the burlap for those events that you choose to participate in."

"Thank you, sir," the pledges said in unison.

"Tommy and Kyle, Al Martin and I will be watching over both of you tomorrow, as your brothers are away for tomorrow's game. Make sure you report directly to me in the morning."

"Yes, sir," the twosome responded.

Oscar nodded. "The only other items that you are going to have to concentrate on during the next week are finishing your paddle and getting your tattoo, if you haven't already done so."

"Yes, sir," the group responded.

Oscar finished up the meeting with a discussion of fraternity business. The brothers, minus the football players who were already en route to their game, and the pledges mingled and partied for the remainder of the evening.

"*Hola, hermanos,*" Oscar exclaimed as Dave and Mark walked into his room on their return from the road trip. "We were expecting you guys home last night. What happened?"

"Halfway back to campus, the bus broke down in the middle of nowhere," Mark groaned, scowling at Oscar's clear, well-rested look.

"We had to sleep on the bus last night. They finally got it fixed around nine o'clock this morning," Dave added.

Oscar gestured for them to sit down. "Sorry about how the game turned out. Seems like you boys could have used the skills of some of our pledges."

"We saw the trophy as we walked through the living room." Dave smiled. "The Pledge Sports Competition trophy is back where it belongs!"

Mark nodded. "I can't believe we got it back. This bunch of pledges are mostly academics."

"Then you'll both be happy to know that the two best academics in our pledge group were the ones that won the trophy back for us." He briefly savored their looks of surprise. "Your little brothers destroyed the competition for the overall points. I never expected Tommy and Kyle to be the most athletic among this group of pledges."

"All right, already, tell us the results of the challenges," Dave urged.

Oscar pulled out his score sheet from the competition. "Let's see," he muttered, prolonging their anticipation. "Tommy won the 40- and 100-yard dashes, with Kyle as a close second in both races. I didn't realize Tommy could run so fast." Oscar looked over at Mark.

"I've run with him a few times, and I know he can go for long distances without getting winded. He usually maintains a slow, steady pace. I've never raced him, and don't think I'll try now," Mark commented.

"You should have seen Brian. He was trying to help Gamma by distracting Tommy with some pretty blatant flirtation. The Gammas were enjoying the entertainment, but Tommy seemed oblivious."

Mark didn't like hearing that Brian was making moves on Tommy, but he forced a laugh. "Well, it obviously didn't work for Gamma."

"Kyle won the burlap bag race, and Carlos came in second, leaving Gamma a distant third again," Oscar recounted. "Tommy and Kyle teamed up to win the three-legged race. Those two work very well together, by the way. I've noticed that they have been supporting and challenging each other throughout the pledge period." Oscar looked over at his two brothers. "Sort of like the three of us did during our pledge."

Mark had seen Kyle running with Tommy some mornings. He wondered whether there could be something going on between the two. The sudden surge of jealousy was something that he had never experienced in regards to another man.

"Tommy, Kyle, Carlos, and Benjamin teamed up to win the relay race. Gamma won the tug of war, and we came in third." Oscar paused for dramatic effect. "But the best race of the day was the cycles race. Carlos rode the unicycle around the track in excellent time. Kyle extended the lead riding the bicycle." He looked over at Dave, then at Mark. "Tommy was chosen to do the tricycle because he's the shortest pledge. He pedaled that tricycle faster than I imagined a six-footer could." Oscar laughed.

"I bet Brian was plenty upset, handing over the trophy that he helped Gamma win last year to the boy he tried to rush this year," Mark said with a smirk.

"Damn," Dave exclaimed. "Six out of seven events won by Kappa. Those boys deserve some reward for that, Oscar."

"I told them that if they won the trophy, they wouldn't have to clean the house this weekend. Guess which two pledges showed up anyway." Oscar raised an eyebrow.

Mark and Dave looked at each other and burst out laughing. "Kyle and Tommy," they said in unison.

"Yes, gentlemen. After six hours of competition in burlap undies, and then the victory party last night, both of those young men were back at the house this morning. I allowed them to clean your rooms, but stopped them from cleaning up the first floor and basement."

"Good. They certainly deserved a break," Dave said with approval.

After returning to his dorm room from taking Mark's clean laundry back to Kappa house earlier in the day, Tommy opened his grandmother's trunk and carefully stowed the clear crystal that had been under Mark's mattress. The topaz crystal had been left under Mark's mattress. He pulled out the dragon head dagger and carved four symbols into the top of the trunk lid. He used a black marker to write the same four symbols onto the strap of Mark's jockstrap, before burying the jockstrap at the bottom of the trunk. Afterward, he placed a candle in the center of a plate, surrounded the outer edge of the plate with dirt from outside the dorm, and poured spring water in between the dirt mound and candle. He lit the candle and left it sitting on his desk. Then he sat on his bed, chanting before he prepared to carve runes into the back of his paddle.

> *Element of Air; I ask for your blessings on my work.*
> *Bring your knowledge and discernment.*
> *Help me see the bright new beginning I undertake*
> *The sunrise of my path.*
> *Element of Fire; I ask for your blessings on my work.*
> *Bring your passion and warmth,*
> *Throught the transformation of the flames.*
> *Help me to dance, love and grow.*
> *Element of Water; I ask for your blessings of my work.*
> *Bring your emotion, intuition, flow.*
> *Help me to swim with the changes.*
> *Element of Earth; I ask for your blessings on my work.*
> *Bring me your wisdom, your deep ancestral knowing.*
> *Help me know nurturance, sustenance, abundance.*
> *Help me to go within.*

Tommy had spent hours researching runic alphabets, looking for the best symbols for his purpose. He had discovered many versions, each with its own variations in names, shapes, esoteric meanings, and magical usage. He finally decided to use the Elder Futhark runic alphabet, which was the one most commonly still in use in northern Europe. He studied each of the twenty-four symbols and chose the fifteen runes that he felt were meaningful for both him and Mark. He then spent several hours creating the design and layout for the back of the paddle.

Before and after carving each of the fifteen symbols, Tommy chanted a portion of his grandmother's spell book. When he had finished carving all of the rune symbols, he stained the oak paddle a dark cherry. These preparations had to be completed before he went out into the woods on Tuesday night, when he wouldn't be able to see clearly what he was doing.

Brent, Rick, and Larry were laughing and joking at lunch on Monday afternoon when they saw Tommy enter the cafeteria with a group of three girls. The pledge and the girls sat on the opposite side of the cafeteria from the three Kappa seniors. All three brothers were members of the house council that would help select the new brothers from the pledge group, as well as being members of the college tennis team.

"What did you think of Simon's accusation against Tommy?" Rick asked his brothers.

"I think Simon's full of shit, and I'm glad he stopped hanging around the house after Herb was kicked out," Brent replied harshly. "Tommy's a cool guy and a lot of fun to talk with."

Larry nodded. "He gets along with everybody in the fraternity; his upbeat attitude has even rubbed off on Mark."

"Mark was a real prick earlier this semester, that's for sure," Rick observed.

Larry looked at Tommy and the girls, then back at his tablemates. "Do you think there's any truth to Simon's accusation?"

The pledge was laughing and joking with the girls at the table. "I don't know." Brent looked at his brothers. "I've seen him with Brian a few times, but that girl sitting on his left has also been hanging around him a lot."

"Maybe they have a class together," Rick suggested.

"That could be. But he smiles a lot when he's around her." Brent smiled broadly. "When I've seen him around Brian, Tommy always looks like he's picking up dog shit."

"I'd hate to have to tutor an asshole like Brian," Larry said with a laugh.

Rick looked speculatively at their prospective brother. "But what if he is queer?" he persisted

"As long as he doesn't make a move on me, I don't give a damn," Brent said.

"Do we want a queer in the fraternity?" Larry asked.

Brent laughed. "We already have a couple in the fraternity, and a couple of other guys that play both sides."

"Who?" Rick and Larry asked in surprise.

"Sorry, brothers." Brent smiled at them. "It's their secret and I'm not going to divulge who they are. You'll just have to try and figure it out for yourselves."

"Have you had dinner yet?" Mark asked when Tommy answered the phone.

"No, sir."

"Good. Meet me at The Gold Spike in fifteen minutes," Mark said, then hung up.

Tommy stared at the receiver in his hand and shook his head. *The brothers sure have a way of making a pledge feel like a human being.* He chuckled to himself as he put away his things.

Ten minutes later, Tommy walked into the restaurant and spotted Mark at a table in the back corner. Tommy smiled brightly as he approached the table. Mark stood up to shake hands and invited Tommy to sit with a wave at the chair opposite him.

"To what do I owe the honor of dining with my big brother?" Tommy asked as he sat down.

"I don't need a reason to invite you to dinner."

Tommy dipped his head in acknowledgement. "Thank you, sir."

"Congratulations for having had such a good fraternity competition," Mark said after the waiter took their orders. "I'm sorry I couldn't be there to give you support, but we were in the middle of having our asses handed to us."

"Thank you. I felt your presence at the competition, which is probably why you had such a bad game."

Mark ignored the implied criticism as he sipped his water. "I've always had an easy time running with you; I wasn't aware that you were so fast until Oscar told us about the races. I'm glad that I haven't challenged you to a race."

Tommy laughed. "A small guy gets very little attention from others, especially jocks."

"You're not that small a guy, little brother. I don't consider six foot tall to be small."

"Standing next to you and the other brothers makes me feel small sometimes," Tommy grimaced, "but riding a tricycle doesn't."

Mark cleared his throat. "Actually, I invited you to dinner to see how the pledge period has been going for you and to make sure you're ready for initiation at the end of the week."

"I believe I'm doing well," Tommy replied. "I just have to finish my paddle before Friday."

"That's good to hear."

The waiter brought their meals and they began eating their dinner.

"How are those burlap undies working for you?" Mark looked over at Tommy and laughed.

"Just fine," Tommy reported. "As long as you don't think about them, they don't itch. So thank you for mentioning it."

"I remember. I thought boxers wouldn't itch as much." He chuckled at the memory. "I discovered that it didn't matter what the style, burlap itches."

"When do we get to stop wearing them?"

"After the final initiation process on Saturday night."

"I can't wait to get them off."

Mark shot a contemplative glance at Tommy. "How are the other pledges holding up? Have there been any problems since Herbie was dropped?"

"We tried really hard to keep Herbie in the group, but we all became frustrated with him. We got to the point where we thought it might be best for the rest of us if we just let him fail. I guess that doesn't say too much for the idea of brotherhood." Tommy avoided looking at Mark, fearing he would see disapproval.

"Not really, Tommy. The rest of you have been working together and doing all the things that you need to do to get into the fraternity. I can understand the frustration you must have experienced. Herbie was a mess, and a serious drinker to boot. I think it was best that you guys let him fail on his own, rather than let him cause problems for the rest of you. Sometimes you just have to let go."

Tommy stared into Mark's blue eyes and smiled. "Thank you. Some of us talked to him afterward. We felt really bad that he was dropped, but he didn't seem too upset about it. I would have been devastated."

"That's the difference between you and Herbie." Mark looked away from Tommy's eyes. "So, how are the other guys doing?"

"Everyone seems to be doing really well. We're all tired from our class work and the extra duties assigned by the brothers, but I think we're all enjoying the experience and helping one another get through it."

"That's good to hear." Mark looked up from his meal. "You and Kyle certainly seem to be getting along well."

Tommy stared at Mark for a moment, startled by his accusatory tone. He wondered whether he should be irritated that Mark would intimate that he and Kyle were more than just friends, or whether he should be flattered that Mark was showing a little jealousy.

"Kyle's a great guy. We met the first day of the semester and got along very well. We've been challenging one another during the pledge period. He's become my best friend here." Tommy looked directly at Mark. "If you're worried that there's some tawdry affair going on between the two of us, rest assured that there is not. We're just friends, so you needn't worry about a scandal within Kappa."

"I'm sorry. I didn't mean anything by the comment. I just thought it was great that you guys are getting along so well. Dave, Oscar, and I were quite the trio in our pledge class," he said.

"Your apology is accepted. I'm sorry I was defensive."

"I deserved it," Mark said with a smile, then changed the subject. "Dessert?"

"I don't think so. I couldn't eat another thing." The meal had been fantastic, but once again, the time spent with Mark had been priceless.

"Do you have any questions about the initiation this weekend?"

"No, I don't think so."

Mark squinted. "You don't have any questions?"

"I'd rather be surprised."

"Hmm. Very interesting."

Tommy worked up the courage to make his request. "I need to be able to have Tuesday evening for myself. I have some things to do, and Tuesday night is the only night that I can do them. Will that be okay?"

"I'll make sure you get Tuesday to yourself," Mark replied, wondering what Tommy was up to.

"Thank you. I really appreciate it."

When the check came for the meal, Mark picked it up with a smile. "This is on me, pledge."

Tommy gave Mark a devilish look. "Now that you've paid for my dinner, I'm not going to have to put out, am I, sir?"

Mark returned the grin. "Not tonight. I'll take a rain check."

Making A Paddle

Early Tuesday evening, Tommy packed his backpack with his paddle, the paddle attachments, varnish, a paint brush, Band-Aids, a couple of rags, a hammer, matches, a small bowl, and three small bottles of spring water. To these, he added his grandmother's ancient spell book, his dragon head dagger, and the black pouch that contained the clear crystal that had been under Mark's mattress for over three weeks. He closed the backpack, slung it over his shoulder, and embarked on his mission. He drove twenty miles out to the woods on the other side of the river from the town and parked his car in a secluded spot, then hiked along a path for a quarter of a mile before he found the ideal spot to perform his ritual.

Tommy cleared a circular area, then gathered some sticks and dead wood which he placed in the center. He stood in the area and chanted:

Uphold the rules of the Wiccan Rede.
Be high in spirit and you shall succeed.
The Power of the Five Elements,
Will help keep Mother Nature alive.
From the grains of Earth to the moving Air.
Past the burning Fire that magic flares.
Flow with Water, streams, lakes, and oceans;
Around the Spirit's aura and dreams.

He sat down and lit the wood, quietly meditating on what he was about to do. Sitting in front of the fire, he spread a small white towel on the ground between himself and the flames, then placed all the necessary items on the towel in front of him. He opened his grandmother's book to the pre-selected page.

Tommy picked up the crystal that he had kept under Mark's mattress, wrapped it in a white hand cloth, and began crushing it with a hammer. He checked frequently to see if the fragments were small enough. When he had pounded it down to a fine powder, he placed the paddle across his lap and chanted, all the while using the dragon head dagger to carve a fresh line through the center of each of the ancient rune symbols on the back of his paddle. When he was finished, he pricked the middle finger of his right hand and let a drop of blood drip into each of the symbols, then smeared it into the wood. He held up the paddle so that he could see the back in the light of the fire. Happy with the work he had done, he hoped that Mark would be proud.

He sat back and quietly meditated on his project. After several moments, he began applying the wooden attachments to the front of the paddle. As with the carvings, Tommy chanted before and after applying each one with wood glue. It took him almost an hour to place all fifteen attachments in exactly the right spots. When he was finished, he held it up to the firelight and stared at it with pride.

Again, he sat back and meditated. He took a sip from the bottle of water and looked for the envelope that contained the loose black hairs from Mark's hairbrush, along with some of his own which he had collected and kept inside his grandmother's trunk until they were needed. He pulled the envelope out of the backpack and placed it next to the book.

He removed a small bowl from his pack and placed it on the towel next to the paddle. He poured some of the varnish into the bowl, sprinkled in a portion of the crystal dust. He checked the book and chanted the incantation aloud while stirring the mixture with a stick. Next, he put several of the loose hairs into the bowl and stirred them in, chanting the incantation a second time. Finally, he took the dagger and made a small cut across the palm of his left hand. He let the blood drip into the bowl, then placed a cloth in his palm to stop the bleeding. Again, he said the incantation as he stirred the mixture. The firelight gave the mixture a dark pinkish hue and made it appear to sparkle.

Tommy dipped a paintbrush into the bowl of varnish and covered the back of the paddle. He dipped his thumb and forefinger into the bowl and pulled out some of the loose hairs, which he placed over the back of the freshly varnished paddle, making sure that they did not cross over any of the rune symbols. When he finished the back of the paddle, he sprinkled a small portion of the crystal dust over it. He leaned the paddle against a stand of sticks that he had set up to keep the paddle from sticking to the towel or ground, and so that the heat from the fire would help it to dry faster.

He took a sip of water and meditated as he waited for the back of the paddle to dry, then he repeated the actions for the front of the paddle. He added more varnish to what remained in the bowl, added another portion of the crystal dust and the last of the loose hairs. He squeezed open the cut on his left palm, mixing in the blood as he repeated the incantation. With the rag in his palm to stop the bleeding, he brushed on the varnish and then placed the hairs on the front of the paddle.

When he was done, Tommy sat back and took a long drink from the bottle of water and meditated on his actions, then quietly chanted as he sprinkled a portion of the crystal dust onto the front of the paddle. He mixed the remainder of the crystal dust into the last of the varnish mixture in the bowl, then poured the contents of the bowl into an empty water bottle to be used later on the inside of his grandmother's trunk. Still chanting incantations, he packed his things into his backpack. Tommy leaned back against a tree and drank more water, staring at the paddle.

After an hour of meditating while the paddle dried, Tommy stood up and flung his backpack over his shoulder. He poured the last bottle of water onto the fire and made sure that it was out. He looked up into the starry night sky, took a deep breath, and carefully picked up his paddle. He chanted as he walked back to his car, where he carefully placed the paddle on a piece of plastic and drove back to the campus.

It was after eleven o'clock when Tommy entered his empty dorm room. He placed his backpack on the floor by his bed and the paddle on the desk, then opened his grandmother's trunk. From the backpack, he pulled the water bottle with the varnish in it. He chanted as he lightly brushed the inside top of the lid, covering the four symbols he had carved there earlier. The remainder of the varnish, which had been empowered and could not be dumped down the drain or thrown away, he brushed onto the front and back of the paddle. After carefully standing the paddle on his desk to dry, he closed the trunk and tidied up the room before going to bed.

The next morning, Tommy rose and opened the curtains to let in the early morning light, then looked at his paddle. Against the dark stain, he couldn't see any of the hairs he had applied. The blood had mixed well with the varnish, and that gave the paddle a richer shade of dark red cherry, and the crystal dust made the paddle glitter if held correctly against the light. He was well pleased with the way it had turned out.

"Care to join me for a morning run?" Mark asked when he joined Jack in the kitchen early Wednesday morning.

"Sure. I'm ready whenever you are. What route do you want to take?" He was curious to know whether Mark was still following Tommy on his morning runs.

"Through town and then down to the river."

Half a block away from Main Street, they watched as Tommy crossed the street and ran further down Main. The pair turned left at Main Street and followed the pledge. They both noticed the white bandage covering Tommy's left hand and wondered what had happened, but neither mentioned it.

Jack started laughing. "Is there a reason we're following Tommy?"

Mark stared at the body half a block ahead of him and smiled. "I need to talk to you about him."

"Is there a problem?"

"I don't know. Is there any truth to the accusation that Simon made?"

"You're going to have to ask him that question," Jack said seriously.

Mark glanced over at him. "I don't know what to do about these feelings that I'm having about him." He returned to watching the taut body in front of him. "It's like I'm looking at a goal in front of me. There's a part of me that wants to reach that goal, but another part of me is scared to death."

"Well, to begin with, it would be a good thing if you knew what you wanted." Jack glanced over at Mark and then returned his attention to what was in front of him. "You and Tommy seem to be getting along well."

"He's a great little brother," Mark said. "My problem is that I don't know if I want something more to happen between us."

Jack glanced over at his confused friend. "I can't tell you what to do, Mark.

It's a personal decision that you have to make for yourself."

"What would you do?"

"Keep in mind that I've already accepted the fact that I'm gay. I know what I want in my life. I'm not confused about it." He looked at Mark, trying to gauge his response. "If I were still single and interested in somebody like Tommy, and knew that he was interested in me, I'd go out on a date with him. I'd get to know him, and then find out whether he was interested in more than just friendship." He smiled at Mark. "Or you could try it the Brian way and get turned down."

Mark watched Tommy turn the corner and head toward the cemetery. "I thought gay guys were always making moves on other guys."

Jack shook his head. "Not every gay guy is trying to put as many notches on his bedpost as he can. With AIDS being such an epidemic, it's too dangerous. I'm the old-fashioned type of guy. I like to be pampered, wined and dined, and neck at the movies. I also like going out with a guy more than one time, getting to know that guy, and hopefully things will work out between us." He studied Mark. "Kind of like you straight guys who are hoping to find the right woman to spend the rest of your life with. There are as many types of gay guys as there are straight guys, Mark."

"Why can't this be easy?" Mark frowned as they ran down the hill to the river.

"Oh, it could be easy." Jack shot Mark a grin. "I know a couple of guys who would love to be fucked by you, no strings attached. Just do them and they'd be happy."

Mark was unamused. "I guess I'm more interested in what Tommy has to offer than a quickie," he said with a scowl. "I'd much rather be with somebody that I care about. But there are two problems with that scenario."

"Which are?"

"What happens if I really like it? Or what happens if I decide that it's not right for me?"

"Meaning what, exactly?" Jack asked.

"There is a chance, however small, that I could be drafted by the NFL. It wouldn't be a good thing to have a boyfriend." Mark glanced over at Jack. "So if I liked being with Tommy, my life would be completely upside down."

"And if you didn't like being with him?"

"Well, then I'd end up hurting Tommy, and that wouldn't be fair to him."

"You have a real dilemma."

They reached the river and turned to run back up the hill. "And that's why I asked you for help."

Jack shook his head. "Then why don't you just try to convince Tommy that one night with you would be more than enough to remember you by?"

"Fuck off," Mark growled. "Either give me some good advice or shut up." He looked over at Jack and smiled ingratiatingly. "Seriously, how do I solve this dilemma?"

"All right. If you really do care about him and you don't want to do anything that might hurt him, talk to him about your feelings and find out whether he'd want to let you bang him for the night."

"That just sounds so tacky."

"What the hell do you want, Mark?" Jack asked, frustrated. "You say that you're not sure what you want, but I bet somewhere inside that thick head, you do. You don't want to hurt Tommy, but you also don't want to miss the chance to fuck him."

"That's not what I said."

"Maybe not, but that's the bottom line. You want to go to bed with him, but you don't want to do anything that might turn you queer or hurt Tommy. You can't have it both ways, buddy," Jack said. "Take him to bed and see what happens when you wake up in the morning. You can always say you were drunk. Fags like me and Tommy are used to hearing that shit," Jack spat angrily, then he sped up his pace, leaving Mark behind.

"Jack!" Mark ran to catch up. "I'm sorry. I didn't mean to upset you. I wasn't saying things right. I'm scared to death about the feelings that I have for Tommy. I've never felt this way about another guy." He looked apprehensively at Jack. "When I was a teenager, I fooled around with a close buddy. You know how things are when you first start realizing that boys and girls are different. You get curious about other boys and compare size and shit like that. Or you have those contests where you see who can get off first and shoot their load the farthest. Once I started dating girls, I stopped messing around with guys. I told myself that had just been a phase I was going through. I've never been attracted to my male friends."

"I'm sorry, Mark, I could have been a little more understanding," Jack said quietly. "But as a gay man, it's frustrating when straight guys just want to play with you to see if they like it, and then pretend nothing happened." Jack took a deep breath. "If you're not sure that you want to have a relationship with Tommy, then just leave him alone. Don't lead him on the way Sally does you. He'll get hurt and be upset, and then I'll have to kick your ass." Jack offered a tentative smile.

"I understand." Mark patted Jack on the back. "I'll think about it a lot more before I decide what to do."

"What did you do to your hand, Ford Tommy?" Kyle asked when he saw Tommy at lunch on Wednesday.

Tommy looked down at the bandage on his palm. "I was carving something into my paddle and the knife slipped. It's just a little cut and should heal quickly."

"Have you finished your paddle?"

"Yes, I have." Tommy smiled. "Have you finished yours?"

"Yes. I'll show you mine, if you show me yours."

Tommy gave him a look of feigned shock. "Here in the cafeteria? You cad."

Kyle punched Tommy's arm. "Are you ready for Friday night?"

"I'm excited and scared at the same time." Tommy began eating his lunch. "I think I'm ready for whatever they toss at us, but I keep wondering what's going to happen."

"I know what you mean. We've come this far and gotten through all the tasks." Kyle looked thoughtful. "But what new twists are they going to throw at us on Friday night? It's a little scary, Ford Tommy."

"Well, we'll be scared together and get through it together, Welby Kyle," Tommy said reassuringly.

7: KAPPA LAMBDA PI INITIATION, PART I

Tommy had been anxious for the week to end. The anticipation of initiation, showing off his paddle and tattoo in order to gain acceptance into the fraternity, were almost more than he could handle. He felt as if he were bouncing off the walls as he struggled through his normal routine those last days.

Friday evening, he and Kyle walked over to Kappa house in silence, each lost in his own thoughts. Each was carrying his paddle inside a pillowcase. "Are you as nervous as I am?" Tommy asked quietly.

Kyle blew out a deep breath. "Yes, I'm scared to death."

As they approached the front door, the two pledges noticed the number of Kappa brothers hanging around outside the house, more brothers than attended the regular Friday night meetings. The only difference between this meeting and the regular meetings was that everyone was quiet and subdued as they awaited the initiation process. Several of the brothers welcomed Tommy and Kyle; a senior member escorted the two pledges inside.

Tommy was surprised at the appearance inside the house. Candles lit the three large front rooms. All of the shades on the windows had been pulled down so that outsiders would not be able to peep in and witness the secrets of the initiation. A senior member stood at each of the doors to the first floor to keep out anyone who did not belong to the Kappa fraternity. Tommy and Kyle were led to the front of the living room and took their places in two of the seats that awaited the pledge class.

As he arrived, each pledge was seated with Tommy and Kyle. They did not see any of the members of the house council or their big brothers. Heads lowered, none of them said a word.

At exactly seven o'clock, the members of the house council entered the living room. They were wearing red and black robes. They took their places along the side wall, facing the pledges.

Oscar stood at the front of the room and looked out at the twenty-four members of the fraternity standing in the large living room and dining room, and spilling out into the side hallway. Tommy felt a lot of tension in the air, even from those who had already been through the process.

"Welcome, brothers and pledges," Oscar began, as members took available seats or had to remain standing in the crowded living room. "Please join hands as we recite the fraternity oath." Everyone joined hands in such a way that each brother was connected to another.

Tommy had been sitting in the first pledge seat and held Oscar's hand as the brotherhood recited the fraternity oath. The pledges would recite another, formal, oath at the end of the initiation period. When they finished, Oscar patted Tommy on the back and waited for everyone to settle down.

"We're here this evening to assess the worthiness of these nine pledges for induction into the brotherhood of Kappa Lambda Pi. This evening they will be judged on two tasks that were assigned to them early in the pledge period: whether they obtained their tattoos, and whether their paddles are acceptable. Tomorrow we will judge the pledges on their overall worthiness to become brothers. If they pass tonight's tests, they'll become Initiates for tomorrow night's final rite of initiation into the fraternity."

Cheers roared up from the brotherhood while the pledges sat in nervous silence. Mark, Dave, Jack, and the other big brothers seemed as nervous as the pledges. Mark kept looking up front at Tommy. Oscar turned and faced the pledges. "Pledges, are you ready to be judged?" he asked aloud.

"Yes, sir," the pledges responded loudly in unison.

Oscar turned to face the members. "We are fortunate this year that the football team does not have to play a game tomorrow. Their schedule the past few years caused us to wait until Sunday before we could finish the initiation process. This year we'll be able to complete the initiation on Saturday and then have one hell of a party."

Again, cheers rose from the brotherhood.

Oscar turned to the pledges. "All right, pledges, it's time for you to show your tattoo."

The pledges stood and rolled up the shirtsleeve that covered the fraternity crest. All nine pledges had obtained the red and black tattoo.

Oscar roughly rubbed a wet rag over each tattoo, checking to see if anyone had cheated by using a marking pen. He smiled at each pledge as it was confirmed that his tattoo was genuine. He turned and faced the brotherhood. "The tattoos are real, brothers." The brotherhood cheered.

"All right, brothers. We will take a brief, ten-minute break before judging the paddles. When we resume, the big brothers should assume a position beside their little brothers." Oscar struck the gavel to start the break.

Some in the brotherhood used the time to get another drink or to go to the bathroom. Mark went out to the kitchen, poured a shot of brandy into a glass, and got a bottle of water from the refrigerator. He chatted briefly with a few people as he made his way through the crowd to stand beside Tommy. Mark handed over the shot of brandy, which Tommy downed in one gulp. Several of the members cheered as Tommy handed the empty glass back to Mark.

"Thank you, sir. I needed that," Tommy said. "I'm so damn nervous." He smiled as he accepted the bottle of water and took a large gulp.

"I thought you were looking pretty calm, cool, and collected. I'm very proud of you," he whispered.

"We're ready to continue, brothers," Oscar announced as he returned to the front of the room. He turned to face the pledges. "We will now judge each of your paddles. I'll call you forward in alphabetical order by first name. You'll hand the bag or case over to your big brother, who will take your paddle out for inspection. After all the paddles are inspected, we will recess and vote on their acceptance." He waited for their nods of understanding. "We hope to see two things in your paddles — a little imagination, and some individuality. Points will be assessed against you for either plain wooden paddles or gaudy paddles." He stopped again and looked at each of the pledges. "Are you ready, pledges?"

"Yes, sir," the pledges chorused.

The process of judging the paddles took time, as each paddle had to be inspected by the big brother and the pledge master. The other members of the house council would get a chance to view the paddles later. After Oscar finished inspecting a paddle, he returned it to the big brother.

Adam, Alex, Benjamin, Carlos, and Jason had their paddles inspected, then it was Kyle's turn. Dave pulled the paddle from the pillowcase and held it up in front of him. The oak paddle had been stained a light cherry color and had the requisite personal attachments on the front. Each had been painted in the fraternity colors, which added to the style. Tommy thought Kyle's paddle was one of the best so far.

Tommy's was next to be appraised. Mark reached into the pillowcase and grabbed hold of the handle, and a startled expression passed over his face. Mark looked over at Tommy, but Tommy only smiled as Mark performed a careful inspection. Mark had appeared a bit nervous at first, but there was serenity in his face as he handed the paddle over to Oscar.

When Mark looked over at him, Tommy smiled again. He could see that Mark wanted to say something to him, but the ritual did not allow the big brother to converse with the pledge.

The final two paddles were inspected and returned to the big brothers. Oscar stood up in front of the brotherhood. "Brothers and pledges, we will now take a recess as the house council and big brothers vote on acceptance of the paddles. You're free to mingle for the next half hour." Oscar strode out of the living room with the house council and two senior big brothers following. Those fourteen Kappa members went upstairs to the third floor and into the private living room, locking the door behind them.

Oscar and the other members briefly chatted with one another as they made themselves drinks from the bar and began to relax. Oscar called them to order, and they all sat around the coffee table viewing the nine paddles.

Jack picked up Tommy's paddle and balanced it in his hand. He could sense the energy captured within it. "What did you feel when you touched this paddle?" Jack asked quietly so that others wouldn't hear him.

Mark acted as if he didn't understand the question. "What?"

"I saw the look on your face when you reached into the pillowcase and touched the paddle. You seemed surprised or caught off guard. I just want to know what you felt."

Mark and Jack both read the same type of books and often discussed extra-sensory or paranormal sensations, so Mark knew he could talk with Jack about what he had felt, but he knew the others might think he was crazy. He took the paddle from Jack and walked away from the group, Jack following. Mark looked back at the group and then whispered, "There was a strange sensation when I grabbed the handle, like there was an energy inside it. I felt a warm, tingling flash through my body." Mark looked into Jack's eyes. "Am I imagining things?"

Jack shook his head. "I can sense the energy in the paddle, but I can't feel it."

Mark turned the paddle over and showed Jack the back. "These are rune symbols, aren't they?"

Jack examined the back of the paddle closely. "Damn, those are good. He must have used a really sharp knife." He looked up at Mark. "That's probably how he cut his hand earlier this week."

What Jack said made sense. Mark looked at the paddle. "What's making it shimmer in the light, I wonder?"

Jack watched as Mark turned the paddle back and forth. "It doesn't appear to be bottled glitter. It must be something else, but I don't know what."

"Hey, what are you guys talking about?" Dave asked, his voice slurring. He stood between them and placed an arm on each of their shoulders. "Ah, it's Tommy's paddle. He did a damn good job. He's got this dark, blood red color going for it."

Jack and Mark looked at each other and started laughing. Dave was drunk, and he didn't really understand or believe in the paranormal.

"Yes, Dave, it's a pretty paddle." Mark slapped it against Dave's ass. "Works, too." Mark and Jack laughed as Dave rubbed his butt.

The three walked back to the group and joined the discussion of the other paddles. They were all nicely done, with personal touches that reflected both the pledge and his big brother. Tommy's and Kyle's designs were the most creative. They couldn't decide which one was the best, but they really liked the personal touches that both pledges had added to their paddles.

Those gathered in the kitchen on the first floor heard Oscar and his entourage coming down the stairs and began to regroup in the living room. The pledges had already taken their seats. The big brothers stood beside their pledges, holding their paddles. Once everyone was gathered, Oscar stood up in front of the group.

He smiled as he looked around the room and then at the pledges. "Brothers of Kappa Lambda Pi, I'd like to introduce you to our new Initiates." A loud cheer rose from the assemblage and everyone stood to clap for the Initiates. Oscar motioned for them to quiet down. When they complied, Oscar faced the Initiates. "Beginning at nine o'clock tomorrow morning, you will face the final ordeal before initiation tomorrow night. You will first face the brotherhood and answer any questions that they may have regarding your character, academics, community service, fellowship with others, reasons for joining Kappa Lambda Pi, and trivia." He paused for a moment and looked at each of the Initiates.

"After two hours of questioning, each of you will meet individually with the house council for half an hour. They will be asking you similar questions, and more. Your big brother will not be present during your individual session. Once the questioning is completed, which should be by four-thirty or five o'clock, the house council will gather and make the final decision as to whether you will be initiated into the fraternity." Oscar knew that he was adding to the pledges' nervousness, even though he really liked all of these guys. "Shall we let them have their paddles back, brothers?"

"Not until they've had their whacks," the nine big brothers said in unison. A chant of "whacks, whacks, whacks" went up from the brotherhood.

Oscar smiled at the Initiates. "In order to get your paddle back from your big brother, you must be whacked." He paused and looked at their pale faces. "Basically, you get as many whacks as you have negative points."

Tommy felt a sense of relief, knowing that he didn't have any points against him. The other Initiates looked nervous, as most of them had accumulated more than ten points, and two had twenty points. Only Kyle wasn't as nervous as the others were because he had only three points, due to lateness when he had tried to help Herbie get to a meeting on time.

"Now, we don't want you to get too comfortable, Tommy boy. Just because you didn't have any points against you, doesn't mean that you won't get whacked." Oscar watched as the look on Tommy's face went from happy to unsure.

Oscar turned to face the brotherhood. "Tommy boy is the first pledge since his big brother Mark not to have any points against him during the pledge period. Because of that earlier achievement by Mark, a new rule was instituted that all pledges with less than ten points against them would automatically receive ten whacks." He paused for a split second. "Ain't that right, brothers?"

"Yes!" the entire room roared.

"So, that includes you also, Kyle." Oscar smiled, looking at both Kyle and Tommy. "We always begin with the Initiate with the fewest points against him. So, Tommy, you have the honor of being the first Initiate to get your paddle back from your big brother. Aren't you glad about that, Tommy boy?"

"Yes, sir," Tommy yelled.

The crowd cheered its approval of Tommy's acceptance of the rules.

"Pants up or down, Tommy boy?" Oscar asked the surprised Initiate.

"Up, sir." Tommy looked over at Mark, who had been slapping the paddle against his hand for several minutes.

Mark smiled evilly at him. "All right, little brother, bend over and grab the chair. I recall a biscuit being thrown at me during the pledge sing."

The crowd counted each whack as Mark delivered them sharply on Tommy's behind. By the fifth whack, Tommy felt the stinging on his ass. He was relieved when he heard the crowd shout "ten". He stood up and turned around to face Mark, who was smiling broadly. Mark handed the paddle over, and as Tommy took it, Mark wrapped his arm around Tommy's neck. As they were walking out of the living room, some in the crowd began counting whacks for Kyle while others went outside or down into the basement.

Mark poured a little brandy into a glass and gave it to Tommy, then grabbed a beer for himself. He put his hand on Tommy's neck and propelled him out of the house. It was a cool October evening, which felt good to Tommy since it had been hot inside the crowded living room. From where they were standing by the big oak tree, they could still hear the counting and cheering.

Mark smiled at Tommy. "Tell me about the rune symbols on that paddle."

Tommy hoped that Mark couldn't see him blushing. "Just a few things I thought I'd add for decoration."

"Any significance to the symbols?"

"Maybe." Tommy smiled broadly as he looked at Mark. "But I'm not going to tell."

Mark raised his eyebrows. "Oh, really, little brother?" he said with mock seriousness, but quickly broke into a smile. "I thought all the personal touches you added to your paddle were great. I'll tell you something." He looked around to make sure there were no other brothers around to hear. "If a pledge makes it this far into the process, he's pretty much guaranteed to make it into the fraternity. That is, if he doesn't totally blow it in the questioning."

Tommy smiled confidently. "I don't think I'm going to blow it during the questioning. I want to make sure that you're proud of having picked me as your little brother."

"I am proud of you, Tommy," Mark said softly.

Tommy lowered his head for a minute before looking back at Mark. "Will you still be my big brother after tomorrow?" he asked hopefully. "I never had a real brother, and I like having you as mine."

"I'm always going to be your big brother and you're always going to be my little brother." Mark tousled Tommy's hair. "Nothing will ever change that, I promise."

They stared at each other for a couple of minutes before Mark broke the eye contact. "I think we should go back inside and watch the last of the whackings," he said nervously.

Mark put his arm around Tommy's shoulder and steered him back into the house. They stood together at the back of the room and counted along with the other brothers as the last of the pledges received their whacks.

After the last pledge had received his whacks, Oscar stood in front of the brotherhood. "Gentlemen, we are adjourned until nine o'clock tomorrow morning." The gavel pounded loudly on the table.

The lights had been turned back on and the candles blown out, while the brothers mingled and talked in small groups. The Initiates had a chance to show off their paddles to the other members of the fraternity. Mark stayed near Tommy as they mingled with the crowd.

Sleep Over At Kappa House

Mark was nervous about the step he was about to take, more afraid of being rejected by Tommy than of discovering that he was gay. He had been caught off-guard by the intimacy in Tommy's earlier question, whether Mark would remain his big brother. Mark had thought he might be reading more into it than was there, but the look in Tommy's eyes had indicated that he was very serious. Now, after three beers, his inhibitions were lowered and he wanted to know what it would feel like to be with Tommy intimately.

"Are you going back to your dorm room or spending the night at the house?" Mark asked quietly, looking around to see if anyone was watching them.

"I was going to go back to my dorm room. Sleeping on the living room floor with a bunch of snoring brothers wouldn't be restful."

"Who said you had to sleep on the living room floor? There's plenty of space on the floor in my room." Mark smiled devilishly.

"As tempting as that sounds, I should go—"

Mark's finger pressed against his lips. "No, little brother, you shouldn't go. I want you to stay and spend the night with me."

"Are you sure?"

Mark beamed a warm smile. "Yes, I'm sure."

Tommy looked around the hallway and realized that nobody was paying any attention to them. He looked at Mark and handed him the paddle. "Are you collecting on your rain check?"

In answer, Mark gripped Tommy's neck and nudged the young man up the stairs.

Mark led Tommy into his room, then shut and locked the door. He became painfully aware of the heat from Tommy's body. Mark stopped Tommy in the middle of the room, walked over to the bed and dropped the paddle on it. He brushed past Tommy, allowing their arms to touch. He lit a couple of candles that were on top of his dresser and then a couple more on his desk.

Mark returned and stood in front of Tommy. He reached out and touched Tommy's chin, lifting his face so that he could look into Tommy's eyes, then he bent down, eliminating his four inch height advantage, and brushed his lips against Tommy's. He heard Tommy's sigh as he pressed their lips together more firmly.

Their tongues met in a passionate kiss while their hands began roaming over backs and sides. Mark grabbed a handful of Tommy's hair and held his face closer as he kissed Tommy harder, more passionately. Tommy wrapped his arms around Mark and returned the kisses with equal fervor.

Mark pulled the bottom of Tommy's polo shirt and the burlap t-shirt out of his jeans, and his hands roamed over the warm, smooth skin of Tommy's back. He had been getting hard from the moment he pressed his lips against Tommy's, and the longer they kissed, the harder he became.

Mark grabbed Tommy's shirts and began lifting them. He broke away from Tommy's lips only long enough to remove the shirts and toss them on the floor. He pulled him closer and kissed him passionately. Mark had never kissed another man like that, and yet it felt so good, so right. He pressed his hands against Tommy's face and pulled away. Mark looked into Tommy's eyes and smiled. He put one of his fingers against Tommy's lips so that Tommy would understand not to say anything. Mark did not want words to intrude on the moment.

Mark's hands roamed down past the crystal around Tommy's neck to the smooth chest. He gently pinched Tommy's nipples, eliciting a soft moan. His hand moved up to Tommy's shoulder and gently slid down his bicep. Mark leaned close and kissed the fraternity crest on Tommy's left arm. He couldn't believe how much he wanted this man.

Tommy stood still as Mark's hands wandered over his chest and as Mark kissed his bicep. Tommy reached over, pushed the red and black robe off Mark's shoulders, and tugged on his jersey. Mark allowed Tommy to pull the jersey up his torso, and then leaned forward so that the jersey could be pulled off over his head. Tommy let out a deep breath as his hands touched Mark's chest for the first time and rubbed his hands over the silky, soft hair. Tommy gently pinched Mark's nipples and heard Mark sigh. When Mark led Tommy over to the bed, he went eagerly.

After their lovemaking, the two young men remained still for several moments as they struggled to regain some semblance of composure. Mark rolled onto his side and looked at Tommy. He brushed his hand across Tommy's cheek and leaned over to kiss him. Then he pulled back and looked into Tommy's eyes, smiling brightly. "That was awesome."

"It was awesome." Tommy gently pushed Mark onto his back and laid his head on Mark's chest.

"What is that black spot on your ass?" Mark asked softly, wrapping an arm around Tommy's back and running his other hand through Tommy's hair.

Tommy chuckled. "It's not a spot, it's a scorpion. It was my first tattoo. My uncle let me get it when I was fifteen."

"Then you got the ankh when you were sixteen."

"Yeah, and the Kappa crest at seventeen." Tommy lifted his head and smiled. "Wanna do it again?"

"I can't believe that I'm going to say this, but I'm a little worn out right now." Mark kissed him on the forehead. "Let's just cuddle up and go to sleep."

"Sounds good to me." Tommy tilted his head down and kissed Mark.

Mark touched the crystal resting against Tommy's chest. "Do you ever take this off?"

Tommy took the crystal in his hand. "I usually take it off and put it under my pillow when I go to bed. It belonged to my grandmother."

"I see." Mark softly kissed Tommy, then pulled the blankets over their bodies.

Tommy curled up with his head on Mark's chest and his arm across Mark's body. Mark's arm wrapped around Tommy and he kissed the top of Tommy's head. The two men fell into a deep, peaceful sleep.

Trying to quietly slip out from the back of the bed, where he was between the wall and Mark, Tommy felt a strong hand grip his wrist.

Mark grinned up at him. "Where do you think you're going, little brother?"

"It's six-thirty and I'm late for my morning run. Would you like to join me?"

"You have the energy to go running this morning?"

Tommy chuckled. "Yes. Now, do you want to come or not?"

Mark grinned evilly as he pulled Tommy down on top of him. "Oh, I'd love to come again." He kissed Tommy, then let him up.

Tommy ignored the innuendo, laughing as he stood up. "Well then, haul your nightstick out of bed and let's go. May I borrow a pair of your shorts?"

"Of course." Mark got out of bed. "You know where everything is, so help yourself." Mark watched Tommy walking away from him, paying special attention to the scorpion tattoo on his ass cheek. He smiled as Tommy put on the burlap underwear and started getting dressed. "You make burlap boxers look sexy, little brother," he teased.

Tommy found a pair of Mark's gray gym shorts and one of Mark's football jerseys to wear. "Shut up," Tommy said softly as he pulled the gym shorts over the burlap. "Just get dressed and let's go."

"You're awfully bossy in the morning."

"If everyone was a morning person, I wouldn't have to be bossy," Tommy said, laughing. He waited while Mark got dressed, and then they both quietly walked downstairs and out of the house without waking anyone.

"I can't believe you have enough energy left over from last night to go running this morning," Mark said as they turned the corner and started down Main Street.

"Why not? I had fun last night, and I slept extremely well after our little workout."

Mark glanced over at Tommy. "You're not as innocent as you look, little brother."

Tommy blushed. "And you're not as inhibited as I thought a straight jock would be, big brother."

"Touché." Mark kept pace with Tommy for a couple of blocks before speaking again. "How old were you when you realized you were gay?"

"Ten or eleven, but I didn't start accepting it until I was twelve." Tommy glanced over at Mark. "My best friend and I were altar boys at church and had been in the Cub Scouts together. When we became adolescents, we naturally became curious and played around with each other. We used to share the same tent on camping trips when we were in Boy Scouts." Tommy chuckled. "Once we entered high school, he developed physically more quickly than I did, and he started dating girls. He was a linebacker for our high school football team, which is why I'm infatuated with the sport."

"And the players?" Mark suggested.

"Yeah, and the players," Tommy agreed with a smile. "I never developed an interest in girls, but that didn't stop my friend and me from fooling around whenever he didn't have a date. Of course, that all ended when we graduated and left for different colleges."

"Were you guys partners or something?"

"No. We were best friends who understood and loved each other, but we each wanted different things. He wanted to get married and have a family; I wanted to find a partner to share my life with."

"Have you found that partner?" Mark queried.

"Not yet. Maybe someday I will."

"Are you seeing anyone?"

"Some guy who thinks he's a quarterback." Tommy chuckled. "But nobody special."

"Jerk." Mark punched Tommy's arm. "May I ask you a personal question?"

"I thought you were asking me a lot of personal questions."

"All right, just one more, then," Mark said with a laugh. "I'm not actually sure how to ask this without offending you."

"Just ask. I won't be offended."

"Do you always prefer the submissive position?" Mark asked, embarrassed at even asking the question.

Tommy laughed and slapped Mark on the back. "With a guy like you, oh yeah."

"I didn't hurt you, did I?"

"Not at all. But my ass is still tingling inside." Tommy sped up while Mark slowed, surprised by the comment.

"I've had complaints about my size and my enthusiasm," he said after catching up.

"You aren't going to hear any complaints from me, big brother."

Mark's cheeks flamed. They continued running through the trailer park and then back toward Kappa house. "Hey, I have another question." Mark looked over at Tommy. "Why are you and Jack so secretive about being gay?"

"To avoid being harassed," Tommy said quietly. "I knew some guys in high school who were severely harassed for being out. I wasn't out, but I was teased and hassled by some guys. Being able to defend myself kept them from bothering me too much."

"I'm sorry to hear that. I never realized how hard high school could be for people who felt different from the rest of the crowd."

"It could be difficult, but I knew who I was, and I was happy with myself. Being gay is a part of who I am, but it's not the only thing that makes me who I am. The music and books that I enjoy are a part of who I am." He looked meaningfully at Mark. "The people that I choose to hang out with are a part of who I am."

"It can't be good for you to be seen hanging out with me," Mark joked as they got closer to Kappa house.

"It's a lot better than being seen with Brian." Tommy laughed and ran on ahead.

As they entered Kappa house through the kitchen door, Mark and Tommy cheerfully greeted Oscar and Jack. "Good morning, brothers."

Oscar was sitting at the kitchen table, and Jack was making coffee. "Fuck both of you," Oscar groaned.

"There's nothing wrong with starting the day off in a good mood, brother Oscar." Mark laughed, rubbing both of his hands over Oscar's head.

"Fuck. Tommy's attitude is rubbing off on you," Oscar grumbled, dropping his head down onto his arms.

Mark and Tommy laughed. "You," Mark looked at Tommy, "go get your shower and I'll get us something to eat." Mark slapped him on the back and watched him go up the stairs. He was humming "Slow Boat to China" as he put some bread into the toaster and poured two glasses of orange juice.

Jack smiled as he recognized the tune. "Did you have a good run, brother

Mark?"

"It was very refreshing, brother Jack," Mark replied as he buttered the toast. "We'll see you later, brothers. Got to get ready for the long day ahead." Mark left the kitchen, humming happily as he went upstairs with the tray of toast and orange juice.

Oscar lifted his head and looked at Jack, who was sitting at the table and smiling like a clown. "What the fuck got into him?"

Jack smiled broadly. "I have no idea, but it's better than the way he was behaving a few weeks ago."

"Ugh," Oscar growled. "Is the coffee ready?"

Jack poured each of them a cup. Oscar took a sip of coffee, trying to stop his headache, as well as attempting to wake himself up. He looked at the stove, then the kitchen doorway, before sitting up straight in his chair. He turned to Jack with an inquisitive look on his face. "What do you know?"

"I don't know anything."

Oscar's face lit up with a smile. "Yes, you do, and I bet I know the same thing."

"Well, what do you think you know?"

"I don't know if I should say anything," Oscar stated evasively.

"Then we'll never know if we both know the same thing," Jack said, getting a box of cereal from a cupboard.

Oscar thought for a couple of minutes. When Jack sat down with his bowl of cereal, Oscar smiled over at him and whispered, "Tommy finally nailed him."

Jack smiled as he put a spoonful of cereal into his mouth. After swallowing, he asked, "What makes you think that?"

"Slow Boat to China," Oscar said with a laugh, "and the way Tommy looks at him."

"How would you know anything about that?" Jack asked, spooning up more cereal.

Oscar's expression was serious. "Because I like to play the whole outfield, not just one side. Why do you think I'm such a good centerfielder?" He waggled his eyebrows at Jack.

"You dog, I never knew that about you."

"You have to beware of quiet types; we like to watch things going on around us. And we keep a lot of things to ourselves," Oscar stated reassuringly. "I also know that your boyfriend is the president of Gamma." Oscar grinned wickedly.

"You haven't told anyone, have you?" Jack said, surprised by Oscar's revelation.

"Of course not. It's none of my business who you play with. And it's certainly not my place to say anything." He laughed, knowing that he had made Jack a little uncomfortable.

"You asshole." Jack laughed with him. "Thanks."

"No problem."

"Other than the accusation that Simon made, do you think anyone else noticed that Tommy has been infatuated with Mark?" Jack asked quietly.

"I'm not sure. If they did, they kept it to themselves, just like you and I have done, and will continue to do." He slapped Jack on the back and got up to get something to eat.

Tommy returned from his shower with a towel wrapped around his waist. He shut the door and turned to see Mark smiling at him from the desk. "What?" Tommy asked self-consciously as he walked across the room.

"Stop right there, little brother," Mark commanded. "Drop the towel."

Tommy stopped in the middle of the room. "What?"

"I said drop the towel. Now."

Tommy undid the slip knot and let the towel fall to the floor. He could feel the warm, early autumn breeze through the open windows caressing his skin.

"The candles in the room and the dim light from outside last night gave you an ethereal beauty, but they didn't do justice to your body." Wearing only his gym shorts, Mark moved close to Tommy. "You have a smooth chest and nice abs," Mark whispered into Tommy's ear as he slowly ran his hand along Tommy's upper torso and moved to stand behind Tommy.

Standing naked in the middle of the room, Tommy blushed. He was getting turned on feeling Mark's intimate touch and warm breath at his ear.

"But this..." Mark's hand slowly slid up Tommy's thigh and stroked the scorpion tattoo on Tommy's ass cheek.

"The tattoo?" Tommy asked timidly. The feel of Mark's calloused hand was exciting him.

"No." Mark slapped the taut ass. He felt the muscles flinch under his hand and saw Tommy's jaw muscle tighten, but Tommy remained silent. His hand still on Tommy's ass, Mark leaned forward and breathed, "This is the hottest ass that I have ever had the pleasure of playing with." He gently bit Tommy's earlobe.

Tommy moaned and grew hard as he felt the soft hair of Mark's chest pressing against his back and Mark's tongue licking his ear.

Mark continued to fondle Tommy's ass as he pulled Tommy close and gave him a kiss on the cheek. "Those mornings that I followed you on your run," he whispered, "I had to turn around at the trailer park because I was turned on." Tommy's face turned pink. "I watched your muscles flexing as you ran. I watched the sweat from your hair and back soak your t-shirt. And I watched your shorts tighten against this hot little ass." He roughly grasped the hard buttocks. "It's a good thing that there was no one else along that road, or they would have seen one very excited man following you." Mark slid a hand down to Tommy's erection. "Just like you've got right now."

"Why are you doing this?" Tommy's breathing was labored.

"Because I wanted to see if I could turn you on as easily as you turn me on, little brother." Mark turned Tommy around so that they were facing each other. He kissed Tommy and then smiled. "And now I'm going to leave you alone in here while I take a cold shower."

"You bastard," Tommy gasped. "What am I supposed to do about this?" He wrapped his hand around his erection.

Mark chuckled. "I'm sure you know how to deal with that problem, or you can wait until tonight and I'll take care of it for you." Mark kissed Tommy again. "Don't forget that you have to get ready for the second half of your initiation."

8: KAPPA LAMBDA PI INITIATION, PART II

Oscar began the Saturday portion of initiation at exactly nine o'clock. The Initiates were again seated in the chairs at the front of the room, facing the brotherhood. The members of the house council, in their red and black robes, stood at the back of the room. "*Buenos dias, hermanos,*" Oscar shouted.

"Good morning, brother Oscar," the subdued crowd responded.

"I hope everyone slept well." His eyes darted to Mark at the back of the room. "Some of us woke up very happy this morning, while others are suffering from the effects of a few too many drinks." He raised a hand to quiet their murmuring. "We're going to get started right away. The boys behind me have a very long day ahead of them, and we want to have a party this evening."

Oscar turned and faced the nine hopefuls. "Initiates, you have reached the final stages of this pledge period and should soon be initiated into the brotherhood of Kappa Lambda Pi. This first part will involve the brothers asking you questions. Some of the questions will be serious and will cover such things as your character, your community service, the history of the Kappas, and your reasons for wanting to be a brother in this fraternity." He paused to make sure all of them were paying close attention. "Other questions will be funny and mostly for our amusement. What those questions are will depend upon the personality of the brother asking the question. You won't know what type of question is going to be asked or when. It's a free-for-all."

Oscar turned to the brothers. "All of you should give each Initiate the same number of questions. We don't want to leave any of the Initiates out, nor do we want to overwhelm just one or two. So pick and choose evenly." He looked back at the Initiates one more time, then turned to the brotherhood. "Let the games begin!"

The questions came fast and furious. Trivia questions, history questions, character questions, proper verb usage questions, fraternity history questions. A question would be asked of one Initiate, and no sooner had that Initiate answered than the next question was asked of another Initiate. There was no rhyme or reason to the questions, nor to the order of which Initiate would be asked. How the brotherhood managed to take turns asking questions and make sure that each Initiate was given an equitable number of questions was beyond the Initiates' understanding. On and on it went, for two hours without a break.

When Oscar appeared in the front of the room at eleven o'clock, the brotherhood went silent. Oscar smiled at them and turned to face the shell-shocked Initiates. "Wasn't that fun, boys?" They stared at him, their minds still reeling from the pace of the questioning. "We certainly did have a good time on this side of the room." Oscar laughed and turned back to the brothers.

"There will be a thirty-minute break so that the house council can move up to the third floor for the individual questioning, and so that our Initiates can get their heads to stop spinning." The brotherhood laughed. "We have nine Initiates and estimate that the individual questioning should take four and a half hours. If anyone wants to leave and return later, feel free to come and go as you please. The Initiates are to remain around the house at all times until the completion of the individual questioning."

He then addressed the entire group. "Brothers and Initiates, we are all to follow the 'secrecy and silence' rule." To the Initiates, he said, "This is the first thing you will learn. There will be no discussion of what is said during the individual questioning. You will each be called to meet with the house council in random order. While you are waiting your turn, and after you are done, you are allowed to mingle with others and talk about anything but what goes on during the questioning. Is that understood?" He eyed the Initiates sharply.

"Yes, sir," all nine Initiates responded.

"The brotherhood will reconvene at five o'clock this afternoon." Oscar slammed his gavel on the table.

The brotherhood cheered and began scattering throughout the house. Some of the Kappas left the house; they would return later in the day. Several others went downstairs to the basement, while the remainder turned on the TV to watch college football.

Mark walked by Tommy and tousled his hair. "Good luck."

"Thank you, sir." Tommy smiled at Mark, who was following the other members of the house council up to the third floor.

Tommy and the other eight Initiates went into the kitchen to get bottles of water, then went outside to try and cool off and gather their thoughts. Kyle stood near Tommy. "Damn, that was tough."

"I can't believe how fast they were firing questions. I felt like a jack-in-the-box most of the time." Tommy wiped his brow.

"So did I," Kyle said. "Even the easy questions seemed hard."

"Do you think the individual questioning will be the same way?"

"No. I think they're really going to concentrate on our character," Kyle responded.

"Probably," Tommy agreed. "The waiting is going to be a killer."

"You said it. I don't know if it would be better to be first or last."

Tommy considered that. "I don't think I'd want to have to wait all day and be the last one."

"Good point."

The house council gathered in the private living room on the third floor. Some of the members went to the bar and got themselves drinks. Dave and some of the others grabbed bottles of water from the mini-fridge. Mark got himself a glass of orange juice and sat quietly on one of the sofas.

Jack sat down next to Mark. "You seem happy this morning."

Mark smiled. "I *am* happy this morning." He wondered if he had given away anything that would lead Jack to know about him and Tommy.

Jack waited until Mark had taken a drink before quietly asking, "Did the sire nurture the childe?"

Surprised by the question, Mark almost choked on his orange juice. He looked over at Jack, who grinned as he patted Mark on the back. None of the others had overheard the question, but they did turn around when they heard the choking sounds.

"Shut the fuck up."

"I'm happy for you, brother Mark," Jack said, trying to keep a straight face.

"Does anyone else know?" Mark whispered as others began to gather around the coffee table.

"Not that I'm aware of," he said quietly, glancing around the room. "Don't worry, your secret is safe with me."

Tommy found that he was right — the waiting was the worst part of the afternoon. He couldn't concentrate on any one thing. He wandered through the first floor and yard, talking briefly with the other pledges, then went back to the living room to watch football on TV. Unable to enjoy the game, he found a quiet spot and tried to focus on what questions might be asked by the house council, and how he would answer them. Often his thoughts drifted to what had happened between him and Mark. It had been wonderful to finally be that close to Mark. When his turn came, he was almost relieved.

When Tommy was called by the house council, Mark slapped him on the back and wished him luck, then went down to the basement and got a beer to take back to his room. There he picked up Tommy's paddle and stared at it. It shimmered in the sunlight. He decided to go on-line and see if he could find out more about the runes.

Mark eventually found a website that showed pictures of runes similar to those that Tommy had used; the site also explained their symbolism. Comparing them to those on the paddle, he realized that Tommy didn't have them in the order that they were listed on the webpage. He jotted down a few notes about each of the runes, then tried to determine how the meanings might be affected by the order Tommy had placed them in. After a while, he sat back with a satisfied smile. He would have an interesting chat with Tommy later.

When he'd completed his questioning, Tommy was drained. He felt that he had answered all the questions thoroughly and with some intelligence, but he wouldn't know how the house council felt about his responses until later that afternoon. He hoped he'd passed the ordeal. Again, the waiting was the hard part, and Tommy spent the next hours wandering about the house and yard.

The last Initiate finally walked out of the private living room and down the stairs at four-fifteen. The house council remained behind closed doors. Many of the brothers had returned to the house shortly after four o'clock and were also waiting for the house council to render their verdicts. Although anxiously awaiting the end of the pledge process, the Initiates looked as if they were ready to fall asleep in their chairs.

Finally, at five o'clock, Oscar and the house council walked solemnly into the living room. The brotherhood stood up as they entered the room. The Initiates took their cue from the brotherhood and stood up while the house council went to the back of the room.

"Please remain standing as we say the pledge," Oscar commanded. In unison, the entire brotherhood and Initiates said the pledge. "If you have a chair, you may be seated." Oscar waited until everyone finished moving around before continuing. "Brothers, we are gathered here this afternoon to finalize this pledge period that started four weeks ago. For the past month, these young men have endured and survived every challenge, task, and ordeal put to them. Last night, they proved their sincere interest in joining Kappa Lambda Pi. Today they stood up to the two-hour questioning by the brotherhood, then the half-hour individual grilling by our house council." For dramatic effect, and to keep the Initiates on edge, Oscar paused for a drink of water before he turned and faced the Initiates. "Please stand, Initiates." His voice gave no indication as to whether they had all been accepted. Even the brotherhood remained silent.

"As pledge master of Kappa Lambda Pi," he said, "allow me to be the first brother to welcome you into the brotherhood. Congratulations, brothers." For the first time, he smiled. The Initiates let out deep breaths as relief rushed through them. A roaring cheer went up from the brotherhood.

"*Silencio, por favor*," Oscar yelled out over the noise. "Brothers, we have not yet finished our business." He waited until everyone stopped cheering. "Before we administer the oath making these Initiates full-fledged brothers, I have one more piece of business." Oscar smiled at the looks of surprise. "During the dinner pledge sing, where we so dearly enjoyed having our pledges perform for the cafeteria crowd, two of our new brothers showed some talent."

Kyle went pale, and Tommy felt his own face turn cold.

"As all of you are aware, our fraternity has never won the All-Greek Halloween Talent Competition." The brotherhood booed and hissed loudly. "We can't force brothers to perform for the fraternity, even if any of you had any talent." Oscar looked out over the Kappas, who were jeering him for his comment. "So," Oscar turned to look at Tommy and Kyle, "we would like to request that Tommy and Kyle enter this year's talent competition."

The two Initiates looked at one another. They turned away from the brotherhood and whispered conspiratorially between themselves. Tommy sneaked a glance at Mark and Dave, who looked at each other nervously, while the rest of the brotherhood watched the two Initiates. Tommy and Kyle moved to stand beside one another, pulled off their shirts, and placed their tattoos together. They grasped hands, raised them in the air, and shouted, "For Kappa Lambda Pi, yes, sir. We'd be proud to represent, sir."

The brotherhood shouted their approval. Dave and Mark cuffed each other, and Kyle and Tommy high-fived and then put their shirts back on. This time Oscar didn't ask the brotherhood for quiet; he was enjoying the enthusiasm.

"Thank you, brothers," Oscar finally yelled out. "Now, would our newest brothers please stand up to take the Kappa Lambda Pi oath?" As the nine new brothers completed the oath, the brotherhood broke out in whistles and applause. Oscar let it go on for a few minutes before he banged his gavel on the table. "We have not yet adjourned, brothers," he stated loudly but with a smile. "Let us all join hands and say the Kappa Lambda Pi brotherhood prayer."

Once all the brothers were joined, one to the other, Oscar started the prayer and the others chimed in. Everyone remained standing and quiet after the amen.

Oscar stood before the brotherhood and lifted his gavel, smiling brightly. "This initiation has now been completed. We are adjourned. Let's party!" The gavel slammed loudly on top of the table and the brotherhood went wild.

The new brothers were surrounded and congratulated with a lot of hand shaking and back slapping. Tommy and Kyle were also singled out for agreeing to represent Kappa in the talent competition.

Tommy was talking with a couple of brothers when Mark walked up from behind and handed him a 7-Up. Tommy beamed as he faced Mark.

"Congratulations, brother Tommy. I can't tell you how proud I am of you." He was smiling mischievously as he leaned close to Tommy's ear. "But I'd sure love to show you how much, later." He pulled back and winked.

Tommy smiled, as his face began to redden. "Thank you, brother Mark, for all of your support." Tommy leaned closer to Mark to whisper into his ear, "You're on."

Dave and Kyle came up to talk with Tommy and Mark. "We're going to go out for a celebratory dinner with a few other brothers. Would you like to join us?" Dave asked.

"That would be great." Mark wrapped his arm around Tommy's neck. "You're still my little brother, so you'll just have to do as I say."

Initiation Party

The party was still going strong when Dave and company returned to the house around nine o'clock. They got themselves drinks and mingled with the other Kappas. An hour later, Tommy was standing in the back yard, taking a break from the emotional overload. It was hot and noisy inside the house, but outside was cool and clear. He looked up at the sky, bright with stars, and began to smile as he thought about Mark.

"Are you okay?"

Tommy stopped stargazing and turned around to smile at Mark. "I'm fine, but I am getting a little tired."

Mark put his arm around Tommy's shoulder and pulled him close. "You hung in there very well today. You should be proud of yourself; I know I'm proud of you." He let go of Tommy but stayed close to him as he looked up into the sky. "There are a lot of constellations visible tonight."

"I know. When I can't sleep, I run out to the cemetery and lie on the back hillside, watching the stars. It's very relaxing."

"I, uh, was wondering if you'd like to, uh, go upstairs to my room."

"I'd love to. It won't be crowded, and it won't be as noisy."

"Oh, I bet we could make some noise." Mark grinned evilly.

Tommy shook his head. "I think I've created a satyr."

Mark's smile widened, and his eyes lit up at the opportunity to reveal his discovery about Tommy's paddle. "You should have thought about that before you cast your spell."

Tommy was startled by the comment. "What?"

"I was on-line while you were being questioned." He grinned at Tommy. "Fascinating explanations on the meaning of runes."

"Oh, goddess." His face hot, Tommy turned away from Mark.

Mark turned Tommy around so that he could look into his eyes. "Hey, look at me." He put his hand under Tommy's chin and tipped his head back. "You didn't just carve a bunch of runes on the back of your paddle. You put a lot of thought into which ones you were going to use and in what order they were going to be placed. I was impressed." Mark wrapped his arm around Tommy's neck, pulled him close, and rubbed his knuckles on the top of Tommy's head, which made Tommy smile.

"That's better. I love seeing that smile on your face," Mark said gently. "Let's go inside and talk some more about that paddle of yours. Or maybe I'll use it on you instead."

They made a stop in the kitchen to refill their drinks and talked to a few people as they made their way through the living room and upstairs to the third floor. Mark opened his door and let Tommy go in first. He followed Tommy inside, switched on the lights, and then locked the door behind him.

"You," Mark said, smiling at Tommy, "come over here."

Tommy stood in front of Mark. "Yes, sir."

"I didn't tell you to talk," Mark said. He put his mouth on Tommy's and kissed him. "I've needed to taste those lips all day."

Tommy blushed as he leaned in and kissed Mark back. "So have I."

Mark took Tommy's hand and led him over to the bed. "Sit down and get comfortable." He went over to his desk and picked up Tommy's paddle. He returned to the bed and sat down. "Now, let's talk about this. I'm very curious about it."

"Okay," Tommy said shyly. "What do you want to know?"

"First of all," Mark started, "I'm dying to know what you used to make it shimmer." He turned the paddle back and forth, watching the light glisten off of it. "It's not glitter."

Tommy chuckled. "No, it's not glitter. I ground a crystal into a fine powder, mixed some of it into the varnish, and then sprinkled the remaining powder over the paddle before the varnish dried."

"Awesome." Mark continued turning the paddle back and forth. "Very nice balance." He smiled as he handed the paddle to Tommy.

The instant Tommy had the paddle back in his hands, he felt the energy surge from within it, as if he were being rejuvenated.

"What did you feel?" he asked quietly.

"Energy." He looked down at the paddle.

"Jack and Oscar can sense the energy, but I can feel it flow through me," Mark said. "I don't know how to explain it, but it makes me feel good." Mark lifted Tommy's head so that he could see his eyes. "What did you do to give it that much energy?"

"I spent a couple of weeks planning and designing my paddle." He looked down at the cut that was still healing, and noticed that Mark's gaze followed his. "I guess I put a lot of blood, sweat, and tears into making it perfect." He looked up at Mark. "But more than that, I put my whole heart and soul into creating it. I wasn't just doing this for me."

"You were doing it for me." Mark leaned over to kiss Tommy, then pulled back and looked into Tommy's eyes. "I've spent my college life searching for somebody who would give me exactly what you have this past month a real and close friendship where I was comfortable being myself, without having sex be the primary motivation in that friendship." He chuckled. "I just thought it was going to be a woman that I would be sharing that type of relationship with. Instead, I met you — a strong, independent young man with a positive attitude toward life."

Tommy's heart was pounding. It seemed surreal, but Mark turning his head for a kiss allowed him to believe that it was real.

"I have a confession to make." Mark's voice was soft, shy. "I can't remember the last time I made love with somebody who could match my intensity. We seemed to be in synch with one another."

"How could I not match your intensity? You're incredible. Besides, I connected with your energy the first time we shook hands, and I haven't been able to get you off my mind." Tommy blushed. "You're the guy that has been in my fantasies and daydreams since the beginning of the semester."

Mark kissed Tommy and laid him down, then positioned himself over Tommy's body and looked down into smoky brown eyes. "If you tell me what fantasy you'd like me to fulfill for you right now, I'd be happy to do it."

After they had made love, Tommy and Mark rolled onto their sides, facing one another with radiant smiles. Mark drew Tommy close, and they kissed passionately. "So, what happens now that I'm caught up in your spell?" Mark whispered.

"You're not under a spell," he said softly, running a finger down Mark's crooked nose.

Mark pushed him back so that he could look into Tommy's eyes, and his tone was serious. "I don't want to lose you now that I have you in my life."

"You won't lose me, Mark." Tommy's voice was subdued. *But you might let me go* if she *returns.*

Mark lay on his side, his head resting in his hand, as he looked down at Tommy. "Seriously, though, what happens now?"

"That's up to you," Tommy said softly, looking up into Mark's intent eyes.

"What do you want?"

"I want to share my life with somebody who loves me as much as I love him. But I've been told that the *happily-ever-after* fairy tale is just a dream when it's for two guys," Tommy said without smiling. "This isn't about what I want, Mark. I'm gay. I could love you for a long time. This is about you, the straight jock. You have to decide what you want."

Mark lay on his back and stared up at the ceiling. "You're not making it easier for me."

"I can't make this decision for you."

"Why not?"

Tommy leaned up on his elbow and looked down at Mark. "Because if I tell you that I want you to be with me and you decide later that you want to be with women, then you'll resent me for encouraging you to choose to be gay. I don't ever want you to accuse me of asking you to do something that you don't want to do."

Mark looked into Tommy's eyes. "Right now, I want to be with you."

"But?"

"I don't know if I'm ready to accept being openly gay," Mark said sadly. "Will you stick with me while I work through it?"

"Yes, big brother," Tommy leaned down and kissed Mark gently on the lips, then pulled back. "But I'm not going to pressure you or convince you to make a decision."

"You'll just tempt me with your hot body." Mark pulled Tommy down on top of his body and kissed him.

Tommy pulled away from the kiss and smirked. "I'm not going to make it easy for you, but I won't be a slave driver either."

Mark laughed. "Using my own words against me. You're going to have to be punished for that one, little brother."

In answer, Tommy kissed Mark deeply, passionately. Mark held Tommy tightly and then pulled the sheet up to cover their sweaty bodies. They fell asleep the same way they had the previous night Tommy's head on Mark's chest and Mark's arms wrapped around Tommy.

Tommy woke up early and looked over at Mark sleeping. He rubbed his hand over Mark's chest, and Mark slowly began rubbing his back in response.

Tommy reached down for Mark's free hand and sized it against his own. "Look how big your hand is compared to mine. You've got long, thick fingers that feel nice against my skin."

"Ugh, my hands are rough and calloused from playing football."

"Well, I like the way they feel because they turn me on." Tommy kissed Mark's chest and then looked up at him. "I'm glad you haven't shaved; I like the stubble on your cheeks."

"Is there anything about me that you don't like?" Mark teased.

Tommy slowly ran his finger down Mark's crooked nose. "Maybe." He paused for a second, allowing Mark to think it might be his nose. "Nope, I love everything about you."

Mark chuckled. "Sally used to make me shave before making out. And I had to use hand lotion to soften my hands for her."

Tommy kissed Mark's cheek. "That's because she's a girl and I'm a boy."

Mark rolled Tommy over onto his back and looked down into his eyes. "No, little brother, you're not a boy, you're an insatiable young man." Tommy's laugh was smothered by Mark's mouth and a passionate kiss. "Should we have been using some type of protection?" Mark asked.

"Don't worry, big brother, I can't get pregnant."

"That's not what I was concerned about, smartass," Mark said as he tweaked Tommy's nose.

"I'm sorry, I couldn't help myself," Tommy said contritely. "I had an HIV test before coming to college, so I know that I'm okay. I assume that you've only been with girls, so you should be okay."

"Ah, but you don't know what kind of girls I've been with." Mark winked.

"Have you been with a lot of skanky whores? Should I be worried?" Tommy asked with mock concern.

Mark tickled Tommy's sides until Tommy cried uncle. "No, I have not been with any skanky whores."

"What about all those sorority sisters you were trying to impress?"

"Well, the ones that I managed to hook up with seemed to be pretty clean," Mark claimed.

"You thought I was innocent until you got me into bed."

"Then I discovered that you're a little sex slut." He kissed Tommy. "I don't think you have anything to worry about from me. I did use protection when I was with those girls," he said. "Shall we go for our morning run?"

When Jack walked into the kitchen, Mark was making an omelet.

"Good morning, Mark. You're up early."

"Tommy and I have already gone for our morning run, and he's getting his shower. We had a great night's sleep and are ready to start a new day, Jack," he stated smugly, flipping the omelet expertly.

Jack looked indignant. "Weren't you both drinking last night? My head is pounding."

"Tommy wasn't drinking, and I didn't have as much as most of the guys that are sleeping on the living room floor."

"Thanks for making coffee," Jack said as he poured himself a cup.

"No problem." Mark dished the omelet onto two plates.

"By the way," Jack sat down at the table, "I was doing some on-line research and discovered some websites that have rune information. If we could get Tommy's paddle, we could find out what they mean."

Mark laughed as he poured two glasses of orange juice. "Tommy and I talked about his paddle last night; I already know what the runes mean." He picked up the tray and glanced over at Jack. "The shimmer on the paddle is from a crushed crystal."

Jack stared at Mark's back as his brother left the kitchen. "Son of a bitch."

Mark passed Oscar on his way upstairs. "Good morning, brother Oscar," Mark sang sweetly.

"Fuck you," Oscar grumbled as he continued downstairs. In the kitchen, Oscar poured himself a cup of coffee and sat down across the table from Jack. "These fucking happy morning people are going to drive me crazy," he grumbled.

Jack nodded. "Me, too."

"I assume Tommy's still in the house."

Jack smiled broadly. "I didn't ask and he didn't tell."

They both laughed, then Oscar stopped abruptly and looked over at Jack with a serious expression. "How long do you think it's going to last?"

Jack looked at him thoughtfully. "If Mark feels the same way as Tommy does, and by the look on his face he does, it could last a long time."

Oscar was less sure. "That's a fast turn around for Mark, don't you think?"

"It's possible Mark was just waiting for the right person to come along, and Tommy was that person."

"Maybe." Oscar was still concerned. "What's going to happen to Tommy if Mark wakes up one morning and decides that he wants to go back to girls?"

"I'm trying not to think about that right now."

Oscar shook his head. "You always have been one of those damned optimists."

"Try it sometime, big guy. Maybe you won't be so grouchy in the mornings." Jack was laughing as he left Oscar sitting alone in the kitchen.

"I thought you said big brothers weren't in the habit of making breakfast for their little brothers," Tommy said as he returned from showering.

"When little brothers do to their big brothers what you did to me, we make adjustments to the rules." Mark was sitting at his desk with another chair nearby for Tommy.

"I think you were the one who did things to me, big brother." Leaving the towel around his waist, Tommy sat down next to Mark.

"Okay, I took advantage of you and now I'm trying to make up for it," he admitted.

Tommy laughed. "Maybe I let you take advantage of me."

"Maybe you did," Mark said with a smile. "But neither of us seemed to mind."

Tommy leaned over and kissed him on the cheek. They ate their breakfast in silence.

"I think your paddle would look great hanging next to mine," Mark said as he finished eating and looked at his own paddle on the wall above his bed.

"That sounds fine to me."

"Where do we go from here, Tommy?"

Tommy leaned back and sighed. "I already told you — wherever you want. You're not under my spell, and I'm not going to make you choose between me and women." He watched Mark closely. "I don't expect you to switch from being a ladies' man overnight, and I'm not going to do anything to jeopardize what you want in your life."

Mark sat quietly for several minutes. "That's not the answer I was expecting to hear, Tommy." He ran a shaking hand through his hair. "I've never done anything that would jeopardize who I am or what I want, and I don't believe that I'm doing that now." He touched the tip of Tommy's nose. "Whether you know it or not, I am under a spell, and I really feel good being with you."

"Are you sure?"

Mark kissed him passionately. "I'm sure," he said as he pulled away. "And I believe the question that I asked you was where do we go from here?"

Tommy beamed. "I guess we go wherever you say we go, big brother."

Sunday Night

Scott laughed as Tommy came into their room early Sunday evening. "It's about time you came back. I think the room was getting lonely with both of us gone."

Tommy chuckled. "It was initiation weekend. I've been at Kappa house since Friday night."

"How'd that go?"

"It was a lot of fun," Tommy said, falling down onto his bed.

"You'll never catch me joining some group. I'm a free spirit, can't be bothered with some group's rules."

Tommy looked over at his unorthodox roommate. "I'm surprised to see you here."

Scott laughed. "Your timing is right on. I'm getting ready to go again. I just came back to shower and change clothes."

"Well, it was good seeing you," Tommy said with a chuckle.

"Have a good night. See ya in English class tomorrow." Scott waved at Tommy as he opened the door. "Hey, Jack," he said as he exited.

Tommy was puzzled at the unexpected appearance of his new brother. "Jack. What are you doing here?"

"I just came by to see how you're doing." Jack sat in the green chair. "I was curious as to what you thought about the weekend."

Tommy smiled knowingly. "Are you curious about my reaction to the initiation, or to Mark?"

Jack smiled back. "Both, if you must know. I just want to make sure you're okay."

"I'm glad that I made it through the pledge period and the initiation." Tommy exhaled sharply. "I've made a lot of friends in Kappa; the Kappa brothers are great guys."

"I'm glad to hear it." Jack followed his intuition. "I imagine one brother in particular is even greater than the others."

"After that first week, Mark has been a great big brother, and we've become really good friends. I enjoy being with him, whether we're having meals or running together." He looked over at Jack shyly. "Maybe even more than just friends. I've never felt this close to another person, not even my best friend back home."

"What about when you were with him in bed?"

"He was very romantic." Tommy's cheeks turned scarlet. "He's handsome, well-built, and a great lover. What more could a boy want?"

"I'm not going to tell you not to fall in love with Mark; I might be too late for that." Jack shrugged. "Just be careful, Tommy. Don't forget that he's always consorted with the female of the species."

"I know. I just enjoy being with him and want it to go on as long as possible."

"Have you and Mark talked about where this relationship might go?"

"Yes," Tommy said quickly. "I told him that it's his choice where it goes. I don't want him to feel that he's being trapped into a relationship that he's not ready for."

Jack stood to leave. "Just remember, if you ever need anyone to talk with, I'm available."

"Thanks, Jack. I appreciate that."

The door to Mark's room was ajar. Jack peeked inside and saw lighted candles in several spots around the room. He knocked gently and walked in. "You okay, buddy?" He closed the door and sat down at Mark's desk; Mark continued to stare out the window.

Eventually, Mark turned around to face Jack. "I'm fine. I was just standing here and thinking. It's been a very eventful weekend."

"Thinking about Tommy?"

"Yes. He's an amazing young man." Mark looked back out the window. "I never thought that I'd be in an intimate relationship with a guy, but he's really brightened my life these past few weeks." He turned back to Jack. "I was scared of this kid when we first met. He made me feel uncomfortable because he caused some unfamiliar desires to surface."

"How was it sleeping with him?" Jack asked directly.

"I thought it was going to be awkward being with another guy, but feeling his soft, smooth body next to me was a major turn on." He looked into Jack's eyes. "Is it supposed to feel that natural and comfortable?"

"With the right person it does." Jack smiled as he thought about some of the guys that he had been with before meeting Ken.

Mark emitted a deep sigh, turned around, and walked over to his bed. "I don't know what to think about what happened this weekend." He sat on the bed, a smile spreading across his face as he thought about Tommy. "After making out, Sally always wanted to talk about female shit, like fashion or make-up. Tommy curled up next to me, put his head on my chest, his arm across my body, and fell asleep."

Jack smiled at Mark's new openness. "Maybe you made him feel comfortable. Is that a problem for you?"

"No. It was nice holding him while he fell asleep. I stared at the ceiling and wondered what I had gotten myself into. When I woke up, we were still in the same position. I can't remember ever sleeping that comfortably with anyone." He laughed a little and rested his head against the wall. "Sally usually turned her back on me when she was done talking, and she'd steal the blankets during the night."

"It sounds to me like you and Tommy had a good weekend."

Mark was glad that the only light in the room came from the candles and the outside light, because he could feel the blood rushing to his cheeks. "I know that I had a good weekend, buddy. I just hope Tommy had a good weekend too."

"He looked happy when he left here earlier."

"You have to swear that you won't say anything about this, Jack," Mark demanded.

Jack raised his right hand in the air. "I swear, Mark. Nobody is going to hear anything from me."

"Tommy seemed so desperate when we made love, as if he couldn't get enough of me," Mark said quietly, leaning forward on the bed. "I've never had anyone offer themselves to me so freely. And I've never made love to anyone that roughly before. Maybe I couldn't get enough from him either."

"Did he complain about being hurt?"

"No, he kept urging me on. Then he bit my nipple and made me come like I've never come before. I thought I was going to hurt him by thrusting so hard."

Jack whistled appreciatively. "He doesn't look like the wild boy type."

Mark shook his head. "He was practically insatiable. He'll give me a heart attack if we keep that up."

Jack laughed. "What a way to go."

"I don't ever remember my boyhood buddy going at it like Tommy did. Is it always like that with guys?" Mark asked seriously, standing up and moving back to the window.

"It depends, Mark. Sometimes the passion between two people just heats them up to where they screw like beasts." He smiled as he thought about Ken. "And sometimes two people will make love slowly and passionately. It's possible that Tommy really wanted to be with you and wanted to let you know just how much."

"He doesn't have to kill me to prove it," Mark said with a chuckle.

"So where do you think this relationship will go?"

"I don't know, Jack." Mark sighed, leaning back against the window casement. "I'm not sure what the future holds. Right now, I'm going to keep Tommy with me. I enjoy his company, both in and out of bed." He stared over at Jack. "Tommy gave me an out this morning. I think he's worried about trapping me into a relationship."

"What do you plan on doing?"

"I don't know."

Jack could hear the uncertainty in Mark's voice. "What do you want?"

"I don't know, Jack." Mark stared out at the stars. "Right now, I'm really confused about everything that happened to me this weekend."

Jack stood up to leave. "If you change your mind, don't hurt him by cutting him out completely. Don't do to him what Sally has done to you."

"I won't, Jack."

"If you ever need to talk to anyone, I hope you know that you can talk to me."

"Thanks. I may take you up on that offer someday." Mark turned to look at Jack. "But right now, I need to work this through on my own. I believe I've made a good decision about the new course of my life. I couldn't be happier about it, or more scared." He chuckled wryly.

Jack smiled sympathetically. "Well, let me just say that I don't think you could have picked a better little brother." He patted Mark on the shoulder. "Good night."

As Jack left the room, Mark stared out the window. "You've got that right, Jack. I picked a good little brother," he whispered softly at his reflection in the window.

On Monday morning, as Brian entered the dining hall with his tray in hand, he noticed Tommy sitting in the back corner with his head in a book. Despite the fact that Tommy had turned down his offers to join Gamma and to sleep with him, Brian was still attracted to the freshman. During the past month, while both Gamma and Kappa were holding their pledge periods, Tommy had remained cordial to Brian, both in their psychology class and during their tutoring sessions. Tommy didn't seem to be holding a grudge for Brian's rude comments about Mark or his trying to distract Tommy during the pledge sports competition.

"Hey, sweet boy," Brian whispered into Tommy's ear as he sat down. "How was your initiation? I'm sure they let you into their group." Brian's words were slurred, as he was still feeling the effects of the alcohol and drugs he had taken during Gamma's initiation weekend.

"Why do you have to do that, Brian? You can be a nice guy some of the time, and a real jackass other times." Tommy looked at Brian with disdain.

"That's just me, sweet boy. If you'd joined Gamma, I'd always be nice to you." He smiled lewdly. "Especially when it came time to tuck you into bed."

Tommy took a deep breath and let it out loudly. "Why are you even sitting with me, Brian?"

"Because I like you and wanted to hear all about the initiation."

"You know we don't talk about what happened at initiation."

Brian smiled. "All right, party pooper. How did everything go for you?"

Tommy wasn't sure if Brian was trying to be civil or setting him up for more crass comments, but he decided to give him the benefit of doubt. "Everything went well," Tommy said. "We had a really good time over the weekend, even though it was emotionally draining. I completed all the tasks that I had to and survived the questioning by the fraternity council. It was great being accepted by the Kappa brothers."

"That sounds so sweet." Brian chuckled derisively. "We had an orgy after our initiation. Fraternity paddles were broken in over hot asses." He saw the look of disgust on Tommy's face and smiled wider. "I had a good time with my little brother. Was your big brother a prince in shining armor? Or did he finally dissuade you of that fantasy?"

"You're fucking disgusting, Brian."

"Don't be such a fucking prude, Tommy. By now you have to want to get it on with somebody. Even though you're a Kappa, I'd still be willing to make you a happy boy."

Tommy glared at him and stood up from the table. "Then I suggest you hold your breath and keep waiting." He picked up his tray and left Brian alone at the table.

Late Monday afternoon, Brian and Andy were sitting under a tree near the back of the library, smoking a joint. Brian spotted Mark, Dave, and Oscar walking down a nearby path. Brian stood up and headed toward the Kappa brothers; Andy quickly followed.

"Hey, Mark," Brian called as he caught up to the threesome.

"What do you want, Brian?" Mark's expression clearly showed his dislike.

"Tommy was telling me that he had a great time over the weekend, but he wouldn't give me any details about his initiation." Brian smiled at the Kappas. "I was wondering if he was tight as a virgin or sloppy as a slut."

Mark's books hit the ground about the same time that his fist connected with Brian's nose, causing him to fall to the ground. "You fucking son of a bitch," Mark yelled down at the fallen Gamma.

Holding his bleeding nose, Brian looked up at Mark and laughed, while Oscar and Dave grabbed onto Mark. "Is he tighter than that slut you date?"

The few students who had been walking along the path stopped to watch the altercation between the two jocks. "Fucker!" Mark tried to break away from Oscar and Dave, but they held him securely.

"Why don't you keep your perverted thoughts to yourself, Brian?" Dave looked over at Andy. "You should get his mouth taped before somebody rips his tongue out."

"Don't ever talk about them again, bastard fuck," Mark yelled. "I'll beat the shit out of you."

Dave let go of Mark long enough to pick up his books, and then went back to help steer Mark away from Brian.

"Hey, Mark," Brian yelled out. When Mark turned around to face him, Brian was standing and laughing. He grabbed his crotch and held it. "I'll find out for myself how sweet Tommy's ass is. I don't mind getting sloppy seconds."

Mark tore himself free of Oscar and Dave and ran after Brian, who turned and quickly escaped from the area. Oscar ran after Mark and tackled him to the ground.

"He's not worth it, Mark," Oscar cajoled, kneeling on Mark's back. "Let him go. You don't want to get into any trouble."

Mark was steaming mad. "Let me up," he said, turning his head and looking back at Oscar, letting out a deep breath. "Fucker," he mumbled. As he stood up, he noticed the other students standing around, watching the spectacle. "Sorry, everyone," he said to those nearby. He and Oscar returned to Dave. "I'll beat the shit out of that bastard if he says anything else about Tommy."

Oscar patted Mark on the back. "It's okay, big guy. Don't worry about that little cockroach."

Shower Room Assault

As he went to take his shower before breakfast, Tommy was still exhilarated from the weekend initiation and an early Tuesday morning run with Mark. Three other guys from the floor were already in the dorm showers and waved in greeting when Tommy entered. Since the beginning of the semester, he had been friendly toward everyone and had never had any problems with any of the guys on his floor or in the dorm.

Tommy took the fourth space in the left corner of the shower room. As he began showering, he noticed two junior wrestlers coming into the room. Both were in the heavyweight class, each exceeding 225 pounds, and were known potheads and troublemakers in the dorm. He knew, from talking with Jay and others, that they had a history of harassing others, and often were seen drunk and disorderly late at night. He watched as they stumbled into the shower room, taking the stalls nearest the doorway. While he was rinsing shampoo out of his hair, Tommy felt a hand grab his ass and squeeze. Then he felt a hard-on press against his other ass cheek, the one with the scorpion tattoo.

"Hey, pretty painted boy," the wrestler growled. "I've got a stinger for that sweet ass, Kappa baby." The other three guys in the shower room scrambled to get out as fast as they could.

Tommy took a deep breath, smelling alcohol and pot on the wrestler's breath, and concentrated on his next moves. He reached behind him, grabbed the wrestler's wrist and began squeezing it. As he turned around to face his attacker, Tommy twisted the wrist he was holding. The sound of bones snapping could be heard even over the running showers.

Caught off-guard by the move and surprised by the strength in Tommy's grip, the wrestler cried out in pain and fell to his knees. "Motherfucker!" he yelled as Tommy continued twisting his wrist.

Tommy glared into the wrestler's eyes. He could see the fear there. "If you *ever* touch me again, I'll break your fucking neck." He let go of the wrestler's wrist and glanced over at the other wrestler, who looked as if he might want to get some payback for his buddy. "I'd think twice before coming after me, asshole." The wrestler turned away and went to help his friend. Tommy looked at the two guys who stood just outside the shower room. "Thanks for the help. I'll remember you if you're ever in a similar situation." They lowered their heads in shame.

Tommy wrapped his towel around his waist and stormed back to his room. Other guys walking toward the shower room, moved quickly out of his way. The third guy who had been in the shower room had gone to get help. He and Jay stood out in the hallway as Tommy approached.

"What happened, Tommy?" Jay asked, concerned about the normally happy student.

"That asshole tried to attack me. If he ever touches me again, I'll kill him," he said angrily, stalking toward his room.

Tommy slammed the door to his room and then sat quietly on the end of his bed, his grandmother's crystal in his hand. He ignored the knock on his door as he tried to regain his composure.

"Tommy," Kyle opened the door and walked inside, "are you okay?"

Tommy glared over at him, then saw the shocked look on Kyle's face. "I'll be fine. Just leave me alone. Please," he said through gritted teeth.

Without another word, Kyle turned and left the room.

"I've been looking for you all morning, Mark," Kyle said as he joined Mark at lunch. Dave, Jack, and Oscar were also at the table.

"What's up?"

"One of the jackass wrestlers tried to attack Tommy in the shower this morning." Kyle watched the expected look of horror come across the brothers' faces.

"Is Tommy okay?" Oscar asked before Mark could say anything.

"He wasn't hurt, but he's... I don't know how to explain it, but he's not the same right now." Kyle shook his head in puzzlement. "I went into his room afterward and received the coldest look I've ever seen. Jay said the look of anger in Tommy's eyes as he walked down the hall afterwards was terrifying."

"Where is Tommy now?" Mark asked, anxious.

"If he's not in his class, Jay said that he might be meeting with the Resident Director and the Dean about the incident." Kyle smiled briefly. "He has to explain how he broke a wrestler's wrist."

The Kappas started chuckling. Mark tried not to smile, but couldn't help himself. "Excuse me. Would you repeat that?"

"There were a couple of witnesses in the shower room who reported that when Howard grabbed him, Tommy grabbed his wrist and wrenched it. They could hear the bones cracking."

"Isn't Howard a heavyweight wrestler?" Jack asked, a bemused smile on his face. "He must have a good fifty pounds or more over Tommy."

"I'm going to go see if Tommy is in his class," Mark said as he stood and left abruptly.

When he got to the classroom, the lecture was still in session. He had time before his next class, so he decided to wait. When Tommy finally came out, Mark sensed nothing was amiss and saw no evidence Tommy was concerned about anything that had happened.

"What brings you here?" Tommy walked toward Mark with a happy smile.

Mark couldn't return the smile; he was too concerned. "I heard a story at lunch about something that happened in your dorm this morning."

Tommy's smile disappeared. "Oh, that. It was nothing; I handled it."

"It was nothing, you say. You could have been hurt." He was upset, but kept his voice low so that the students passing them would not overhear.

"I learned how to defend myself a long time ago." He smiled reassuringly. "That wasn't the first time somebody thought they could take advantage of me. People don't know that I've had training in both karate and judo. I promise you that nobody has ever made a second attempt against me."

Mark stared at him incredulously. "I don't know why you aren't more concerned about what happened."

Tommy gave him a gentle smile. "Mark, thank you for the concern. I spoke with the Resident Director and the Dean this morning. It was self-defense, and I'm not hurt. Now stop worrying about it. It's over."

"You never stop amazing me." Mark put his arm around Tommy's shoulder and they walked out into the sunshine.

Overhearing a Conversation

"Have you seen Mark?" Sally asked one of the brothers, as she entered the Kappa house one late October evening. She had decided it was time to bring Mark back into her life before the upcoming holidays.

"If he's not in his room, I don't know where he is," the brother replied, passing her on his way out the door.

It was quiet in the house, as most of the brothers were still at dinner. Sally went up to the third floor and opened Mark's door. She noted that the room was unusually clean, but Mark was not inside.

"He's been a little upset lately."

Sally heard a voice coming from another room, and quietly walked along the hall until she stood outside Oscar's room, where the door was ajar.

"Yeah." Oscar was speaking on his cell phone. "Mark said that his grandmother's house was sold last week and it upset him. ... No, he knew the house was being sold, but it was still upsetting. ... She died this past summer and left everything to him. Mark said it surprised his family when they learned how much she was worth. ... He even inherited a cabin in the Poconos." Oscar chuckled. "That lucky bastard is set for life."

I certainly can't let him go now. Imagine, Mark getting an inheritance! Sally quietly walked down the stairs and out of the house, a smile on her face.

9: HALLOWEEN TALENT COMPETITION

There was still half an hour before the start of the All Greek Halloween Talent Competition when Tommy entered the backstage area of the auditorium. He walked through the milling contestants, trying to find his best friend, when he spotted an overly rotund character that looked familiar. He moved toward Kyle, making his way through the groups of competitors, stagehands, and other workers, who were running around, talking and yelling.

"How did you gain so much weight, Welby Kyle? It can't have been from the cafeteria food," Tommy teased.

Kyle laughed as he turned around to see his fellow Kappa costumed as Merlin the Magician. Neither of them had seen the other since having dinner with some of their fraternity brothers. Each had been very secretive about how he was going to dress for the Talent Competition. "Wow. Look at you, Ford Tommy. You look great!" Kyle waved a white dishtowel. "Can I pass as Pavarotti?"

"It looks like you have enough padding." Tommy patted Kyle's padded belly. "Do I look like Merlin?"

"Yes, you do." Kyle tugged at Tommy's gray beard. "That's on really well."

"Are you as nervous as I am?" Tommy asked.

"You bet I am." Kyle managed a weak grin. "I could barely eat dinner tonight, in case you didn't notice."

"Nope. I've been too nervous myself to notice what anybody else was doing."

Kyle glanced at his watch. "I hope Dave and Mark get back from the game in time for the competition."

Tommy hoped Mark would be at the talent show, but he was worried about Mark's reaction to the song he had chosen to do. "So do I," he said, wavering between emotions.

The auditorium was packed with over five hundred enthusiastic students, all talking amongst themselves as they waited for the show to begin. Most of the students were fraternity and sorority members, dressed in Halloween costumes and ready to attend the many Halloween parties afterward. Only two members from each fraternity or sorority were allowed to compete in singing, dancing, or acting. The sororities almost always won the competition, while the fraternity entries typically ended up being the comic relief. The Kappa brothers were hoping that would change this time, especially since they had doubled their chances of winning by entering Kyle and Tommy.

Twenty of the Kappa brothers were sitting in a group in the middle of the auditorium. The Kappa football players were not among them because the team had been delayed in returning from the away game they had played, and lost, earlier that day. When they finally arrived, just before the start of the competition, they were stuck standing in the back of the auditorium.

The crowd erupted in cheers as the MC bounded out onto the stage to start the competition. Jeremy Waters was a senior member of the theater department, well-known throughout the student body, and not a member of any fraternity.

"Happy Halloween, brothers and sisters, students and faculty," the MC greeted the crowd as they quieted. "Welcome to the All Greek Halloween Talent Competition. I am your host for the evening, Jeremy Waters. We have twelve anxious brothers and sisters backstage, waiting to entertain you."

Jeremy waited for the cheering to stop. "As you are aware, we will follow a girl/boy order throughout the competition. Six members of the Performing Arts Department will judge the contestants and select a winner. The winner will do a final performance before the competition officially concludes."

The six judges were seated throughout the auditorium, rather than all together in the front row to judge whether the performers could be heard over the crowd of students, as well as on their performances.

"All right, let's get started with Rita from Delta sorority," Jeremy stated and walked off the stage.

Rita appeared on the stage in a floor length, tight-fitting, low-cut red dress that had a stuffed bodice, and she wore a huge blond wig. She sang the Dolly Parton song, "I Will Always Love You", from the movie *The Best Little Whorehouse in Texas*.

Joe from Omega followed Rita. He was a seven-foot tall, African-American basketball player, who took possession of the stage in bright yellow dashiki pants and no shirt. He sang M.C. Hammer's "Can't Touch This".

Alice from Alpha, a beautiful African-American woman, was next. She wore a short dress and long-haired wig as she sang "What's Love Got To Do With It?" moving across the stage just like Tina Turner. The crowd went wild as Alice sang, and she received a standing ovation when she finished.

"That was amazing, Alice. Wow!" the MC exclaimed. "Now, please welcome Kyle from Kappa."

The crowd began laughing as Kyle walked onto stage, but Kyle remained composed. He had slicked back his hair with styling gel and was wearing a silk Mandarin prince's costume. The costume was three times larger than would have fit him, had it not been for the padding that he had used to stuff the outfit. He held a plain white dishtowel in his right hand as a handkerchief, similar to the manner in which Pavarotti appears on stage. Those in the crowd familiar with Pavarotti reacted by cheering for Kyle.

Kyle stood in the center of the stage and looked around as the cheering and laughter quieted down. The music began, and Kyle started singing the aria "Nessun Dorma" from the opera *Turandot*. He put his whole heart and soul into the song, and his voice rang out strong and clear through the auditorium. When he finished, Kyle received a two-minute standing ovation. The sorority sisters, who were more familiar with operatic pieces, yelled out bravos for the young man. Most of the fraternities gave Kyle a grudgingly polite standing ovation. But the Kappa brothers stood hooting, hollering, and whistling for their brother.

"Where did that guy come from? Wow! That was amazing," a surprised Jeremy lauded, clapping his hands loudly. "Coming up next is Marcia from Sigma sorority."

Marcia tiptoed onto the stage in a white tutu and danced the death scene of *Swan Lake*. Her performance was perfect, although the majority of the student body was bored by the formal dance.

Rob, one of the openly gay members of Gamma, took to the stage telling jokes and juggling tennis balls. The crowd was not impressed with either his juggling or his jokes.

"Bring back the fat singer, huh, crowd," Jeremy commented, returning to the stage after Rob's act. "All right, let's hear it for Victoria from Delta."

Victoria was the president of Delta sorority. She wore a 1930s-style flowing emerald green satin gown that complemented her wavy, auburn hair. She stood in the center of the stage and waited for the applause to stop before singing "My Heart Will Go On" from the movie *Titanic*. When she ended the last note, the audience rose to its feet and cheered. The Delta sisters, who were sitting directly in front of the Kappa brothers, cheered the loudest.

"Your heart might go on, sweetheart, but mine stopped." Jeremy laughed. "Now we have Tommy from Kappa."

Tommy wore a medieval-style, full-length black velvet robe, patterned with silver moons and stars. A long gray wig covered his hair, and a matching gray beard was affixed to his face. In his left hand, he carried a six-foot tall staff with a crystal atop it. As they had when Kyle walked out onto the stage, most of the crowd began laughing, believing that they were going to hear something funny.

Tommy stood in the middle of the stage and looked out at the crowd as they quieted down. A piece of non-descript New Age music began playing as he began reciting his monologue:

Back in the time of lore — when I helped Arthur create a world of peace — Knights were gallant and chivalrous — Ladies were beautiful and virginal — People believed in magic and love.

The peace didn't last — People stopped believing in magic — And love lost its luster — Even I became trapped within my own magic by the spell of love.

But peace and magic and love never die — They always remain within our reach — within our hearts — Belief, faith, and hope are all they need to be reborn.

When the music changed, Tommy began singing "The Rose". Everyone was familiar with Bette Midler's version of the song, but none had ever heard a man sing it. Just as Kyle had done, Tommy put every fiber of his being into the song.

For the second time that night, the crowd was stunned by a fraternity brother's singing. The audience went wild with cheering and applause. Tommy's ovation didn't last as long as Kyle's had, but he smiled at the crowd as he walked off stage. The Kappa brothers were cheering the loudest.

"Where are the Kappa brothers stealing these singers from? Can you believe two great singers in one fraternity?" Jeremy remarked with a light laughter. "Next up is Miranda from Zeta Rho."

Miranda walked onto the stage dressed as Madonna in the movie *Desperately Seeking Susan*, and sang "Like a Virgin".

Stefano from Upsilon followed Miranda. He was a good-looking Hispanic, who pranced onto the stage in tight black pants and a dress shirt open to the waist. He had the crowd clapping and stomping their feet as he sang Ricky Martin's "La Vida Loca".

Melanie from Alpha Kappa Alpha followed Stefano. She performed a modern dance routine to New Age music.

Richard from Theta Chi was the last performer of the competition. Wearing everyday clothes, he stood at center stage, and performed a truly un-PC routine, picking on every minority group imaginable. There were a few chuckles from some and several loud boos from others.

"Is Merlin still in the back? We could use a little magic to make us forget that routine," the MC jested to much laughter from the crowd. "Fortunately, that concludes our competition portion of the show this evening. Let's give a round of applause to all of our participants." The MC waited for the applause to finish before he continued. "We will now take a fifteen-minute intermission while the judges make their decision. Smoke 'em if you got 'em."

Some of the audience members mingled inside the auditorium, talking with friends, while others went outside to get some fresh air or to grab a smoke.

"I think we actually have a chance of placing in this competition, brothers," Oscar observed to several other Kappas who were outside, and then saw the football players. "Glad you guys made it. We saved some seats for you."

"I wasn't at the pledge sing. I didn't know Tommy and Kyle had such good voices," Donald said.

Oscar smiled at him. "That's why we drafted them for the competition. We did hear them sing."

"I thought Kyle was great," Mark commented to Dave. "That deep voice resonated through the auditorium."

"Hey, Tommy wasn't too shabby either," Dave replied. "He looked funny dressed as Merlin, but it certainly worked."

"Do you think they could both place?" Donald wondered aloud.

Paul shook his head. "I don't know. Victoria and Alice were both very good. I think it's going to be tough for both of our brothers to place."

"I think we could take two out of three," Oscar said confidently. "Our brothers were spot on with their singing and their stage presence."

"Since when did you become so damn optimistic?" Jack asked Oscar with a mitigating smile.

Dave and Mark laughed and punched Oscar from both sides. "You're prejudiced in favor of our newest brothers," Dave cautioned. "They were good, but so were others."

Mark winked at Oscar. "Keep the faith, brother Oscar. And so will I."

As the Kappa brothers began walking back into the auditorium, Oscar pulled Mark aside. "Tommy was over at the house today to clean your room and do your laundry. Apparently you haven't told your little brother that he could stop doing that now that he is a full-fledged member of the fraternity."

Mark gave him an impish smile. "And that's a problem because...?"

Oscar shook his head and laughed as he slapped Mark on the back. The two brothers followed the rest of the group to their seats in the auditorium.

Jeremy Waters strolled to the center of the stage and waited for the chatter to die down. "Sisters and brothers," the MC yelled out, "what a competition we had this year! The judges had a very difficult time deciding upon our winners. Let's bring all of the performers out here on stage and give them a huge round of applause."

The crowd cheered, hooted and hollered, and applauded as the competitors walked out onto the stage and stood in a line behind the MC. Various groups called out the names of their brothers or sisters or friends.

Jeremy turned to the participants. "Congratulations on great performances. Good luck to all of you."

Oscar leaned forward in his seat to address Mark and Dave, who were sitting in the row in front of him. "One of our boys better win this thing," he whispered.

Jeremy turned around to face the crowd as he pulled the card from the envelope. "Our third place winner this year is Tommy from Kappa fraternity." The crowd applauded with approval as Tommy walked up to the MC and accepted a bouquet of roses. He bowed to the crowd and took his place back with the others.

"All right. Our second place winner this year is Alice from Alpha sorority," Jeremy announced. The crowd once again applauded with approval as Alice received her flowers. She curtsied to the crowd and waved to her sisters before returning to her place.

"Okay, sisters and brothers," the MC announced, "we have a stunning outcome to announce. For the first time ever, we have two brothers from the same fraternity placing in the top three, and for the first time in over twenty years, we have a brother winning the competition." The MC smiled as the audience cheered. "First place goes to Kyle from Kappa Lambda Pi."

The Kappa brothers stood up as one and roared their approval as Kyle accepted the trophy.

"And now our winner will perform one more song," the MC announced, and led the other contestants off stage.

Kyle pulled Tommy from the group moving off stage. They stood facing each other as the music began, and they started singing "Don't Go Breaking My Heart" which they had secretly practiced in case one of them won and had to do an encore. As they sang, they danced with one another, and the crowd convulsed with laughter at the overly stuffed Mandarin prince dancing with the thin druid Merlin. When they finished, Kyle and Tommy stood in the center of the stage and bowed to the crowd. The Kappas stood, proudly and loudly cheering their newest brothers.

Twenty Kappa brothers waited for Kyle and Tommy outside the auditorium. As they walked out, the two young men were greeted by cheering and surrounded by their brothers. Kyle handed the trophy over to Jack as Dave and Oscar lifted him up on their shoulders. The brothers sang and cheered during the walk back to Kappa house. Tommy walked in the midst of the group next to Mark.

When they arrived at Kappa house, and before everyone got too drunk to pay attention, Oscar stood before the brothers in the living room. "*Hermanos!*" he shouted above the talking. "May I have your attention?" He waited for the noise to quiet down. "First of all, my condolences to Victoria, who might have had a chance to win the competition, had it not been for our brothers Kyle and Tommy."

Victoria was standing next to Dave, his arm around her waist. She took the backhanded compliment in good humor, raising her bottle of beer to Oscar.

"Kyle and Tommy, where are you, boys?" Oscar called out. They walked to the front of the room, Kyle carrying the trophy he had won. Oscar put an arm around each of them. "I knew we did the right thing, requesting these two boys perform for us." The group hooted. "Thank you, Kyle, for giving us the one trophy that we have never won in this fraternity. We would like to place it amongst the others, if you're okay with that."

Kyle handed the trophy to Oscar, who raised it above his head to the cheers of the brothers. Oscar placed the trophy on top of the fireplace mantel until he could reconfigure the trophy case in the living room.

Later that night, Tommy was sipping a small shot of brandy and talking with a group of brothers. He felt a rough hand grip the back of his neck and smiled to himself.

"My room, now," Mark whispered into Tommy's ear.

After following Tommy upstairs and locking his door, Mark turned Tommy around and kissed him,then pulled back with a laugh. "I've never kissed a man with a beard before." He pulled a couple of loose strands of gray hair from his mouth. "I think you need some Grecian Formula, little brother."

Tommy laughed and sat down on the bed. "Do you want me to take this off? Or do you want to know what it's like to make love to a man with a beard?"

"I'd rather be with you, not my grandfather."

Tommy reached into another bag that had been hanging from his waist and pulled out a bottle of hair glue remover that had come with the beard kit. As he took off his costume and beard, Mark undressed and lay naked on top of the bed. When the beard was finally off his face, Tommy slid onto the bed next to him. The two young men began kissing, and then Mark made love to Tommy. Afterward, they lay quietly cuddling and talking until they fell asleep.

10: NOVEMBER ANGST

The golden colors of autumn had fallen from the trees, and there was a chill in the November wind that blew around Kappa house. The fun and excitement of the fraternity pledge period and the Halloween Talent Competition were over. The brothers of Kappa, along with the other students on campus, were preparing for the three weeks of classes before the week-long Thanksgiving break.

Tommy woke up before Mark and stood staring out the window, watching as the rain poured down into the yard. He enjoyed feeling the cold glass against his warm hand and forehead. He was lost in thoughts about Mark when he felt a pair of arms wrap around his body.

"I guess we won't be running this morning," Mark whispered, kissing Tommy's ear.

"Not unless you feel like catching pneumonia." He turned around and looked up into Mark's bright blue eyes. "Think it might turn into snow?"

"If it keeps getting colder, it might." Mark lightly kissed Tommy's lips. "How about we get some clothes on and go have some breakfast? Otherwise, I'm going to get ideas about what we can do together while we're still naked."

Tommy laughed. "It's a tough decision, but my stomach is taking precedence over my...other appetites, right now." He kissed Mark, then they dressed and went down to the Kappa kitchen.

After having breakfast with Oscar and Jack, the two young men returned to Mark's room to finish up some of their coursework. Mark sat on his bed, working on a paper, while Tommy sat at the desk using Mark's computer. He had his own computer in his dorm room but used Mark's whenever he was at the house. In exchange, Tommy was typing Mark's papers. A few of the Kappa brothers, including Oscar and Jack, had learned that Tommy was a fair typist and offered to pay him to type their papers, as well.

A knock sounded on the door and Mark called "Come in." Tommy continued to work, not looking up as Dave entered carrying a book and some papers.

"Mark, I need some help..." He stopped and stared at Tommy, then looked back at Mark. "Sorry, man, I didn't know you had...company."

"If you'd get out of your room once in a while, you might have a better idea of what's going on in the outside world," Mark said with a smile.

"I, uh, was just working on that paper we have due. I know I should have gotten an earlier jump on it, but me and Victoria have been having some..." He blew out a deep breath and dropped that sore subject. "Anyhow, some of this research is confusing, and I hoped you might be able to help."

"You always need help, Dave." Mark laughed.

Dave was slightly irritated, but he walked over and sat down at the bottom of Mark's bed. "I didn't know he was still here."

"*He*," Mark started, looking over at the back of Tommy's head and then back at Dave, "is working on a paper. And *he* is a brother of this fraternity and can be here anytime he wants." Mark smiled hard at Dave. "By the way, *he* has a name."

Tommy was sitting at the desk, facing the computer. He was having a hard time typing and keeping a straight face as he listened to Mark correct Dave.

Dave studied Tommy's back before turning to look at Mark. "I'm sorry. I didn't mean anything by it."

Mark let Dave off the hook. "So, what's the problem?"

Dave began pointing out the part of his research that was confusing him. Mark listened and then gave him some sense of what he thought the answer might be. Dave glanced over at Tommy from time to time, impressed by how fast he was typing.

"I thought he was doing research. Does he always type his notes that fast?" Dave asked.

"He's multi-tasking, Dave. He's researching information, verifying facts, and typing his paper at the same time." Mark laughed as he looked over at Tommy.

"He's fast," Dave said as he stood to leave.

"I know. He's going to type my paper for me."

"Would he type my paper?" Dave asked.

Mark chuckled. "Why don't you ask him yourself? His name is Tommy, and he knows how to talk."

Dave walked over to the desk. "Would you mind typing my paper for me, Tommy?"

Tommy looked up at last, stifling a grin. "No problem, but I charge a dollar a page."

"That's fine." Dave gathered his papers and book and left the room.

Later that evening, Dave saw Oscar and Jack sitting in the den on the first floor. Oscar was using his laptop to do research while taking notes on a pad of paper. Jack had a couple of books open in front of him and was also taking notes. Dave walked into the room and shut the door behind him. At the sound, Oscar and Jack looked up.

"Hi, guys," Dave said quietly. They acknowledged him, then went back to their work.

Dave sat down on one of the chairs in the middle of the room, hesitating over what he was about to ask. Not looking at either of the other two, he asked, "Is there something going on between Mark and Tommy?"

Oscar and Jack looked up from their work, and then at each other, before looking at Dave. "What?" Oscar asked, as if he had not heard correctly.

Dave looked over at him. "I've just realized that Tommy has been spending a lot of time with Mark. He was upstairs earlier, wearing one of Mark's jerseys."

Jack started laughing. "Stop the presses. Kappa little brother is wearing his big brother's jersey. News at 11."

Oscar shrugged. "So what? Tommy's been using Mark's computer to do research, and he's typing papers for those of us who don't type so well."

"Is there a rule in the by-laws that says he shouldn't be doing that?" Jack asked, his laughter subsiding.

"I just thought—"

"There's your problem, Dave," Oscar interrupted. "You've been thinking. You shouldn't do that; it might burn out something in that pretty little head of yours." That made Jack laugh again.

Dave wasn't happy at being the brunt of their amusement, but realized that he had brought it on himself. "It's just that he seems to be here a lot," he persisted.

"He's a brother, Dave," Oscar said. "A lot of brothers are here; they like being in the house."

Jack looked over at Oscar with a broad grin. "Maybe we should get a time clock and schedule brothers so that they aren't hanging around here all the time."

Oscar laughed. "Sorry, dude, you've been here three days this week. Get out."

Dave stood up and glared at each of them. "You guys are assholes," he said, walking out of the room.

During that week, Tommy finished typing six papers for various members of the fraternity. He had double-spaced the papers, the accepted standard set by most professors, and so that the brothers had room to make any necessary revisions on the drafts. Some of the brothers had already returned their papers so that Tommy could prepare the final versions.

Early Saturday morning, Tommy had showered and dressed, and was finalizing papers for the brothers while Mark took a shower before the football game that afternoon. He was sitting cross-legged at the bottom of Mark's bed, several papers spread out in front of him as he was prioritizing assignments before he started typing. When there was a knock at the door, he called, "Come in."

Dave entered, leaving the door ajar. "I was looking for Mark."

"He's in the shower," Tommy supplied as he continued arranging his work.

Dave sat down on the chair by the desk and looked over at Tommy. "You've been spending a lot of time around the house."

Tommy looked up. "Is that a problem?"

Mark was returning from his shower and heard Dave's question from outside the door. Wrapped in his towel, he stood quietly, listening to the conversation.

"No. But I've noticed that you and Mark are spending a lot of time together."

Tommy had always thought Dave was a nice guy and was confused by the change in his attitude. "What are you getting at?"

Dave stared at Tommy as he took a deep breath. "Is there something going on between the two of you?" he asked directly.

They both jumped when they heard the door slam shut and saw Mark standing at the door, eyes flashing with anger.

"Whatever might be going on between whomever in this fraternity house, it's none of your fucking business!" Mark growled. "Tommy is my little brother, and he's welcome in my room any damn time he pleases. If you have a problem with that, you should be talking to me and not to Tommy."

"I, uh, was..." Dave stammered.

"You were what, Dave? Butting your nose in where it didn't belong? Trying to make others as miserable as you've been the past couple of weeks?" Mark asked heatedly.

"I was concerned about you," Dave replied. "You've been spending a lot of time with Tommy, and I was worried that you might not be taking care of business."

Mark laughed, but it wasn't a happy laugh. "As I recall, Dave, you were the one that told me I was supposed to take my responsibilities as a big brother more seriously." Mark glared at him. "Now you think I might be having problems because of the amount of time I'm spending with Tommy."

"Well, I, uh..."

"Correct me if I'm wrong, but didn't you just give Tommy your first draft? I've already finished my paper."

Dave was caught by surprise. "You're finished?"

"Yes, finished." Mark smiled smugly. "Tommy's not a bad influence on me, so you can stop playing daddy and deal with your own business." He went to the door and opened it. "You have a game to get ready for."

When Dave left, Mark slammed the door behind him and went over to the bed and sat down next to Tommy. "So, how were you going to answer his question about us?"

Tommy smiled mischievously. "I was going to tell him that I like riding your dick like it was a pogo stick." Tommy laughed as he rubbed his hand over Mark's chest.

Mark laughed with him. "The truth! That's clever." He kissed Tommy and then went to get dressed for the football game.

Dave went down to the kitchen, shaking his head at what he had just done. Not only had he made a fool of himself, he had offended his best friend and Tommy. Oscar and Jack were sitting at the table. Dave poured himself a cup of coffee and sat down. "I just fucked up royally, guys."

Jack and Oscar stared at him. "What did you do?" Oscar asked.

"I just insinuated to Mark and Tommy that there was something going on between them. I insulted both of them, and I infuriated Mark. I made a complete and total ass of myself," Dave said, looking at each of them.

"Wow!" Jack exclaimed. "And they say the Army does more before nine o'clock than we do," he said with a chuckle.

Oscar turned to look at Dave. "What has your problem been lately? And what do you have against Tommy?"

"I don't have anything against Tommy. It just bothers me that he's been hanging around with Mark so much lately." He looked away from Oscar's glaring eyes.

"Tommy's one of the best things that has happened around the house this semester," Jack said. "His attitude has rubbed off on a lot of the guys. We've had more guys hanging around the house this semester because the mood around here isn't just party and crash. He's very popular. He's also one of the most helpful brothers we have." Jack looked over at Oscar and smiled. "Besides, when was the last time you ever saw Oscar awake and happy this early in the day?" He received a hard glare from Oscar, before Oscar laughed.

"He's a good guy, Dave. So what's the problem?" Oscar asked.

Dave's eyes began watering as he looked over at Oscar. "He's taken my best friend away from me, and I don't have anyone to talk to about my break-up with Victoria." He lowered his head and wiped his eyes.

Oscar and Jack looked at each other, stunned by the admission. "Shit, Dave, what happened?" Jack asked sincerely.

"We'd been having problems since before Halloween. We were always arguing whenever we were together, so we started finding excuses not to see one another. We got together after the talent competition to talk about our problems, and instead of working things out, we broke up."

"Fuck, man, that sucks," Oscar commiserated.

"I know." Dave looked at Oscar. "And I've been trying to talk with Mark about it, but he's always hanging around with Tommy."

Having overheard Dave's story from the doorway, Mark walked into the kitchen and put a hand on Dave's shoulder. "You could have talked to me anytime you wanted, Dave," Mark said quietly. "Tommy wouldn't have complained; he probably would have tried to help. You didn't give either one of us a chance to be there for you."

Dave put his head in his hands. "I know. I know."

Mark sat down at the table next to Dave. "Come on, big guy, talk to us. What's going on?"

"Victoria and I broke up. We've been having some problems, and she finally let me know that she found somebody else."

"Did she give you any reason?" Mark asked.

"None. I didn't even know she was unhappy." Dave looked at Mark. "I thought things were going well."

Jack jumped to the obvious. "Did you forget her birthday or an anniversary?"

"I thought about that, but none that I can think of."

"Were you neglecting her needs? You know how women can be about their needs." Oscar smiled at Mark.

Mark accepted the barb with good grace. "God forbid you overlook their needs."

"I was being attentive," Dave insisted. "Shit, I was even attentive during the rush period. Classes, football, rush, and Victoria; I had all the bases covered." Dave managed a weak smile.

"I think I see the problem." Jack smiled, and Oscar and Mark nodded in agreement.

"Is that the order of priority you had, Dave?" Oscar asked, looking directly at Dave.

"Well, sometimes football or rush took priority," Dave admitted and then slapped his hand against his forehead. "Shit."

Mark shook his head sympathetically. "Women always want to be your number one priority, my friend. I should know."

"But she had her sorority rush to deal with, as well as her classes."

"Sorry, dude." Oscar patted Dave's shoulder. "It's different for women. They can have other priorities over the boyfriend, but you are not allowed to have any higher priority."

"How would you know, Oscar?" Dave asked. "You date a different woman every week. Jack barely ever dates, and Mark has the bitch from hell or some other female groupie."

They all laughed at Dave's assessment, and Oscar pointed over at Mark. "That's how I know, dude. I've watched the shit that Mark has gone through, and he always made her his number one priority."

"What should I do?" Dave asked. "Should I try talking to her?"

The other three guys looked at each other and shrugged their shoulders. "It couldn't hurt," Jack finally responded.

"Let her go," Mark suggested.

Oscar burst out laughing. "This from the man who's been played like a yo-yo for over a year."

Mark smiled over at Oscar. "She always came back."

"Before dumping your ass again," Oscar reminded Mark.

Dave looked at Oscar, then Mark. "Guys, we're talking about me."

"Talk to her, Dave," Jack repeated. "You'll never know if you still have a chance if you don't talk to her."

"I don't know. I'll think about it."

"Why don't you think about it while you get ready for the game." Mark stood up. "We have to leave soon."

Dave followed Tommy outside during the Kappa party that night. "Hey, Tommy," he called.

Tommy turned and waited for Dave to catch up. "Sorry about the game today. That was a tough loss."

"Thanks." Dave noted there was no apparent animosity between them. "I want to apologize for my behavior this morning." Dave looked directly into Tommy's eyes. "I was an ass, and I'm sorry."

"It's okay."

"No, it's not okay. You're a really good guy, and I treated you like shit."

"I just assumed that you have something on your mind. You've been a little distracted lately." Tommy smiled.

"Victoria and I broke up. We had some problems, and she found somebody else."

"I'm sorry, Dave."

"What would you do if you were in love with somebody and they just ended it?" Dave asked.

Tommy thought for a moment about what his reaction would be if Mark ended their relationship. "I don't know," he replied quietly. "I think it would depend on the circumstances."

"Would you try talking to her about it?"

Tommy thought for a while, gazing up at the stars. "I think if she broke my heart," he made sure to use the proper pronoun, "I'd probably just let her go."

"I don't want to let go," Dave replied sadly. "I love her too much."

Tommy took a deep breath. He didn't want to think about how he would feel if Mark ever stopped loving him. "There's an old cliché, Dave." He continued looking at the stars. "If you love somebody, set them free. If they come back to you, it was meant to be. If they don't return, it was never meant to be." He looked at Dave and smiled. "Or something to that effect."

"Is that what you would do?"

"I don't know, Dave." Tommy looked away. He didn't want to think about this subject any longer. "I really don't know how I would react. I've never been in love like that."

"Jack thinks I should try talking to her," Dave repeated.

"Then you should be honest with her. Tell her how you feel about not being with her. Let her know how much she means to you." Tommy looked earnestly at Dave. "Don't bring up the fact that she's with somebody else. I would only talk about the relationship between the two of you."

Dave absorbed that for a moment, then nodded. "I can do that."

"Are you able to do it without getting angry if she decides that she doesn't want to get back together?"

Dave looked away for a moment, then back at Tommy. "That's going to be hard, but I really want to try."

"Good luck, Dave. I hope she'll listen to what you have to say."

"Thanks, Tommy." Dave gave Tommy a one-armed hug. "I'm really sorry that I was such an ass to you."

"You're forgiven," Tommy said with a chuckle.

Torn Between Two Lovers

Mark walked slowly through the campus, his head hunched down between his shoulders. He had agreed to meet Sally for dinner at a restaurant on the far side of campus, and the walk gave him time to think about why he had agreed to get together with her. He loved being with Tommy because they had a lot in common: football, country music, and vampires, to name just a few. He also felt comfortable, even contented, around Tommy, whether they were studying, hanging around with their fraternity brothers, or having sex and sleeping together.

Still, he wanted a long-term monogamous relationship, and he had always taken it for granted that could only happen between a man and a woman. Tommy had mentioned that his uncle had been with the same man for over twenty-five years, but Mark wasn't convinced that was likely to be the case with him and Tommy. The bottom line for Mark was that he was scared of being in love with a man. The possible ramifications of being gay were a constant source of worry, and Mark was beginning to regret that he hadn't listened to Jack and not gotten involved in a relationship with his little brother.

At the door to the Chinese restaurant, Mark took a deep breath and blew it out slowly, trying to expel his doubts and fears and indecision along with the exhalation. Inside, the waiter showed him to the table where Sally was already seated.

"I wasn't sure you were going to join me," Sally said shyly as Mark sat in the chair next to hers.

For Sally, there were a lot of things about Mark that she liked: his blue eyes, his muscular body, his athleticism, his sense of humor, and his family's wealth and status. There were also things that she disliked: his lack of fashion sense and style, his fascination with sports above everything else, his enjoyment of vampire movies and novels. She knew that she had to keep the positives in mind to be able to get through dinner and wheedle him back in her life.

"I wasn't sure I would." His voice was soft, distant.

She noted the detachment and sadness. "So, why did you?"

For the first time since arriving, he looked directly into her eyes. "Fear."

"Of me?"

"No." He looked away from her. "Of love. I tried to love you once, and it didn't work out." That was part of the truth; the other part he kept to himself, fighting the hurt inside.

"I've seen the football player, the fraternity brother," she smiled at him, "and the lover, but I've never seen this sensitive side of you."

"A lot of things have happened this semester, and I've done a lot of thinking about who I am."

They both fell silent as the waiter came and took their order. When he went to get their beverages, Sally picked up the conversation.

"So, who are you, Mark?"

"I wish I knew. I'm confused about everything."

"Do you think I can help you clear up the confusion?"

"I don't know, Sally. You and I have had such a rocky relationship." As he looked at her, for a split second he wished it was Tommy sitting next to him. He pushed away the thought. "When we met last year, it seemed like love at first sight. We had fun dating, going to movies and dances, hanging out at parties, and making love. I thought you were the one that I was going to spend my life with, especially after last Thanksgiving with your family."

Sally reached over and touched his cheek. "You expected too much from me. I wasn't ready to have my life decided for me," she said softly, stroking his cheek before abruptly withdrawing her hand. "You need to shave."

"I like it like that; I'm not going to shave," he responded defensively, knowing that Tommy approved of the stubble that made him look tougher. He lowered his head and closed his eyes. It was thoughts like those that he had to put out of his mind. He looked up at Sally. "I wasn't trying to decide your life for you."

"I'm sorry, Mark. I didn't say you were trying to decide my life, but that's how it felt. You wanted so much from me, and I just wanted to enjoy my freedom until after college. I didn't want to make any long-term decisions so soon."

Mark looked at her intently, evaluating the truth of her explanation. "All I wanted was for us to be a couple until we graduated, and then decide where the future would lead us. I didn't think that was asking too much."

Sally was grateful that the waiter returned with their meals, because it gave her time to decide what response would give her the upper hand. "Mark, you really are a sweet man, and I do love you. I wasn't ready to settle down with one man. I was afraid you would want to get married and have children right after we got out of college, then I'd be stuck raising kids and not being able to live the life I want."

"That's not what I wanted for either of us," he said. "I only wanted for us to be together."

Sally smiled faintly. "Funny, it's usually the girl asking for a commitment from the guy, not the other way around."

Mark grinned. "Ours has been an unusual relationship, and holidays have been especially brutal. Our first semester together was great, then we argued over New Year's. We got back together and broke up three times last semester. We were together again at the end of the semester; you spent some time with my family, and then I spent the Fourth of July with your family. I don't even know what happened that caused us to break up."

It appeared to Sally that he was accusing her for their problems, and her immediate impulse was to get up and walk out. She took a deep breath and reined in her flare of anger at his reluctance to fall back into her arms. "I really want to make things up to you, Mark. I can't begin to tell you how sorry I am. We've had good times together, and I miss being with you. It was only when I thought things were getting too serious, that you wanted marriage and a family, that I freaked out." She gave him a smile. "Do you think we could give our relationship another try? You're the man I want to spend my life with, Mark. When we aren't together, all I do is think about you. I'm lonely and unhappy when you aren't a part of my life."

Mark was a little surprised by her admissions, although he had heard some of them before. But he had never heard such sincerity in her voice before. "I can't believe you're saying all this. What's changed since the last time we were together?"

Sally smiled at him. "Dating a bunch of insensitive jerks helped me realize how much you mean to me. Please give us another chance."

"Are you sure about giving our relationship another try?" he asked, still doubtful. If he believed her and returned to her, then he was going to have to deal with Tommy. He hoped Tommy had been honest when he said the two of them would go as far as Mark wanted to go, and that Mark would be free to end it if that's what he decided. He loved Tommy, but he didn't want to be gay. The normal and right thing to do would be to marry a woman. And he still remembered how much he had loved Sally when they first met.

"I'm sure, Mark. Let's go about this slowly, start having meals and going to movies, try getting to know one another again, like we did last year. I think part of our problem was that we didn't have enough time to do a lot of the fun things we used to like to do together."

"Okay."

She reached over and touched his cheek. "I'll come up to your house for Thanksgiving and spend some time with your family."

"Is that a promise?" he asked skeptically. She had made promises to him before and then broken them.

"Yes, Mark," she said with a bright smile. "You can come down to the Hamptons a few days before Thanksgiving and pick me up so that we can drive up to your parents' house together. Or, if we leave late, we can find a hotel to spend the night."

He grinned at her. "You're a bad girl."

"Promise me that you'll be tender and gentle when we make love."

Mark thought about Tommy and the times they had made love. It was passionate and hot, and Tommy didn't mind the roughness of their sex play. Mark loved being able to totally be himself. But, for the chance to prove to himself that he wasn't gay, he could live without the rough sex. "I can do that," he decided.

Sally leaned over and kissed him gently on the lips. "You mean so much to me, Mark. I just know that our relationship will work out this time. Besides, imagine how happy our parents will be that we're back together."

"You have charmed my dad," he admitted. "He really likes you." Mark wasn't sure that his mother would be as happy for him, but she would be supportive.

As they left the restaurant, Sally had her arm around Mark's waist and her head against Mark's chest. She had a satisfied smile on her face, knowing that she had accomplished what she had set out to do. She would make sure that she kept Mark close, but not so close that she felt trapped.

Mark had his arm around her shoulders, holding her close. He'd take his time getting back with Sally, but he would have to make sure that Tommy didn't see them together. He wasn't ready to deal with the anguish that Tommy was undoubtedly going to feel.

Storm Clouds Move In

As the fall semester drew nearer to the Thanksgiving break, everyone got caught up in the rush. Tommy's classwork kept him in the library more frequently, allowing him little time to spend at Kappa house or with Mark. When he did go to Kappa house to return papers he had typed for the brothers, Mark was rarely around. The team was putting in extra practices, trying to make it into the state championships now that football season was coming to an end. Tommy understood that Mark's classwork had to be a priority, even if it meant time away from him. Still, after all the time that he had spent with Mark during the pledge period and just afterwards, Tommy's heart ached to be with his big brother, to be held in his strong arms as he fell asleep. The loneliness he felt as he sat in his dorm room was something he hadn't experienced since his grandmother's death. For more than a week, Mark had been avoiding him, and he'd seen him with Sally on a couple of occasions. Tommy began to fear it was more than obligations and bad timing that was keeping them apart.

Mark was spending as much time with Sally as he could. Although they'd had some bad times, he was hoping that he would once again love her the way he had that first semester, and that this new start would grow into a lasting relationship. In deference to his ambivalence, he tried to make sure that he and Sally didn't go anywhere that Tommy might see them together. The one thing he could depend on was that Tommy kept to a regular routine. He avoided having meals with Sally in the cafeteria whenever he knew that Tommy might be there. When he did run into Tommy, he invented excuses about classwork and football taking up his time, which made him feel guilty. Although he soothed his conscience by telling himself that he had to give his relationship with Sally a chance, a part of him continued to feel as if he were cheating on Tommy. At the very least, telling Tommy about Sally was the fair thing to do. Then he could stop avoiding Tommy and making up excuses about why they couldn't spend time together. The Monday of the week before Thanksgiving break, he had joined some of the brothers at lunch and had asked Tommy to meet him later that evening.

Mark stood on the hillside in the cemetery, overlooking the fields of snow, waiting for Tommy to arrive. It was a cloudy, cold Monday evening, a perfect match to Mark's mood. He didn't want to hurt Tommy, but he couldn't pass up the opportunity to have a normal relationship with Sally. There was an aching in his heart over losing what he had with Tommy. He hoped they could still be brothers, but that would depend on Tommy's reaction to his ending their loving relationship. At the sound of crunching snow behind him, Mark turned and watched Tommy walking toward him. Tommy had been a friend and a lover. As he watched Tommy getting closer, he once again wondered whether he was doing the right thing.

"You look like you have the weight of the world on your shoulders." Tommy stopped a couple of feet away from Mark, looking into his eyes. "So, what's bothering my big brother?" he asked somberly, dreading what Mark was going to say.

Mark's heart raced and his breath caught at the words "big brother". He let out a deep breath, while he searched for the right words. His throat tightened as he remembered their conversations, their runs, the warm feeling he got as he looked into Tommy's smoky brown eyes, and the feel of Tommy's body next to his as they fell asleep and woke up in the morning. For a moment, he wavered. He knew that he had never been so in love. Then Mark resolutely pushed all of those thoughts away. Regardless of how Tommy made him feel, he was too scared of being gay to accept the love Tommy offered.

"I have made one of the hardest decisions of my life, and it involves you." Mark faced Tommy directly; Tommy deserved that much from him. "You told me that we would go as far as I wanted, and that if I changed my mind, I would be free." Mark closed his eyes for a moment, took another deep breath, and then looked at Tommy. "I've been seeing Sally, and we've been talking, really talking this time, about our relationship. She says she loves me and believes the two of us belong together. I've agreed to try to make a relationship with her work."

Tommy's face showed no emotion. He looked around the hillside and out at the peaceful fields. He took a deep breath and let it out. "Okay." He looked at Mark, his lips tight. "It was fun while it lasted. I have no regrets. I hope you and Sally will be happy together." He turned and started to walk away.

Mark was undone by Tommy's stoic response and by the hurt and pain he saw in Tommy's eyes. It was a look that he would never forget. He felt a constriction in his chest, and his breathing became labored. "Tommy, please," he choked out.

Tommy stopped and turned around to face Mark. "No," he said firmly. "I don't want to hear anything more, and I don't want to talk about it. You're free,

Mark. Now leave me alone."

Mark stood frozen for the long, agonizing moments it took Tommy to walk out of the cemetery gate. He stood there long after the freshman disappeared from sight, the snow falling around him, the chill settling in his bones and in his heart.

Tommy strode through the kitchen at Kappa house without a word to Dave. He was on a mission and polite conversation was not a part of it. Dave stared after him, puzzled. "Mark's not here," he called.

"I know," Tommy replied tersely, reaching the stairs without stopping.

Tommy reached the third floor without encountering anyone else and stalked into Mark's room. He took his paddle down from the wall over Mark's bed, then reached under the mattress and pulled out the topaz crystal that had been hidden there since the start of the pledge period. He slammed the door behind him on his way out.

Oscar was coming out of the bathroom and noticed Tommy. The look on Tommy's face was unlike any he had ever seen on the cheerful brother. "Are you okay?"

"I'm fine," Tommy snapped. "There's nothing to be said."

As Tommy passed Jack on the stairs, he looked into Jack's eyes. "You were right, and I was wrong. There's nothing more to say," he stated flatly.

Tommy made his way back to his dorm room on autopilot. He barely noticed the falling snow or the people moving out of his way as he strode by. When he got back to his room, he put the paddle on his desk and undressed, dropping his clothes in a pile on the floor. He got into his bed, pulled the covers over his head, and cried himself to sleep.

The snow was falling heavily by the time Mark roused himself from his self-inquisition and trudged out of the cemetery. He thought about going to see Sally, but it didn't feel like the right thing to do. Instead, he went into one of the bars on Main Street and had a couple of drinks. Jack, Dave, Oscar and several other brothers were watching the end of *Monday Night Football* when Mark finally stumbled through the living room on his way to bed.

"Hey, buddy," Dave said cheerfully, pretending that nothing out of the ordinary had happened. "How ya doing?"

"Not good," Mark said, forging toward the stairs.

Oscar stood up and started to follow, but Mark rounded on him. "I don't want to talk to anybody. Just leave me the fuck alone!" He stormed up the stairs.

Mark slammed the door to his room, the room that he had all to himself again. He immediately noticed the empty space over the bed, where Tommy's paddle had hung next to his. He threw his jacket on the floor and stood near the window, watching the snow fall. As snow blanketed the ground, Mark imagined it becoming a blank canvas. He wondered what type of painting would depict his future: a blurry Monet, a twisted and warped Picasso, or a contemporary monstrosity that made no sense to him. In his heart, he was convinced that it wouldn't be a peaceful still-life. Tears ran down his face as he walked over to his bed and stared at the blank space on the wall that echoed the emptiness in his heart.

As he entered his Tuesday morning psychology class, Jack looked for Tommy and found him sitting quietly at a desk. He looked okay, but there was no sense of positive energy coming from him. It would have been easier to just leave him alone, but he was a brother. Jack steeled himself. "Hey, Tommy."

"Hi, Jack." Tommy didn't look up from his notebook.

"Are you okay?"

"I'm fine, Jack. I just want to be left alone," he said civilly, still looking at his notebook.

"If you want to talk, I'm available."

"Thanks, Jack. But I don't have anything to say," he replied politely.

Without another word, Jack took his own seat. He watched Tommy during class and noticed that, while Tommy was responding to the professor, he wasn't the same person that he had been just a week or two ago.

Brian followed Tommy into the hall after class and grabbed him around the neck. "Hey, sweet boy, how about some lunch?"

Tommy shoved Brian's arm away and glared at him. "I'm not in the mood to be harassed," Tommy said harshly between gritted teeth. "Just leave me the fuck alone, Brian. I'm not fucking with you." He turned away from Brian and stomped down the hall and out of the building.

Brian stood staring for a moment before he could shake himself out of his surprise. As he turned around, he saw Jack standing nearby. "What the fuck did you guys do to him?" Brian asked. "He used to enjoy my teasing."

Jack shook his head. "I don't know what happened, Brian."

"Did you find out anything from Tommy in class today?" Oscar asked as he and Jack were eating dinner.

"No. He was polite but dismissive. He participated in class as usual, then he went off on Brian after class." Jack sipped his milk. "Tommy's not the same person we initiated. He's closed himself off, kind of like he's a robot pretending to be alive."

"Mark hasn't said a word," Oscar commented. "I wonder what happened."

Jack scanned the cafeteria and then looked back at Oscar. "I think it's walking toward us now."

Oscar followed Jack's gaze and saw Mark and Sally approaching their table.

"Hey, guys," Mark said. "Mind if we join you?"

"Not at all," Jack replied graciously. "I was just leaving." He picked up his half-full tray and walked away.

"Is something wrong with Jack?" Mark asked as they sat down.

"He's just upset about Tommy." Oscar enjoyed the pained expression that appeared on Mark's face. He stood up with his tray and smiled at the couple. "You guys have a good dinner."

Tommy was hurting too much to see Mark, and he especially didn't want to see Mark and Sally together, so he avoided Mark just as Mark had done to him before their break-up. By staying away from Kappa house, he also evaded any of the brothers probing into what was bothering him. When people saw him on campus and asked, he cited his class workload not leaving time for anything else. Tommy began spending his free time in the psychology section of the library.

On his eighteenth birthday, just two days after Mark ended their relationship, Tommy sat alone at the cemetery. He stared out over the snowy fields and pondered the mistake in judgment he had made. Instead of strictly observing his uncle's warning about jocks, he had fallen in love with one. Now he was going to have to find a way to heal himself so that he would be able to be active with his brothers in the fraternity. Either that, or miss out on fraternity events until the following year, after Mark graduated. He opened his hand and stared at the topaz crystal that had been empowered with Mark's energy. His first thought was to simply crush it and be done with it. He couldn't bring himself to do that because it meant too much to him; his grandmother had given it to him. Even so, he knew that he couldn't keep it. Before leaving the cemetery, he had resolved what he would do with the crystal.

Mark was also staying away from Kappa house for much more than just sleeping. He could sense an emptiness inside the house, especially in his own room, and that made him think too much about Tommy. He thought that was the reason he was having restless nights. He and Sally were spending their free time together, going out to dinner and to movies, trying to strengthen their relationship. Sally didn't go running with him in the morning, which gave him time to himself, time that he spent thinking about Tommy. Running alone wasn't as much fun as running with Tommy had been, but it was something that he was going to have to get used to.

Mark had noticed that many of the brothers were avoiding him, and he wondered whether Tommy had been saying things about him. On Thursday morning, he joined his friends in the kitchen.

"Hey, guys, what's up?" When Oscar and Jack kept eating breakfast without answering, he persisted. "Either of you talked to Tommy lately?" The silent glares he received spoke volumes. Sighing, he dropped into a chair at the table. "I just don't know what I should do about Tommy," he began.

"Stay away from him," they said in unison.

"I don't know if I can do that. The brothers have been treating me like a pariah, and if Tommy is saying something—"

"What?" Jack exploded. "You think the cold shoulder is Tommy's fault?" He shook his head in disbelief. "Tommy hasn't said a word about what happened, or even about you. I warned you about this, Mark." He pointed an accusing finger and stomped out of the kitchen.

Oscar set his plate in the sink and followed after Jack. At the doorway, he turned back. "You might start by taking a look at the company you keep." His departure left Mark sitting in the kitchen alone.

A Walk In The Dark

Even on the Friday night before Thanksgiving break, Tommy was in the library working on one of his term papers. Dave sat down across the table from him.

"Hey, brother," Dave said, smiling at him. "I miss you around the house."

Tommy looked up at him. "I've been too busy to come over."

"No, you haven't." Dave looked at him hard. "But I understand what you're going through right now."

"No, Dave, you don't," Tommy said quietly, looking back down at his work.

"You and Jack helped me through the same thing after Halloween."

"It's not the same thing," Tommy mumbled.

Worried about his new brother, Dave took a deep breath. "You're in love with him, aren't you?"

Tommy guessed that Dave was fishing. "I don't think you know what you're talking about."

"Okay, maybe I don't know what I'm talking about." Dave shrugged. "Maybe I don't know that you and Mark have been closer than most of the brothers in the house. And maybe I haven't talked to some of the other brothers and found out that they are also keeping secrets about themselves." He reached over and touched Tommy's arm. "I was surprised to find out that you aren't the only one with a secret, Tommy."

Tommy felt his eyes watering and looked down from Dave's earnest gaze.

"Around Halloween, I was worried that you were fooling around with Mark, keeping him from his studies and trying to make him gay. I was also jealous of the time that you were spending with him." Dave lifted Tommy's chin and looked into the wet eyes. "It wasn't until you walked out of Kappa house with your paddle that I realized how much spirit you had brought into that house. It's gloomy over there now, and the brothers are concerned about you. They miss you; I miss you."

Tommy brushed Dave's hand away and looked down at his paper.

"I started talking privately to some of the brothers, beginning with Oscar and Jack," Dave said softly. "I learned that there are things going on in that house that I was unaware of. A lot of our brothers are very good at keeping secrets."

"I need to finish my paper, Dave." Tommy choked back a sob. He just wanted Dave to leave him alone; he wasn't ready to deal with the Mark issue.

"I'll leave you alone when I'm done talking to you," Dave insisted quietly. "I've done a lot of thinking, Tommy. When I first figured you might be gay, I thought you were going to wreck the spirit around the house. Getting to know you better, and you helping me out with my problem taught me otherwise. You were the spirit in the house this semester.

"Then when I found out that there are other gay brothers in the house, and that they care about you and respect you, I discovered that I felt the same way." Dave lifted Tommy's chin so he could look at him. "You're a great addition to our Kappa brotherhood. I don't want to lose you because Mark decided to go back to Sally."

Tears trickled down Tommy's face. "I'll be fine after I've had some time to pull myself together. I just can't deal with the fact that I fell in love with the wrong person."

Dave smiled at him. "You gave me some great advice on how to deal with Victoria. You should use that advice yourself, brother."

"It's not the same thing, Dave," Tommy said sadly. "He's straight. He decided that being with me was not right for him. I'm not going to try to talk him out of being with the person he wants to be with."

"Are you going to come back to the fraternity?"

"I'm going to spend Thanksgiving getting my head on straight. By the time we return, I should be able to deal with seeing him. Right now, it hurts too much."

"I understand. But I want you to know that if you need somebody to talk with, I'm there for you." Tommy's eyes filled with tears. "Oscar and Jack are also concerned about you, and both of them want to be there for you. All you have to do is call us, and we'll meet you anywhere you want." Dave stood up and turned to leave, then looked back at Tommy. "Good luck with your paper, brother."

As he watched Dave walk away, Tommy let the tears fall freely.

Brian had followed Tommy for over a week, trying to get his routine down. He smiled as he watched the young man walking out of the library at eleven o'clock. He was even happier when Tommy took the unlit shortcut between two administration buildings to get to his dorm. Tommy was right on schedule, keeping to his set pattern.

Tommy was thinking about his term paper and what Dave had told him, inattentive to anything around him. Having taken the path many times before, he moved by rote.

Brian caught up to him in the middle of the shortcut; he had Tommy right where he wanted. He grabbed Tommy's shoulders, spun him around, and pinned him against the wall of a building. "Hey, sweet boy." He smiled evilly. "Didn't anyone warn you about walking alone at night?"

Tommy glared at him. "What the hell do you want?"

Brian pushed his body firmly against Tommy. "I want you, sweet boy. You've been unhappy lately, and I've got just what you need to make you happy." He pressed his lips against Tommy's.

Tommy relaxed his body and shifted his hips so that one of his legs was between Brian's. Thinking that Tommy was giving in, Brian pressed his tongue inside Tommy's mouth. As Tommy bit down on Brian's tongue, he lifted his knee hard into Brian's crotch.

Brian let out a yelp of pain and grabbed his crotch. While he was bent over, Tommy slammed his fist into the side of Brian's face. Brian went down on the ground, curled in a fetal position. Tommy looked down at the failed attacker.

"I told you not to fuck with me, asshole," Tommy growled between his teeth.

A security guard patrolling near the library had heard the yell and came running over. He shone his light on Brian, lying on the ground, and then flashed it up at Tommy's face. "What's going on here?"

"This bastard tried to attack me."

"Do you want to press charges?" the guard asked, recognizing the fallen Gamma.

"No." Tommy looked down at Brian with disgust. "I just want him out of my sight." He looked at the guard. "May I go to my dorm now?"

The guard found it amusing that the smaller guy had gotten the better of the bigger basketball jock, but he kept his amusement to himself. "Just let me have your name and statement for my report," he pulled out his notepad, "then you can go. I'll take care of this guy."

Great fucking way to start the break, Tommy thought sarcastically as he waited for the guard to start asking questions.

11: IS THERE ANYTHING TO BE THANKFUL FOR?

"I spent four fucking hours driving all the way out here to be with you, and you've spent the past two hours dancing with your old boyfriends," Mark growled through clenched teeth, pissed about the turn their holiday plans had taken.

Sally had promised to come to his family's home near Hartford, Connecticut for Thanksgiving. He had wanted the time with her, and his family, to try and make sense of their odd relationship. True to form, she had reneged, calling him on Monday and inviting him to a get-together on Wednesday evening in East Hampton, New York. He argued for her to stick to the plans they had made, but she cajoled and persuaded until he agreed to attend the "small gathering" of her "closest friends".

There were over a hundred people at the party. He had spent over an hour trying to converse with her friends, but he was on the outside looking in. He finally got tired of being ignored or rebuffed and found a quiet spot on a second floor balcony. Half an hour later, Sally found him there, and Mark's resentment had boiled over in his outburst about their change in plans and her behavior.

Sally put her arm around his waist. She had been drinking with her friends since early that afternoon. "They aren't boyfriends, they're jus' friends. And I tol' you to dance with some girls, sweetie."

His hands tightened around the balcony railing as he turned away from her and stared out toward the water. "What the hell am I even doing here? You promised to come to my house for Thanksgiving."

"Tha's not until t'morrow, babe. We can drive there t'morrow."

"Dammit, Sally. We were supposed to be spending the break together." He felt the crystal warming against his chest; the crystal he'd gotten as an unexpected gift from Tommy.

On the Friday before the Thanksgiving break, Kyle had given him a small box during the Kappa meeting and told him it was from Tommy. He packed the box in his suitcase and waited until he was home in Connecticut, in his own bedroom, to open it. Then he left it in the box on top of his dresser. While dressing for his trip to East Hampton, he had seen the crystal and put it on, feeling a comforting warmth from within it.

"We are together, babe," she cooed, trying to calm him.

"No we're not. You're spending time with your *friends* while I walk around this mansion like a ghost. You haven't introduced me to anyone, so it's pretty easy for them to ignore me."

"Then come with me and I introdush you."

Mark glared down at her. "I don't want to meet them, Sally; I want to be with you. I thought that's what we were planning to do this week."

"I been busy with Mommy and Daddy. I had to spend some time with them if I wush goin' to your house for Than'sgivin'," she whined, pulling away from him. "Why ish everything 'bout you?"

"What?" Mark was incredulous.

"Why do we hafta do everythin' tha' you wan' to do? Wha' 'bout wha' I wanna do?" She turned her back on him and walked along the balcony.

"You can't be serious, Sally. We've always done what you want to do." He followed her. "I make plans for us to have a romantic time together, and you find a way to change them to suit your whims."

Sally turned and smiled at him. "Woman's per...pergo...oh fuck it, woman's choice."

"Are you saying that you're choosing not to be with me?"

"No, Mark. I'm with you." She leaned her head against his chest. "Babe, we have our whole future ahead of us."

Mark froze, hands at his sides, and stared out toward the water. "Excuse me! We haven't even discussed a future together, because every time I bring it up, you want to talk about shopping or going to parties, or some other petty crap."

Sally giggled. "It doesn' really matter. Wha's 'mportan' is you and I are t'gether, and we're looking t'ward our future. Sweetie, we don' hafta talk about serious things all the time." She closed her eyes and put her hands on his shoulders.

"No, but it would be nice to talk about serious things, such as our future together, at least once."

"All right, all right." She giggled, nuzzling against his chest. "Yes, I wan' to marry you and make a family t'gether. I'm sure we'll be able to have a won'erful home with the money from your 'heritance."

Confusion and anger swirled in Mark's head until he felt almost dizzy. He gripped her arms and roughly pushed her away from him. "What did you say?"

Sally playfully slapped at his chest. "You know, silly, the money tha' your gran'mother left you and the money you made from the sale of her house."

"Money..." He looked shrewdly at Sally. "Where did you hear about that?" he demanded.

"I went to Kappa house to find you, and I acciden'ally heard Oscar on the phone, I don' know, sometime around Halloween." Her body swaying, she grabbed hold of the balcony railing. "He was saying tha' you inherited your gran'mother's money and sol' her house. He said you were set for life." A drunken giggle escaped her.

Mark distinctly remembered when Tommy had sold his grandmother's house. Clearly, Oscar had been passing that information on to somebody, and Sally had misinterpreted the conversation. It was shortly after that when Sally came back into his life, pleading for another chance to explore their relationship. He had given her that chance, primarily because he was afraid of his feelings for Tommy.

"You conniving bitch!" he snarled, pacing along the balcony. "You played me. You didn't want me back; you wanted the financial security that you thought I could provide. I was a fool to believe that you really loved me. Jack and Oscar warned me about you, but I wouldn't listen. I wouldn't even listen to myself when I met somebody who really did love me. Damn it!"

Sally was dumbfounded by the sudden change of attitude. "I don' unnerstand. Why are you mad at me? We're going to get married and live a life of luxury."

Mark glared at her. "I am not going to marry you." He turned his back on her and stared out toward the ocean. "I was such a fucking fool. I threw away the best thing that ever happened to me because I was too damn scared to accept love." Mark turned and looked at Sally. "The worst thing about giving you another chance wasn't that I made a fool of myself. I've been doing that for over a year. The worst thing is that I hurt somebody the way you've been hurting me." He shook his head in self-loathing as he walked away.

Sally stumbled after him and grabbed his arm. "What about us, baby? We can make it work."

"Let go of me." He shoved her hand away. "There is no *us*. I don't intend to ever get suckered into having anything more to do with you, so you can go back downstairs and find one of your *friends* to help you get home. I'm sure there's more than one that would be happy to escort you."

In the doorway, Mark turned around and sneered. "By the way, sweetheart, neither of my grandmothers is dead. You made the wrong assumption about what you heard Oscar saying." Rushing down the stairs and brushing through the crowd of people, he mumbled, "Foolish, stupid, idiot."

As he drove home from Long Island, he had one hand on the steering wheel and the other around the topaz crystal. His stereo was blasting a Patsy Cline album, and he had the car windows open for fresh air to help him stay awake, since it was getting late. The buzz that he had gotten from the wine had dissipated during his tête-à-tête with Sally. He wasn't as mad at her as he was at himself for having allowed her to play him, again. More than that, he was angry with himself for being afraid to accept the fact that he was in love with Tommy, who had loved him unconditionally.

As he waited at a red light, he fingered the crystal, picturing Tommy. Tommy wouldn't have ditched him. Tommy didn't want anything from him, except his love. Mark shook his head and pounded his fists on the steering wheel. "And why did I break up with him? Because he's a guy and I can't be in love with a guy. It's wrong and sinful to be in love with another guy. Isn't it? Can I be in love with another guy?" He leaned back in his seat and blew out a deep breath of exasperation. "He was in love with me and it didn't bother him. I enjoyed being with him, enjoyed being able to be myself with him. And I'm such a jackass that I went back to Sally because his love scared me." Mark glanced to his left and noticed that the passengers in the car next to his were staring at him. Thankfully, they had their windows up and hadn't heard his ramblings. He had to smile as he realized he must have been waving his hands around as he talked to himself. He directed a civilized wave at the occupants of the other car as the light turned green and he drove off. "I still think about him; I miss being around him, running with him, sleeping with him. All I had to do was accept the fact that I love Tommy and that it's okay to love him. But I fucked that up, didn't I?"

He thought feverishly about whether there was any way to make things up to Tommy, whether he could even get Tommy to talk to him again. He turned up the volume on the car stereo, listening to Patsy Cline and drowning himself in the sorrow, pain, and misery in her songs.

It was almost midnight when Julia Young saw her son walk through the front door, softly singing "Sweet Dreams of You". At first she thought he was singing the Patsy Cline song because he was happy. Then she considered the words of the song and the look on his face, and realized that he was very unhappy.

"When you didn't arrive earlier, I wasn't expecting to see you until noon tomorrow," she said softly, walking up to him and brushing her hand through his hair. "Are you okay, honey?" she asked, assessing his mood and deciding whether she should press him further.

"No, Mom, I'm not okay," he replied quietly, hanging up his coat.

"Do you want to talk?"

"No. I just want to go to bed and forget about today." He kissed her on the cheek. "Sally won't be here for dinner, and I don't want to talk about it. Good night." He walked upstairs, humming the song, and leaving his mother staring after him.

San Francisco Blues

"So, what the hell have you done with my nephew?" Allen asked as he walked into the guest bedroom that Tommy used when he stayed with them. He shut the door behind him, walked over to the stereo, and turned off Dolly Parton's "I Will Always Love You" before sitting down in a chair next to Tommy's bed. "You've been here since Tuesday night, and you've been depressed the whole time. That's not like you, Tommy. I've tried to let you have your space, but now it's time for you to tell me what's going on."

"I'm sorry, Unc." He had been sitting on his bed, writing in his journal about his feelings for Mark and how he had felt when Mark chose Sally. "I've had a lot of things on my mind."

When Tommy left Timian on Saturday morning, he had gone to the cabin in the Poconos. He had spent the weekend attempting to pull himself together before attending a meeting with his attorney in Philadelphia on Monday. After he signed legal papers finalizing the sale of his grandmother's house and several other documents, he had attended a play and spent the night in Philly. On Tuesday afternoon, he had flown to San Francisco to spend Thanksgiving with his uncle and Morgan, Allen's partner.

"Who is he?" Allen asked, smiling at his nephew.

"What makes you think there's a 'he' involved?"

"You've been moping around since you got here. And you've been listening to Patsy Cline or replaying *that* song over and over again. I may be old, and I've lived with Morgan for over twenty-five years, but I do remember what it was like to be in love and have your heart broken." He tousled his nephew's hair. "Would you like to talk about it?"

Tommy wanted to say no, but he knew that his uncle wouldn't stop asking about it until he talked, and he knew that his uncle would be able to help. He pulled two pictures of Mark out of his journal and handed them to his uncle.

Allen looked carefully at both pictures. "I see. A very hot young man." He smiled at Tommy. "You and your football players. So, tell me what happened."

"Mark is a senior, the quarterback of the team," Tommy looked over at his uncle. "He's also my big brother in my fraternity."

"Oh, so this is *the* Mark, the guy you had the crush on. I'm guessing he's the reason you joined the fraternity."

"Partly," Tommy said shyly. "My friend Kyle was also pledging. Jack, one of the brothers, is a really cool guy, and he's gay. He and his boyfriend Ken are really discreet about their relationship. And I know that the friendships you make in a fraternity can last a lifetime."

"Plus, there was the added bonus of being closer to your crush," Allen teased with a laugh.

"I thought that I could be content just being his friend. I wasn't planning on having an affair or a relationship with him; he had a girlfriend. Theirs wasn't a happy relationship because she kept playing head games on him."

"So you thought that if he noticed you, then you'd have a chance to show him how much you cared about him," Allen finished.

"Yeah," Tommy admitted softly. "I felt this connection to Mark the first day of the semester, when he walked through my dorm. He lit up the lobby and my heart.

When Jack introduced us at lunch one day, I felt this electric surge through our hands. After I accepted the invitation to join Kappa, he and I became friends. Sometimes he would join me on my morning run; we would have meals together or with some of the other brothers; or just talk to each other as we walked through campus to our classes. We enjoyed each other's company during the pledge period, and then...he asked me to spend the night with him."

"Please tell me that you didn't use any of your grandmother's spells."

Tommy lowered his head to keep his uncle from looking into his eyes.

"Tommy, Tommy, Tommy." Allen got up from the chair and sat down next to Tommy on the bed. He put an arm around Tommy's shoulder and pulled his nephew close. "I'm certainly not going to tell you that magic doesn't really work, because when I was younger I saw your grandmother do many amazing things. But that stuff can backfire on you if it isn't done properly and if you're not careful." He lifted Tommy's chin and looked into his eyes. "What did you do?"

"Mark and I were getting along, and all I really did was empower the paddle that I had to make for the initiation." He looked up at his uncle.

"I really wish your grandmother hadn't left that trunk for you. You're too young to be messing around with that stuff." He pulled Tommy closer and hugged him. "So, tell me what happened after you did all of that."

"Well, I made it through the initiation, and that weekend, Mark asked me to stay with him." Tommy blushed at the remembrance. "We had a really great time that weekend, and for a few weeks afterward. Then the girlfriend came back into his life."

Allen sighed. "Why couldn't you find a nice gay boy to fall in love with?"

"I didn't want to draw any attention to myself and have others harass and tease me like what happened in high school." Tommy thought for a moment. "There is one gay guy that's after me, but only as a conquest. Besides, he's a self-centered, egotistical jerk."

"What happened after the girlfriend returned?"

"About a week after Halloween, I sensed there was a distance developing between me and Mark. He was busy with football and his classes, and I was busy with my classes and typing papers for some of the brothers. I tried not to let the lack of time we were spending together bother me until I saw him with her a couple of times." He looked at his uncle sadly. "I tried to pull my energy together so that when he told me about her I would be able to handle it maturely, and not act like some spoiled brat who wasn't getting his way. I didn't cause a scene, but I'm not sure I handled it all that well. I just stopped talking and shut everybody out."

He gave Tommy a comforting hug. "It's okay, kid. Everyone, gay or straight, goes through falling in love with the wrong person at least once in his or her life. It's how you handle it and what you learn from it that makes you stronger." He looked into his nephew's watery eyes. "What's going on in your head?"

Tommy looked up at the ceiling. "I want to hate him. I want to despise him. I want to blame him, but I can't." A tear tracked down his cheek as he glanced at his uncle. "I can't stop thinking about him. He was a friend, first, and we had books and music in common. I miss running with him in the mornings. And I miss sleeping next to him," he sobbed. "He has a warm, hairy chest that I love laying my head on. His hands are so beautiful, rough and calloused from playing football, with long fingers. And those damned blue eyes that sparkle when he smiles. It wasn't his fault that I fell in love with him. I should have known better. You told me to stay away from jocks."

Allen held him tightly and rocked him. "First loves are always the hardest to get over." He brushed his hand through Tommy's hair. "I still remember my first love. After all these years, I can still remember how much it hurt when it ended. But it doesn't hurt as much when I think about it now. It will get easier for you as time passes."

"I hope so," Tommy sobbed.

Allen moved back and looked into Tommy's eyes. "If he broke your heart, why did you name him on your legal papers? And why didn't you tell me about this before getting my consent for your lawyer?"

"I didn't tell you because you wouldn't have given me your consent," Tommy declared, wiping his eyes.

"No, I wouldn't have," Allen agreed. "So why did you name him?"

"Because I respect him," Tommy said.

"He broke your heart and you respect him!" Allen exclaimed.

Tommy looked into his uncle's eyes. "I didn't grow up with a family, Unc. I had Nanny, Uncle Morgan, and you. As much as I love all three of you, it's not like having a brother to hang out with. Mark became that brother for me." He slumped against the headboard of the bed. "Besides, I'm the one that said that we'd go as far as he wanted to go with this relationship. I just didn't think that...I hoped that he wouldn't change his mind."

"All right. But I think you're setting yourself up to be hurt again."

"No, I'm not," Tommy declared. "I've learned my lesson about straight boys."

"How do you plan on handling your fraternity when you return to school? You're going to have to participate with the others, and that means you're going to have to see Mark."

"I know." Tommy wiped his eyes. "I'll deal with all of that when I get back to school. Right now, I just want to be miserable."

"Well, you're doing a damn good job of that." Allen laughed. "I hope you don't plan on staying in this mood the entire time you're here with us. Morgan has worked hard planning this Thanksgiving dinner party."

"I'll be okay. I promise."

"Yeah, right." Allen snorted, tousled his hair and quietly left the room.

A Mother's Love and Understanding

"Come in," Julia called out in response to the knock on the door of her home office. She turned away from the computer screen as her son entered. Despite her psychotherapy schedule, she always made time for her son and daughter. Mark had been sullen and withdrawn since he'd arrived home late Wednesday night. He had come out of his room only to have Thanksgiving dinner with the family. She had known it was only a matter of time before he would come to talk with her.

"Do you have time to talk, Mom?" he asked, as he sat down in the big red leather chair near her desk.

"I always have time for you, sweetheart." She moved from behind her desk to sit in the chair next to her son. She gave him a kiss on the cheek, noting the redness of his eyes and sadness on his handsome features. "What's on your mind?" she asked, getting comfortable.

"I broke up with Sally," he said, looking into her eyes.

Julia was well aware of Mark's on-again, off-again relationship with Sally. "How do you feel about that?"

"Please don't play therapist with me, Mom."

"I'm sorry, Mark. It's a habit that's very hard to break, even with my own children." She smiled. "What happened this time?"

"Sally promised me weeks ago that we would spend Thanksgiving break with my family. Then she changed our plans and invited me to that party in the Hamptons. She spent most of her time dancing with a bunch of guys who I believe have been more than just friends." He glanced over at her. "But that wasn't the main reason that I felt I had to end our relationship. This time, there's no chance we'll ever get together again."

"I see," Julia responded softly. She wanted her son to be happy, and he had initially seemed to be that way after meeting Sally. Then the emotional rollercoaster ride began, with Sally breaking off their relationship every few months.

"This time it really is over. For good. She caused me a great deal of pain this time, Mom, and not just by using me to promote her own personal agenda. This time I hurt somebody in order to get back together with her." He reached up and touched his shirt over his chest.

"You've never before mentioned hurting anyone when you and Miss Brown reunited," Julia replied, watching his hand move up to his heart.

"That's because I'd never met anyone that I wanted to be with when I was separated from Sally," he replied, frowning. "I've been dealing with her crap for over a year. When she was hurting just me, it didn't really bother me; I hardly noticed each time. You and a few of my fraternity brothers were the only ones who seemed to be pissed off by my not acknowledging what she was doing to me."

"Some of us care more about you than we do about Miss Brown," Julia replied with a smile. "I hate to tell you this, dear, but you *were* upset and depressed whenever she broke up with you. You were bothered, even if you say you didn't notice the hurt. Then you would become elated whenever you got back together, but I didn't get the sense that you were truly happy when you were with her. I tried not to interfere with your personal business, but I was worried about you, sweetheart."

"I know, Mom." He looked away from his mother, his hand still on his shirt. "Something happened to me in October that changed my perspective about Sally, and about love."

"You seemed truly happy in October." Julia chuckled softly and saw Mark smile at her. "I could hear it in your voice whenever I talked with you on the phone. I don't recall you sounding that way when you were with Miss Brown earlier this year."

Mark stood and walked over to the window that looked out over the back yard. Snow was falling gently. "I met somebody that didn't want anything from me except to be with me," he started. "I wasn't expected to make any changes in who I was or what I wanted for my life. I was only expected to be myself."

Julia noted that Mark didn't say he had met a new girl, but rather that he had met *somebody*. The new person might be the someone that Mark had talked about a lot during his fraternity's pledge period. Even as her mind began putting pieces of the puzzle together, she was interested in knowing how this person had affected her son. Julia went over and stood next to him, placing her hand over his heart and feeling the crystal beneath it. "What does your heart tell you, sweetie?" she asked softly.

Mark put his large hand over his mother's and looked down into her eyes. "It tells me that I was an idiot for letting go of the one person who finally made me feel happy about being me. It tells me that I was a fool for getting back together with

Sally. It tells me—"

Julia placed her fingers against his lips. "You are neither a fool nor an idiot, Mark."

"Oh, yes I am, Mother. I met somebody special and was fool enough to give that up. I was scared about the feelings I was having and how they would affect my future. When Sally wanted me back in her life, I jumped at the chance to escape from a situation that I was afraid to commit to. Then I found out that the only reason Sally wanted me back had nothing to do with loving me." He turned and looked out at the falling snow, a gentle cascade. "Sally overheard Oscar telling somebody about Tommy's inheritance, and she assumed that he was talking about me. I thought she really cared about me, but she only cared about the money that she thought I was inheriting."

Mark closed his eyes and rested his head against the cool window pane. "I hurt him so badly, Mom. I could see the pain in his eyes when I told him that I was going to get back together with Sally. I know I broke his heart."

She knew that Tommy was Mark's little brother. She hadn't realized that Tommy had meant more to Mark than that. "Did he cause a scene, make any threats?" she asked quietly, acutely aware of the change in her son when he mentioned Tommy.

"No, but I wish he had." Mark wiped his eyes and looked over at her. "Instead, he wished me the best, and then quietly walked away, taking a piece of my heart with him. I can't forget the look of hurt in his eyes or the emptiness I felt as he walked away."

Julia patted the crystal beneath his shirt. "I think he may have given you back a piece of your heart." She wiped away the dampness on his cheek. "Tell me more about this young man, starting with the crystal."

Mark looked at her in surprise. "How did you know about that?"

Julia smiled and ran her hand along his cheek. "I saw the open box on your dresser when I went into your room on Monday to put away your clean clothes. And I'm not entirely without knowledge about crystals and their healing ways."

Mark returned her smile. "Tommy wears a clear crystal around his neck that he got from his grandmother. He didn't really tell me anything about it, only that it's comforting to him. This one has been pretty comforting to me." He turned his head and stared out the window. "The first time I met Tommy, I felt this energy pass between us. I've never felt anything like that before. He has the most amazing attitude about life of anyone I've ever known. He makes people feel good just by being around them. I think all of the brothers in the house love spending time with him — so much so, that..." Mark stopped in mid-sentence and stared at his mother. "Fuck. *That* is why the brothers have been treating me like a pariah."

"What do you mean?"

"The other brothers don't know what happened between me and Tommy, but they've apparently been holding me responsible for Tommy staying away from the house and avoiding everybody, and rightfully so."

Julia smiled at Mark. "Aren't revelations wonderful? They can provide us with a whole new perspective on our behavior, and sometimes give us the answers to fix problems."

"I don't know how I'm going to be able to fix this particular problem, but at least I understand why the brothers have been mad at me."

"That's a start, sweetie. Now, let's get back to Tommy."

"His life has been difficult," he said, looking over at his mother. "He has alcoholic parents, and his father fractured his jaw when he was only six. His grandmother took him in and raised him after that. She passed away in June and left everything to Tommy." He smiled briefly. "His parents were not too happy to discover that Tommy's grandmother had a fortune tucked away in the bank and in real estate."

Julia smiled at her son. "It sounds like he deserved to inherit his grandmother's assets."

"Her house was sold around the end of October. That's when everything seemed to go crazy on me. Sally wormed her way back into my life, and I pushed Tommy out."

"Did Tommy pressure you into a relationship?" Julia asked quietly.

"No. He never gave me any reason to believe that he was gay." He looked away shyly. "I chose Tommy to be my little brother. During the pledge period, my feelings for him started changing. By the time we held initiation, I wanted to know what it would be like to hold him in my arms. I made the first move." He looked over at her, to see how she would react.

"How did he respond?"

"Surprisingly, he offered me an out."

Julia raised an eyebrow. "How?"

"He told me that he didn't intend to make me choose between being with women or him. He said it was a choice that I would have to make for myself."

"That's a rather mature attitude for a college freshman," she said, seeing the sad look in his eyes. "So, what happened after Miss Brown weaseled her way back into your life?"

Mark took a deep breath and slowly let it out. "I told him last Monday night, a week ago, that I was going to give Sally another chance." He looked over at his mother. "Whenever I saw him on campus after that night, the look that I received from him made me shiver."

Julia put an arm around her son's waist. "I can't really blame him. I'd have slapped you silly."

"Mom!" Mark frowned. "What am I going to do? He won't talk to me."

"Have you tried to talk to him?"

"No," he replied forlornly.

"Then you really don't know whether he'll talk to you or not." She looked at him intently. "What do you want, Mark?"

"I want him back in my life. I miss our morning runs, and talking with him as we walk through campus or do classwork together. And I miss holding him close to me as I fall asleep at night."

Julia reached over and brushed her hand through his hair. "You broke up with him, so now you're going to have to try and talk to him."

"Brad told me the same thing when I called him yesterday." He frowned, thinking about what his childhood best friend had told him. "That's even scarier than when I broke up with him."

"I have a feeling that Tommy might be ready to talk with you, sweetie." She patted the crystal.

"Do you really think he'll talk to me?" he asked.

"I didn't say that." She gave him an encouraging smile. "I said that he *might* be ready to talk with you. But you're going to have to make the first move because you're the one who ended things."

"What if he doesn't want to talk to me?"

"Then you're going to have to accept it. But you're never going to know unless you take the first step." She gave him a little kiss on the cheek and patted the crystal. "I have a feeling that somebody still cares about you."

Mark looked at her, confusion plain on his face. "Why aren't you shocked, surprised, or even upset that your son is in love with another guy?"

"Well, first and foremost, it's because I love you and will accept you the way you are. As long as you're happy, then I'm going to be happy for you." She smiled at him. "I have friends, colleagues, and clients who are gay. They are all wonderful people, with hearts of gold and problems with life, just like the rest of us. All of them have told me that the hardest thing they had ever done in their lives was to come out as gay. The trauma, anxiety, stress, and mostly confusion, nearly drove them all *crazy*." Julia chuckled. "They agree that once they accepted the fact that they were gay, life became somewhat easier for them. They said the next obstacle was finding that special someone to share their life with."

"I guess I did it backwards," Mark said with a wry grin.

Julia held his face in both of her hands, lowered it to within her reach, and gave him a kiss on the nose. "That's my boy. Why do it the easy way, if there's a hard way to do something?"

"What do I say to Tommy?"

"I suggest you find a private place to speak with him, then be honest with him. Tell him what you feel in your heart." She patted his shoulder. "Just make sure that you are being honest with yourself before you talk with him. Make sure this really is something that you want. Don't hurt him again."

Mark placed a kiss on her cheek. "Now, what do we do about Dad?"

"We don't do anything, sweetheart." She smiled and returned to her desk. "We just go on with our lives and don't say a thing until it's absolutely necessary."

"But he's going to ask about Sally."

"If he asks about Miss Brown, just tell him that you're off-again and leave it alone." Julia laughed. "When he's on these business trips, the only thing he thinks about is business."

"You don't think I should say anything to him?"

"No, dear. You keep that handsome mouth of yours shut. Okay?" She reached up and squeezed his cheeks.

"But what about letting him know about Tommy?"

"You just allow Tommy to become a part of our lives a little at a time. He's your friend and your fraternity little brother." She looked at him with stern resolve. "That's all your father really needs to know right now."

He smiled at her. "I never knew you were so devious, Mother."

"What your father doesn't know won't hurt him." She chuckled. "In time he'll find out, or you can tell him when you're ready. For now, you need this time for yourself. You don't need your father breathing down your neck about being a sinner and an abomination."

"Good point. It would be easier starting a *sinful*," he winked at her, "relationship without having Dad hounding me about it. Thanks, Mom."

"Anytime, sweetheart." She blew him a kiss as he turned to leave.

12: RETURN TO TIMIAN

It was a cold and snowy Sunday as students returned to Timian to settle in and prepare for the last three weeks of the semester. Many of the Kappa brothers were at the house, noisily discussing their Thanksgiving. Loud music came from all three floors. Mark was putting his clothes away and listening to Patsy Cline when he heard a knock on his open door.

"Welcome back, Mark." Dave walked into the room, shut the door behind him and sat down on the desk chair. "How was your Thanksgiving?"

"I had a miserable holiday, Dave. Thank you," Mark shot back.

"Want to talk about it, big guy?"

"Not really, Dave. It's personal, and I don't think you'd understand."

"Hm." Dave picked up a pen from Mark's desk and began twiddling it in his fingers. "We've been friends for a long time, and we've always been able to discuss personal things."

"This is different."

"Does it have something to do with dumping Tommy? Or is it getting dumped by Sally again?" He smiled as Mark stared incredulously. "I saw Tommy before the break. He was working on a term paper in the library and blaming himself for what happened between the two of you. Was it his fault? I remember earlier this month I insinuated that there was something going on between you. Neither of you admitted or denied it."

Mark plopped onto his bed and let out a deep breath. "All right, Dave, there was something going on between me and Tommy. After your intervention, I spent more time with my little brother. The night of initiation, after we inspected the tattoos and paddles, I invited Tommy to spend the night with me. Then I asked him to spend the next night with me. I had been falling in love with Tommy during the pledge period, and the more time we spent together, the deeper I fell." Mark frowned. "It scared the hell out of me to realize that I was in love with a man, to think that I might be gay. So, when Sally asked me to give her another chance, I jumped at the opportunity to prove to myself that I was straight. I told Tommy before the break that I was back with Sally."

Dave sat quietly, absorbing Mark's admissions. "You dumped Tommy for Sally?" Dave said accusingly, surprised that he wasn't shocked by Mark's confession that he was gay. "I had a feeling that it involved a love relationship, but I thought it was because he was in love with you, and you brushed him off."

Mark met Dave's eyes. "You're not surprised that I fell in love with Tommy?"

"That doesn't really bother me. Several of our brothers came to me before the break, asking what happened or speculating about what happened. I've learned that more than a few of our brothers have secrets, including Oscar and Jack. Some were happy that you and Tommy were *friends*, and a couple of them were actually jealous that *you* were with Tommy. But all the brothers that talked to me let me know that they care a great deal about Tommy, and so do I." Dave glanced at him. "How could you dump somebody like Tommy for that bitch?"

Mark started laughing, partly in relief. "Have all my brothers gone mad? I just outed myself, and you and some of the others don't care. Is it supposed to be this easy?"

"Probably not. But this is about you and Tommy, two of the nicest, most respected guys in the fraternity. Both of you have a bunch of positives going for you," Dave said, then added with a smirk, "Of course, you have the big negative — Miss Brown."

"Go to hell." Mark smiled sadly at his brother. "I don't know how to fix things with Tommy. While I might be able to accept him not wanting to be involved with me, I can't accept him not being my friend and little brother."

"Talk to him," Dave said. "He and Jack advised me to talk with Victoria and let her know how much she meant to me. So I talked with her about our relationship and how much I love her. We started dating again and had a great Thanksgiving together. We were able to get rid of a lot of baggage that we had both been holding on to."

"My mother and my best friend told me to do the same thing," Mark said. "I just don't know if Tommy will even talk to me."

"I would suggest talking to him in person and not over the phone," Dave added. "I'd hang up on your sorry ass."

"Thanks a lot. Good thing I'm not trying to patch things up with you, then."

"Maybe you'd like to talk with Oscar and Jack about this. They probably know more about the situation than I do."

"They aren't talking to me."

Dave smiled as he stood up to leave. "As fraternity prez, I can tell them what to do, and they'll do it. It's good to be in a position of power."

"Don't force them to do something they don't want to do."

"Force won't be used, big guy. Threats will be used." Dave laughed maniacally. "I'll be around if you want to talk," he said, shutting the door as he left.

Most of the Gamma brothers returned to their fraternity house Saturday afternoon, wanting to get in a full weekend of partying before classes started. By Sunday night, there was a party going full force.

"I really want a piece of that boy's pretty little ass," Brian said to Andy as he set up another line of speed.

"Who?" Andy lay back and let the drug flow through his system.

"That pretty boy, Tommy."

"You're still obsessed with that Kappa boy?" Andy laughed. "Get over him, dude, he isn't interested."

"Not important if he is or isn't." He thought back to before the Thanksgiving break, when he'd almost had Tommy. Tommy was stronger than he looked, and that was the only reason the freshman had gotten the better of him. He wouldn't make that mistake again. "I'm going downstairs to get more beer. Want anything?" Brian asked, shaking a half bottle of beer in his hand.

"Get a six pack. I have enough pot and snort for us." Andy finished rolling another joint and tossed it to Brian, then started making one for himself.

"Hey, hey, hey, Ken doll." Brian was smoking a joint and carrying a bottle of beer as he stopped in Ken's doorway on his way to the stairs.

"Brian, you look like you've run into a truck."

"Partyin', dude." Brian slumped down on the floor and leaned against the doorframe. "Andy and I have some really good speed. Want to share a little bit with us?" He looked up at Ken with a leer.

"No thanks. I'm not into the drug scene, but you just keep on enjoying yourself."

Brian pushed himself up from the floor and ogled Ken. "Why haven't you and I ever hit the sheets, Ken doll? I could show you a really good time." He grabbed at his crotch. "I'd love to feel that hot body of yours squirming under me, find out if you're a *real* tight end."

"You'd probably be more than my heart could handle, Brian," he said with a placating smile. "I'm going out to dinner. Why don't you think about grabbing something to eat and getting some sleep?"

"I've got to find the right thing to eat. But first, I'm gonna get me a fine piece of pretty boy ass." He turned around and winked at Ken. "Then I'll think about getting some sleep."

Late Sunday Afternoon at Kappa House

"So I left her at the party and drove back home." Mark finished explaining to Jack and Oscar what had happened between him and Sally. "I don't know what to do about this, guys. I've never been in this position before. I've never looked into somebody's eyes and felt that kind of coldness, and I've never felt this empty. What the hell am I supposed to do to make it up to Tommy?"

"*Pendejo*. You got what you deserved," Oscar replied.

Jack shook his head, unsure of the Spanish word's meaning, but assumed it wasn't good. "Please, Oscar. He needs our help. We need to be a little compassionate."

"*Pendejo*." Oscar glared over at Mark. "You had a fucking good thing with Tommy. He's a good kid, cute as a button, worked his ass off to become a brother, and is as discreet as Jack about his lifestyle. He wasn't going to jerk you around like that *puta* did."

Mark sat quietly and took it. There was nothing that he could say in his defense; Oscar was right. He had never realized that Oscar hated Sally so much. He couldn't understand why he had been the last one to see what she was.

"Look, Mark," Jack said calmly, glaring over at Oscar and daring him to interrupt, "you really only have two choices in this matter. You can wait for Tommy to get over the hurt, or you can go over to him and try to get him to listen to you now. There are other options, such as doing nothing and forgetting all about Tommy."

"What do I say to him after what happened?"

"You say 'I'm a scum-sucking fuckwad. I deserve to be kicked in the balls'," Oscar growled. "*Pendejo*."

Jack shook his head in amusement. "Oscar, you're not helping."

"I'm playing bad cop to your good cop." Oscar looked over at Jack with a slight grin. "I'll say what really should be said, and you can make it sound nice."

"Oscar," Mark said softly, "I've been kicking myself in the ass ever since Thanksgiving. There's nothing you can say that's going to make me feel any worse than I already do."

"Keep kicking yourself," Oscar advised. "If a guy, or gal, like Tommy ever came along and wanted me, my playboy days would be over. I wouldn't have been stupid enough to let something that good get away from me, especially not for a conniving soul-sucker like Sally."

Jack tried to soften the big man. "You're being awfully hard on him, Oscar."

"Somebody has to be. He wouldn't listen to us when we tried to warn him about that two-faced shrew. He just let her keep playing him. Then he finds somebody who is crazy in love with him, God only knows why, and he goes and plays Tommy like she played him." Oscar paused only to take a breath. "If I were Tommy, I'd tell him to go fuck himself."

Mark glanced over at Oscar and started chuckling. "I could do that if I wanted to."

"*Pendejo*," Oscar snarled.

"Oscar, I'm really glad you're not Tommy. I might stand a chance with the real Tommy."

Oscar shrugged. "Even if that boy is smart enough not to take your sorry ass back, you make sure that you get him to come back and be a part of this fraternity. I need him in this house to help clear out the bad energy that came in after he walked out of here."

"I thought this kind of stuff only happened in Danielle Steele or Barbara Cartland novels," Mark said, shaking his head.

"Where do you think they get their ideas from?" Oscar retorted. "Real life is much more dramatic than most people realize. You don't get stories like that without somebody having experienced those events at some point in time."

Jack stood up and put his fist in front of his mouth, as if holding a microphone. In a deep voice, he began mimicking a sound voice-over. "Our masculine stud hero, torn between two lovers. One, a beautiful, yet devious woman who would use him for her own financial gain. The other, a handsome young man who would lead him down into the lush gardens of desire, or fiery depths of hell, depending upon your religious leanings. Only one truly loves our hero, as the other plots for his entrapment. Will our hero be trapped by the black widow? Or will he fall in love with the only man who can save him from the spider's web?" Jack burst out laughing.

"You are truly twisted, Jack," Oscar said with a grimace.

"How do I get Tommy to talk to me again?"

Relenting at last, Oscar smiled. "Beg. Plead. Stalk."

"Does anyone know if he's back?" Mark asked.

"I saw Kyle earlier, and he said that Tommy was supposed to come back this evening," Jack supplied. "Ken and I are going out to dinner tonight. We could come over afterward to talk with you."

"I sure could use a pep talk before I try to talk with Tommy," Mark said. "Thanks."

Sunday Evening In Heinz Hall

"Ford Tommy, I know you're in there," Kyle called out as he knocked on Tommy's door Sunday evening. "I'm going to keep on knocking until you let me in." True to his word, he started knocking again.

Before leaving his uncle's house, Tommy had thought that he was prepared to deal with the Mark situation. But once he returned to campus, he started feeling anxious and lost the confidence he had mustered over the holidays. He finally got out of his chair and went over to open the door. "What do you want?" he asked, blocking the doorway with his arm to keep Kyle from entering.

Kyle grabbed Tommy's forearm and pushed his way through the doorway. He shut the door, then pulled Tommy over to the mirror on the wall between the two closet units. "Who the hell is this?" Kyle asked as he stared into the mirror. "This is not my buddy. My buddy was happy and had a positive attitude, even as we went through hell pledging Kappa. I loved hanging out with my buddy." He stared into the reflection of Tommy's eyes in the mirror. "I miss my buddy, and I want him back."

Tommy lowered his head and moved away from the mirror. He sat down in the middle of his bed, drawing his legs up into lotus position. Kyle sat down on the desk chair. "I'm sorry, Kyle, I'm just dealing with a few things and don't feel like being bothered with keeping up appearances."

"Well, you're going to be bothered by me, because I care too much about you to let you continue doing this to yourself. I've never become friends with somebody as quickly as I did with you. Your attitude and personality the first day of the semester charmed the hell out of me. I knew right away that you were the kind of guy that I could hang around with and have a good time. I wasn't wrong about you, Ford Tommy." He smiled and was pleased to see a small return smile on Tommy's face.

"I'm sorry, it's just a bunch of personal stuff."

"About Mark," Kyle interrupted. He grinned as Tommy stared at him in surprise. "The adage about blonds being more fun is true, but the adage about blonds being dumb is not. Furthermore, I'm not blind, either." Kyle smiled brightly.

"I really don't want to talk about that."

"I wasn't asking you if you wanted to talk about it. I'm going to talk to you, and you're going to listen to me," Kyle asserted. "First of all, I don't care that you're gay. You and Jack are both discreet, and neither of you try to push yourselves on other guys. I've never felt uncomfortable around either of you. As a matter of fact, I enjoy being around you two guys more than some of our straight brothers, especially when they get drunk."

"Thank you," Tommy said softly.

"Don't thank me yet. I'm not done with you. I've got a lot more to say, buddy." He laughed at the curious look on Tommy's face. "Secondly, only you and Mark know the truth. I believe there are two other brothers who may know what was going on before Thanksgiving. And there were a few brothers who thought that you might have come on to Mark and that's what caused the problem. Oscar and Jack assured everyone that was not the case. Then, when Oscar and Jack started avoiding Mark, it became apparent that Mark had caused the problem." Kyle smiled over at Tommy. "It's kind of funny when you think about it: a bunch of jocks prefer having their new brother back in the house over some chick. That's the effect that you had on these guys, and how much they like you. You have no idea of how much the brothers dislike Sally, especially after watching her strut around with Mark before the break."

Tommy was starting to feel a little better as Kyle talked. Knowing that the Kappa brothers liked him more than Sally helped a lot. He still couldn't conceive getting to a point where he would be able to see Mark and Sally together and not feel hurt.

Tommy tilted his head and looked at Kyle. "What happened wasn't Mark's fault; it was my fault. I made the mistake of falling in love with a jock and believing that any problems would sort themselves out. For a little while, he was interested." Tommy chuckled at his own gullibility. "Then Sally set her claws into him again. I have a feeling that Mark was scared about changing lifestyles, and that's why he decided to go back to her. I can't blame him for that."

"I can," Kyle interjected. "If I had somebody who cared about me as much as you care about him, I'd switch teams." Kyle nodded earnestly. "You would be worth it."

"Shut up, Welby Kyle." Tommy blushed and lowered his head. "You're full of shit."

"Now that sounds a little more like my pledge brother." Kyle leaned over and tousled Tommy's hair. "So, are you coming to the meeting tomorrow?"

"I don't know yet. I'm embarrassed about what happened, and I'm not sure I'm ready to see Mark just yet. It still hurts."

"Kappa house hasn't been the same since before Thanksgiving. It's really weird and hard to explain, but Oscar has tried to help me understand it. If you won't come to the meeting, would you at least call Oscar or Jack?" Kyle looked into Tommy's eyes. "They are both concerned about you and want to talk to you, if you'll let them." Kyle pulled a piece of paper out of his pants pocket. "They gave me their cell phone numbers so that you don't have to call the house."

Tommy accepted the piece of paper. "Thanks. I'll give them a call. I do miss talking with them."

"Good." Kyle smiled at Tommy. "I don't ever want to see that other Tommy again."

"Neither do I." Tommy stood up and hugged Kyle. "Thank you, Kyle, for being a persistent pain in the ass and making me listen to you."

Kyle returned the hug. "You're welcome." He walked over to the door and turned around to face Tommy. "By the way, I meant what I said earlier. I'd have switched teams for you, Ford Tommy." He winked at Tommy as he left the room.

Sunday Night At Kappa House

"Come in," Mark called out from his desk. He went over to greet Jack and Ken as they entered his room.

"Sorry we're late." Jack grabbed one of the extra chairs by the desk and sat down. "I filled Ken in on your problem over dinner."

Ken smiled as he shook Mark's hand. "It's an honor to be invited into the upper echelon of Kappa house."

Mark laughed. "It's nothing special. Thanks for coming over." Mark shut the door.

"You're a friend in need, buddy. I couldn't say no when Jack asked me to talk with you," Ken said sincerely.

"I assume that Jack told you long before tonight what had happened. Please sit down and let me try to figure out where I should begin."

"Jack and I have few secrets from one another, but we don't run our mouths off to others." Ken sat down on the desk chair. "I understand that Oscar has been rather tough on you about what happened."

"Not any tougher than I've been on myself," Mark said bitterly as he sat down on his bed.

"First of all, you need to stop kicking yourself for what happened," Ken started. "I'm sure it was scary and shocking to realize that you were falling in love with a guy."

"To say the least."

"A lot of us gay guys fight this battle when we're teenagers. Some will fight it until the day they die because they believe what the Religious Right and Moral Majority tell them: being gay is a sin; loving another man is an abomination. Poppycock!" Ken was pleased to see Mark smile. "There are no guidelines that life hands out to tell us how we are supposed to fall in love with the right person. It happens between two people without rhyme or reason. Falling in love is magical. You either accept it, or you don't. Accepting it is a whole lot easier than fighting it."

"I fought it in junior high," Jack continued. "It was frustrating. I gained nothing by pretending to like girls. So I stopped pretending and just accepted things as they were. I met a couple of guys who were just like me, quiet and athletic. We had each other for support and...other things." He smiled self-consciously. "We even met some girls who liked other girls and dated them. Nobody was the wiser that, after dances, the boys paired off and the girls paired off. It was very convenient for all of us."

"How are you able to play football with all the guys around, Ken?" Mark asked.

"Being gay is just one part of who I am; it's not the only thing I am. I've always been athletic and enjoyed playing sports. I'm not sexually interested in the guys that I'm on a team with, unless we meet outside the sport and things go in that direction." He looked squarely at Mark. "It's like seeing you in the shower room and thinking about how hot you look," he teased. "I would never consider making a move on one of my teammates in the locker room or showers. But if I met you at a bar or a club, then maybe I'd consider asking you home."

"Don't lie, Ken," Jack interrupted. "If we were both single and on the prowl, neither one of us would say no to the nightstick." He and Ken burst out laughing.

Mark blushed a deep crimson. "Guys, I'm honored that you think so highly of my appendage, but you're not here to discuss that. I know how to work it." He drew them back on subject. "My problem is being gay and Tommy."

"Sorry, buddy," Ken said. "You're a distracting man."

"For some reason, we're both feeling very comfortable with you. Before this semester, neither one of us would have been this way around you," Jack said.

"Why not?"

"We're discreet with our talk and our actions, especially around straight guys." Ken looked over at Jack. "Although, if I recall correctly, we weren't so discreet the first time you introduced me to Tommy. We were rather playful around him."

Jack smiled over at Ken. "That's because Tommy makes everyone feel comfortable. You don't feel as if you have to hide anything from him."

"Good point." Ken looked over at Mark. "That's why we wouldn't have felt this comfortable around you."

"But Jack and I have always gotten along."

"Yes, but as brothers and friends. I've never really discussed my being gay with you, except during that run when we talked about Tommy," Jack commented.

"What are you worried about, Mark?" Ken asked. "Are you worried that once you admit you love another man, everyone in the school is going to know about it? Are you worried that once you admit you're gay, you'll start coming on to every male on campus? Are you worried that if you accept the fact that you're gay, you'll want to start dressing in drag?"

Mark pondered all the questions that Ken threw his way. "No, I'm not worried about any of that. I don't think anyone knew that Tommy and I were involved with one another after his initiation. If they did," Mark looked over at Jack, "they certainly didn't say anything about it."

Jack smiled and nodded. "Just as you never mentioned that you were aware that Ken and I were more than just friends."

"I'm also not worried about other men on campus, because there's only one that I am interested in being with," Mark added. "As for drag," he smiled, "I'm not sure I have the legs for a slit skirt, and I highly doubt that I could walk in stilettos."

Ken and Jack burst out laughing. "But you do have the legs for one of those leather Roman warrior skirts," Ken said.

"Oooh, and the gold-plated chest piece," Jack added.

Mark was laughing, but stopped himself. "Guys, you're not helping here."

"On the contrary..." Ken winked. "Look inside yourself and see how much fun you're having right now. And then think about when you were spending time with Tommy. Are you hiding anything from yourself right now? Did you hide anything from yourself when you and Tommy were together?"

All the joy seemed to go out of Mark as he thought seriously about Ken's questions. "No. I wasn't hiding anything from myself when I was with Tommy. I was enjoying every minute I spent with him, whether we were running, or talking at dinner, or just lying together. I never felt freer than when I was with Tommy."

"So what happened? What made you want to not be that happy person?" Ken asked.

"I've seen how some of the gay guys on campus are treated by *straight* guys. They stay in little cliques and are laughed at and looked down upon by the *normal* students. Plus there was Howard, the wrestler who tried to attack Tommy in the shower room. I mean, he just assumed Tommy was gay, when nobody else even knew at that time," Mark responded. "So, it was the fear of being an outcast, being harassed, and being different that made me hide inside myself."

Ken looked over at Jack. "Sounds familiar, doesn't it?"

Jack smiled at Ken and then looked over at Mark. "See, you're no different from any other guy who has struggled with being gay. But the difference between those of us who accept being gay and those who don't is the freedom to be ourselves."

"But you guys really aren't free because you have to hide who you are on campus and in the fraternities."

"That's a choice we made for ourselves," Ken corrected. "We both know that we're gay and that we're in love with each other. We don't have to let the whole campus know; it's our business. No offense to the other gay guys on campus, but we would rather be closeted about our sexuality than out there. There's a lot less bullshit to deal with this way."

"Besides," Jack cut in, "once we graduate and move to a place where we can be out, we won't feel the need to be so damn discreet."

"And I'll be able to wear my poodle skirt and saddle shoes to the dance," Ken lisped.

Mark laughed with them, as he thought about the things they had discussed. "So, tell me guys, how do I get Tommy to talk to me so that I can apologize to him?"

"Well, big guy, that's a problem," Ken said seriously. "I can only imagine how devastated Tommy was when you chose Sally over him. I wouldn't want to speak to you ever again." He saw the hurt appear in Mark's eyes. "However, you'd better take advantage of the opportunity that was opened for you."

Mark looked at him curiously. "I don't understand. What do you mean?"

Ken asked Jack, "Is he always this thick-headed?"

"Sometimes." Jack laughed, then went over to Mark and lightly cuffed his head. "Kyle told me about the box that Tommy gave him to give to you." He watched as Mark's hand reached up to his chest.

"He gave you a gift, Mark. He was making a statement." Ken spoke slowly.

Mark snatched at the ray of hope. "Do you really think so?"

Jack slapped Mark on the head again. "Listen to us. That gift is as close as

Tommy is going to come to talking with you. You hurt him and he's angry about that, but he still cares about you. It's up to you to make the next move."

"The sooner you make the move, the better your chances." Ken looked into Mark's eyes. "If you wait too long to acknowledge the gift, or to ask him to forgive you, you risk not getting a second chance. It's up to you, big guy."

"As they say in tennis, Mark, the ball is in your court. Either do something with it, or the game is over," Jack said as Mark looked up at him. "He isn't going to give you another chance unless you do something."

"First my best friend from high school, and then my mother. Everyone keeps telling me the same thing." Mark smiled briefly.

"Then maybe you should listen to what everybody is telling you," Ken said.

Mark looked at his friends. "I'm even more afraid of asking him to forgive me than I was about discovering that I might be gay."

"You're the one who broke his heart, so you're going to have to be the one that fixes it."

"What am I going to do if he won't give me a second chance?"

"You're going to have to accept whatever decision he makes," Jack said, putting his arm around Mark's shoulder. "If Sally hadn't been Sally, Tommy was going to have to accept your decision to stay with her. Sometimes what ultimately happens is out of your hands."

"But being with him is the only thing that I have been thinking about since Thanksgiving." Mark could feel his eyes starting to water. "I've made a lot of decisions since that night, and I really want Tommy to be a part of my choices."

Ken gathered Mark into a hug. "These are things that you should be telling Tommy, not us. Be honest when you talk to him. He's going to be a lot more understanding if you're open about your feelings."

"Thank you both," Mark said quietly.

"It's getting late, so I better get out of here," Ken said. "Don't wait too long before you talk to Tommy."

"I'll walk you out," Jack said as he joined Ken at the door.

Mark waved them out, then plopped down on his bed. He was grateful that Jack and Ken had come over to talk to him, but the hard part was ahead of him.

13: ATTACK ON TOMMY

Tommy returned to his dorm room late Sunday evening after having spent a couple of hours at the library doing research for a term paper. It didn't surprise him that Scott wasn't in the room. He undressed for bed and read for a while before falling asleep around eleven o'clock. Shortly before midnight, Tommy thought he heard Scott come into the room. He turned toward the wall and started to fall back to sleep.

Tommy vaguely felt the blanket yanked away from his body and then a heavy body on his naked back, a stiff shaft pressing urgently against his ass. Before he could fully wake up or react, he felt the blade of a knife against his throat. Fear flickered at the touch of the steel and the smell of alcohol.

"Hey, sweet boy. If you say anything, I'll slice your fucking throat," Brian threatened in a raspy voice.

Tommy recognized the voice. With the knife blade tight against his throat, he let the rape happen. He held still as Brian positioned himself and began pushing into him. Brian was rough and forceful, panting with his exertions as his thrusts became faster.

"You should have given in, you cocksucker. I wouldn't have had to do this if you had pledged Gamma. Fucking little dick tease." Brian moaned as he plowed deeper. "I knew you'd have a hot little hole, Tommy boy." He grabbed a fistful of Tommy's hair and shoved Tommy's face into the pillow as he groaned and shot his load.

He pulled himself free and sat back on Tommy's legs. "You brought this on yourself," he snarled. He repeatedly plunged the knife into Tommy — both shoulders, then his thigh. "Next time, you'll let me have what I want." Brian slid off the bed and pulled up his pants with one hand, dropping the knife on the floor as he headed for the door.

When Scott returned to the dorm, he discovered he didn't have his room key. He staggered down the hallway and pounded on Jay's door.

Jay threw open the door and glared sleepily at the wasted student. "Damn it, Scott, I bet you forgot your fucking keys again," he growled. Turning back into his room to grab his robe, he saw that his clock showed twelve-ten. "This happens too fucking often."

"I'm sorry, Jay," Scott apologized. "I must've lost my keys at the party, or left them on my desk."

"Why didn't you just wake Tommy?" Jay wrapped his robe around his body, grabbed his master key, and walked out his door.

"I did that the last time." Scott chuckled a little. "It was your turn."

"You take turns waking us up?" Jay stopped abruptly as his attention turned to somebody slinking out of Tommy's room. "Who's that?"

Scott stared down the hall. "I think it's Brian from Gamma house. He was at the same party I was." Scott smiled and waved. "Hey, Brian," he called out.

Brian turned and stared for a moment as the two men walked toward him. Then he ran to the stairwell and out of the dorm.

Jay and Scott entered the dorm room and turned on the lights. "Holy shit," Jay gaped at the sight of a bloodied Tommy lying face down on his bed. "Call 9-1-1," he shouted to Scott, as he checked for a pulse.

Scott collapsed onto his bed in shock. His set of keys was lying on the floor near a bloody knife. "Oh, shit!"

"Call 9-1-1, Scott," Jay yelled again. "Now, goddammit!"

Awakened by the shouting, Kyle rushed to Tommy's room. "What's going on — oh, fuck!"

"He's still alive, but losing a lot of blood," Jay said.

Kyle grabbed the phone and dialed 9-1-1, explained the emergency and where to send the ambulance. After he hung up, he looked over at Scott, who was staring at his keys and mumbling the word "shit", over and over.

"Did Scott do this?" Kyle asked, confused.

"Brian Walker," Jay said. "We saw him in the hallway."

"Son of a bitch." Kyle picked up the phone again. "I'm going to call Mark. He's Tommy's big brother and needs to know what's going on."

"NO!" Mark sat bolt upright in his bed. His heart was racing, his breathing was labored, and he could feel the cool air of the room chilling the sweat on his body. He tried to remember if he had been dreaming when he'd felt a sharp pain lance through him, but he couldn't recall any dream. He grabbed hold of the crystal around his neck, a warmth and comfort washed through him.

"Mark, are you okay?" Oscar asked, poking his head inside the dark room.

"Huh?"

Oscar entered the room, shut the door behind him, and then sat at the end of Mark's bed. "I heard you yell out. What happened?"

"I don't really know." Confused by the rude awakening, Mark was trying to gather his thoughts into a coherent arrangement. "Before falling asleep, I was trying to figure out what to say to Tommy that didn't sound like some of the bullshit I've heard from Sally. I fell asleep thinking about everything that you and others have been telling me. The next thing I knew, this shooting pain woke me up."

Oscar looked at Mark with concern, seeing the crystal hanging against Mark's chest. "How long have you been wearing that crystal?"

"Since before Thanksgiving," he replied, lifting the gem and holding it in his hand. "Tommy told me that he once wore a topaz before he started wearing his grandmother's crystal. He said they were comforting."

"Hm," Oscar grunted. *If the crystal had been Tommy's...* Before he could put words to his sudden worry, Larry burst into the room.

"Mark, Kyle's on the house phone. He said it was an emergency."

"An emergency?" Mark mumbled. As the adrenaline rush jolted him awake, his mind flashed to the bolt of pain and the throbbing of the crystal against his chest. And Kyle lived across the hall from... "Oh, no, not Tommy!" A sinking feeling in his gut, he dashed to the phone at the end of the hall and snatched it up. "Kyle? What the hell's going on?"

Tumbling over one another, Kyle's words came out in a rush. "Tommy's been stabbed. By Brian Walker. I heard Jay yelling for someone to call 9-1-1 and—"

"For Christ's sake, Kyle, how he is? Is he alive?"

Mark heard a deep breath on the other end of the line as Kyle began to speak more coherently. "He's lost a lot of blood, and he might need surgery for the stab wounds. The ambulance is here, and the medics are getting ready to take him to the hospital. I thought you should know."

"Thanks for calling. I'll see what I can find out at the hospital, and I'll let you know."

Mark slammed the phone into its cradle and raced back to his room. As he pulled on a pair of jeans over his gym shorts and put on a sweatshirt, he quickly told Oscar what he knew about the attack on Tommy, and that he was going to the hospital.

"I'm here to see about Tommy Ford," Mark told the emergency room nurse.

She looked at the youth dubiously. "Are you a family member?"

"No, his family isn't here. I'm his fraternity brother."

"Sorry, we do not provide medical information about a patient to anyone who is not a member of the family." She turned back to her charts dismissively.

"He doesn't have any other family here right now!" he repeated loudly, angrily.

"Please, keep your voice down." The nurse looked at him with a modicum of sympathy. "I understand your frustration, but that is hospital policy. When somebody from his family arrives, they will be given a full update on his status."

"I want to talk to somebody about this," Mark demanded. He felt a hand on his shoulder and turned to see Al Martin, dressed in green scrubs with his stethoscope over his shoulder.

"Hey, Mark." Al put his arm around Mark and led him away from the desk. "You aren't going to get any help from the nurse by yelling at her. She's just doing her job."

"My little brother was brought in here a little while ago," he said. "I'm just trying to find out how he's doing."

"I know. I was here when they brought Tommy in."

"How is he?" Mark asked with hesitation, fearful that the prognosis might not be good.

Al glanced around the waiting area; no one was close enough to overhear. "We truly don't know anything for sure yet. He's in surgery right now. He has four really deep knife wounds, and he's lost a lot of blood."

Mark rolled up his sleeve. "Let's go. I'll donate blood, and if I don't match his type, we can wake up the brothers. The Kappas will get you all the blood you need."

Al put both of his hands on Mark's shoulders and looked directly into his eyes. "Mark, everything is under control, I promise you. The hospital has its own blood bank, already typed and cross-matched and ready for transfusion." His look was sympathetic. "Tommy is getting the best possible care."

"So what can I do to help?" he asked, anxious that Al wasn't giving him any solid information about Tommy's condition.

"There's nothing you can do. I suggest you go home and get some sleep. I'll call you at the house tomorrow morning after I get off my shift."

Mark shook his head. He knew there wouldn't be any sleep for him until Tommy was out of danger. There was little sense in going back to Kappa house. "When can I see him?" he persisted.

"If there are any complications, or they discover any serious punctures of major organs, he's probably going to be in the intensive care unit after surgery. Seriously, Mark, you might as well go back to the house where you'll at least be more comfortable. They won't let you into ICU unless you're family."

"Except for an uncle in San Francisco, Tommy's estranged from his family. The Kappas are his family, and I'm his big brother," Mark argued.

"I'm sorry, but the hospital has rules that it can't break. Federal privacy regulations, and all that." Al looked at him sympathetically. "Why don't you get hold of a member of his family and have them contact the hospital on your behalf?"

Al patted Mark on the back, as Mark sighed and put his head in his hands. "Unless you can get authorization from a family member, the hospital won't let you see him until after he's released from Intensive Care. And they won't give you any information about his condition." Al gave Mark a sympathetic smile. "I'll keep you updated, if you promise not to tell anybody."

"That's a promise. Thanks, Al. I guess I'd better go let the guys know what's happening." Mark took a few reluctant steps toward the door, then stopped and turned around. "Al," he called out.

"Yes?"

"Was Tommy wearing a crystal?"

"No, but there was one clutched tightly in his hand. They put it in an envelope and are keeping it at the nurse's station for him."

"Would you do me a favor and put it under his pillow? It belonged to his grandmother. He's never been without it."

"All right, dude. If you get out of here and go try and get some rest, I'll make sure it gets put under his pillow," Al bartered.

Mark nodded. "Thanks, Al." His step was a little lighter as he left the hospital than when he had arrived.

Oscar, Jack, and Dave were waiting in the kitchen when Mark returned from the hospital at one thirty on Monday morning. Oscar had wakened them and told them what had happened to Tommy.

"How's Tommy?" Jack asked.

Fatigue catching up with him, Mark plopped down into a chair. "They won't tell me anything because I'm not a family member." He looked at each of the brothers. "Al's working tonight. At least he told me that Tommy's in surgery. He was stabbed four times and lost a lot of blood."

"Shit," Dave grumbled. "Why the fuck would anyone want to hurt Tommy? He's a great kid."

Jack shook his head. "Ken said Brian has been obsessed with Tommy."

"So he has to stab the kid?" Dave asked, perplexed. The other guys around the table looked at one another and shrugged.

"He's just fucking nuts, is what!" Jack could see that their comments were just upsetting Mark even more. "Forget about that for now. There must be something we can do for Tommy. And I suppose Tommy's family should be notified." He put a hand on Mark's arm. "Do you think you should give Tommy's uncle a call?"

Mark's thoughts were with Tommy, and he had missed Jack's question. "I'm sorry. What?"

"You could call Tommy's uncle."

"It's a good idea, Jack. I'm just afraid that Tommy might have said something to him about me over the break, and then I'd be the last person he'd give any kind of permission to. Plus, there's the problem of getting Tommy's address book out of his room with police hanging around." He pushed back his chair and stood up. "Goodnight, gentlemen, I'm going to up to my room. I can't deal with anything else right now." Mark left the other three sitting at the table.

14: MONDAY MADNESS

Mark didn't sleep well and was awake again at six o'clock. He dressed and went downstairs to get something to eat. Oscar was sitting at the kitchen table drinking coffee.

"Did you even go to bed last night?" Mark asked wearily.

"Yeah, but I couldn't sleep. I was worried about Tommy," Oscar replied. "I thought I'd go with you to help find his address book and to bring his grandmother's trunk back to the house."

Mark stared at Oscar. "How do you know about the trunk?"

Oscar smiled at Mark's expression. "Do you think you're the only one in this house that Tommy spent time with? Tommy and I talk; we're friends."

"Why are you so concerned about that trunk?" Mark asked, sitting down at the table with a bagel and some coffee.

"Tommy's grandmother was a special lady. I'm sure there are some...unique items in that trunk that other people shouldn't touch." Oscar tapped his spoon against the rim of his coffee cup. "I think Tommy's trunk would be safer in our house than sitting in his dorm room." He took a sip of coffee. "And besides, it's something we can do for him."

Mark Calls Tommy's Uncle

Mark and Oscar contacted Housing for permission to remove the trunk and some of Tommy's more personal things from his room. At the dorm, a haggard Kyle told them that the crime scene team had taken a bunch of photos, especially of the bloody handprint on the exit door of the dorm, and that Jay and Scott had formally identified Brian for the police. Mark and Oscar also heard through the fraternity grapevine, courtesy of a Gamma in Campus Security, that Brian had been picked up and booked for aggravated assault with a deadly weapon and attempted murder, according to the preliminary police report.

Now Mark sat with Tommy's address book, trying to work up his nerve to call and relate what little he knew to Tommy's uncle, hoping that he could somehow convince the man he had never met to let the hospital release information on Tommy's medical condition to him. His fingers trembled as he punched in the number.

"Hello?" a sleepy male voice answered.

"Is this Allen Potter?"

"Just a minute."

Mark heard the sleepy voice calling for Allen. He smiled at the thought of Tommy's uncles having been together for so long. He had never thought that he would be in a position to hope for a relationship that might last as long as theirs. He glanced at the time and realized that it was a little after five o'clock in the morning in San Francisco.

"Allen, wake up. It's for you," the first voice was saying.

"It better be fucking important," the second voice said grouchily in the background. "Who the hell is this? Do you have any fucking idea of what time it is?"

"My name is Mark Young. I'm—"

"I know who you are, *Mister* Young," Allen said, fully awake now that he heard the caller's name. "My normally happy nephew spent his entire holiday moping over you."

"Sir," Mark interrupted, "while I justly deserve your anger for what I did to Tommy, and for waking you this early, it's not as important as the reason I called." He paused to be certain the man was listening. "Tommy was stabbed last night. He was rushed to the hospital and went into surgery around twelve thirty this morning."

"What! How did the surgery go? Is he going to be okay?" Allen shouted.

"I think so. But the hospital won't give me any information because I'm not a family member."

"What happened?"

"Some guy who was obsessed with Tommy got into his room and stabbed him. That's all I know right now."

"Was it that Brian kid?"

"You know about Brian?" Mark asked, surprised.

"Tommy and I are very close. He's told us everything about his semester at college."

Marked fumbled for something to say, but couldn't manage anything more than, "I'm really sorry, sir."

"Not as sorry as you would have been if I were there," Tommy's uncle replied with brutal honesty.

"Sir, I was wondering if you would contact the hospital and find out how Tommy is doing."

"I'm not sure they would believe that I'm his uncle over the phone. You should call Tommy's attorney, Steven Parker. He has an office in Philadelphia and will be able to help you."

"I was going to call him when his office opens this morning," Mark said. "I thought I should call you first."

"Thank you. As much as I would like to tell you off, I do appreciate your letting me know about Tommy." There was a brief pause as Allen spoke to his partner, then he added, "Tommy's attorney has some paperwork that will get you the access you need for the hospital."

"Thank you, sir."

"Mister Young."

"Yes, sir."

"If you ever hurt my nephew again, you're going to find a pair of size twelve leather boots implanted in your ass. That's not a threat, Mister Young, that's a promise."

"I understand, sir."

"I hope you do," Allen said quietly. "I'm going to rearrange my work schedule and find a flight over there. It may take us a day or two to get things in order. Please keep us informed about Tommy's condition. And let him know that I'll be there as soon as possible."

"Yes, sir."

"And, Mister Young...you'd better take excellent care of him until I get there."

"I will, sir. I promise."

Mark hung up the phone with a sigh of relief. After talking with Tommy's uncle, he had renewed hope that Tommy would give him a second chance if that bastard Brian hadn't run them out of time.

Mark Calls Tommy's Attorney

Mark glanced at the trunk that he and Oscar had placed in the corner of his room and then looked up at Tommy's paddle that was once again hanging next to his own. They looked good together, and he smiled faintly as he dialed the number from Tommy's address book and waited for somebody on the other end of the line to answer.

"Steven Parker's office. How may I help you?"

"May I speak with Mister Parker, please?"

"Mister Parker is not available right now. Would you like his voicemail?" the receptionist asked politely.

"I'm calling about Tommy Ford, and it's really important that I speak with him," Mark pleaded.

"Hold on a moment. I'll see if I can locate him."

"This is Steven Parker," a deep voice responded a long moment later.

"Mister Parker, my name is Mark Young. I'm Tommy Ford's big brother in Kappa Lambda Pi," Mark began. "Tommy was stabbed last night and is in the hospital, and they won't tell us anything about his condition because we're not members of his family. Is there anything you can do to help us?"

"I'm really sorry to hear about Tommy. Will he be okay?" the lawyer asked.

"As far as I know," Mark said, "but we can't get any details without being family."

"Do they know who stabbed him?"

"Yes, it was a guy who was obsessed with Tommy. The police have arrested him." Mark empathized with the lawyer's concern, but his primary objective was to get permission to see Tommy, and he turned the topic back to that. "Can you help us find out about Tommy's current condition?"

"I can do a lot better than that, Mister Young," Parker responded. "Tommy and I had a meeting last Monday. He updated all of his legal papers, and gave you power of attorney in the event of emergency while he was at college. Tommy's uncle is still his guardian and has final say over everything regarding Tommy until after he graduates from college; that's the way his grandmother had things set up. But these general powers of attorney grant you limited rights, Mister Young."

Mark was flabbergasted by the information. Tommy had changed his legal papers *after* Mark had broken up with him. Mark sighed as he thought about how he'd let Tommy down.

"There was a conference call last Monday. Tommy convinced his uncle to approve putting your name on these papers because you are his fraternity big brother, and he respects you. Afterward, he and I had a lengthy discussion. His primary concern was that there be somebody at Timian in the event of an emergency. Despite his insistence, I wasn't sure he was doing the right thing by naming you on his powers of attorney. I did, however, understand his reasoning. If he's told his uncle the same thing he told me after the conference call, his uncle is not going to be happy with you."

"I spoke with Tommy's uncle before calling you, sir. He promised to shove a pair of size twelve boots up my ass if I did anything to hurt Tommy."

Parker laughed. "You must have caught him off guard. That's kind and gentle for Allen Potter."

"It was around five o'clock this morning in California."

"Then it had to be the news about Tommy that made him polite," Parker said, laughing again. "I'm afraid you have made a bad first impression on the uncles,

Mister Young. They work in tandem where Tommy is concerned. One day you may come to understand the phrase 'good cop, bad cop'."

"Two of my fraternity brothers have already gone that route with me for what I did to Tommy," Mark admitted.

"You'll wish it was your fraternity brothers again, if you ever meet Tommy's uncles."

Mark had thought the same thing after talking with Allen Potter, but for the moment he just wanted to get the papers and see Tommy. "So, what do I have to do to get the hospital to give me information?"

"I could either fax or e-mail a copy of the powers of attorney to you."

"We don't have a fax machine in the fraternity house, so e-mail would be better."

"Let me have your e-mail address, and I'll have my secretary send you PDF versions of the signed, notarized documents. I'll include a cover letter in case the hospital has any hesitation."

"Thank you so much. You don't know how relieved I am."

"It's okay, Mark. I understand how you feel," Parker said.

"Tommy's a difficult young man to figure out," Mark observed, thinking of how he had been named in the power of attorney even after he disappointed Tommy.

Parker laughed. "No, he's not difficult to figure out at all. He's a confident, honest, mature young man. It's other people who are difficult to understand, because they're busy playing games with one another. They don't know how to deal with a person who isn't playing games."

Mark flashed on Sally's intrigues. "You're probably right about that."

"Mister Young," Parker said seriously, "I'm Tommy's attorney, and I'll be watching out for his best interests. If you use these documents to do anything that appears to be out of line, I'll be there to stop you. This is not a threat, it's a promise."

Mark was glad that Tommy was well cared for by both his uncle and his attorney. "I understand. I have no intention of doing anything that would hurt Tommy."

"One final thought, Mark," Parker said before they ended their call. "You should be very thankful that Tommy's grandmother isn't alive. She was the sweetest, most diminutive woman you would ever want to meet," he paused for effect, "but she would have had your balls on a platter for hurting her grandson."

Mark swallowed hard. "Yes, sir." He gave Steven Parker his e-mail address and thanked him again for his help before he turned off his cell phone. He went over to his desk and switched on his computer to wait for the e-mail that would allow him access to Tommy.

Return to Hospital

"I'm Mark Young, and I'm here to see Tommy Ford," Mark said as he stood patiently at the reception desk. It was after lunch, as he had attended his morning class before going to the hospital.

"Are you a member of the family?" the day nurse asked.

"No, I'm not. However, I believe these papers will permit me to see Tommy. This is a power of attorney." He slapped the first paper on the counter and smiled smugly at the nurse. "This is a health care power of attorney." He waggled his eyebrows as he slapped the second paper on the counter. "And this is a letter from

Tommy's attorney." Mark stood back and folded his arms. "Please feel free to contact Mister Parker's law firm if you have any questions or concerns about these documents," he added politely.

The nurse chuckled before scooping up the documents. "Have a seat, Mister Young," she said, and then left the reception area. When she returned, she walked over to where he was sitting. "Doctor Lang will be with you shortly."

"Thank you," Mark replied, looking up with a smile.

Five minutes later, a doctor appeared. "Mister Young?"

"Yes. I'm Mark Young."

"I'm Doctor Lang." He gripped Mark's hand tightly. "I'm glad to meet you."

"How's Tommy doing?" Mark asked anxiously. "May I see him?"

Doctor Lang beckoned Mark to follow him. "Tommy is doing well," he reported as they walked down the hallway to the elevators. "There were four stab wounds: two in his left shoulder, one in his right shoulder, and then one in his left thigh. One of the knife wounds to his left shoulder punctured his lung."

The two men stopped talking as they got onto the crowded elevator, and Doctor Lang pressed the button for the fifth floor. When they exited, Mark followed Doctor Lang into the Intensive Care Unit where they stopped outside of Room 517. The window shade had been drawn to keep the bright lights from disturbing the patient, and Mark couldn't see inside the room.

"The puncture to the lung is our biggest concern right now. He may have some difficulty breathing for several days, or even weeks. Tommy lost a lot of blood, and he is asleep due to the pain medications that we have him on. Try not to be too concerned about that; he needs the rest to mend. He may initially lose some shoulder girdle flexibility because of the damage, but with physical therapy, he should regain full range of motion," Doctor Lang looked directly at Mark. "Were you aware that Tommy was also sexually assaulted?"

Mark stared at the doctor in disbelief. Kyle had only told him Tommy had been stabbed, and there had been no mention in the preliminary police report. "No."

"They discovered semen on his back and thighs when they were prepping him for surgery. We are doing blood tests for sexually transmitted diseases and AIDS, and should have the results in a few days."

Mark wasn't sure how to respond. "Thank you for telling me, Doctor. May I see him now?"

"Go ahead inside. Please keep your visit to five minutes. He's still listed in critical condition until he fully regains consciousness."

"Thank you," Mark said again and opened the door.

He was shocked by Tommy's pallor. There were monitors checking Tommy's heart rate and other bodily functions, along with tubes that provided him with oxygen and nutrition, as well as medication. Mark's eyes watered as he looked down at his little brother. The Tommy he loved was vibrant and full of energy. Lying there on his stomach with a sheet covering his body, this Tommy looked frail.

Overwhelmed by his emotions, Mark could hardly bear to stay in the room. Tears rolled down his face as he thought about what Tommy had been through. More than anything else, he wanted to hold Tommy in his arms and comfort him. He reached down and felt beneath the pillow for the crystal, making sure that it was there. As he pulled his hand out from under the pillow, he brushed some hair away from Tommy's forehead. He bent down and lightly kissed Tommy on the cheek. "I promise I'll be here when you wake up," he whispered.

Opening The Trunk

After the nurse's assurance that Tommy was on high doses of pain meds and was unlikely to wake for several hours, Mark returned to campus and attended his early afternoon class. During the lecture, his mind was on Tommy and how much he loved him, on the mischievous sparkle in Tommy's smoky brown eyes when he sang "Slow Boat to China" during the pledge sing in the cafeteria, and how Tommy's voice had pierced his heart and soul when he sang "The Rose" for the Halloween Talent Competition. Mostly, he relived how good it had felt holding Tommy close to his body after they made love. After the class, he drew a blank when he tried to recall a single thing the professor had talked about.

Outside his room at Kappa house, Mark could smell incense burning. Opening the door, he saw lit candles near Tommy's trunk and Oscar and Jack looking up at him guiltily. "What the hell are you guys doing?" Mark asked as he closed the door and stared from one brother to the other.

"I figure that Tommy's grandmother had a healing crystal, and it has to be inside the trunk," Oscar said. "So, we've been trying to get the trunk open."

Mark looked down at the two brothers and at the trunk. It was made from oak that had darkened over the years. There were owl-headed metal handles on each of its sides. Mark did not see any hinges indicating an opening, or any visible lock. "Where's the seam for the lid?"

"It's a seamless trunk, created by a master druid or Wiccan craftsman," Oscar guessed. "The seam is hidden within the grain of the wood. The trunks are sealed by spells that are cast by the owner to prevent theft." Oscar smiled at the other two. "My grandmother had one, and it always amazed me when she opened it."

"If it's sealed by a spell, then only Tommy can open it," Mark concluded. "So why were you trying?"

Oscar laughed. "Because I know a few secrets for opening these types of trunks, but so far they haven't worked. I even called my grandmother for advice, but she couldn't help, either." He looked up at Mark. "Maybe if you were to try, it would open."

"Why me? You and Jack have more expertise in this field."

"Because you're emotionally closer to Tommy than either one of us," Oscar said, as if that were the most logical thing in the world.

Mark was skeptical, but if there was something inside that could enhance whatever the doctors were doing, he would do whatever was necessary to get to it. "What do I have to do?"

"You need to sit down in front of the trunk and meditate," Oscar clarified. "If anything happens while you're meditating, don't freak out. Just stay relaxed and concentrate on opening the trunk. We'll discuss anything that happens afterwards."

"What do you mean 'if anything happens'?" Mark asked suspiciously.

Oscar looked over at Jack before returning his attention to Mark. "It's possible that you may hear someone speaking to you. It may be a wandering spirit, or it may be the spirit of Tommy's grandmother."

Mark was having second thoughts about messing with things he didn't understand. "Is it safe to do something like this?"

"We're going to be here with you," Jack reassured him.

"How do you know it's not locked by black magic?"

"Do you think Tommy would be the kind of person he is if he had been raised by a grandmother that practiced black magic?" Oscar smiled at Mark. "Besides, if Tommy were a practitioner of black magic, I highly doubt he would have let you get away with dumping him."

Mark nodded thoughtfully. "That's a good point." He sat down in the lotus position in front of the trunk. "So, what do I have to do?"

"Concentrate on Tommy and how to open the trunk. Whatever happens, maintain your meditation and let it happen," Oscar instructed.

Mark took a deep breath and looked up at Tommy's paddle, glittering in the candlelight. "Give me Tommy's paddle, please," he said to Jack. He placed the paddle in his lap and pulled his topaz crystal out from under his shirt. Closing his eyes, he began to meditate.

After several minutes, Mark reached for the trunk and easily lifted the lid. A strong scent of lilac and a sense of energy came from within the trunk. Mark reached inside and laid the royal blue velvet material onto the floor in front of him. He pulled out three red velvet pouches and placed them on the blue velvet. "I smell lilacs," Mark said as his body slumped forward and he reached out to brace himself. He shook his head a few times and looked at Oscar and Jack. "I smell lilacs. What the hell just happened?"

"*Hermano*, you just had a spiritual moment." Oscar chuckled and reached over to pat Mark on the shoulder. "The smell is coming from the trunk."

"That was the strangest thing I have ever experienced." Mark looked over at Jack and then back at Oscar. "First, I saw this swirling gold light, which was joined by a white light. Then this beautiful older woman was standing beside me, smiling at me. It felt as if she held my hand before she started chanting something that I couldn't understand. When she finished chanting, she nodded her head at me and I felt myself opening the trunk. She told me what I needed to take out, and then she smiled at me before disappearing."

"Mark," Oscar said, "you *have* become attuned to that crystal around your neck."

Mark reached up and held the topaz. "Tommy said she gave it to him when he was six years old, when he first began living with her."

"Oh." Oscar nodded. "That crystal and his crystal are in synch. That's why you sensed his pain the other night."

"Al said that Tommy was clutching the crystal when he was brought into the hospital."

"He must have been holding it when he was stabbed. The two crystals resonated with the pain, and you sensed the blackness." Oscar shook his head in amazement. "No wonder you're so attuned, those two crystals have some strong energy within them."

"This is a little scary, Oscar," Mark replied nervously. "I'm not used to being around this magic stuff."

"You better get used to it. If you plan on hanging around Tommy, he's only going to become stronger with the energy," Oscar said. "It's not something to be afraid of when used properly. If Tommy's grandmother smiled at you, then the energy is good and you have nothing to fear from Tommy." He looked down at the three red velvet pouches. "I assume one of these is the healing crystal?"

"Tommy's grandmother said that we should use all three." He looked down in front of him and then inside the trunk. "She said that you would be able to explain this stuff, Oscar." He looked over at Oscar expectantly.

Oscar looked surprised. "Me?"

"She said you would know and understand," Mark insisted.

"That's a lot of pressure from a spirit," Oscar muttered as he picked up one of the red velvet pouches and traced his finger along the gold thread of the protective symbol.

"What is that, Oscar? If I'm going to be involved with Tommy, then I'd better start learning more about this Wiccan stuff."

"It's a protective symbol, possibly Norse or Celtic." He looked at Mark. "It's from about the same period as the rune symbols on Tommy's paddle. It protects the energy of the crystal from escaping, as well as keeping bad energy from getting in."

"Wow!" all three exclaimed at the dark purple, terminated crystal that came into view. The slender amethyst was six inches long, a half-inch thick at the base, and a quarter-inch near the point.

Oscar took a deep breath. "Crystals are a natural part of the Earth and have been endowed with certain natural energies. Those energies can be enhanced and empowered by those who use the energies of Earth. Druids, such as Merlin, and Wiccans are believers in the use and powers of the natural energies. My ancestors have beliefs in these energies that go all the way back to the time of the Aztecs. Rarely are these energies used for evil purposes because that goes against nature." He smiled. "Feel free to ask me any questions if I'm going too fast or am not making myself clear." Mark and Jack nodded.

"Any crystal can be used for any purpose, so long as it is properly empowered." Oscar held up the purple crystal. "This amethyst crystal is normally used as a generic healing crystal." He handed the crystal to Mark and then opened a second pouch. "Nice." He held up a brown and gold terminated crystal, which was the same size as the amethyst.

"Is that a tiger's eye?" Mark asked, surprised at seeing another stone he recognized.

"Yes. This crystal is used mostly for the healing of wounds. I've never seen one quite this large." Oscar again passed the crystal before opening the third pouch. "*Dios mio!*" He smiled as he handed Mark a red and gold rutilated oval stone. "One of the modern uses of this crystal is for tissue regeneration."

"So we've got crystals for wound and tissue healing." Mark held the crystal up to the light from the window and gazed at the colors within it. He was amazed that he could feel its energy.

"Let's see what else we have in this fabulous trunk." Oscar knelt and pulled out the other nine pouches. He looked over at Mark. "Put the three healing crystals into one of these empty pouches and keep them with you as we look through the trunk." Oscar neatly placed the nine pouches onto the blue velvet material. He pulled out the crystal ball and gently placed it on top of the pouches. Next, he pulled out a deck of Tarot cards and laid them next to the pouches. When Oscar pulled out the dagger, both Jack and Mark gasped.

"Wow! What the hell is that?" Mark asked.

Oscar chuckled. "My grandmother told me stories about these daggers. I always thought they were a myth." He looked over at Mark. "It's a dragon dagger. The dragon's head is the handle, and the curved blade is its tail. If this is a real dragon dagger and not a replica, then it's believed to have been empowered by the dragon's own blood during the forging of the dagger."

"Shit," Jack whispered, looking at the dagger. "That's amazing."

As Mark and Jack examined the dagger, Oscar continued his search through the contents of the trunk. "Hmmm." Oscar smiled at Mark. "Does this belong to you, brother Mark?" He waved a white jockstrap in the air.

Mark blushed. "How the hell did that get in there?"

"Our newest brother either used this in some of his spell casting," Oscar grinned at Mark, "or he has a sexy little fetish that we were unaware of."

"May I have that back?" Mark asked, holding out his hand.

"No. You need to put it back inside the trunk. We can't take anything that we're not supposed to," Oscar warned. "We're being allowed access for the healing crystals only. Everything else has to go back inside."

"Would something bad happen?" Jack asked.

"I don't know," Oscar looked at him meaningfully, "but I don't want to take a chance. I can feel the energy coming from this trunk. It's almost the same as when I was with my grandmother. I'm not willing to take any risks."

"Okay, it will go back inside." Mark shook his head, bemused. "I can't believe he took one of my jocks."

Oscar pulled out four books and looked them over, paying attention to one in particular. *Journal of Spells*. He held it up to the light. "And it has a stain in that same dark red varnish and glitter." He put it down on the blue velvet material.

"It's not glitter," Mark corrected.

Oscar looked over at him curiously. "What is it?"

"A crushed crystal. Tommy mixed it into the varnish." Mark picked up the *Journal of Spells*. "Why doesn't it open?"

"It's sealed shut. Only the owner can open it." Oscar shook his head at Mark's lack of understanding.

"But we opened the sealed trunk," Mark protested.

"We were given guidance to open the trunk. We weren't trying to open the journal." Oscar pulled the final item from the trunk. He fell back against Mark's desk with a start. "*Dios mio!*" Mark and Jack stared at the book he was holding. "It's a copy of the *Malleus Maleficarium*."

"The whateus whatium?" they both exclaimed in unison, and laughed.

"The *Malleus Maleficarium* was a guidebook unofficially authorized by Pope Innocent in 1484. It was used by inquisitors as a guide for hunting down and killing witches."

"If Tommy's a witch, why would he have a copy of that book?" Jack asked.

"To find out what the other side thinks and feels." Oscar shot a glance at Jack. "Haven't you ever read *Mein Kampf* or some other book that ranted against the Jewish people?"

"Yes," Jack replied softly.

"But Tommy doesn't have any books around about being gay or what the Religious Right is doing to crush gays. I never officially knew he was gay until the night we first had sex," Mark said.

Jack started chuckling. "First of all, no gay person in his right mind would have those books lying around his dorm room. That's an open invitation to harassment." Jack looked at the artwork hanging on the wall behind him. "He had that picture hanging on his wall. How many college guys do you know that have a two hundred dollar piece of art in their dorm room?"

"Here, none," Mark admitted.

"Did he ever tell you about it?"

"He said it was his ideal vampire," Mark said. "And that he'd accept an offer to spend eternity with him if asked." Realization hit him. Tommy had told him that he was gay, but he had done it discreetly and without having said the words.

Jack smiled at Mark's epiphany. "Tommy and I enjoy reading vampire novels because vampires are outcasts from society, much like gays. We can empathize and relate to the characters because they are strong and independent beings, albeit misunderstood."

"I read vampire novels, but I never thought of it that way."

"Sorry, guys, I got a little distracted," Oscar said as he looked up from the ancient manuscript. "Did Tommy mention what he used to get the dark red color in the varnish?"

"He didn't say it in so many words, but I suspect he used his own blood, and that's how he got the cut on the palm of his hand." Mark held up the dagger. "He said he cut his hand while carving the symbols in the back of the paddle. However, there was just the one cut on his palm, and I would think carving that many symbols, using this dagger, would have resulted in a few more cuts, especially on his fingers."

"Very observant, *hermano*." Oscar flipped through some of the pages of the manuscript. "Blood is a conduit to empower and enhance natural energies. Using his own blood made it very personal." Oscar paused. "Tommy has some very strong natural psychic abilities. He was probably trained by his grandmother to use those abilities, as well as to harness other natural energies, such as those from the crystals." He looked over at Mark. "We've all sensed this connection to Tommy and his positive persona, his magnetism. A lot of people have that, including the three of us. It's just that Tommy knows how to use his a lot better than we do."

"The first time I shook his hand," Mark's hand tingled at the recollection, "I felt this electric surge through my body. Is that what you're talking about?"

"Exactly. It's always through the eyes and hands that you can feel the connection of energy. Sometimes you sense the energy that surrounds a person." Oscar thought about Tommy's magnetism. "A person's aura surrounds them and you can feel it if you're sensitive. Tommy is extremely sensitive, both inwardly and outwardly."

Mark's face was drawn. "I'll never forget the night I told Tommy that I was getting back together with Sally. The expression on his face never changed, but the light went out of his eyes, and I felt physically cold. When he turned and walked out of the cemetery, I felt as if a piece of my heart had been carved out. The connection that I'd felt with him was gone."

Oscar reached over and patted Mark's shoulder. "You're sensitive to these things also, *hermano*. You had the choice of any pledge to be your little brother, but you picked Tommy."

"Then that's what happened inside the house after Tommy removed his paddle, a...disconnection," Jack said. "Tommy never seemed the same after that, and the house seemed empty."

"That's right. The house lost all the positive energy that Tommy had brought into it," Oscar said. "I also suspect that Tommy pulled his energy tightly around himself to protect against any further emotional upheaval. Unfortunately, that may have caused him to be unaware of the danger from Brian."

"You know a lot more about this stuff than you ever let on, Oscar," Mark commented.

"Like our new brother, I lived with my grandmother. She *dabbled*, as did her mother, in the Arts. We can trace our bloodline back to the Aztecs. So while my grandmother dabbled, I watched and learned. It was a helluva lot more fun than watching the cactus grow in Arizona." Oscar looked at the magnificent assortment of magical implements sitting on the blue velvet. "Our brother has quite a valuable collection here. I'm impressed."

"Financially valuable?" Jack asked.

"Well, that too, but that would be secondary. These items are mostly for those who dabble in the arts of spell-casting and magic. For them, it's an extremely valuable, possibly priceless collection. These books and this gorgeous sixteenth century manuscript, and possibly that dagger, if it's authentic, are the most valuable items inside this trunk. The crystals would only be of value to those who know what to do with them."

"It makes me a little nervous to have such rare things just lying about. We should probably put this stuff away now," Mark suggested. "We have what we need to help Tommy."

The three began repacking the trunk, putting everything neatly back into place and then putting the blue velvet material back on top. As they were preparing to close the lid, the light shone on the inside of it. "What's this?" Mark asked, touching the dark red stain on the inside of the lid.

Oscar moved closer for a better look. "It's the same dark red varnish as on Tommy's paddle and the spell journal."

"Are those symbols carved into the lid?" Mark asked.

"Yes," Oscar murmured as he brushed his fingers over the carvings. He reached over onto Mark's desk for a piece of paper and pencil, then did a rubbing of the carving.

ᚠ ᛁ ᚱ ᛈ

"What is it?" Mark asked.

"It's an old alphabet." Oscar studied the rubbing he had picked up on the paper. "I'll check on-line to see if I can find a website that will tell me exactly what alphabet these are from." He looked over at Mark and smiled. "But I think I know why you were able to open the trunk."

"Why?" Mark asked curiously.

"If my hunch is correct, these letters spell out your name."

"Why would he put my name inside his grandmother's trunk?"

"That's a question that only Tommy can answer. But it's a really good thing that he did, otherwise we might never have been able to get it open."

"How deeply do you believe in all this stuff?" Mark asked thoughtfully.

Oscar let out a deep breath and leaned back against Mark's bed. "I was born and raised in the Catholic faith, but I have issues with organized religion. Churches don't appear to practice what they preach. Still, my faith and belief are rooted in the way I was brought up. I attend church with my family, but I've stopped going when I'm not with them. My grandmother attends mass every Sunday, even though she also uses heathen or pagan items similar to these." Oscar pointed toward Tommy's trunk. "There was a time in history when the use of herbs was the only way to cure people. If we believe that a Creator God or Goddess or Higher Power exists and created all that is on Earth, then it can't be wrong for us to use these things. Wiccan beliefs are about the use of the natural resources and energies that surround us. It says very little about organized religion."

Oscar looked over at Mark and Jack, then held up one of the healing crystals. "Yes, I believe strongly in this stuff. Does it hurt anyone else that I believe there is energy that can heal contained inside this rock? No. Does it take away from my own personal religious beliefs? No. Nature provides us with its energy, but the majority of people in this world simply ignore it because they don't believe in its use any longer." He looked directly at Mark. "Do you remember what Tommy said during the talent competition?"

"People stopped believing in magic, and love lost its luster, but that those ideals never die. Belief, faith and hope are all that's needed for them to be reborn," Mark recited softly.

Oscar was impressed by Mark's attention to what Tommy had said. "Mark, you've sensed and felt those energies around Tommy, and you experienced them this afternoon. You don't have to believe in the unseen, but he does. It's something that is going to be a part of his life for as long as he lives."

"One last question, Oscar." Mark looked serious. "Am I under some sort of a spell?"

"Are you in love with Tommy?"

Mark's face reddened. "Yes. I am in love with him."

"Then, *mi hermano*, you are under a spell." Oscar smiled reassuringly. "It's a spell that may or may not have been cast by your little brother. Who's to say what causes us to fall in love?"

Monday Night

Brent saw Sally Brown stroll into Kappa House and start walking down the hallway that separated the living room from the other side of the first floor. He moved to intercept her at the end of the corridor before she could go upstairs, catching up with her at the bottom of the stairway.

"May I help you?" he asked, glaring at the intruder. He was one of the few brothers in the house who knew about Mark's history with Sally. Like Oscar and Jack, he was not fond of the beautiful blonde.

"I'm here to see Mark," she snapped.

Brent stood his ground. "Why? Haven't you hurt him enough?"

"You don't know anything about what we have between us. Now get out of my way," she requested curtly.

Six brothers were sitting in the living room, watching the events unfold at the stairway. They also knew about Mark's history with Sally, had heard about Mark's Thanksgiving, and knew that he had finally broken off their relationship. There was little love for Sally Brown in Kappa House.

Brent wouldn't let her by. "Oscar," he yelled up the stairway, "the bitch is here." He would have called for Dave, but he was out of the house with Victoria.

Sally glared at him, then turned to look into the living room at the other brothers, who were laughing. Brent stayed at the bottom of the stairs until Oscar appeared.

"What the hell are you doing here?" Oscar growled. He grabbed her arm and pushed her into the den, shutting the door behind them.

"You don't have to be so rough," she complained, jerking her arm from his grasp.

"You're not welcome here," he barked. "You've done enough to hurt Mark; it's past time for you to leave him the hell alone."

"That's for Mark to decide." She stared haughtily at him, but when he didn't wither, she quickly turned away from the anger in his eyes.

"He said he made that decision already."

"That was a misunderstanding." She tried smiling.

"That's not what Mark said," he contradicted calmly. "He said that you invited him to a party and spent that evening dancing with old *friends*."

"It was a party. He could have danced with any of the other girls that were there."

"He wanted to be with you." Oscar shook his head. "For whatever reason, he's wanted to be with you for a long time, but you couldn't see that. Now he's done with you."

"You don't know what you're talking about. This is between me and Mark. Now, where is he? I came here to talk to him about our misunderstanding." As an after thought, she added, "And to comfort him about what happened to his little brother."

A smile crept across Oscar's face. "Aw, that's so sweet. You came all the way over here thinking that you could take advantage of Mark's vulnerability because his little brother was attacked." The anger that radiated from Oscar belied the smile on his face. "Mark doesn't need your sympathy. He has his brothers to support him. The only reason you're here is because you thought you saw an opportunity to worm your way back into his life."

Sally raised her hand to slap Oscar, but his hand was quicker as he grabbed her wrist. "Don't even think about it, bitch," he growled. "Find Mark on your own time, but don't come back into this house. You're not welcome here."

"We'll see about that." She whirled and stormed out of the den, slamming the door behind her.

Brent smiled at Oscar, who came in and sat down in one of the chairs. "She didn't seem too happy with you, brother. Did you offend her?"

Oscar laughed. "If I didn't, I wasn't trying hard enough."

Mark returned to the hospital at nine o'clock Monday night. "Hey, Al," he said as he reached the fifth floor nurse's station. "Thanks for the call this morning. You won't have to do that again." Mark smiled as he waved the power of attorney documents.

Al laughed. "I heard about that. One of the day nurses said you were gloating."

"May I go in and see him? I promise to keep my visit to five minutes."

"Don't worry, Mark. He's resting comfortably, and all his vitals are good. As long as you sit quietly," Al said, lowering his voice, "you can stay as long as you want. It's very quiet up here at night, and nobody will know any differently."

"What about the rules, Al?" Mark smirked.

"Some of the rules can be stretched, brother," he replied with a smile.

"Thanks, Al."

Mark entered Tommy's room and sat down on a chair next to the bed, encouraged to see that there was a little more color in Tommy's face. He was starting to look more like the Tommy he was used to. Mark pulled Tommy's crystal out from under the pillow and put it into the velvet pouch with the others they had taken from the trunk. He gently placed the pouch underneath Tommy's pillow and gave him a kiss on the cheek.

Mark sat quietly listening to the beeping and buzzing of the machines as he fondled the crystal around his neck. It had been a long and eventful day: phone calls to Tommy's uncle and attorney, moving Tommy's trunk over to his room, attending classes, opening the trunk, and three visits to the hospital. He was exhausted, but he felt an exhilaration within himself that had come after opening

Tommy's trunk. There was a lot more to Tommy than he had ever realized.

Mark looked away from Tommy's sleeping form and out the window. A shadowy image, reflecting on the window was one that he couldn't forget — that look of hurt and pain in Tommy's eyes when he'd ended their relationship. That image always returned when Mark was at his most vulnerable. He turned away from that dark glass.

Now all Mark wanted was for Tommy to wake up so that he could talk with him. There was a lot that he wanted to say. He really hoped that Jack and Ken were right that the gifting of the crystal meant that Tommy was willing to talk with him. His last thoughts before falling asleep were of making love to Tommy and holding him in his arms.

"Mark," a soft voice called, "wake up."

Mark opened his eyes and looked up at Al. "Huh?"

"Here." Al put a second chair near Mark. "Use this to prop up your feet. You'll be a little more comfortable." He handed him a blanket. "Just in case you get cold."

"I should leave," Mark responded sleepily.

"Don't worry. The nurses are aware that Tommy doesn't have any family nearby and that you're his fraternity brother. It can be helpful to the patient if they have somebody near who cares about them and loves them." Al winked as he helped Mark get comfortable.

"Thanks, Al. I want to make sure that I'm here when he wakes up." He looked over at Tommy. "He looks so frail."

"He's going to be fine. His condition is stable, and his vital signs are improving." Al put his hand on Mark's shoulder and smiled widely. "The crystal he had with him is working."

"What do you know about all that?" Mark whispered.

"Other than the fact that I talked with Tommy at the barbecue in October?" Al looked from Tommy to Mark. "My great-grandmother was considered a vodun witch in New Orleans. The family doesn't like to talk about her, but I idolized that woman."

Mark chuckled softly. "What is with all you guys and grandmother witches? You, Oscar, Tommy. Things I've never known about are all around me these days."

"Get some rest. You're going to need it if you plan on staying here all night."

"Will that be all right?"

"Sure. I'm one of the lead nurses at night."

"Thanks, Al."

"Good night."

15: TOMMY AWAKENS

His brain surfacing from its deep sleep, Tommy felt the energy from the crystals flowing through his aching body. As he wondered how the crystals had gotten underneath his pillow, he became aware that he was lying on his stomach. He opened his eyes, and the darkened room swam into focus. The first thing that he saw was a sleeping form next to the bed. Beyond that was a large window looking out onto a nursing station, where he saw the fuzzy figure of a large, dark-skinned man.

His eyes focused on the body sleeping next to his bed, and he realized that the features were Mark's. He smiled at the gold chain around Mark's neck. His fuzzy thoughts caromed from the feeling of desolation when Mark broke up with him, to the anger he had felt afterward, to the bittersweet feelings he'd had when he realized he was partly to blame for what had happened. He felt his anxiety on returning to Timian and having to interact with Mark again, and then the joy of seeing Mark there in his room. The thoughts flitting through his mind confused him until the pain shooting through his lung, shoulders, and leg demanded his attention.

Tommy slowly moved his hand out from underneath the pillow and grabbed the black call button that was lying on the stark white sheet. As he pressed the button, he saw the dark man out in the hallway turn and move toward his room.

Al walked quietly over to the bed, bent down, and put his hand on Tommy's head. "How are you feeling, brother?" he whispered.

"Like I was run over by a truck." Tommy groaned softly. Looking up, he recognized Al. "Hey Al, it's you."

Al chuckled. "Yes, it's me. Surprise."

A faint smile came to Tommy's lips. "How long have I been here?"

"They brought you into surgery at twelve-thirty yesterday morning. You've been here in the ICU since about four o'clock that same day. So it's been a little over twenty-five hours." Al checked the machines and readings, making sure that everything was as it should be and marking it on Tommy's chart. "Are the crystals working?"

"Yeah, I can feel their energy. How did they get here?"

"You'll have to talk to your sleeping friend about that," Al looked at Mark and then at Tommy. "He's been quite the nuisance since you were brought into surgery: harassing the nurses for information, and then gloating as he waved powers of attorney in their faces later on Monday. He fell asleep during my shift last night." Al laughed softly. "He's been very concerned about you, Tommy."

"That's really sweet of him," he gasped, trying to catch his breath and feeling pain in his lung. "Would you let him know that I appreciate him being here?"

"Sure thing." Al's face creased with concern. "I assume you need more pain medication?"

"Yes. My lung hurts, and my back and leg feel like they're on fire."

"Do you remember what happened to you?" Al asked as he adjusted the medication IV.

"Sadly, I do," Tommy grunted.

Al looked down at Tommy with a smile. "Well, you're doing much better than you were yesterday. You're going to be fine."

Tommy could feel the medication seeping into his body, and his tiredness began to overwhelm him. "Don't forget to thank Mark for me," he said as his eyes closed.

Al smiled and brushed his hand through Tommy's hair. "No worries, brother." As he left the room, he looked back at the two sleeping men and smiled.

Before going off shift at eight o'clock on Tuesday morning, Al went into Tommy's room and woke Mark. "Let's go, big guy. It's time for you to get out of here."

Mark slowly became alert and immediately looked over at Tommy. He was sleeping peacefully, with more color in his face than he'd had the night before. "How's he doing?"

"He's doing just fine." Al smiled at Tommy, then turned his attention back to Mark. "He woke up at five-thirty this morning. He asked me to thank you for being here."

Mark felt a great joy at knowing that Tommy had been happy to have him there. "I'm sorry I missed that."

"Don't worry, he should be awake later today. You'll be able to talk to him then." Al put an arm around Mark's shoulders. "You in love, big guy?"

Mark looked at Al, surprised by the question. "Yes," he answered honestly, for the first time not afraid that he was admitting his love for Tommy.

"There's a lot of good juju surrounding that kid. I'd keep that one on my side, if I were you. The world could be your oyster, brother."

Mark stared at Al, then looked down at Tommy. "I'm going to try."

Mark grabbed a quick lunch in the cafeteria before his afternoon class. He was hoping that Tommy would be awake when he returned to the hospital. Engrossed in working out what he might say, he didn't see Sally approaching his table until she sat down next to him.

"Hey, babe." She smiled sweetly at him, then recoiled at the angry look that flashed across his face. "I was sorry to hear about your little brother," she said. "I came over to the house last night to see you, but Oscar was rude to me and wouldn't let me upstairs." She laid a hand on his arm with a suggestive smile. "I hope you'll talk to him about that."

Mark stared at her in disbelief. She was sitting there, pretending that nothing had happened between them. "What the fuck are you doing here?" he growled. "I told you that we're through. Done. Finished. No more. I've had enough of your bullshit." His kept his voice low, not wanting to draw attention to them, but he could not suppress the anger that oozed out. He was happy at the shock registering in her face, knowing that he'd finally been able to get through her self-absorption.

"Mark, please," she pleaded, "you have to understand—"

He raised his hand. "I understand only too well," he assured her bitterly. "You want me when you need an escort or a meal ticket, but I'm not worthy of your love. You toss me aside when you're bored with me and expect me to be honored when you want me back in your life." Mark glared at her as her eyes began to water. He couldn't tell if she was really hurt, or if she was trying to force a few tears so that he would give her what she wanted. Whichever, he didn't care any longer. "I tried really hard to love you, to give you what you wanted, but that wasn't good enough for you. I don't know what you want and I don't care anymore. I'm not going to be at your beck and call any longer. You and I are through."

"Don't do this, Mark," she sobbed pathetically.

"Don't even try that little crying game, Sally. You lied about your feelings for me to get me back in your life. Then you made a promise to me and broke it. So it's not going to work this time," he stated flatly. "Right now, I'm concerned about Tommy. And after he wakes up, I'm going to be involved in his recovery. You don't fit anywhere in that equation."

"But Mark," she said, a single tear trickling down her cheek.

"As for Oscar," he said, ignoring the sadness in her face, "he can treat you as rudely as you deserve." He stood, picked up his tray, and left her sitting alone with her crocodile tears.

Tuesday Evening

Mark sat quietly beside Tommy's bed. The nurses said that he'd woken up once during the day, but had received more pain medication and gone back to sleep. Mark thought he had sensed that awakening while he was in class; he'd felt a warmth emanating from his crystal.

He had classwork with him, giving him something to do while he waited for Tommy to wake, but he found it difficult to concentrate. He walked over to the window and stared out, looking at the leafless trees covered in snow and ice. Some of the trees looked like his heart felt — empty and cold. If Tommy wouldn't give him a chance to make up for his disastrous decision, the rest of his life might feel as bleak as the landscape outside the window. He hoped it was only stress making him feel so melodramatic.

Before he even opened his eyes, Tommy sensed the energy from Mark's crystal. Focusing his vision, he saw Mark standing by the window, staring out into the darkness. The joy he felt at Mark's presence was tempered by the anger and frustration he still felt over being dumped. Although he knew he was partially at fault for what had happened, he still held Mark accountable. However, the anxiety he had felt on Sunday over seeing and talking with Mark again seemed to have dissipated.

"Hey, big brother," Tommy called out hoarsely.

Joy bubbled through Mark's despair as he heard the soft voice. He turned away from the window to smile at Tommy. "Hey, little brother. I was wondering if you were going to wake up while I was here." He moved over to the bed and brushed his fingers through Tommy's hair. "How are you doing?"

"Not so good." Tommy grimaced. "This isn't the way I planned on returning." He squinted up at Mark. "What day is it?"

"It's about seven o'clock, Tuesday night." Mark sat down on the chair beside the bed.

"I think I woke up earlier this morning and saw you sleeping right where you're sitting," Tommy said groggily, gasping for breath. "My mind isn't exactly clear about things." He closed his eyes against the jolt of pain that rushed through him. "Did they get Brian?"

"They sure did. Scott and Jay both saw Brian leaving your room." Mark looked Tommy with concern. "So, there were two witnesses. Plus, he was pretty careless about leaving his fingerprints on the knife and on the door."

"Good." Tommy groaned as the pain shot through his body. "Good."

"Do you need more painkiller? Would you like me to leave?"

"No, please stay with me for a little while." Tommy opened his eyes and looked at Mark. "You look ragged, big brother."

Mark smiled. "You look pretty ragged yourself, little brother." He put a hand on Tommy's. "I've been really worried about you. Actually, I've been scared to death that..." he took a deep breath, "...that you might not make it, and I wouldn't get the chance to talk with you again. I missed you, Tommy."

"I missed you, too. More than you'll ever know." Tommy's eyes began to water. "I can't tell you how happy I was to see you here this morning."

"I wasn't sure how you were going to react to my being here. I was afraid that you might have Security escort me out, but I knew I had to be here with you." Mark smiled shyly and ducked his head. "I'm sorry about what happened, Tommy. Not this..." He gestured around the room. "I mean...well, yeah, this too, of course, but I meant about what happened between us. It was a huge mistake for me to let you go." He looked up. "When you're feeling better, I hope we can talk about it. And I hope that you'll consider giving me a second chance."

"I'd like that, Mark." Tommy moistened his lips. "Especially after what you did for me."

Mark was perplexed by that. "What do you mean?"

"The crystals under my pillow. How did you know which ones to get?"

Mark's smile broadened. "I guess it was your grandmother who helped guide us to the right ones, and then Oscar explained them to me and Jack."

"I see." Tommy grinned at him. "Then maybe it's Oscar that I should be talking to instead of you."

Mark raised his eyebrows. "Hey, if I hadn't been there to help open the trunk, Oscar would never have gotten into it."

"That's true," Tommy agreed, closing his eyes.

"Are you okay?"

"Another flash of pain." Tommy reached for the call button. "I think it's time for more drugs." He tried to smile, but didn't make it past a grimace.

"I should leave and let you get some rest."

"You could stay until the drugs knock me out," Tommy said as the nurse entered. "Hey, Al."

"Hey there, little bro," Al said with a big smile. He slapped Mark on the back. "How are you doing, big guy?"

"A lot better now that I see my little brother is awake and once again becoming a smartass." Mark smiled at Tommy.

"Good to hear." Al chuckled. "We know we're doing something right when the patients have the strength to be smartasses." He finished adjusting the dosage in the tubes leading into Tommy's arm. "You've got about five minutes, little bro, then it's lights out for you." He slapped Mark on the back as he left the room.

Mark cleared his throat. "I, uh, called your uncle yesterday morning to let him know what happened to you. He's a scary man. He said something about shoving a size twelve leather boot up my ass."

Tommy chuckled softly. "Probably the same boot I...almost had shoved up my ass...over the break because I was so out of sorts."

"I'm really sorry that your break was spoiled because of me."

"You're wearing the crystal." Tommy's words were blurring as the medication nudged him toward sleep.

"How did you know that?"

"It used to be my crystal. I can sense your energy flowing through it when you're wearing it." Tommy smiled sleepily. "What were we talking about?" he asked as he looked at Mark. As the painkillers took effect, Tommy's eyes began to glaze.

"It doesn't matter right now. All that really matters is that you're talking to me again." He brushed his hand through Tommy's hair. "We'll talk again tomorrow. I'll be back."

"You better be back." Tommy's eyes were closing. "Or you won't get that second chance."

Mark leaned down and kissed Tommy on the cheek. "Trust me, little brother. I'm going to be back here bothering you until they let you out."

"I still love you, Mark," Tommy whispered before he fell into a deep sleep.

"I still love you too, Tommy." He squeezed Tommy's hand. "More than I ever knew."

Early Wednesday Morning

Mark smiled as he walked into the hospital early Wednesday morning, carrying a vase of red roses. The sun was shining brightly and the snow had finally stopped falling. After talking with Tommy the previous night, he had gone back to Kappa house and had a restful night sleep. He planned to put the roses in Tommy's room before going to his morning class.

"We'll take those for you, Mister Young," the nurse at the desk stated firmly but with a smile. "Sorry, but flowers are not allowed in ICU. We'll leave them here on the desk, and he'll be able to see them through the window." She took the vase from him and set them down. "He was given more painkillers a little while ago, so he won't be awake much longer," she said as Mark turned toward the room.

As Mark opened the door, he was greeted by a big smile. Tommy was still lying on his stomach with his head turned toward the door. Mark was happy to see the sparkle had returned to those brown eyes.

"Good morning," he said, smiling brightly. "It's good to see you awake again. How are you feeling?" Mark gently brushed a finger along Tommy's cheek.

"Better than yesterday. But maybe that's the drugs."

"You look better, especially when you smile." Mark pulled the chair over next to the bed.

"It really was nice to have you here next to me when I woke up yesterday."

Mark looked into the eyes he loved. "You're still my little brother, even if you don't want to be."

"I still want to be your little brother," Tommy said. "I'm sorry that I was avoiding you."

"You're not the one that should be sorry." Mark looked directly at Tommy. "It was all my fault. I made a horrendously bad decision. The stupidest thing I've ever done in my life was to let you go."

"You weren't stupid, Mark." Tommy lowered his eyes. "I shouldn't have fallen in love with a straight guy."

"You didn't fall in love with a straight guy; you fell in love with a confused and scared guy."

"You? Confused and scared?" he teased.

"Yeah." Mark took Tommy's hand. "The difference being that the confused guy can get himself unconfused and can stop being scared. I don't want to exhaust you right now, but I really want to talk with you about us. I'm hoping that you're still willing to give me another chance."

"I'll think about it. However..." Tommy yawned.

"However, what?"

"There won't be a third chance."

"I'm not going to be foolish enough to need a third chance." Mark quirked an eyebrow. "Why are you letting me off the hook so easily?"

"Who said I was letting you off the hook?" Tommy yawned again.

"Maybe we should talk about this some other time."

"I'm sorry, Mark, the meds are kicking in. Will you be around later?"

Mark reached over and brushed Tommy's cheek. "Go ahead and get some rest, little brother. I plan on being around for a long time."

As Mark returned to visit Tommy after his morning class, he snagged one of the roses from the vase at the nurse's station. As the door closed behind him, he dropped to his knees, a pleading look on his face as he held the rose in front of him and began to sing "So Wrong".

At first, Tommy was confused. When Mark started singing, off key and out of tune, he began to laugh. "Stop, please. It's too painful, and Patsy must be spinning in her grave."

"Punk." Mark got up off his knees and walked over to the bed.

"You're not going to sing again, are you?"

"Only if you want me to," he replied, laying the rose on the bedside stand.

"No, thank you." Tommy was glad to see Mark's mood so buoyant. "I guess you spent a lot of time with Patsy recently, too."

"Who else can sing a song and make you feel your own pain?" Mark asked, a smile on his face as he stood next to the bed. "You have a lot more color in your cheeks and a gleam in your eyes." Mark tousled Tommy's hair. "And greasy hair," he added, as he made a face and wiped his hand on his jeans.

Tommy laughed. "We've been able to do the sponge bath, but not the shampoo."

"Have you been able to get out of bed and walk around?"

"Maybe later today or tomorrow. Are you between classes or something?" Tommy asked as Mark sat down.

"I just got out of my morning class, and I don't have another one until two."

"So you thought you'd join me for lunch," Tommy said drolly.

Mark made a sour face. "I hadn't thought to go that far," he said, causing Tommy to laugh.

"Good afternoon, gentlemen," the nurse said as she entered the room with a walker. "Once you finish your lunch, Mister Ford, we'd like you to start working out those muscles before they atrophy."

Tommy groaned. "Yes, Nurse Ratched." His smile took any sting out of the jibe.

"You keep that up, young man, and I'll have them put the catheter back in." She laughed as she checked Tommy's vitals. When she finished, she looked over at Mark. All the nurses knew who Mark was after the incidents on Monday. "Would you like us to bring you a lunch as well, Mister Young? A few patients left earlier this morning, and there are some extra plates available. Afterwards, you could help Tommy with his physical therapy." She grinned at Mark as she put a thermometer in Tommy's mouth.

Mark gave her a dour look. "Couldn't I just watch Tommy eat?"

"Not if you want to stay here any longer. We'll have to ask you to leave while he has lunch."

Tommy chuckled despite the thermometer. Mark glared at him, then started laughing. "Then I guess it'll be two for lunch. Is there a choice of entrée?" He smiled engagingly.

"Of course, Mister Young. You can have the baked chicken or the baked chicken. It comes with mashed potatoes and green beans. We have red Jell-O or orange Jell-O for dessert." The nurse removed the thermometer, giving Mark a sideways glance. "I'll give you time to think about your choices," she said, chuckling as she left the room.

"She's a real card," Mark said after the door closed.

"After Al, she's my favorite nurse."

"You probably don't get to see much of Al because he works nights."

"Actually, he and I did talk. I was awake early this morning before he got off his shift. He told me about my entrance into the emergency room early Monday morning, and your attitude problem because you couldn't get inside." Tommy chuckled.

"I didn't have an attitude problem," Mark argued. "I was concerned about you, but they wouldn't let me see you because I wasn't a family member."

"They have to keep out the riff-raff, you know," Tommy teased.

"You were a lot sweeter when you were asleep." Mark leaned over and planted a kiss on Tommy's cheek. "Where are those drug lines?" he asked, looking around the room, a smile on his face.

"Ha ha. I can take pills now, like a big boy," Tommy said in a child-like voice. He was still in pain, but he was feeling better now that Mark was around.

"Why don't you tell me about how you guys got the trunk open?" Tommy asked as he and Mark were walking slowly down the hallway after lunch. Tommy hadn't thought using a walker would be difficult, but his lung hurt when he took deep breaths, his shoulder and thigh muscles were stiff and ached, and the wheels on the walker were sticky.

Mark looked over and smiled before giving Tommy a quick recap of the events surrounding the opening of his grandmother's trunk. Before finishing, he recollected something else about the trunk incident. "Is there a reason that one of my jockstraps is inside that trunk?"

Tommy laughed out loud. "It's a keepsake."

Mark grinned. "So, what's it like being a witch?"

"I don't know what you're talking about."

"All those things in your grandmother's trunk," Mark said, "Oscar said that they are powerful. Even I could feel the energy coming from inside the trunk."

Tommy looked over at him bashfully. "My grandmother was the practitioner. I'm just an apprentice."

Mark put his arm around Tommy's shoulders and whispered into his ear, "Are you a good witch or a bad witch?"

"I'm a good witch." Tommy turned serious. "*That which you do, comes back threefold.*" He quoted his grandmother's mantra. "If I cause any harm to others, I'll be in serious trouble."

"So how does the vampire thing play into your life? I didn't think witches and vampires got along," Mark teased.

"First of all, I'm not a one-dimensional person," Tommy said in earnest. "I'm a Wiccan apprentice, a gay man, a football fan, a country music fan, and a lot of other things. And you're not just a jock."

"Okay, that's one point for you," Mark allowed.

"Secondly, the vampire thing is just a game," he smiled over at Mark, "at least until I meet a real vampire."

"Two points for you."

Tommy laughed out loud. "What do you want to hear? That when I go to the cabin in the Poconos, I stand over a boiling cauldron and cast spells over people while listening to New Age music?"

"I'm sorry." Mark rephrased his earlier question. "I'm just a little curious about this witch stuff and how I'm going to be affected by being with you."

"We'll have plenty of time to discuss the witch stuff." Tommy looked away from Mark shyly. "It's not a simple matter of saying abracadabra or hocus-pocus. Besides, I'm not that kind of witch. I use the Earth's energies to empower myself for positive things to happen." Tommy looked over at Mark, a glint of mischief in his eyes. "You don't have to worry about being affected by being around me unless a coven chases after me. Then I'm going to hide behind you."

Mark laughed loudly and hugged Tommy. "I'll do my best to protect you." They reached the end of the hallway, and he asked, "Do you want to go back to the room now?"

"No. I'd like to try to make it around the whole floor," Tommy said. "I'm feeling pretty good."

"I'm glad to hear that." Mark tousled Tommy's still greasy hair. "I called your uncles and let them know that you were awake and recovering well."

"Thank you." Tommy looked at Mark with curiosity. "Did my uncle give you a hard time again?"

"No." Mark chuckled. "He seems to be more concerned about your health and getting out here to see you."

"Did he say when he was going to be here?"

Mark checked the hallway ahead, making sure that there were no obstacles in Tommy's way. "He's still working on it."

Tommy smiled, knowing that his uncle wouldn't tell Mark when he was going to arrive. "They're going to move me out of ICU tonight and put me into a semi-private room. I won't have a roommate because they don't have a full house."

Mark was encouraged. "Hey, that's great. That must mean that you're doing well, and they'll let you out of here soon."

Tommy's smile left his face. "I'm a little anxious about going back to the dorm. Usually, nothing scares me."

"Don't worry about it. Things will take care of themselves."

"You sound like my grandmother." Tommy laughed. "Are you sure you let her back out of your mind?"

"Yes, I did." Mark laughed and gently patted Tommy's arm. "Let's get you back to your room so that I can get to my class."

Tommy sat quietly on the side of the bed, a little winded from his first walk in three days. "It felt good to walk around, but I have to admit that I'm tired out." He settled himself in the bed. "However, I can't wait to start running again."

Mark cupped Tommy's face and tilted it up. "You be a good boy this afternoon." He smiled down into Tommy's eyes before leaning down and giving him a light kiss on the lips. "There's a house meeting at six o'clock. I'll be here as soon as it's over."

Tommy smiled brightly. "Will I get another one of those?"

"Only if you're a good boy."

Mark arrived at the hospital shortly after eight o'clock and was directed to Tommy's new room on the first floor. As he walked into the room, he saw that the second bed was not made up. Tommy was lying on the bed near the windows. He smiled as he approached and gave Tommy a kiss on the cheek. "How are you feeling, little brother?"

"Better," Tommy replied, waiting until Mark sat down next to him. "I talked with the police this afternoon. They said that Brian didn't put up any resistance when they arrested him."

The smile left Mark's face as he thought about what Brian had done to Tommy, beyond the stabbing. "I haven't paid much attention to what happened to Brian; I've been worried about you. I was scared that I was going to lose you before I had the chance to get you back." He fidgeted a bit, then steeled himself to ask, "Why didn't you tell anyone when Brian assaulted you by the admin building?"

Tommy closed his eyes for a couple of moments, recalling the attack on the solitary path. "How did you find out about that?"

"One of the Gamma brothers works for campus security, and Monday he came over with Ken to talk with me, Jack, Oscar, and Dave. He told us that the police had requested all security incident reports concerning either you or Brian. There was the report regarding you and the wrestler, and several reports involving Brian, most for drunk and disorderly behavior. But the last report involved Brian attacking you in an alley." Mark looked into Tommy's brown eyes. "Why didn't you tell anyone?"

"Because I handled it myself." Tommy's response was clipped.

"That's what the attached infirmary report implied." Mark chuckled. "Brian had been kneed in the groin and punched in the jaw, dislocating it. It also said that he had bitten his tongue so hard that it required two stitches."

"He didn't bite his tongue; I bit his tongue." Tommy allowed a smile. "He had me pinned against a wall and was trying to kiss me. As I was positioning myself for the knee jerk, I opened my mouth and let his tongue inside. When I was ready to knee him in the balls, I bit down on his tongue."

Mark cringed. "Ouch!"

Tommy laughed a little. "No, not like that. It was a scream. A very high-pitched scream."

"You're a dangerous little guy," Mark said, his tone clearly indicating admiration as well as gentle teasing.

"Not dangerous enough, or I wouldn't be here now."

Mark took a deep breath. "How did he get you?"

"I was asleep. When I woke up, he already had me pinned face down on the bed with a knife at my throat." Tommy lifted his head enough for Mark to see the small cut below his jaw. "If I'd known he was going to stab me after raping me, I would have risked getting my throat sliced to kick his ass."

"I'm sure you would have." Mark stood up and walked over to the window. "It's started snowing again."

Tommy watched Mark's reflection in the window. "What's on your mind?"

"Do you feel like talking?"

"Sounds serious."

"It is to me," Mark confirmed. "I have a lot of things that I want to say to you, but if you're not feeling up to it, then I'll wait."

Tommy looked into Mark's eyes. "I'm not in any position to walk out of here, so I guess I'm going to have to listen to you."

Mark smiled. "You're definitely getting better because you're getting sassier."

"So, what's on your mind, big brother?"

Mark sat down with a sigh. It wasn't as easy as when he had rehearsed what he would say. "I want you to know that I love you. The more time I spent with you during the pledge period, the deeper I fell. But falling in love with you scared the hell out of me. I've never been in love with another guy. So I ran away from you. I thought that would be the end of it."

Mark lowered his head. "I'm never going to be able to forget the look of desolation in your eyes when I told you that I had decided to go back with Sally. When you turned your back to me and walked out of the cemetery, I felt a disconnection such as I have never felt in my life. It felt as if a piece of my heart was leaving with you." He looked into Tommy's eyes. "Afterwards, when I saw you on campus, I could see the coldness in your eyes and feel the gulf between us. That was painful for me, but I just know it didn't come close to how badly I hurt you. I don't ever want to hurt you like that again, Tommy."

He tenderly rubbed Tommy's cheek. "Do you want to know what I did over the Thanksgiving break?" He looked directly into Tommy's eyes. "I was at a party with Sally and a bunch of her friends. I sat alone, with a bottle of red wine, on the second floor balcony watching the ocean. The only thing I could think about was how much more fun I would have been having with you. I really missed being with you, Tommy. I hope that you can forgive me for not having had the courage to love you. I'd really like to see where this relationship can go."

"That's the sweetest apology I've ever heard," Tommy said softly, his eyes stinging with tears. "I spent the break trying to get you out of my mind, but I couldn't. I really wanted to hate you for what you did, but I couldn't even do that. The only thing that I could do was kick myself for falling in love with a straight jock." He looked up into Mark's dark, wet eyes. "I forgave you the other morning, when I woke up and saw you sleeping in that chair." He smiled playfully. "Goddess, I was pissed that you were able to sneak back into my heart and life when I was in no condition to punch you."

"I'll let you punch me when you get out of here." Mark laughed. "Besides, you caught me off guard during the pledge period when you snuck into my heart. Doesn't that make us even?"

"Yes, sir, big brother. I think that makes us even," Tommy said with a broad smile.

"The other day you said that you would give me a second chance, but not a third. Do you remember that? And does it still apply?"

"Yes, I do remember saying that, and yes, it still applies."

"Thank you, Tommy." Mark leaned forward and lightly kissed Tommy's lips. "You didn't let me down during pledge, and I'm going to do my best not to let you down again."

"So, what happened at the house meeting?"

"Nothing for you to be concerned about," Mark replied with a smile.

Tommy became suspicious, but because he was tiring, he decided to let it drop.

"Can I ask you for a favor?"

"Anything."

"Please bring me some chocolate. The food in here is going to kill me."

Mark laughed. "Now that's my little brother — a sparkle in his eyes and chocolate on his mind."

16: FAMILY VISITATIONS

Mark stopped short as he walked into Tommy's hospital room on Thursday morning and saw two men standing at the side of the bed. The closer man was about the same height as Tommy, with thinning light brown hair and similar facial features. The man standing at the end of the bed was only an inch shorter but more muscular and had thinning dark brown hair. Both men turned their heads toward the door as Mark entered.

"Mister Young," the taller man said. "I'm Allen, and this is my partner, Morgan." Allen offered his hand.

Mark cautiously shook hands as he studied the man who had threatened to shove a boot up his ass. Allen didn't look like a fighter, and Mark was larger than either of Tommy's uncles. However, knowing that Tommy had been able to handle a wrestler that was more than fifty pounds heavier caused him to think twice about the capabilities of the older man.

Tommy started laughing because he had never seen Mark intimidated. "Relax, Mark, he's not wearing his old boots."

Allen chuckled as he released his firm grip on Mark's hand. "I'm not about to ruin a new pair of boots."

Mark smiled nervously. "It's nice to meet you, sir."

"I'm glad you think so," Allen said smugly as they moved toward Tommy's bed. "You wouldn't have said that last week."

Mark looked at Allen and then over at Morgan. "Did you have a good flight?"

Morgan laughed. "Nice move, Mark. Change the subject."

"Yes, we did have a good flight," Allen said, "although our landing was delayed for over an hour because of these damn snow showers. Our rental car had been given to somebody else, and we had to wait an hour while they arranged for another. And then it was slow driving from the airport because of the snow. We didn't get to our hotel until one o'clock this morning." A hint of a smile crossed Allen's face as he looked at Tommy. "You couldn't have chosen Berkeley?"

Tommy laughed. "No. This is where I wanted to go."

"Have you had lunch, Mark?" Morgan asked.

"No. I'm between classes and wanted to see Tommy first."

"Good. We haven't had lunch either." Allen glanced at his watch. "What time is your next class?"

"Not until two," he replied reluctantly.

"Even better." Allen looked down at Tommy and ruffled his hair. "We're going to take your friend out to lunch." He turned his head to peer over at Mark. "He might even be returned to you in one piece."

"You don't have to do that," Mark said nervously.

"Oh, but we do, Mister Young." Allen moved toward the door.

Morgan put his arm on Mark's shoulder and led him away from Tommy's bed. Mark looked back at Tommy pleadingly, hoping that Tommy would ask for him to stay, but Tommy just smiled and waved at Mark as the three men left his room.

Before closing the door, Morgan looked back at Tommy and winked. "We'll let you know where we leave the body."

Julia Young watched from behind a post and a magazine as two men led her son out of the hospital, then she went over to the nurse's station. "May I please have the room number for Thomas Ford?"

The nurse consulted her charge sheet. "He's in room 137. Just down the hall and to your right."

"Thank you so much," Julia said with a pleasant smile.

As she opened the door of Tommy's hospital room, she could feel the energy. She immediately grasped that this young man was more steeped in the Wiccan ways than she and her college girlfriends could have imagined. "I hope I'm not disturbing you, Mister Ford," she said considerately as she approached the bed.

Tommy immediately recognized her as Mark's mother from the pictures in Mark's room. She had the same magnetic blue eyes and the same aquiline nose, but in a smaller, more feminine size. Her wavy black hair elegantly framed her round face and hung gently over her shoulders. She was impeccably dressed in a tailored black woolen skirt and top, her overcoat neatly over her arm. He smiled as he looked at the long, manicured fingers holding the railing of the bed. He smiled up at her. "Jungle Red, Doctor Young?"

"I find it appropriate when I'm protecting my young." She placed her coat and purse on the empty bed, then moved the chair closer to Tommy and sat down. "Who were the men with Mark?"

"My uncles," he replied. "They came out here to make sure that I was okay and to help Mark understand that male relationships can work." The fact that Mark's mother was there told Tommy he wasn't revealing any secrets.

"I want to know what you did to my son, Mister Ford."

"I didn't do anything to your son, Doctor Young," he stated firmly. "I merely provided Mark with an alternative direction for his life. And a better direction, I might add, than the trap that Miss Brown was setting for him."

Julia sat back in the chair, smiling. "I see Miss Brown wasn't able to charm all males, only my husband and my son." Her smile disappeared just as quickly as it had come. "What type of spell did you put on him?"

"I don't know what you're talking about, Doctor Young." Tommy knew that was an outright lie, but he wanted to know exactly how much this woman understood of Wiccan magic before he admitted to any of his actions.

Julia leaned forward and stared directly into Tommy's eyes. "There are three sources of energy within that topaz crystal you gave my son." She had hoped to provoke a reaction from Tommy, but none was forthcoming. "One is his own energy, and now I recognize that another is yours. The third energy is in this room and is a part of you. And from what Mark told me about you, I would venture a guess that the third energy belongs to your grandmother." A slight smile spread across her face. "It'll be easier for us to become friends if you tell me what you did to him, rather than forcing me to drag the facts from you one at a time, Mister Ford. And I do intend to get the facts from you."

Tommy stared deeply into her dark blue eyes and smiled. "Technically, Doctor Young, I didn't do anything to Mark." He noted the look of disbelief on her face as she sat back in her chair and waited for him to continue. "It was your son who captured my heart, the day I registered. He is the most captivating man that I have ever met. When he walked through the lobby of my dorm, it seemed as if all the movement in the room stopped, and the noise died away. He was the only person in that lobby whose inner spirit was so full of life that it spilled out into the physical world." Tommy closed his eyes and smiled to himself as he remembered that first day of college. He sighed deeply. "The first time that we were introduced, a charge of electricity went through me. I've met a number of people that I knew I could connect with on a personal level, but I've never felt that type of connection with anyone. I fell in love with Mark at that instant."

"And so you cast some spells on Mark to make him fall in love with you," she suggested, raising an eyebrow.

He met her gaze evenly. "I did not cast any spells directly on Mark."

A wide smile spread on Julia's face. "So you influenced him indirectly." Redness suffused Tommy's face, and she knew it wasn't because he was angry with her.

"Are you aware of how many women were throwing themselves at Mark whenever he and Sally were apart? All of those women were just like her, only wanting him as a trophy. The hot quarterback stud that made them look better whenever they were with him."

"And what did you want him for, Mister Ford?" she asked. "I imagine that there are just as many gay men out there who would love to have a hot quarterback stud hanging on their arm." Challenge issued, she folded her arms across her chest.

Tommy's eyes narrowed, but his voice was soft when he began speaking. "I envision two men sharing their lives together, allowing each other the space to grow as individuals, yet depending on one another for the support and love they need to survive and thrive in this world. Together there would be nothing that would keep them from doing anything they wanted to do, or being whoever they wanted to be. Together they would share all the ups and downs that the world threw at them. Together they would love each other until death parted them." He smiled at her. "Pretty much the same as what you and Mister Young have together."

Julia stared at him for several moments. "You are aware that our family is quite wealthy?" she blurted, trying to evoke a response.

"I'm financially secure, Doctor Young; I don't want or need your family's wealth. I didn't know a thing about your son when I first saw him. I only want to be able to love Mark for as long as he'll let me."

"And whatever you *indirectly*," she grinned, "did to him, will help you toward that end?"

Tommy continued looking into her eyes — he wanted her to know how much he loved Mark. "As I told you, Doctor Young," he grinned, "I didn't do anything to Mark. *He* picked me to be his little brother."

"And after that, what did you do," her look was smug, "*indirectly*?"

"I placed two crystals beneath his mattress," Tommy admitted. "A clear crystal that had never been used for any purpose, and the topaz crystal that I gave to him."

A puzzled look crossed Julia's face. "No," she insisted quietly, looking down at the floor and then up at Tommy. "There has to be more to it than that. You have to have done something."

Tommy shook his head. "I helped Mark open his mind and make choices for himself, Doctor Young. The two crystals were used as conduits to collect his energy and allow him to clear his mind of the crap that Sally had put into it. I used the clear crystal to finish my fraternity paddle and left the topaz crystal beneath his mattress."

"Calming and clearing his energy." She glanced at him. "He did mention that he had been sleeping better during pledge period. I thought it was just because *she* wasn't around him."

"She wasn't around him after the first week," Tommy said. "And I wasn't sleeping with him either. It was all Mark and only Mark."

Julia stood and walked over to the window, looking out at the fresh blanket of white that covered the ground and trees. "I'm confused, Tommy," she said, using his name for the first time. "What is all the energy that I feel surrounding you and Mark?"

"The topaz crystal originally belonged to my grandmother. When I was six years old and moved in with her, she gave me the topaz crystal and later taught me how to empower it. She told me that the topaz would be comforting. It was, but it also allowed me to open my mind to all potentialities."

"So you let Mark add his own energy to that crystal and at the same time opened his mind to other options available to him." Julia leaned against the window sill and watched Tommy. "You're only a freshman in college, Tommy. How is it you think you can guide somebody else's life in a direction that might not be right for him?"

It was not meant as a reprimand but as an effort to understand what was happening, and Tommy took it as such. "I'm not guiding anybody's life but my own, Doctor Young," he said softly. "My grandmother warned me against casting love spells when she first began teaching me about magic. I certainly don't want to be with somebody who doesn't want to be with me. I want to be loved in return. I crushed the plain crystal from under Mark's mattress and sprinkled it on both the back and front of my fraternity paddle. The only spell I cast into my paddle was one that would make him take notice of me. The rest happened on its own before he even saw my paddle. I was simply being myself around Mark. I wasn't playing any games with him, and I wasn't trying to persuade him to prefer men to women."

"You got him to notice you, and you got him to open his mind. I'd have to say you worked your magic on him," she argued. "*Indirectly*, of course."

"I love Mark, and I want to share my life with him," Tommy said. "If there had been any spells on those crystals, or Mark, he wouldn't have chosen to leave me and go back to Miss Brown."

"Ah, now there's another thing that confuses me." She frowned. "A lot of things changed for Mark before Thanksgiving. He told me that he was having trouble sleeping and that his concentration was poor."

"When Mark went back to Sally, I took my paddle and the topaz crystal out of his room and back to my dorm."

Julia started laughing. "You say you love him, and yet you left him to fend for himself against that woman?"

"He made the choice."

"And you didn't do anything to make his life miserable?" she asked softly, already knowing what the answer was going to be.

"I didn't do anything except leave him alone so that he could be with her."

Julia sat back in her chair and smiled. "I noticed that little box on his dresser with the crystal inside. I felt the energy emanating from that crystal and was quite curious about where he had gotten it. He never said anything about it until after Thanksgiving."

"I couldn't keep it because it stirred up too many memories for me, but I couldn't destroy it either. So I decided to give it to him."

"And once again, making him notice you." Her smile lit up her eyes.

"I just wanted him to know that I was thinking about him."

"He knew, Tommy," she said softly, brushing her hand over his hair. "He was beating himself up over how badly he had hurt you. He was scared to death that you would never speak to him again. He told me that he would understand if you didn't want to be with him, but he didn't want you to stop being friends. I think he was lying about the first part, Tommy. He may have understood it, but it certainly would have hurt him. And I'm not trying to defend him for what happened between you," she said. "I'm just letting you know."

"I already know." Tommy's eyes were wet with tears. "Mark told me the other night when I was fully awake. Actually," a smile spread across his face, "he's been telling me ever since I woke up."

"How do you even know what you want out of life, Tommy? You've had little experience with the world."

"I've had more experience than I care to think about, Doctor Young." His smile was sad, wistful. "As for knowing what I want in life, I discovered that with my best friend in junior high school. I want to share my life with another man. I found that man when he walked through the lobby of my dorm and later chose me to be his little brother. I intend to do everything in my power to make sure that Mark never regrets falling in love with me."

Julia stood up and walked over to the window. She stared out as she absorbed their conversation. "Mark said you were a remarkable young man." She shook her head and turned around. "I knew I was going to like you when he told me what your major was."

A smile spread over Tommy's face. "Then why did you come here and scare me like you did? I've been sweating bullets for fear that you were going to try and make me let go of Mark."

"Would I have gotten honest responses from you if I had walked in here, all sweet and demure, fully supporting a man falling in love with my son?" she asked.

"Yes, you would have," Tommy responded.

"Well, I didn't want you to think that I was a pushover."

"With all due respect, Doctor Young, any woman who raises two children and works her way to a doctorate in psychology is not a woman that's going to be a pushover." He smiled at her, a gleam in his eye. "Especially if she's behind the wheel of a pink Cadillac."

"So he told you about that." She laughed softly, the smile softening her face and making her look younger than her years. "I raised my children to find themselves and to have faith in themselves. Miss Brown slowly took that away from Mark by rejecting him over and over again. He always seemed okay when they were together, and then would be depressed after they broke up." Julia leaned against the window frame and looked over at Tommy. "He talked about you during your pledge period, Tommy. I heard about all of your accomplishments and how proud he was of the way you were handling your pledge responsibilities. I certainly didn't think it was because he was falling in love with you. I only knew that he sounded happier than any time when he had been with Miss Brown. He sounded confident again."

Julia walked slowly back to the chair. "Before Thanksgiving, I knew something was wrong and that it had to do with Miss Brown. He didn't come to me right away, and I later learned it was because he was trying to find a way to tell me about you. He was devastated by what he had done to you and didn't know how to fix it. It was hard for me to believe that he would give up somebody who loved him unconditionally for somebody who was using him. I wanted to slap him when he told me about it." She shook her head. "Of course, I couldn't do that when he had come to me for help. That's when I knew how much you meant to him. And if I needed any further proof that he loved you, I got it Monday morning." She leaned forward. "It took me several minutes to calm him down before I could make sense of what he was saying. Mark was frantic about what had happened to you, and he was scared that you were going to die before he could talk to you."

"I'm not ready to die," Tommy said, as if that settled the matter.

"He wasn't sure if he should stick around and wait for you to wake up. He was afraid that you might be upset at seeing him here."

"I almost cried when I saw him sitting by the bed."

"If this terrible thing hadn't happened to you, would you have let him back into your life, Tommy?"

Tommy smiled. "I was going to wait for him to talk to me, and then I was going to take my time thinking about it," he admitted. "But I wasn't going to let him get away. I'm not stupid."

Julia's light laughter filled the room. "When you're ready to look for a master's program, let me know. I have some friends that I can put you in touch with to help guide you to the right school."

"Why would you do that? You don't even know if he and I are going to be together by the time I'm ready to think about where to go for my master's. Mark might change his mind again."

"That's true," she said with a smile. "However, there was a look of joy in his eyes when he came to me and talked about you. There was also pain and hurt when he told me what he had done and how you had reacted. When he called me at two in the morning on Monday, there was fear in his voice. But when he called me on Tuesday, after you woke up and talked to him, there was that sound of joy again. I believe that you and he are going to be together for a long time. Besides, I think you're going to be very good for my son."

"Thank you, Doctor Young. I'll do my best not to let either one of you down." Tommy smiled up at her. "What about your husband? How is he going to react to all of this?"

"I'm going to tell you the same thing I told Mark." She smiled. "What he doesn't know, won't hurt him." Her laugh brought a smile to Tommy's face. "Mark has enough to deal with right now; he doesn't need his father berating him. When the time is right, Mark will talk to him. Right now, neither of us is going to say a thing to Mister Young. As far as he is concerned, you are Mark's fraternity brother and friend. You will slowly become a part of our family, and Mister Young won't even realize what's going on."

"You're good, Doctor Young." Tommy chuckled. "It's no wonder I was scared of you when you came in here. They never would have found my body, would they?"

Julia laughed again, brushing her hand over Tommy's hair. "No, they wouldn't have. When I'm protecting my children, Tommy, no telltale trace is left behind."

"I'll remember that." He smiled at her. "I think I'm going to like you very much."

"I already like you." She leaned down and kissed him on the cheek, then sat back for a couple of minutes. "How are you dealing with what happened to you?"

"I'm doing okay," Tommy replied honestly. "I have my grandmother watching over me, and I have Mark back in my life."

"But what about your feelings about what happened the other night?"

Tommy took a deep breath and blew it out slowly, wincing at the pain in his lung. "I think I'm dealing with all of those feelings and emotions rather well." He sighed. "After what my father did to me, my grandmother came into my life and took care of me. When I woke up on Tuesday after being raped and stabbed, Mark was sitting in a chair by the hospital bed. I've had two really horrible experiences in my life, and in the aftermath, both times I've had the person I've loved the most next to me. I'm going to be fine, Doctor Young."

Julia nodded. "You're a very strong young man, Tommy, but if you ever need or want to talk with anyone about what happened, please call me. I'll be happy to listen."

"I appreciate that," he said quietly.

"I know you handled Mark's going back with Miss Brown well," she said with a twinkle in her eyes, "but didn't you want to rip her conniving eyes out of her head?"

"And rip her blonde hair out by the roots," he added with a laugh.

"That's good to hear. For a moment I thought you might be too good to be true."

"I can protect what's mine, too, Doctor Young. I just didn't want to make a scene which would cause Mark to turn against me. I had to walk away with dignity and let him know that he was free to make his own choices."

"Which was even worse than causing a scene," she remarked.

"I think he respected me more because of it."

"I know that he respected you more." She smiled. "But, oh how I would have loved to have seen you take that little bitch down."

Tommy laughed out loud. "Several of our fraternity brothers would have loved that, too."

"Well, it's time for me to be leaving." She stood up and put on her overcoat. "Neither Mark nor my husband are aware that I'm here. I came here to meet you and get to know more about you. Our conversation is strictly covered by doctor-patient privilege. I'm the doctor and you are the patient." She smiled conspiratorially. "Nothing we said goes any further than this room. And that means that you are not going to tell Mark that I was here. Understand?"

"Yes, sir, Doctor Young, sir." Tommy saluted.

She smiled at his antics and leaned down to kiss him on the cheek. "You take care of yourself, and please call me if you need to talk." She stopped at the door. "I'll look forward to officially meeting you some day. Be surprised when we're introduced."

At The Restaurant

They had been seated and placed their orders before Allen spoke. "You're a fortunate young man, Mister Young."

The ride from the hospital to the restaurant had been silent, and Mark's nervousness had been growing exponentially. "I don't understand."

"Tommy thought you might benefit from getting to know us better," Morgan explained. "He felt that we might be able to help you deal with your uncertainty about male relationships, answer any questions that you might have."

"We've been together for over twenty-five years," Allen said slowly.

"My parents have been married for twenty-five years," Mark said.

"Were things always peachy?" Allen asked. "Did they ever have any difficulties?"

"I guess our family had some tough times. My parents kept personal issues between themselves and away from my sister and me," Mark said thoughtfully.

Morgan smiled at Allen. "Normal life goes on in a relationship, regardless of the sex of the two parties involved."

"If anything, Mark, we might consider that we had a more difficult time than your parents, since we already had a strike against us because we're gay. But we don't think that way," Allen added. "Our life together has had ups and downs, great moments and tough moments. We've watched friends die from AIDS. Some of those friends had been in long-term relationships, while others were single and loving it. We miss them all equally."

Morgan nodded. "We've been able to last this long because of mutual respect and understanding. We allow each other to grow and remain independent, while holding on to each other for support."

"More importantly, we communicate with one another, openly and honestly," Allen said.

"That doesn't mean that we tell each other absolutely everything," Morgan quickly added, smiling at Allen before looking back at Mark. "Mostly it's little stuff that I discuss with friends and my family, stuff that I consider unimportant and that he'll learn sooner or later."

Allen laughed. "Like what you and Tommy discussed about Mark?"

"I told Tommy that he should scratch her eyes out in a cat fight in the cafeteria," Morgan admitted.

Mark burst out laughing. "No question, Tommy could take her."

"That wasn't what I told him," Allen said, looking from Morgan back to Mark. "Tommy has been a part of our lives since he moved in with his grandmother when he was six. His mother and father were not keen on our being around him. Most of the time they were too drunk to know what was going on, but that's a different story."

They waited quietly as the waiter placed their food on the table and left.

"Tommy has been out to visit with us every summer since he was eight years old," Morgan recounted. "He's met all of our friends, from the laid back and mellow to the wild and crazy. Couples, singles, lesbians, and a few drag queens. He was exposed to gay people even before he realized that he was gay."

"He knows what he wants in a relationship, Mark," Allen said seriously. "He's looking for the same thing that we have: a long-term, monogamous relationship with a guy that he can share his life with." Allen looked directly at Mark. "What are you looking for in a relationship, Mark?"

He paused to think about his response. "I've been looking for the same thing, only I thought I was supposed to be looking for that in a woman. I certainly didn't expect somebody like Tommy to come into my life."

Allen smiled wryly. "People rarely get what they expect, Mark," Allen said, looking at Morgan. "We met quite by accident at a Fourth of July picnic. Morgan didn't really like me when we first met because I was quite outspoken." He switched his gaze to Mark. "I guess we grew on each other."

Morgan looked at Mark. "He was obnoxiously political then. I was quite comfortable being the quiet little closet case."

"What got you together?" Mark asked, curious about the differences that they had overcome to become a couple.

"Anita Bryant," they said in unison, and laughed.

"She was a little before your time, kid," Morgan continued. "That's when the Religious Right and the Moral Majority started coming down on gays and lesbians. Allen convinced me that if I wasn't going to help do something to stop those people, then I deserved to have my closet door nailed shut."

"Why are you being so nice to me after what I did to Tommy?"

Allen sighed. "Tommy was very excited about coming to college. By the third week of the semester, we began hearing about Mark," Allen smiled at him. "Mark is a football player. Mark is in a fraternity. Mark is going to be my big brother. Mark this and Mark that. On and on, *ad nauseum.*"

"The only thing he hadn't told us was what had taken place after initiation," Morgan interjected. "We knew that Tommy had a crush on you, but we weren't aware that it had gone farther until he talked about it over Thanksgiving."

Allen looked at Mark appraisingly. "What happened?"

Mark lowered his head in shame. "I was scared," he said as he looked up. "Maybe if I had grown up with uncles like you, I would have felt more at ease falling in love with Tommy, but I had decided how my life was going to be. I had hopes of getting into the NFL, then marrying and having a family." He looked at Allen. "It was all so simple until Tommy came into my life."

"Who said you had to change your plans?" Morgan asked.

Mark shook his head. "I may be a good quarterback at a small school like Timian, but I'm probably not NFL caliber. Even if I took a couple of years to play in another league, there would be even more quality quarterbacks available every year."

"No, Mark," Allen said. "What he meant was why do your plans for having a family have to change? There are many gay couples raising children."

Mark stared at Allen for a minute. "To be honest with you, I wasn't thinking about having a family right away. I wanted to spend some time traveling if I didn't go to the NFL. I had thought there would be one woman in my life, but I never considered having a man in my life."

"So, what are your plans now, Mister Young?" Allen waited patiently as Mark considered his response.

"I've been doing a lot of thinking about that since Thanksgiving, when I finally opened my mind and heart. But I haven't talked to Tommy about any of this, and I believe that he should be the first one to hear my plans for the future."

"Is Tommy a part of those plans?" Allen asked.

"Yes," Mark affirmed without hesitation. "I've learned a lot about myself. The first thing I learned was that I enjoy my life a lot more when Tommy is a part of it. The second thing I learned was that I had made a mistake and had to figure out a way to get him to talk to me again." Mark frowned. "I certainly never expected it to be with him in a hospital bed."

"You want to know something, Mark?" Allen fiddled with his napkin. "If you and Tommy were in the opposite positions, he would have done the same thing you did. He would have sat by your bedside, waiting for you to wake up."

"I know," Mark said softly. "I realized that when he gave me this crystal."

"Did Tommy tell you about that crystal?"

"He told me that his grandmother gave it to him when he moved in with her. And that he had put it beneath my mattress during the pledge period."

"Tommy is a strong young man who doesn't like people feeling sorry for him or showing him pity because of the way his parents treated him. Did Tommy tell you why his grandmother gave him that crystal?" Allen looked into Mark's eyes.

"No, sir."

"Tommy's mother didn't stop drinking while she was pregnant, although she didn't get drunk as frequently. She smoked pot but didn't use hard drugs during her pregnancy. Tommy was born a couple of weeks premature." The look of surprise on Mark's face told Allen that Tommy hadn't shared the whole story. "His mother left the hospital two days after he was born, but his grandmother stayed with him until he was released. During the weeks that he remained in the hospital, she used that crystal to heal him."

Mark pressed the crystal over his heart.

"I don't know exactly what my mother did to Tommy during his first weeks of life, but she completely skewed the medical Bell curve." Allen smiled briefly. "She allowed the hospital staff to believe that they had helped Tommy become a miracle baby. Now he's a stronger person because of what she did."

He waited for his words to sink in. "She couldn't completely protect him after he left the hospital to live with his parents, but she did threaten to take him away if they harmed him. He had to deal with a lot of psychological abuse during his early years, but there was never any physical abuse, at least, not until the night that his father fractured his jaw. After he was released from the emergency room, she took Tommy into her home and raised him herself. The first thing she did was to give the crystal to Tommy in order to help him heal."

"Why would he part with it?" Mark asked softly.

"He had charged the topaz with your energy, and it hurt him too much to keep it, but he couldn't destroy it. He gave it to you because he felt that you might need some healing." Allen looked intently into Mark's eyes. "Even though you broke up with him, Tommy never stopped loving you."

Mark felt his eyes sting. "I may have broken up with him, but I don't believe that I stopped loving him, either."

"Just remember one thing, Mark," Allen warned. "I have an old pair of size twelve leather boots in my closet." His smile held as much promise as levity.

"I'll remember that, sir." Mark laughed. "Trust me, I'll remember that."

"If you ever need to talk to anybody, or if you have any questions, please call us," Allen said. "If you're going to be a part of Tommy's life, then you're going to be a part of ours. You'll be welcome in our home and to call us whenever you need to."

"Thank you, sir. I really appreciate that."

"What did you do with Mark?" Tommy asked his uncles when they returned to his room later that afternoon. They had been gone much longer than he had expected. He wasn't worried about them hurting Mark; he knew that his uncle's bark was worse than his bite.

"We took him for a ride." Allen cackled fiendishly. "And then we had a little talk with him before taking him for another ride."

"We took him to lunch and then dropped him off back at *Animal House*," Morgan interpreted, laughing.

"Kappa house is not as bad as that," Tommy objected.

"We also walked around your campus for a while. It's very nice. Some of the older buildings are beautiful." Allen looked at his nephew and gave a deep, dramatic sigh. "Are you sure you don't want to try to find a nice gay boy to fall in love with?"

"No, Unc," Tommy replied softly. "I love Mark."

"Well, kid, he's a nice guy."

"And pretty nice to look at, also," Morgan added.

"Keep your eyes to yourself," Allen teased, and then looked over at Tommy. "I'm going to remind you again that jocks don't easily switch teams. I don't want you to get hurt again."

"I know, Unc."

"I don't think you do, Tommy," Allen said. "Mark is a nice guy, and we had a good talk with him at lunch, but there are no guarantees that he won't decide later on that he wants to be with women. Then you'll be right back where you were before Thanksgiving: miserable."

Tommy mulled that over. "Actually, I should be able to handle it better if it happens again, but I don't think it's going to. You didn't see the look in Mark's eyes when I woke up. He was really concerned about me, and he told me how much he loved me."

"You know what's going to happen to you if you ever again come to my house and behave the way you did at Thanksgiving," Allen stated seriously, but with a smile on his face.

"A size twelve leather boot will be shoved up my ass," Tommy guessed with a laugh.

"I'm serious when I tell you that I don't want you to get hurt again, Tommy." Allen looked into Tommy's eyes. "I want to believe and trust Mark when he says he wants to be with you, but I'm concerned about him dumping you again."

"I don't fully understand why I fell in love with him, Unc, but I did. I told him that I would give him a second chance, but that he wouldn't get a third. I'm going to trust him and hope that he meant it when he said he loves me."

"All right, kid. You've been warned about the jock and the boot." Allen stood and looked down at his nephew. "You give us a call if you need anything."

"You're leaving already?" Tommy asked, perplexed. "You just got here."

"We could only get a couple of days off," Morgan said. "We have an early evening flight back to San Francisco."

Allen put a hand on Tommy's arm. "We came out here for two reasons: first, to see you for ourselves and make sure that you're going to be okay; and second, to check out that football player you love so much."

Tommy smiled up at his uncle. "So you're satisfied that everything is okay?"

"Not at all," Allen grumbled. "I think you've lost your mind, getting involved with a jock. But I must agree with Morgan, he is a really nice looking boy. Still, that's not a reason to fall in love, but..." He shook his head, looking at his nephew. "There's no use in arguing with you; I won't win." He gave Tommy a kiss on the forehead. "You be good and do everything the doctors tell you."

"Yes, sir," Tommy replied sharply.

Morgan smiled down at Tommy and brushed his fingers through the young man's hair. "We'll be hoping that Mark doesn't change his mind again. Call us if you need us."

Allen looked over at Morgan in mock dismay. "He couldn't find an artist or dancer or actor. No. He has to fall for a football player."

They were laughing as Allen opened the hospital room door and saw Mark standing there. He glared at Mark, then broke into a smile. "You'll get the second boot if you don't take good care of my nephew."

"I intend to take good care of him for as long as he'll let me."

"See that you do," Allen said, shaking Mark's hand.

Morgan laughed and slapped Mark on the back as he left the room behind Allen.

"I see my uncles weren't too hard on you."

Mark smiled at him. "Your uncle is a scary man, but he let me live." He sat down in the chair next to Tommy's bed. "They were very nice to me; I learned a lot from them."

Tommy looked into Mark's blue eyes. "Would you do me a favor?"

"Your wish is my command, little brother." Mark sketched a seated half bow.

"Would you give me a real kiss? Not one of those little pecks on the lips."

Mark willingly complied, then smiled after pulling back. "I wasn't sure if it would hurt or not."

"My lips weren't stabbed, Mark."

Mark leaned over and kissed Tommy again. "That one was for me." Mark sat back in the chair. "Damn, I've missed those kisses."

"So have I."

"I'd like to talk about something important," Mark said, serious. "I was going to tell you earlier, before I was abducted by your uncles."

"Okay. What's on your mind?"

"Oscar, Jack, and I didn't think you would want to move back into your dorm room." He noted the sour look on Tommy's face and couldn't help but smile. "So I talked with the ruling council and all the resident brothers because freshmen are not permitted to live in the house. However, due to your circumstances, all of the brothers agreed that your moving in would be the right thing. Jack and Oscar helped me move all of your belongings into my room." He was pleased by Tommy's immediate smile. "There's an old cot in the room also, just so others don't think there's anything inappropriate going on between us."

"Who gets to sleep on the cot?" Tommy asked mischievously.

"I'll let you decide. You can either let me hold you at night as we fall asleep, or I'll sleep on the cot." Mark waited for an answer.

"I like the first option."

"Good. I was hoping you'd like that one." Mark's smile slowly faded as he prepared himself to ask about the attack. "Other than being stabbed, did he hurt you?"

The gleam in Tommy's eyes dimmed as he thought about what had happened. He closed his eyes for a moment before responding. "Other than my pride being hurt because I was caught off guard by the attack, and the stab wounds, he didn't hurt me." A slight smile replaced the sad look in his eyes. "If he'd been carrying a nightstick like you do, then there could have been some damage, but he wasn't even as big as me."

"I'm sorry I asked. I didn't mean to bring back those memories. I just wanted to make sure that he hadn't done any additional damage."

"It's okay."

"No, it's not okay. It's probably embarrassing and humiliating that it happened." Mark gave him a sympathetic look. "Some of the residents in your hall were awakened by the commotion, but Kyle and Jay kept everyone out of your room, except for the paramedics. So Kyle, Jay, Scott, and I are the only ones that know about the assault. The brothers are aware only that you were stabbed, and it was a good thing that Brian was already in police custody. They were ready to storm over to Gamma house and beat the crap out of him."

"That's really nice of the brothers," Tommy said softly.

"They really care about you." Mark chuckled. "Most of them stopped talking to me and went out of their way to avoid me. At first, I thought that you might have been saying something about me. Oscar and Jack set me straight on that issue. They assured me that if there was a reason people were avoiding me, I should be looking at the company I was keeping."

Tommy laughed out loud. "When your brothers are avoiding you because of the woman you're with, you should get the hint."

"Sometimes I'm bullheaded," Mark acknowledged.

"But you're very handsome," Tommy soothed.

"Okay, smartass." Mark grinned. "Oscar, Jack, and I have talked to your professors. They were all quite understanding about what had happened." He paused dramatically. "We'll have all of your classwork waiting for you when you get out of here."

"You guys are pricks," Tommy said with a chuckle. "But I love and appreciate all of you, especially you, big brother."

Stranded at the Airport

All flights leaving the airport that evening were delayed due to a snow squall. Passengers waiting for their flights were hoping that it would be a short delay, and that the squall would not turn into a full-blown blizzard. Allen was staring out at the snow while Morgan read a magazine. Neither man paid any attention to the other stranded passengers around them.

"He's a nice guy and a good looking one, but I'm not sure," Allen commented.

"Give him a chance," Morgan answered, not looking up from his magazine.

"What if he does it again?" Allen asked, looking over at his partner.

"Then I'm sure Tommy will handle it as well as he did the last time." Morgan glanced over the top of the magazine. "He knows what he's getting himself into," he said before returning his attention to the magazine.

Allen shook his head in dismay. "Why did it have to be a jock?"

"Because we don't choose who we fall in love with. It just happens."

"And when some broad with big tits comes by and catches jock boy's attention, Tommy will be crushed again," Allen complained.

"What if some other jock comes along and catches your Tommy's attention?" a female voice asked from behind Allen. "What happens to jock boy? He could end up just as devastated." Julia turned around in her seat to face the two startled men. She had seen them in the airport and had purposely sat in the seats to their backs, hoping to get an opportunity to introduce herself.

"This conversation is none of your business," Allen said with a bit of a huff.

Julia smiled at him. "Then you shouldn't be having it when somebody is sitting behind you and can overhear it."

Allen raised an eyebrow at her audacity as Morgan started laughing. "I'm Morgan, and this is my partner, Allen." He held out his hand. He hadn't felt uncomfortable introducing them as partners, since the woman seemed to be open-minded and considering the calmness with which she had intruded into their discussion. "We were visiting our nephew."

"I'm Julia," she replied, shaking hands with both of them. "I was in the area visiting. Bad time of year for traveling in this part of the country."

"It is that," Allen replied, "but my nephew is in the hospital and we had to make sure he was doing okay."

"I'm sorry to hear that. I hope it's nothing serious."

"It's serious enough, but he's doing well and is expected to be released by the weekend."

"That's good." She smiled at the two men. "So, your nephew fell in love with a jock," she said offhandedly.

"It's really none of your concern," Allen said tersely.

Julia laughed at his umbrage. "But we're stuck here in the airport, and I overheard your concerns about your nephew, so I'm curious about the story."

Allen looked at her dismissively, then continued the conversation as he tried to figure out what seemed familiar about her. "If you must know, my nephew recently turned eighteen, and his hormones are causing him to make bad decisions. He got himself involved with a fraternity. Then he fell in love with his big brother, who also happened to be the college's quarterback. This jock was having difficulties with his girlfriend, decided to have a good time with my nephew, and then went back to the girlfriend."

Although Allen kept his voice low so that others wouldn't overhear, Julia could hear the underlying anger and frustration. "Now the jock is back?" she asked softly.

"Yeah, he's back." Allen's voice changed again. He had vented his anger and was now talking in a more normal tone. "We had lunch with him today, as a favor to my nephew."

"You don't like the jock," Julia observed.

"I don't trust the jock," Allen corrected, raising an eyebrow. "Jocks don't switch teams, if you know what I mean."

"Anybody can change, Allen," she said softly. "There's no reason why the jock can't decide that he might be better off with your nephew."

"I still don't trust him."

Julia chuckled. "Let me tell you a story." She cleared her throat. "My son was dating a girl that had charmed both him and his father. I disliked the conniving bitch." She smiled as Morgan laughed.

"Tommy thought the same thing about the jock's girlfriend," Morgan commented.

"She played with my son's emotions and dragged him along on a string. A mother can tell things just from the sound of her child's voice, even if it is over the telephone." She glanced at both men. "I could tell that my son was unhappy. Even when he was with this girl, he had a strained voice, one that was pretending to be happy. Then he met somebody earlier this semester and I could hear a newfound joy when he talked to me. He told me how much he enjoyed being with this person and how much fun he was having.

"Despite his connection with the new romantic interest, my son began dating his old girlfriend again. Naturally, I supported his decision. After all, a mother is supposed to be supportive of her children. But the strain was back, and I knew that he wasn't really happy. He was very moody at Thanksgiving, and I wanted to slap some sense into him."

"Tommy was the same way," Morgan offered. "He wouldn't come out of his shell, seemed to prefer being miserable."

"Yes, same with my son." Julia smiled. "Then something happened, and my son broke up with his girlfriend, once and for all. I wanted to interfere and ask him what was going on but decided to wait for him to come to me. When he did, I learned the truth."

Allen's eyes had narrowed as he watched the woman. The wavy black hair, slightly bent nose, and bright blue eyes... The pieces didn't quite fit together.

Julia smiled at Allen, knowing that he was starting to figure out who she was. "My son came into my office one day and laid it all out for me. He had met a guy and fallen in love. He was so scared about being gay and all that entails that he went back to the girlfriend, and he ended up hurting the other guy by dumping him."

Julia saw that Morgan also had an inkling of who she was. "I could see the pain in his eyes because of the hurt that he had caused this other young man. I could also see the desperation and fear that he would never be able to heal that hurt. He was determined to try and fix things when he returned after the break." She took the opportunity to let one of them say something, but they just stared at her.

"I received a call very early Monday morning from my son. He was frantic because his friend had been stabbed and was in the hospital. He was scared to death that this young man was going to die before he could talk to him, but on Tuesday evening when he called me, that joy was back in his voice." She smiled as they became certain who she was. "His friend had survived and had been happy that my son was waiting for him to wake up. My son hasn't *shut up* about how much he loves this boy since," she said with a laugh.

Morgan nodded his awareness. "I thought there was something familiar about you."

"How did you know who we were?" Allen queried.

"I was at the hospital this morning, but there were already three people in Tommy's room, and they wouldn't allow me to go in until somebody came out." She smiled. "I watched as you left the hospital with my son, and then I went to meet the young witch that had stolen Mark's heart."

"My nephew is not a witch," Allen objected sternly.

"Your nephew is Wiccan," Julia allowed. "I saw the crystal that he gave my son, and I felt its energy. I was simply making sure that Tommy wasn't a bad witch who had cast some sort of sick spell over my son. I was completely satisfied as to Tommy's honesty. I think he's going to be good for Mark."

"My concern is whether Mark is going to be good for Tommy," Allen responded, daring her to contradict him.

Julia took a moment to gather her thoughts. "Mark has made few bad decisions in his short life. I always thought that he made a mistake when he thought he was in love with Miss Brown. For over a year, he wouldn't admit that she was a mistake. One of his faults, or virtues, depending on how you look at it, is that he tends to be very loyal. He'll stand by a friend for a long time, sometimes longer than he should. Another one of his faults is that he will very rarely admit that he has made a mistake. He admitted to me that he made a mistake when he broke up with Tommy." She looked at both men. "That told me a lot more about Mark's feelings for Tommy than if he had admitted he made a mistake in going back to Miss Brown. My son is in love with your nephew, and it scared him to have somebody besides his family love him unconditionally, as Tommy did. That type of relationship is rare."

"Can you be sure that he won't dump Tommy again?" Allen asked.

"Can you be sure that Tommy won't dump him for some other jock?" she shot back.

A smile slowly crept across Allen's face. "All I can say is that Tommy has done nothing but talk about Mark since he first met him. I was growing sick of hearing about this Mark person until it suddenly stopped. That's when I knew there was a problem, but Tommy wouldn't talk about it until I forced him to. He told me about Mark, and what had happened with the girlfriend. He also told me what he had done with the crystals and his fraternity paddle. I reprimanded him for playing around with that stuff," he said gruffly. "I've always thought he was too young for his grandmother to have left her collection to him."

"Allen," Julia said softly, "Tommy and I had a very long talk about what he did and didn't do. I'm aware that he employed the crystals, even used one on his paddle, but he didn't cast any spells on Mark." Julia's smile widened. "What he did do was let Mark know what love was truly about. He showed Mark how much fun two people could have together and let him know that he could be happy and be in love with another guy. Mark was given more options than he ever received from Miss Brown."

Morgan and Allen looked at one another and then back at Julia. Allen was surprised that this woman wasn't upset that her jock son was in love with another man. "Why are you accepting all of this so readily, Julia?"

"I told you earlier." She smiled. "Mark is my son, and I love him, unconditionally. I'm very proud of the way he manages his life and of how he is working toward his future. I would prefer that he not be gay because I'm sure it's not any easier in this day and age than it was before the gay movement started."

"It's not even easier when you're living in a city like San Francisco," Allen agreed. "But it's not as difficult there as in some small town in the middle of the Bible Belt."

"Mark is in love with Tommy, and I can either let him go or support him," Julia continued. "I'm not about to give up my son just because he loves another man. Although I might think twice about that if the other man wasn't as sweet and charming as Tommy."

"Did he put a spell on *you*?" Morgan teased with a laugh. "Sweet and charming! He was anything but that over the break. We invited some friends to a Thanksgiving party and several brought their gay sons or nephews. Some of those young men were athletic and charming, but Tommy ignored them all."

Julia laughed along with Morgan and Allen, then she stopped abruptly and looked at them seriously. "Do you think Tommy would have given Mark a second chance if this incident hadn't happened?" She knew the answer that Tommy had given her, but wanted to know what these two men thought.

"Yes," Allen said without even thinking about it, then he smiled brightly. "But he would have made Mark sweat it out waiting for an answer."

"Mark would have deserved that," Julia replied honestly. "And I would have done the same thing to him if I were Tommy."

Allen stared at her for a moment. "I just realized that Mark didn't mention that you were visiting him."

"That's because I'm not visiting Mark." She enjoyed the look of surprise on their faces. "I came here today strictly to visit Tommy. I knew he was in the hospital and wouldn't be able to avoid me. After you left with Mark, I went into his room and began questioning him about his Wiccan activities in regard to my son. We had a delightful conversation, one which I am not at liberty to divulge. And I would appreciate it if neither of you mention that I spoke with you either. Neither Mark nor my husband are aware that I'm here, and I would prefer to keep it that way for the time being."

The loudspeaker overhead sounded. "Flight 53 for Boston, now boarding at Gate 16."

"Well, gentlemen," Julia stood up, "that's my flight. I hope yours will be boarding shortly. It's been a pleasure talking with you. I have the feeling that we'll be seeing more of one another in the future."

"It's been a pleasure meeting you, Julia," Allen returned, standing up and putting out his hand. He felt the warmth of her hand as she grasped his. "May I ask what you do for a living?"

A wide smile crossed Julia's face. "I used to sell cosmetics until I earned my doctorate in psychology." She shook hands with Morgan.

"You're a shrink?" Morgan asked.

"Don't worry, gentlemen." She smiled as she started to walk away. "I'm bound by the doctor-patient privilege and won't divulge anything we discussed." She waved her hand in the air and disappeared into the gangway.

Morgan looked over at Allen. "I think I like her."

"You can't fault a woman wearing basic black and Jungle Red nail polish," Allen observed with a laugh.

17: RELEASE FROM THE HOSPITAL

The doctors were surprised at how quickly Tommy was healing, attributing it to good medicine and Tommy's positive attitude. Late Friday morning, they signed Tommy's release. Mark arrived at the hospital after his morning class and drove him back to Kappa house. Most of the brothers were at their classes, but the few inside welcomed Tommy and offered him any assistance that he might need to get around.

"Wow," Tommy exclaimed as he entered Mark's bedroom, "not only is it completely changed, but it's clean." He laughed, as Mark cuffed him lightly on the head.

"Smartass. I did this so that you could get in and out of bed easily and not be trapped against the wall."

Mark had rearranged his bedroom. The double bed now had the headboard against the wall. Both sides of the bed were open so that he and Tommy would each be able to get out of the bed without disturbing the other.

"I see my paddle is back up on the wall next to yours." Tommy also noticed that his grandmother's trunk was prominently located at the end of the bed with two red roses in the white vase, and his de Lempicka was hanging above the cot. "Very nice, Mark. You must have been really confident that I was going to stay with you."

Mark walked over to Tommy and held him in his arms. "I was more hopeful than confident. Now that you're back in here, I don't have any intentions of letting you leave." He gave Tommy a kiss on the lips and then pulled back. "Now get comfortable on the bed, and I'll get your classwork. You've missed a week of classes and have some catching up to do before finals in two weeks."

Tommy grimaced but did as he was told, mumbling "the downside of having a big brother" just loud enough for Mark to almost hear.

"What was that?"

"Nothing," Tommy replied cheerfully, stacking several pillows behind his back and getting comfortable. "I said I was happy to have a big brother."

"Hm." Mark stood by the side of the bed and looked down at the smiling young man. He put Tommy's books and several notes from professors near Tommy's leg. "You better behave yourself, or I'll have Nurse Ratched come over to look after you."

"Yes, sir," Tommy said, smiling and saluting.

"Don't push it, punk, or you'll be sleeping on that cot. I'm going to my afternoon classes, and I'll be back around five." Mark gave him a quick kiss. "Don't run away."

"Now who's the smartass?" he called as Mark left. Tommy looked at the books and papers surrounding him, then picked up the notes from the professors and started on the work that he had missed while his life had been on hold.

"*Gracias*, Oscar. That was an awesome meal." Tommy sat in the recliner in the third floor living room, a dinner tray over his lap. The group of friends had just finished a Mexican dinner, that Oscar had specially prepared as a welcoming gesture for Tommy.

"I figured that after four days of hospital food, you'd want something real to eat." Oscar chuckled, removing the tray and setting it on a side table.

"Technically, I only had two days of their food. The first two days of nutrition came from an inverted plastic bag on a hook." The other six guys joined in Tommy's laughter.

"Sorry the chips and dip were store bought. It's a bitch trying to find fresh avocado and tomatoes in the winter."

"You should cook for the house more often," Dave said.

"And you should go to hell," Oscar replied.

When the laughter died down, Ken looked over at Dave. "Are the Kappas ever going to forgive the Gammas for what happened to Tommy?"

"We don't hold the Gammas responsible, Ken," Dave replied.

"The looks I received as I walked into the house, even with Jack escorting me, were pretty angry."

"We're just a little sensitive about what Brian did to our brother."

"Guys," Tommy interjected, looking around at them all, "you're all my friends, and I'm glad that you're all here. Let's not talk about Brian. This is supposed to be a fun evening."

"Tommy's right," Mark said. "What do you want to talk about, little brother?"

Tommy looked over at Kyle. "I want to know what happened to Scott, and what's being said around the dorm."

"Wow!" Kyle took a deep breath and sat back in his seat. "When he and Jay came in and found you, Scott freaked out. He just sat on his bed blubbering. After the paramedics left, Jay and I calmed him down and got him to call some friends and go stay with them. He moved out of the dorm the next day without saying a word to anyone but me. He wanted me to tell you he was sorry about what happened, it being his keys that Brian used and all, and he hoped you'd get better fast.

"The guys in the dorm were shocked that anyone would want to hurt you. You are quite popular, Ford Tommy," he said with a smile. "There were some rumors that you came on to Brian and he was retaliating, even though most people knew what an asshole Brian could be. People also knew that Brian was a heavy drinker and pot smoker. So I let it slip that Brian was drunk and was after the cash you kept in that trunk." A grin spread over his face. "They were surprised that you would keep cash in your dorm room."

"Thanks, Welby Kyle." Tommy laughed at the diversion Kyle had created to keep anyone from learning about the assault.

"No problem." Kyle looking knowingly from Tommy to Mark. "Besides, I happen to know that you have better taste."

Mark blushed, and the group broke out laughing.

"What *do* you keep in that trunk?" Dave asked.

"Books," Oscar said, quickly jumping into the conversation. "Some very old books," he looked over at Tommy, "that I would really enjoy looking at someday."

"You'd be welcome to read them anytime, Oscar." Tommy smiled over at Oscar, grateful to him for having changed the subject away from his trunk.

Later that night, when Tommy tired, Mark slid into bed next to him. He lay on his side and gently rubbed a hand over Tommy's back, feeling the dressings covering the stab wounds. He kissed Tommy's shoulder, elated to be lying next to him again.

Tommy was lying on his stomach, enjoying the feel of Mark's calloused hands rubbing his back. He sighed deeply as Mark kissed his shoulder. "You better stop that or you're going to make me horny. I don't think my muscles are ready for that type of therapy yet."

"I'm sorry. I'm just happy to have you back in my bed again. I'll stop if you want me to."

"As long as you know I can't do anything yet, you can keep rubbing my back."

Mark kissed Tommy's ear. "I don't expect anything from you until you're ready. I just want to touch you so that I can believe you really are here."

"Mmm," Tommy sighed as he closed his eyes. "I missed those hands touching me and hearing that deep voice whispering in my ear."

Mark moved closer to Tommy, resting his head on the same pillow. "Why did you pick me, Tommy?" he asked quietly, watching as Tommy opened his eyes and looked at him.

"I was seventeen, horny, and thought a straight football player would be the best choice for somebody to spend the rest of my life with."

Mark grabbed a handful of Tommy's hair and gently tugged on it. "Stop being a smartass." He stared into Tommy's eyes. "I'm being serious. Why me?"

Tommy let out a deep breath and closed his eyes for just a second before returning Mark's gaze. "When you walked through the lobby of my dorm that first day, your aura was bursting with life. Everything around me seemed to pause, except for you. I felt your energy and spirit filling the room as I had only ever felt from my grandmother. I decided that you were the type of man that I was looking for to spend my life with. It wasn't until we shook hands and I felt your energy flowing into me that I began fantasizing about being with you."

"But as far as either of us knew, I was a straight jock with a girlfriend."

"I really wanted to be with you, Mark, but I couldn't do anything to let you know that I was in love with you. I was afraid that you would get angry about being hit on by a gay boy and have me tossed out of the pledge group. So I decided that being your little brother and friend would have to be enough for me."

Mark chuckled as he turned onto his side again. "But it wasn't good enough for you. You let me be myself and allowed that energy to come out. Buried feelings began surfacing, and I started seeing you as more than just my little brother. While you were figuring out a way to get me, I was trying to figure out what to do with my feelings for you." Mark leaned down and kissed Tommy's cheek. "I made my decision even before you could work your magic on me with that enchanted paddle."

"I told you that you weren't under a spell. I certainly wouldn't have let you go back to her if I had cast a spell on you."

"Maybe not. However, you did let me know what real love between two people could feel like. You even let yourself suffer through my breaking up with you."

"I wanted you to love me as much as I loved you. I didn't want you to feel trapped in a relationship that you didn't want. If she was what you wanted, I loved you too much to not let you go."

"I felt more trapped with her than I ever felt around you. I was scared about being gay until I almost lost you for good. Now that you're back in my life, I don't feel trapped or scared."

"Are you sure?"

Mark grabbed a handful of Tommy's hair and leaned down to kiss him fully on the lips. "I'm sure, little brother," he said softly, rubbing a hand over Tommy's cheek. "I don't intend to let you go again. Not after all the thoughts that I had as I watched you lying in the hospital, connected to all those machines. I love you too much."

Tommy grasped Mark's hand and brought it to his lips. "I love you, Mark."

As Mark lay on his back, Tommy moved closer and laid his head on Mark's chest. He put his arm across Mark's body and held tightly, afraid that he might discover he was dreaming.

"So, why don't you tell me more about this witch thing," Mark urged. "Tell me what you did to the crystals."

"Actually, I didn't do anything to the crystals, you did." Tommy smiled at the frown that creased Mark's forehead. "When I pledged Kappa, I put my topaz crystal and a clear crystal under your mattress. I couldn't put them under your pillow because you might have accidentally moved them. I wrapped them in one of your jockstraps. That worked as a conduit to pull your energy into the crystals. The clear crystal was used on my paddle, and the topaz crystal stayed under your mattress. You empowered the crystals with your energy."

"Ah, I see," Mark said thoughtfully, gently tightening his hold on Tommy. "You used me," he teased.

"I'm sorry. I needed to have a crystal that had your energy in it to finish my paddle."

"So after I broke up with you and you came in here to reclaim your paddle, you took the crystals back."

"I only took the topaz crystal back," Tommy corrected. "I had used the clear crystal on my paddle." He laughed in realization. "I guess I did take both of them."

"You stole my energy," Mark accused. "I had restless nights after you took the crystals back. Of course, I blamed it on my conscience, since I didn't know there had been crystals under my bed." He kissed Tommy, then stroked Tommy's soft hair as he thought about the holidays. "I first wore the crystal to that party in the Hamptons. As angry as I was with Sally that night, I remained relatively calm as I finally ended that disaster of a relationship. I'm not sure, but I think I fondled the crystal the entire drive home that night, thinking about you and wondering how to get you back." He kissed Tommy's head. "I haven't taken it off since then."

"You can put it under your pillow when you go to sleep."

"No, little brother. I need to keep you close to my heart. The night you were attacked, I had fallen asleep thinking about you and holding the crystal. I woke up with a sharp pain shooting through my body. Oscar heard me yell out, and a few minutes later Larry came into the room. He told me that Kyle was on the phone, babbling about an emergency."

Tommy stared into Mark's eyes, incredulous at the implications.

Mark smiled at him and pressed his finger against Tommy's nose. "Oscar tells me that I'm attuned to the connection between our crystals."

Tommy raised an eyebrow. "Your energy is a lot stronger than I thought. You're supposed to be a regular jock, not a connector."

"You picked the wrong jock to charm, little brother." Mark passionately kissed him. "I did a lot of thinking about my future during the break and wanted to talk to you about it. Fortunately, because you were stuck in that hospital bed, you had no choice but to listen to me." Tommy pulled another hair from his chest. "Ouch! Stop that or you'll make me bald-chested," Mark complained.

"You've got plenty of hair on this chest, stud." Tommy kissed him over the heart.

"I've talked to my counselors about staying at Timian to get my master's degree, and I'm planning on renting an off-campus apartment for next semester. Would you be interested in living with me?"

Tommy feigned indignation. "You want me to live with you? In sin?"

"You would probably have the choice of staying in Kappa house, even though you are a freshman, or you could move back up to the dorms. Either way, you're going to have a roommate. I just thought you might like it to be me," Mark said hopefully.

"I'd love to live with you," Tommy replied, kissing Mark's chest again. "If you're sure that's what you want."

"How many more times do I have to tell you, I'm very sure about that. I don't want to lose you again." Mark tweaked Tommy's nose. "You are so cute. I'm glad that you're giving me another chance."

"So am I."

"Would you have pledged Gamma if we hadn't invited you to pledge Kappa?" Mark asked.

"No," Tommy answered quickly. "There was only one fraternity that I was going to pledge, and it wasn't Gamma."

"What if I hadn't been your big brother?"

A devilish smile crossed Tommy's face. "Then it would have been harder for me to get you."

Mark pulled Tommy close, enjoying the warmth of his body. "Did I ever tell you that I had first choice among the pledge class?"

"No," Tommy replied, surprised by the admission.

"I stared at your picture and knew you were going to cause me a lot of trouble. I picked you anyway." Mark kissed Tommy on the head, enjoying the sound of Tommy's chuckle. "Where do you see us going?"

"I told you initiation weekend" A hand covered his mouth.

"No! Not this time, little brother. The last time you left me in charge of where we were going, I fucked it up," he said, gently chastising Tommy. "This time, I'm going to follow you. So tell me what you see in our future."

Tommy felt a warmth surge through him at the words "our future". He tightened his grip around Mark's chest. "I see two extremely happy guys. One, an independent businessman with his own company, and the other, a therapist who helps teens and young adults cope with the harsh realities of the world. They live on the wooded hillsides near Lake Tahoe, in the house that they built."

"We build our own house?" Mark asked, yawning.

"No. We hire people to build the house because we're too busy living our lives to the fullest." Tommy yawned, too. "We have lots of friends to entertain — gay, lesbian, and straight couples. Of course, we wouldn't forget our single friends, the ones who haven't found that one special person to share their lives." He tried to stifle another yawn, but couldn't. "I can imagine the sun rising over the mountains and shining down on a sparkling blue lake as we take our early morning run. I can almost smell the autumn leaves as they crumple beneath our feet along the paths through the woods behind our house. I also see fresh, untouched snow and hear it crunching beneath our cross-country skis."

"I like the sounds of that future." Mark craned his neck forward and gave Tommy a lingering kiss. "Close your eyes and get some sleep. I'm going to dream about your happy ending. Good night, little brother."

Tommy nestled closer to Mark, holding tightly. "Good night, big brother."

When Mark woke up Saturday morning, the sun was just starting to shine through the rime-frosted windows. He thought he detected the delicate scent of lilacs. He was lying on his back, Tommy's head on his chest and an arm holding Mark tightly. Tommy's body provided a warmth and comfort that he hadn't felt with any other. Mark reveled in being held by somebody who wanted to be with him, someone who loved him and would never let him go. He had been surprised by the mutual passion and intimacy that they had shared earlier in the semester. No woman had ever matched his vigor the way Tommy had done. He smiled up at the ceiling and thought about Tommy's vision of their future together. Whatever the future held for them, he was going to make sure that their love never lost its luster, and that he never stopped believing in its magic.

The Beginning

Larry Coles moved from a small town in southern New Jersey to San Francisco in May of 1982, shortly after having graduated with a B.A. in psychology/sociology from a small state college in Pennsylvania. He has been a legal secretary for over 20 years, and a part-time writer for the past 10 years; writing after work as a way of relaxing. He has participated in National Novel Writing Month (NaNoWriMo): in November of 2004, completing a 60,000+ word vampire novel before Thanksgiving; in November 2005, completing a 104,660 word warlock/vampire romance novel; and again in November 2006, completing a 59,000+ word gay romance novel involving two of the fraternity brothers from *Freshman Pledge*. He started writing stories based on erotic short stories, wanting to flesh out and give depth to the characters and the story. Larry is a romantic at heart and desires for all of his characters to find and have romantic relationships, much like the one he found in 2001.

Larry lives in San Francisco with his partner of five years, Darrin, and their three year old chocolate brown cat, Armand. On February 20, 2004, after Mayor Gavin Newsom allowed same sex marriages to be performed, Larry and Darrin were married at S.F. City Hall. In August of 2004, the California Supreme Court ruled all 4,000+ same sex marriages that had been performed in S.F. were illegal and had them annulled. Larry and Darrin hope that one day the Court's ruling will be overturned and they will once again be allowed to legally marry.